We hope you enjoy  renew it by the due

You can renew it at norfolk.gov.uk/libraries or by using our free library app.

Otherwise you can phone 0344 800 8020 - please have your library card and PIN ready.

You can sign up for email reminders too.

NORFOLK ITEM

30129 083 615 238

NORFOLK COUNTY COUNCIL
LIBRARY AND INFORMATION SERVICE

Hit
Girls

Dreda Say Mitchell

HODDER

First published in Great Britain in 2011 by Hodder & Stoughton
First published in paperback in 2011
An Hachette UK company

6

Copyright © Dreda Say Mitchell 2011

The right of Dreda Say Mitchell to be identified as the
Author of the Work has been asserted by her in accordance
with the Copyright, Designs and Patents Act 1988.

A CIP catalogue record for this title
is available from the British Library

Paperback ISBN 978 0 340 99322 4
Ebook ISBN 978 1 848 94209 7

Typeset in Rotis Serif by Hewer Text UK Ltd, Edinburgh
Printed and bound by Clays Ltd, Elcograf S.p.A.

Hodder & Stoughton policy is to use papers that are natural, renewable
and recyclable products and made from wood grown in sustainable
forests. The logging and manufacturing processes are expected to
conform to the environmental regulations of the country of origin.

Hodder & Stoughton Ltd
338 Euston Road
London NW1 3BH

www.hodder.co.uk

This one is for my geezer girl crew, the Geezerettes, who have hit the streets helping me promote all my books and for Uncle Moses for being a one-man band.

Acknowledgements

To the librarians who I met at the W.F. Howes lunch for giving me one of the blinder ideas for the book and for Allison and her mates for all their help with the medical stuff. And massive thanks to Paul for the scaffolding pole tip.

one

The twin girls ran across the playground.

They were laughing their heads off.

Five minutes later they would be dead.

Three thirty on the dot the kids were streaming out at home time at Parkhurst Primary School on Claremont Road in the heart of London's East End.

'Oranges and lemons' played temptingly from an ice-cream van in a neighbouring street. The July sun dazzled in the clear, blue sky. The heat was hitting twenty-nine degrees C.

'Mum! Mum! Look at my picture,' one of the ten-year-old girls yelled as she waved a piece of paper in the air.

Their mum, twenty-seven-year-old Marina Lewis, smiled tightly back as she waited just inside the playground, near the former school keeper's house. She was size-zero thin, medium height, shoulder length blonde hair she had done up every two weeks at Betty's hair salon, and blue eyes that darted behind false eyelashes as if she were looking for something better in life. But it didn't matter how hard she tried to copy those celebs she read about in mags she bought for 99p a time, she always looked like something that came from a bargain bucket.

She knew which of her daughters was calling out to her. Molly. Most people couldn't tell the twins apart, but she could. Minnie was the talker, took after her, while Molly was the naughty one taking after her dad. Although she'd never been quite as naughty as her dad. She'd never murdered anyone in cold blood for a start.

Although she felt the sun on her skin, she shivered. If he knew what she was planning to do ... She let the terrifying thought hang in the air.

She needed to get them away quick. Into the car where their suitcases and passports were packed ready to go. Hit Gatwick before her bastard of an ex realised what was going on. Whatever else was wrong with her life, and there was plenty wrong with it, her daughters had always been what was right about it. She'd lost faith in everything and everybody else but she'd kill and be killed for these girls, she'd never been in any doubt about that.

Oranges and lemons.

The sound of the ice-cream van got closer. Her nails dug into her Chloe Paddington shoulder bag as Minnie and Molly continued to run towards her. The girls' excitement added to the beautiful summer's day. They had the sun behind them shining through their blonde hair and in the crowd of other children rushing towards their parents, they seemed to be floating rather than running towards her.

'My little angels,' she whispered.

Her blue eyes shifted momentarily away from her beloved girls as she flicked her gaze onto a group of other parents. Seeing her eye them up they almost took a step back. *Wankers.* The other parents milling at the gate might nod to her, but they never came anywhere near her. Mind you she couldn't blame them really. They knew what she was. Or rather had been. Stanley Lewis's missus. Well ex-missus now. Been divorced for the last two years. But Stanley wasn't your normal husband or run-of-the-mill dad, no, he was what he liked to call the 'managing director' of East London's notorious Lewis gang. Well at least he was while the old man, Kenny, was doing bird for robbery in Oldgate Prison, something Stan didn't thank you for reminding him of. She felt the looks of the other mums, the fear and envy, the respect and contempt. Marina's gaze stopped on the only parent who had the nuts to look her straight in the eye like a normal person. Jackie Jarvis. Short cropped red hair, green eyes, freckles and maybe barely a couple of inches above five foot but as tough as nails. Jackie had a strength in her face that Marina knew she would never have. The other woman boldly met Marina's blue gaze. Nodded and sent her a whatsup? smile. Marina nodded back but didn't smile. She didn't have time for that not with her worrying about . . .

'Mum, mum.' She forgot about Jackie as a small body barrelled into her. Minnie looked up at her with her pearly white teeth and excitedly gushed, 'Look at what I drew.'

No kisses and hugs for her little ladies today.

'We ain't got time for that now.' Marina pushed Minnie back. 'We need to get going.'

She quickly turned, missing Minnie's look of disappointment as she headed out of the school gate. Her hand shook, dipping into her bag, searching for a smoke. She needed to calm down her nerves. The other parents and kids pushed out with her onto the street.

'Oh mum, please . . .' Minnie whined behind her.

'Not now, get moving,' she snapped not bothering to turn around. She found her pack of Bensons. Pulled it out. Popped one to her painted lips as she gazed idly down the street. That's when the smoke caught in the back of her throat, when she saw the black Merc, with the black-tinted windows, picking up speed as it came down the street towards the school.

Thirty-six-year-old Jackie Jarvis knew there was going to be Trouble as soon as she saw the Merc, tyres squealing, coming to a halt outside her sons' school. If there was one thing that she had learned in her life it was how to spot Trouble when it came blowing down the street.

Oranges and lemons.

The ice-cream van was around the corner. She hugged her ten-year-old twin boys, Darius and Preston, looking over their heads as the passenger door of the car flung open.

'Mum, can I get an ice-cream?' Preston asked eagerly.

Darius was the sparkier of the twins taking after his dad, while Preston was still mummy's little boy. They both had their dad's smooth, brown, Caribbean skin and Preston liked to have small flicked up dreads in his hair at the front just like his dad wore all over. But Jackie didn't give her son the nod that he could go anywhere as her gaze skidded back to the Merc outside the school. She knew Trouble was in the air . . .

'Oh, please mum,' Preston pleaded.

Jackie looked at the face her son pulled and it tugged at her heartstrings. She found it hard to say 'no' to her boys sometimes.

'Mum . . .'

'Alright,' she finally agreed. She pointed her finger at him as she added, 'But no hanging around . . .'

Before she could finish he let out a whoop as he hopped, skipped and jumped down the street. Jackie let her gaze go back to the car. She sucked in her breath when she saw who got out.

Twenty-five-year-old Stanley Lewis. Leather jacket, gelled brown hair, D&G shades and that mean look he wore when he was on duty as an East End street thug. Two other men got out of the motor, leaned against the bodywork and watched their boss get on with his work.

She drew Darius closer to her side, her arm curling around the Arsenal rucksack on his back.

Oranges and lemons.

'You thinking about taking my kids away, bird?' Stanley shouted at his ex-missus. 'Who do you think you're dealing with here? A social worker or something?' But he didn't wait for an answer, instead he swaggered up to his ex-wife like a pop star on a shoot.

An unnatural hush fell over the other parents as they drew their kids protectively to their side. Darius looked across at Molly with frightened eyes. Jackie knew her boy was sweet on the little cutie, although he'd never admit it in a million years. They were tight those two, always getting up to all kinds of naughties at school. Her son's first love and it had to be some villain's daughter. She held him tight as the street soap turned dirty.

Marina grabbed her daughters' hands as she tried to march past her former husband.

'You know the rules Stan – or do I have to go back to court and remind you of them? Today ain't one of your visiting days so fuck off.'

A few of the parents let out shocked noises on hearing the F word and put their hands over their kids' ears. But they didn't leave. *Two-faced creeps,* Jackie thought. They should be belting the other way with their kids, the way they always treated Marina like a leper, but they couldn't resist watching a bit of good old-fashioned East End drama. Beats having to pay West End theatre prices any day of the week.

Stanley pushed himself threateningly towards his former old lady. 'I know what your game is babe. I've seen the suitcases in the back of your motor.'

Marina's face whitened, but she stood her ground. 'Ain't there a tart on a barstool waiting for you somewhere?' She spat the words in his face.

His arm came up so quick that not even Jackie saw it coming. He struck Marina a stinging blow across her flushed face. Some moved forward to intervene and then caught the eye of Stan's goons and thought better of it. The crowd sucked in their breath as she stumbled onto the outer wall of the school. Minnie and Molly shifted quickly to the side, out of harm's way. But didn't cry, as if they had seen this all before. Seeing the distress of his friend, Darius tried to wriggle out of his mum's arms, but Jackie held him tight. No way was her boy getting involved in this mess.

Oranges and lemons.

Jackie's gaze flicked down the road as she heard the ice-cream van once more, checking on Preston. But she couldn't see him or the van.

Marina launched herself off the wall. 'Some kind of tough guy, aren't you . . . ?' She swung her arm and clawed at her Stan's face with her four-inch, bubblegum pink acrylic nails.

He let out a yelp as her nails dug into his skin. He bashed her arm to the side with a vicious blow. Used both hands to shove her in the belly. She slammed back into the wall. He grabbed her hair with one hand. Yanked her head to the side. Swung his other hand and belted her in the face. She cried out. He twisted his hand and backhanded her across the other cheek. This time he split her lip. Maybe it was the taste of blood in her mouth that finally tipped

Marina over the edge, but Jackie watched as she screamed and flew at her ex-husband with both arms raised. Surprised by her attack he stumbled back, his shades falling and smashing on the ground.

'You ain't having 'em,' she screamed as she hit him, over and over again, with her fists.

Everyone's eyes were on the fighting couple so no one noticed as their girls hurried further away, along the wall. Jackie hugged a shocked Darius and debated whether she should step in. Pull them apart. Remind them that their daughters and the whole friggin' world were watching them.

She made her decision. 'Don't move,' she whispered to her son.

But just as she stepped away from him another voice yelled out. 'What is going on here?'

Everyone turned to find the head teacher, Mrs Moran, standing just outside the school gate. Jackie stopped moving. If there was one person who could sort this out it was Mrs Moran. No one fucked with her, including the parents. It was one of the reasons Jackie had opted to send the boys to the school. Mrs Moran ran a tight ship, put excellent results at the top of the school's priority list and didn't take shit from no one.

Even Marina and Stanley stopped their scrap when they saw her. Jackie would say later, along with a couple of the other parents, that maybe they could've done something if they hadn't had their eyes glued to Mrs Moran. But they had and no one saw what came next.

The sound on the street was an odd echo of Stan's earlier arrival, for another vehicle was accelerating down the street at high speed. Jackie looked up the road towards it, as did everyone else. Marina's eyes peered through the swollen flesh of her face in horror when she saw what was coming down the road. A 4x4 jeep with tinted windows was veering down the road, picking up speed as it headed towards the school wall. Jackie grabbed Darius by the arm and leapt backwards. Other parents did the same, pulling their children clear by their limbs or their hair. But some parents remained rooted to the ground in shock, others with hands pulled over their heads as if by that they would avoid the danger.

Yards from where Jackie was standing she saw the jeep bounce as it mounted the kerb. Pulled slightly to the left. Headed straight for Marina and Stanley Lewis's twin girls. The terrified girls, who were pressed up against the wall, didn't stand a chance. The bumper smashed into both girls, crushing them against the wall.

'No,' Marina whispered. She rushed towards the wall as the car skidded into reverse. Swung in to a one-eighty turn. It juddered backwards. Then screeched back down the road.

Horrified, Jackie watched as Stanley rushed after Marina. Sobbing, the distraught mum fell to the pavement on her knees and picked up Minnie's shattered body. The girl's limbs were at an awkward angle. Gently, she cradled her daughter's limp head, rocking back and forth whispering, 'My little angel. My little angel.'

'Where's Molly?' Stanley shouted as he crouched over his ex-wife.

Jackie and everyone else swung into action. Looked at the car disappearing at high speed down the road. Jackie covered her mouth and shook her head in despair at what she saw. A pair of small legs, that's all that were visible from the back end of the car, bumping and swaying against the hard road. A pair of trainers were scattered in the road. Molly Lewis was trapped under the car. Stanley was the first to move. Then everyone else – parents, Mrs Moran, Jackie – belted after him. Suddenly the car stopped. Stood still for a few seconds. People got closer. And closer. Then the engine re-ignited like thunder. The car took off again, swerving down the street. Everyone staggered to a collective halt. Stared at what the car had left behind. *Ohmygod*. Molly's bloody, broken body.

His face frozen in disbelief, Stanley juddered forward like a zombie.

'Oh no. No, no, no, no . . .' he screamed as he looked at the wrecked and battered body of his daughter. He dropped to his knees beside her as Jackie and the others reached him.

'Ambulance. Get a fuckin' ambulance someone for Christ's sake,' someone yelled frantically into a mobile phone. Jackie looked across at the speaker and realised that it was Scott Miller, the Chair of the school's Governing Body. His ten-year-old son stood terrified by his side.

Then came a moment of absolute silence. Absolute stillness. Only muffled weeping disturbed the quiet. No one wanted to move or believe what they had just seen. Then the silence snapped as Marina Lewis staggered down the street, her blouse wet with blood, carrying the broken body of her other daughter. The child's arms and angelic blonde hair hung limply flecked with red smears. Her head flopped back in an unnatural angle. In one of her hands Marina clutched the picture Minnie had drawn.

'You shouldn't be carrying her.' It sounded like Mrs Moran.

But Marina ignored the desperate advice and only stopped when she reached her former husband and other daughter. She took one look at Molly and started screaming at the same time there was a screech of wheels from around the corner. The picture she held in her hand fluttered to the ground revealing to everyone what the little girl had drawn – a picture of Stanley Lewis, now splattered with blood.

A shout and a scream came from around the corner. Jackie and a few of the other parents ran down the street. Turned the corner. Stopped. Jackie scanned the scene. A smashed pink ice-cream in the road. A crowd of people gathered around something. Someone moved out of the tight circle. That's when she saw what they were all looking at. A small body, twisted in the road. Blood. Looked like a kid. Blue school blazer. Spiky hair. No, they looked like small dreads. Same ones that her Preston wore with pride . . . No, her mind suddenly screamed. Preston!

She started running. And running. And running as Oranges and Lemons started playing again.

two

The door crashed open. The three occupants of the room, all at the bar, looked up sharply. The newcomer remained in the doorway. Positioned herself into a cocky pose – hands on swaying hips, feet slightly apart. Then started singing, a tune about your girlfriend being hot like me. Every time she sang the word 'hot' it was like she was breathing slowly, open-mouthed onto a window.

The others shook their heads and rolled their eyes as they checked her out. Anna Crane. She was a total knockout, black, tall, filled out in all the right places, wearing a short, sexy, floral number with heels that made her legs go on and on and on. She was a party monster through and through, but had a big heart and a matching sized mouth to go with it.

Anna did a happy little dance, shopping bags jiggling at her side, as she stepped into the main room of the Shim-Sham-Shimmy Club in Wapping. The club was one of the hottest nightspots in town. And Anna still got a thrill that she part-owned it with the three other people in the room – Misty, Roxy and Ollie. Anna's face grew puzzled as she checked out the rest of the room looking for the other co-owner. Where the heck was Jackie? She of all people should be here as they were meeting to plan her kids' confirmation party.

'Stop that bloody racket,' Misty McKenzie groaned in mock horror, her mobile next to her as she leaned on the bar, as if she were ready to dish out drinks. A choppy Paris Hilton style hairdo weaved around her face and neck and she wore everyday leggings and a T-shirt. Only her lime green, peep-toe heels shouted out about the more outrageous lifestyle she lived when day turned into night. She was really a he and had once been one of the city's most talked about drag queens. But those who were in the know hadn't forgotten the days she had once been a baseball-wielding member of the McKenzie family crew. What age Misty was, not many people knew and she wasn't telling.

Anna just grinned. 'The problem with you lot,' she said as she strutted towards them, her shiny black hair weaving against her back, 'is you ain't got no taste.' She settled herself on a lipstick-coloured kettledrum stool at the bar between Roxy and Ollie. Roxy was a buttermilk blonde, plump and could talk anyone under the table. Ollie was the quiet one, her dark skin, finger-combed small Afro and thick rimmed glasses making her look like a radical black sister. Anna, Ollie and Roxy were the same age as Jackie, all having met at the age of fifteen in St Nicholas care home for kids. A place they all tried hard to forget about.

'What you having?' Misty asked as she heaved herself off her elbows.

'Pina Colada. I'm feeling all "exotic" today.' Anna settled her bags on the floor beside her.

'How's Bell?' Misty asked as she placed Anna's drink in front of her in a long-necked cocktail glass. Bell Dream was one of the country's most sought after lawyers and had also been Anna's girlfriend for the last ten years. None of them had thought it would last – Bell being part of the professional establishment and a good twelve years older than her partner and Anna the rave queen who in her day, freely admitted, had been quite a tart. But to everyone's amazement Anna had settled into domestic bliss like she'd been waiting for it all her life.

'Still thanking God that she chose me to spend the rest of her days with,' she answered cheekily. She started humming the tune she'd been torturing them with in the doorway, swaying to the rhythm on her seat. They all looked at her and chuckled.

Anna stopped singing and tucked into her drink. She licked some of the cream from her lips. 'So where's Jackie?'

'Dunno.' It was Roxy who spoke in that little squeaky mouse voice she'd always had. 'Should've been here ages ago.'

'Think she had to go to the hospital first,' Ollie replied, pushing her glasses higher on her nose.

'Ozzie?' Misty's voice was puzzled. 'What for? She sick or something?'

Ollie just shrugged her shoulders. The women all tucked into their drinks for a few minutes. Then Anna said, 'Well, might as well start. So what kind of bash are we throwing here?'

They were organising a party to celebrate Jackie's twin boys' Confirmation in three weeks' time. The boys had made their Holy Communion a couple of years back and now were getting ready to take the next step in becoming young members of the Catholic faith.

Misty was back leaning on her elbows. 'What do kids like these days?'

Anna flicked her black hair back. 'They're boys for a start, so maybe something rough and tumble. Maybe Jackie should ask Schoolboy?'

On hearing the name of Jackie's other half they all dropped into an uncomfortable silence. None of them wanted to say it, but they all knew that something was going on between Jackie and her old man. Jackie would barely talk about him these days.

'We should really ask her what's up,' Roxy muttered quietly.

Ollie answered. 'When she's ready she'll tell us.' Her take on life was that you didn't meddle in anyone's business unless they asked you. Never asking questions was something she'd learned back in her days as a child soldier in Africa. Asking questions could mean a death sentence at the end of a gun or wicked-looking machete.

Anna kissed her teeth, a classic Caribbean gesture for showing annoyance, dismissing her friend's remark. 'Look, we're her mates, yeah?' She wriggled her head to emphasise her words. 'We can all see something's up so we should just point blank ask her. Schoolboy used to pop in here all the time and now I can't remember the last time we saw his face.'

'He's busy with his *own* business,' Ollie persisted.

'No, I think Anna's right.' Misty took a sip from her G&T before she continued. 'I weren't happy, as you all know, about Jackie hooking up with him, but I've got to say he proved me well wrong. You couldn't ask for a more blindin' husband and dad than Schoolboy.'

'So we're all agreed then.' Anna stared at them, her tone clearly saying she wasn't asking but telling. 'We're going to ask her what's—'

But before she could finish Misty's mobile started going. With a sigh she picked it up.

'Yeah?' As she listened she slowly straightened to her six-two height as the blood drained away from her face. 'We'll be right there.' She cut the call. Looked at the concerned faces of the others.

'What is it?' Ollie asked.

'We need to get to the hospital.' Misty started moving frantically from behind the bar.

'Ohmygod.' A distressed Anna shot to her feet. 'Is it Jackie?'

Misty stopped moving. Shook her head. 'It's one of her boys. I think he might be dead.'

three

Across town the brakes of the jeep screeched to a halt outside the garage. The windscreen was shattered and the front crunched in on the left side. The driver got out. Bulky man, with a hooded top hiding his face. His breathing heaved in his chest as he moved swiftly towards the dirty splattered white door. Opened it. The garage was empty. Cold. He jumped back in the car. Drove inside. Got out of the car again. Headed for the door. Stepped outside. Bang. He slammed the door behind him. Then he ran, his hood still hiding his face.

The air ambulance touched down on the rooftop of the Royal London Hospital in Whitechapel in a whirl of noise. For those that had time to worry about such things, the views across the capital were mouth dropping, with the Gherkin building jutting out of the skyline to the west and Canary Wharf and the HSBC building to the south. But the occupants of the ambulance didn't notice any of that, all they focused on was the boy inside hanging onto his life.

Jackie held her son's hand, her mind spinning as fast as the helicopter blades, as she stared at the tubes coming out of him. Her little Preston. Mummy's little boy. *Jesus, Mary and all the saints please don't let my little boy die. Please.* Jackie snapped out of her prayer when the paramedic beside her flung open the door. A blast of cool air rushed inside.

He looked at her and said, 'Keep your head down and just follow us.'

She nodded. With quick efficiency the doctor and paramedic moved the gurney that Preston lay on outside. They moved without glancing back at Jackie. She followed. Kept pace with them as the noise of the blades got slower and slower behind them. They stopped at a lift and were soon inside. Jackie's trembling hand smoothed her son's springboard locks back as she whispered, 'You're going to be alright, you're going to be alright.' Her mind skidded back to the horror show she'd witnessed half an hour ago.

She'd run towards Preston's prone, bloody body. Knelt by his side, yelling for an ambulance at the same time. She'd looked at him, the tears washing her cheeks. And when she'd seen the blood pooling by his head . . . Oh Christ . . . she'd almost fainted dead away. But instead she'd reached for him. Wanted to pick him up. Squeeze him to her crazy beating heart. But someone had dragged her back, who it was she didn't know. Told her not to touch him. Not touch him? Were they bonkers? No way could she leave her little boy there, broken in the road. That's when she'd struggled, fought, whoever held her. But they wouldn't let go. Her sobs had torn up the street like a wounded animal. The voices of the people around her had started floating over her, one voice merging into another, but she was able to pick out what one of them was saying. The jeep had ploughed into Preston as he crossed the road. Must've been the same car that had mowed down the Lewis girls outside the school. After that everything had become a blur and the next thing she knew she was riding beside her son, high above London in the air ambulance taking them to the hospital.

The lift doors opened, pushing her thoughts to the side. Another doctor was waiting for them. Female, Asian, a pretty young thing, whose eyebrows wriggled together as she looked at Preston. They raced along the corridor, the new doctor speaking with the other medical staff as they moved. She wanted them to just shut up and do something. At the end of a corridor they hit A&E and swung through its doors.

Jackie stepped eagerly forward to go inside, but a hand on her arm stopped her. Her hand dropped away from the moving gurney as she looked sideways. The paramedic looked at her gently. 'Miss—?' He started.

'Jarvis.' She hadn't taken Schoolboy's surname of Campbell when they'd tied the knot. Keeping her name somehow made her feel her own woman still. 'But people just call me Jackie, never Jack mind you,' she babbled back. If she kept talking then there was no space for bad news.

The pressure of his hands increased as he smiled softly. She looked over his shoulder as they settled the trolley in the centre of the room. She tried to move forward but the increased pressure of his hands stopped her. 'Best if you remain here so the medical team can work—'

'But—' she protested back.

'Let them do their work.'

She wanted to argue back but knew he was right. She might just get in the way. She nodded back, her arms wrapping around her tense tummy. But she moved until she stood looking in the window of the room Preston was in. Her breath tumbled in her chest as the medical team cut off his clothes quickly and efficiently with a pair of scissors. Then she heard them talking, using words she didn't know the meaning of:

RTA

Hypotensive

Tachycardic

FBC

ABG

She gasped when she saw the large bruise and blood clinging to his side. Her legs almost gave out then and there. *Stay strong. Stay strong.* Her arms tightened around herself. The tears gathered in her green eyes. One of the nurses turned around and caught her distressed stare. Walked over to her. 'Why don't you take a seat in the waiting area and we'll come and get you—'

Jackie shook her head. 'No disrespect – but sod off, I ain't going anywhere—'

But, as if she hadn't spoken, the nurse calmly took her arm and started leading her away. Jackie twisted her head and yelled,

'Hang in there son.' Then she was in the corridor, the noise of other people about not registering with her. Suddenly her mind started filling up with images. Preston bawling his head off as the Priest dropped water on his head as he was christened in a beautiful, white gown in church; Preston leaping in the air after scoring his first goal at Saturday footie club; Preston looking up at her with his adoring dark eyes as he lay with her on the sofa, whispering in her ear, 'No one's got a smile like my mum.'

She sniffed as she wrapped her arms tighter around herself. 'Mum loves you.'

'Ms Jarvis?'

Jackie twisted around at the sound of her name. It was Mrs Moran, the boys' headteacher, who stood a few feet away from Jackie. Clutching her hand was Jackie's other boy, Darius. He let go of Mrs Moran's hand as Jackie opened her arms and flew into her embrace. She held him close as his little body shook with sobs. She knew he was crippled by the thought of his twin seriously hurt. She rocked him whispering words of comfort. Finally she raised her eyes to Mrs Moran and said, 'Thank you.' And she meant it with all her heart. Mrs Moran was here for her just as she had been for the school for the last six years. Parents couldn't ask for a better head teacher than the woman standing in front of her.

Mrs Moran's face was pinched, the paleness of her face matching the stark white of the blouse she wore under her navy skirt suit. The older woman nodded, making a stray strand of hair escape her no-nonsense brunette-tinted bob. She took a step closer to Jackie. 'How's Preston?'

Jackie opened her mouth but the words stuck in her throat. She swallowed and tried to speak again but the words just wouldn't come out. Misreading her reaction the eyes of the older woman grew large. 'I'm so sorry . . .'

'No,' Jackie finally uttered with a swift shake of her head. 'They're working on him now. He's going to be alright, I know he is.'

Mrs Moran took another tentative step closer as if she were debating whether to take the plunge and haul Jackie into her arms. But instead she stopped and drew her shoulders back as if remembering she was still doing her job. Still had to be one of the people who were the backbone of her pupils' community. 'I'm sure he will be,' she responded softly. 'I would stay but I need to get back. The police want to talk to me.' Without waiting for Jackie to respond she half turned, but Jackie's next words stopped her.

'How are the girls?'

The other woman slowly turned as Jackie felt Darius's body tense in her arms. Suddenly he started sobbing harder.

Mrs Moran faced her. 'They were pronounced dead at the scene.'

four

Detective Inspector Ricardo Smart, Ricky to his mates, should've been on the job back at the office when he got the call. Instead he was on the job with his girlfriend between the sheets in their duplex in Wapping. Ricky was a couple of inches over six foot, had the right blend of Irish and Jamaican to attract the female eye and was one of the top black cops in the Metropolitan force. What made him most attractive to his superiors was that he was not only damn good at his job, but he understood the underworld inside out. He'd been a street hood himself once upon a time.

But gangland was the furthest thing from his mind at the moment. Naked, his smooth, brown skin glistened as Daisy did her thing on top of him. Her black hair tumbled over her shoulders as she moved and moaned. His mobile went off as his sexed-up leer watched his thumb flick a nipple just the way he knew she liked it. She groaned. Arched. Did that playful swivel of her hips as the phone rang for a second time. They both ignored it. Kept going at it until Ricky knew whoever the caller was wasn't going to give up.

He shifted their bodies sideways as his left hand leaned over and picked up the phone on the bedside cabinet.

'Smart,' he mumbled, his other hand never missing a beat as it continued its down and dirty exploration of Daisy. He relaxed as he realised that the voice on the other end belonged to one of his junior officers. 'This better be good.'

He listened, barely suppressing a groan as Daisy's hips took him onto the next level of his sexual journey. He cut in, 'This is one for the Bill in Mile End.'

Deciding that the conversation was finished, he started to move the receiver away, but was stopped when he caught some of what the officer said next. '. . . kids dead?' His thumb stopped moving. But Daisy kept on going. 'Give it to Begum to sort out . . . Why do they want me?'

The officer's next words made his body shoot forward, unseating Daisy.

'Whose kids?' He was already swinging off the bed. His face became bleak as the answer was repeated. 'I'll be there in twenty.'

He stood up at the same time he cut the call.

'Ricky, you aren't going to leave me like this?' Daisy complained. She lay on her side looking at him with her intense, blue eyes, the beauty spot looking playful at the corner of her mouth.

'One kid's badly injured and two kids are dead. There's going to be some reverb on this one.' He saw her face shift gear from sexy to shocked surprise. 'Someone just mowed down Stanley Lewis's kids outside their school.'

Daisy shot upright. In her line of work as a lawyer defending some of London's more notorious characters she knew all about the Lewis family. 'Was it an accident?'

Ricky grabbed his trousers as he answered. 'That's what I'm going to have to find out.'

Fifty-year-old Kenny 'Bulldog' Lewis got the news about his grandkids while he was doing his Tai Chi routine in his prison cell on the outskirts of South London. Oldgate was one of the previous government's new prisons built in partnership with a private company – a couple of wings remained incomplete and were likely to remain so for some time as the new government had axed funding in its bid to deal with the economic recession. Kenny wasn't a big man but his own name was all the muscle he needed. He kept his greying brown hair clipped short, his brown eyes alert and his nose in the middle of most of the dealings that went on inside. And each day, like clockwork, he practised his Tai Chi at five o'clock.

He'd been doing Tai Chi since he was eighteen years old. Picked it up from a Sri Lankan dope smuggler who he'd shared a cell with during his first stretch. He'd laughed at his cellie at first, calling him a tosser for all his primping and preening. One day the guy had dared him to try it. Never one to back away from anything in life he had given it a go. The first move he'd been taught was to move his arms and hands as lightly as a butterfly. *Stretch your arms out and move them up in an arch as if you were reaching for the moon.* His Sri Lankan friend was right; inner calm turned out to be very healthy for a ruthless gangland boss like Kenny.

He reached for the moon now as his cell door opened. He knew something was up because no one interrupted his 5 p.m. routine. He didn't turn around. Instead he brought his arms down until his fingers lightly touched his thighs. Inhaled through his nose. Exhaled through his mouth. Finally turned.

When he saw it was the Number One flanked by two guards he knew some serious shit was up. Especially when he saw a counsellor bringing up the rear. Mind you, that was no surprise; this prison had more counsellors than it did screws. The most likely reasons, Kenny decided, were a successful, high profile appeal – or someone was dead. And as he had no appeals outstanding . . .

'Oh dear. Someone gone coffin-wise?' he asked calmly.

The Governor did a nervous cough before he quietly said. 'Kenny, I think it's better that—'

The Governor tailed off. Kenny had a think. It might be his son, Stan. The way that kid carried on it was surprising no one had stiffed him long ago. Kenny had been tempted to do it himself on occasion. But it was more likely to be his mum. The amount of fags the old dear smoked, she was a one-woman cremation machine.

'My mum?' The Governor just shifted his gaze nervously. 'Come on mate, we're all grown ups here—'

'Mr Lewis, Kenny—'

'Stan?'

No surprise there. Kenny's heart sank as he realised he was going to have to go to all the trouble of organising revenge killings. In gangland, revenge arrangements always came before funeral ones.

The Governor gave a tiny shake of his head. Then Kenny wondered briefly about the other son, the son that didn't exist. How could anyone have killed the son that didn't exist . . . ?

'There's no one else—' That's when he saw it in the Governor's eyes. No way. No fucking way. Not his beautiful girls? No wonder the Governor had come mob-handed because he knew what was going to happen next.

The Governor held up his hands in a peace gesture. 'Kenny, I want you to take it easy—'

But it was too late. Kenny clenched his fists and pushed forward, swinging at the guards, and then he reeled backwards onto the floor under quick blows from their batons which they'd held ready. They knew who they were dealing with. He was lifted to his feet, a guard holding each arm, but Lewis didn't need restraining any more, he needed support as he sank under his own weight as the news caught up with him. He looked up. 'Minnie and Molly.' He looked up at the Governor. 'What happened?'

The other man swallowed. 'There was an accident outside their school.'

'What?' Kenny shook his head. That couldn't be right. Outside their school? 'How?'

'They were hit by a car. I'm afraid we don't know the details yet but obviously the police have launched a full investigation and we'll keep you fully informed. A drunk driver looks most likely. Perhaps you'd like to speak to a counsellor? Mr James here can provide you with any support you might need at this difficult time.'

Lewis shook off the guards. He looked at Mr James and then back at the Governor,

'Why? Does Mr James here know anything about revenge killings? Because God help the bastard who killed my grandkids.'

'Why did that car hurt Molly mum?'

Jackie tightened her arm around her shaking son as they sat on the plastic chairs in the corridor waiting for news about Preston. She didn't know how long they'd been waiting, but the sunlight was still seeping through the window. She squeezed her eyes shut for a moment realising that her boy had to somehow deal with the death of his little Molly. She didn't have an answer for him. Couldn't tell him why he might never see his twin alive again. The pressure of her arm increased. Somehow she was going to make sure that *this* son stayed close by her side. Why hadn't she put her foot down this afternoon? Told Preston to forget the bloody ice-cream and stay put? Told him . . . Shit she wanted to get up a scream. Tell the world that this just wasn't right. Her boy was three weeks off doing his Confirmation for crying out loud.

'Jackie.'

She looked up to find her man rushing towards her. As she stood up Darius leapt out of his seat and into the arms of his dad, Elijah 'Schoolboy' Campbell. Most people still name-checked him as Schoolboy, the nickname he'd earned in his days ducking and diving on the street. Every time she saw him she was struck by how much he'd changed. And she didn't like it. Not one bloody bit. They'd both met while they lived in Ernest Bevin House, a council block in the south end of Hackney. She'd been on the second floor, he'd lived on the fourth, right at the top. She'd been the unofficial spokeswoman of the block while he'd been the sweet-talking bad boy, dealing drugs and getting up to all kinds of naughties. First time she'd clapped her green eyes on him she'd got the hots for him. His street swagger, his cheek popping dimples, his bad boy clothes and that beautiful brown face of his made her feel like she'd gone to heaven and back every time she saw it. Not a woman to let anything stand in her way she'd gone after him . . . He'd resisted for a long time, not the type of guy to put down roots or let people crowd him too much. That was until the day he'd got into all that bother with two gangs and a mobile phone. With her help he'd managed to kiss goodbye to the underworld and take up his old passion of cooking. Finally they'd got hitched, eleven years back, in a wedding that East London was unlikely to forget any time soon for all the wrong reasons.

Now he owned a restaurant up on Church Street in Stoke Newington, which was so famous it had a waiting list of two months. And to top it all he was negotiating with a TV production company to film a cooking programme called *The Bad Boy Chef*. She didn't begrudge him his success, no way, but she didn't like some of the changes it had bought. She ran her gaze over him. He looked like a friggin' City banker for crying out loud; crisp, lined designer suit, Italian shoes and briefcase. He'd even considered cutting off his shoulder-length dreads, but she'd put her foot well and truly down about that. Her old Schoolboy was disappearing before her eyes.

'Where is he?' Schoolboy's voice was frantic as he loosened one of his arms from around Darius and moved towards her. At least his voice hadn't changed, thank the Lord. It was still Cockney wide boy with a hint of Caribbean rude boy threaded through it. His arm came out as if to touch her, but she locked her arms around herself like barbed wire. His arm fell by his side. They each stood in their own space looking at each other. Things hadn't been good between them for a while.

Jackie swallowed as a shudder pulsed through her. 'He's in the emergency room.' She shook her head. 'His head's all smashed up . . .'

Schoolboy swore, his head moving from side to side as if he couldn't believe what he was hearing. He thought the world of his boys. If anyone had told him years ago that he'd be the father of twins he would've told them they needed to visit the quack. He'd lived his life a loner, on the wrong side of the law for years and finding love hadn't figured high on his list of priorities. Then he'd met Jackie and that had all changed. 'The other kids involved are dead,' she announced starkly, interrupting his thoughts.

'Fucking hell.' His fingers rushed madly through his locks. 'Have you told Ryan?'

Ryan was her eldest boy. Eighteen. She'd had him when she was a dizzy seventeen-year-old looking for the man of her dreams. But the man of her dreams had pissed off quicker than you could say child support. Schoolboy was the only dad her Ryan had ever really known.

She shook her head. 'I tried to call him, but he weren't around.' She twisted her teeth into her lip, as she thought about her eldest.

He was living away from home now and she couldn't help but worry about him. She still worried about what had happened to him at her wedding all those years ago. She just wanted all her boys close to her right now.

'The dead kids' parents must be going out of their mind,' Schoolboy uttered, shaking his head.

'They were Stanley Lewis's girls.'

His mouth fell open. Schoolboy knew who Stan Lewis was alright, he'd been part of that world back in the day. Suddenly his dark eyes blazed at her. 'Tell me you ain't been involved with these people?' The Caribbean part of his accent grew stronger.

The blood shot to her face in anger. Who the fuck did he think he was, coming here and mouthing off at her, with their kid lying in his own blood, maybe halfway to heaven by now? He had no right, no right. 'Do I look like a friggin' fool to you? 'Course I'm not involved with them, I just sorta know the girls' mum, Marina. You've heard the boys chat about the girls, the twins, especially Darius who is . . . was . . . great mates with Molly.'

'Never realised who they were,' he threw back defensively.

She folded her arm. 'Well you might've if you'd been at home more often.'

Oh, she wanted a row did she? Well he'd give her one. 'Why wasn't Preston with you anyway?'

Jackie's arms tightened around herself. 'He just wanted an ice-cream—'

'Yeah, but I thought we agreed that the boys shouldn't eat any junk before they—'

Her hands flew in the air. 'What you saying? That this is all my fault?'

''Course I ain't—'

She cut over him, her voice hitting the roof. 'Don't you think I've asked myself over and over what if I hadn't let him go? Let him . . .' The tears bolted down her pale face. And before she knew it she was wrapped in the arms of the man she loved. Just like they used to be in the old days. Her body heaved as he whispered, 'Jackie, Jackie.' His hand stroked her short, red hair. Then she felt the smaller body of her son pressed against her side. They stood there, arms wrapped around each other, like the tight family they had once been, praying for a miracle.

'There they are,' someone shouted.

Jackie and Schoolboy broke apart as they both looked down the corridor. Jackie let out a huge wave of relief when she saw who it was – her girls. Misty, Ollie, Anna and Roxy. The women swarmed around her, hugging and throwing questions at her at the same time. Just seeing them made her feel so much better. Quickly she answered all their questions. A stunned silence fell when she explained where Preston now was.

'Want me to find out what's going on?' Misty asked, taking control as she usually did in an emergency. Her grey eyes were fired up and the uneven ends of her golden hair flapped against her face.

It was Schoolboy who answered in a low tone. 'No. The doctors will let us know.'

He took Darius's hand and pulled him towards the chairs. Collapsed with his head bent, his locks falling over his head. Jackie felt the others' eyes on her, knowing that if she looked up she'd see a similar expression in all of them – one of them urging her to go to her man and comfort him. They hadn't said anything to her, but she knew they knew something was up between her and Schoolboy. Without looking at them she moved slowly towards him. He looked up at her, his dark eyes bloodshot, sensing her presence. She slid her arm across his shoulder and he buried his head into her side. 'It's going to be alright babe, you'll see,' she soothed, not sure if she believed her own words.

'Ms Jarvis?' They both shot to their feet as they heard someone call Jackie. A female nurse stood outside the emergency room. They rushed towards her, pulling Darius with them.

'The doctor would like to speak to you.' She pushed the swing doors and they disappeared inside.

The nurse walked briskly down the corridor. When she reached the group of women Misty stopped her.

'What's happening?'

Instead the nurse gave her a grave look and just shook her head. Then walked off.

Misty looked at the others. 'I think he's gone,' she whispered. She slumped back against the wall.

'I can't believe it,' Anna said, shaking her head in a daze. 'A couple of hours ago we were planning a party for him and his bruv and now it looks like we'll be planning his funeral.'

Roxy pulled out her inhaler and took huge sucks on it. On her fifth pull of air she started to cry. Calmly Ollie took her into her arms soothing her.

Then Jackie and Schoolboy emerged from the room, closely followed by the doctor. Jackie's friends rushed over to her. 'Jackie?' Misty asked, her face showing the dread she was expecting to get worse.

'They've stabilised him and he's breathing on his own, but he's unconscious. He's got a fractured right thigh and his head . . .' She took in a deep breath. 'They've given him oxygen and pain relief.' Her mouth wobbled at the thought of her little boy in pain. 'They're going to move him into Intensive Care.'

'Ohmygod,' Anna let out.

Suddenly Jackie raised her tear-streaked face. Her eyes frozen jade.

'No one will be able to keep me away from the scumbag who did this. No one.'

five

Have you planned your funeral?

Pinkie Lewis read the flyer that had just come through her front door the same time the sun slipped behind a cloud. Pinkie looked like she'd just stepped out of the 60s – blue rinse hair plus hairpiece done up into a beehive at one end, gold glitter slingbacks at the other and in the middle a strawberry pink baby doll miniskirt that showcased legs that looked years younger than her sixty-nine. Shame about the many wrinkles that were still visible through the packed powder on her face.

'Planned my own funeral?' she muttered. Bloody cheek. For Christ's sake she had plenty of years left in her yet. 'The grim reaper knows better than to mess with Kenny Lewis's mum, you cheeky sods.'

She screwed the flyer up. Some scammers having one over on the old folks; telling them to put money aside for their own deaths. Her Kenny was going to sort her out when her time came. She made her way back into the sitting room, Elvis's 'The Wonder Of You' playing softly in the background. She'd lived in this three-bed flat on the tenth floor of what had once been called Parkview Towers in Hackney for the last forty years. Except for that time the council had shipped everyone out so they could tart the block up. And when she'd returned the place had looked spanking new with a new name – Parkview Garden. What a steaming pile that was. Parkview Garden my arse. They'd need to put a park opposite for a start. Did the council really think that giving it a lick of paint, a steam clean

and writing a new name in big silver writing above the security
door – which rarely worked – was going to turn it into Buck House?
(They needed a security door on the inside anyway, without some
of the residents they'd been saddled with.) Ken wanted to move her
out, somewhere in Essex, but all her mates were here, well those
that were still alive. And she'd brought up her Kenny and Glenda
here and some of the best memories she had of her Phil were here
too. Her happy feelings disappeared as she thought about Glenda.
She hadn't seen her daughter in over fifteen years. Mind you who
could blame Glenda after what had happened. After . . .

Pinkie dropped into her armchair as she shook off best-left-
alone thoughts of the past. She picked up the glass on the table
next to her. Her favourite poison, cough mixture with a stick of
cinnamon – her Bingo mate Matilda kept her supplied with the
spice every time she went to Grenada in the Caribbean – and a
dollop of water. Her little finger with the two rings on flapped as
she took a healthy slug. That's why everyone called her Pinkie
because she liked to wear two rings on her little pinkie.

She popped the glass down with a sigh and picked up the library
book and the thick black felt-tip pen on the arm of the chair. She
squinted as she began her favourite pastime, after Bingo that was,
scrubbing out swear words in library books. 'Filth,' she muttered
as she came across the F word again. The book was a tale about
a young girl looking for her real mum. So what was with all that
fruity language? Her own great grand babies, Minnie and Molly,
could go into the library and pick it up for heaven's sake. Her
late husband had drawn bras in felt-tip on topless models in the
tabloids. They had standards. They were a standards family.

A furious pounding at the front door came just as she raised
her pen again. She eased back. For a minute she thought it must
be her Kenny. Then she remembered he was banged up in that
new swanky slammer. Her long-dead Phil had seen the inside of
Brixton a couple of times before some scum had gunned him down
in a pub on The Old Kent Road. The pounding came again.

'Hold your horses,' she muttered as she pushed herself up. She
made her way into the passage, past the bedroom that she always

kept locked. Opened the door. Shocked, she peered up to find her grandson.

'Stan?' He looked a total mess, hair going this way and that, shirt hanging out of his pants and . . . blood? What the hell had he been up to? Reminded her of the days he used to come home from school after playing a game of 'dodge my fist' with some kid in the playground. Reminded her of that night . . . Pinkie jumped out of her thoughts quickly. She didn't want to think about *that* night.

'Gran–' Then he burst into tears. She poked her head out and quickly looked around. That's all she needed was for the twitchy curtain neighbours of hers to see her grandson blubbing for all the world to see. Her boy Kenny would go bonkers if he heard his son had been booing in public.

Quickly she ushered him indoors. She put her arm around him. 'Now, tell your Nan what's been going on.' All the men in her family were little boys really.

Whatever it was she knew it was bad from the haunted look in his teary eyes.

'Minnie . . .' He choked. 'Molly . . .'

He carried on talking and she started to shake. There weren't many times in her life that Pinkie Lewis had cried. The last time had really been that night that dreadful business happened in the bedroom she kept locked. But she cried now as she covered her mouth. Why, oh why, was God taking two more kids from her family? She'd already lost two others before they were full grown.

Jackie's words exploded around them like a grenade. They all stared at her as if she'd lost the plot. Misty. Ollie. Anna. Roxy. Schoolboy. Even Darius gave his mum a stunned look under his eyelashes.

Roxy surprised everyone by being the first one to respond. She shook her buttermilk bob and squeaked, 'Calm down Jackie, you can't take the law into your own hands.'

Jackie's finger pointed down the corridor. 'You seen what whoever the bastard is has done to my kid? No one does that to one of mine and gets away with it.' Her eyes shot to her husband. 'Do they?'

Instead of answering he remained silent, his lips twisting together. Jackie reared towards him. 'You ain't going to help me, is that what you're saying?' Still Schoolboy said nothing. With a huff of fury she stabbed her finger into his chest. 'Back in the old days you wouldn't have thought twice. You would've been with me all the way. Oh, but I forgot,' she continued sarcastically, slamming her fists onto her hips. 'You're all suited and booted these days. Mr Respectable. With his own business and his la-di-da nosh-loving mates. But you know what? You've lost something along the way and you know what that is?' One of her hands flew off her hips. Pointed her finger razor-straight into his face. 'Your fucking backbone.'

'That's enough my girl.' It was Misty who spoke, her tone saying clearly that Jackie had crossed a line.

As if suddenly realising what she'd said, Jackie snapped her mouth shut. Without a word Schoolboy grabbed his son's hand and calmly walked back to the area with the seats.

Misty hustled closer to Jackie. 'That was way out of order.' Jackie opened her mouth but Misty carried on. 'You're not the only one who's hurting. Poor bloke looks like he's just done 15 rounds down Bethnal Green ABA—'

'I don't fucking care,' Jackie exploded, hands going in the air. 'He should be stood right here next to me now.'

Anna moved closer, her brown face creased in disbelief. She spoke in a clenched whisper. 'He was until you started flapping your mouth. What are you going to do? Go around London playing the Caped Crusader while he has to do Robin? Give the brother a break.'

The sound of a mobile ringing cut through the tense atmosphere. Misty whipped her hand into her lilac shoulder bag and pulled out her phone. As she moved away from the group to take the call, Ollie spoke quietly, addressing Jackie, her dark face solemn. 'They are right Jackie. You must leave this to the police.'

Misty rejoined the group, before Jackie could respond to Ollie, her face looking slightly worried. She shoved the mobile back into her bag as Jackie looked frantically between her friends. 'What are you all saying? You ain't going to help me?' When one of them was in a tight fix they always banded together and got whatever was up sorted out. It was a serious bit of bother that they'd all been involved in when they were fifteen, and God knows how old Misty had been since she didn't let on about her age, that had made them the tight five-person circle they were. Now she couldn't believe that they weren't going to lift a finger to help her out. Didn't they get it? Some scumbag had almost killed her own flesh and blood? Had killed two girls in one of the places they should've felt the safest, their school.

Misty put on her bossette of the group face. 'You need to be thinking about your boy. Preston needs you—'

'That's what I'm bloody doing,' Jackie yelled back. 'Thinking of him. I don't care that this might be some accident, no one . . .' She stabbed her finger at Misty. 'No one has got the right to do what they did to him today.'

'Jackie . . .' This time it was Schoolboy.

She sent him a look filled with so much scorn that he winced. Her small body trembled as she said contemptuously, 'I don't need you lot anyway. I can do this my own.' Swiftly she turned but someone grabbed her. She half turned, running her gaze over the hand, up the arm until she found the face it belonged to. Misty. 'Listen to me—'

'Let. Go. Of. My. Arm.' Every word sliced through Jackie's teeth.

But Misty's hold grew tighter. She dipped her face closer to the woman she had been looking out for since she was fifteen years old. 'I'm not letting you—'

No one saw it coming. Not even Misty. Jackie slapped Misty with all the fury and anger she'd felt since seeing her son, broken and bleeding in the road. Misty staggered back as the others gasped. No one moved as Misty rubbed her palm against her stinging cheek. She stared at Jackie with dismay. Not once, no matter how many times they'd locked horns, had Jackie ever hit her. That's why Misty had stumbled back, not because of the pain – she'd had much worse growing up on the streets of East London – but because it was Jackie who had bloody walloped her one. Right there, in front of the others.

Schoolboy broke the silence. 'What is going on with you?' he threw at his wife.

'My son, your son, might be brown bread any moment now and I'm going to find who did this . . .'

But this time it was Misty's turn to point her finger at Jackie. 'Me and you . . .' her voice so soft that Jackie knew the woman she'd seen as a second mum was about ready to explode, 'will need to have a chat about what you just did, but for now you're going to park your arse and stay put.'

Tears glistened in Jackie's eyes. 'But I've got to—'

Finally Misty lost her rag and started shooting her mouth off. 'You don't know what you're getting into. Guys like . . .' Her fingers pressed against her lips when she realised what she was about to reveal.

'Guys?' Jackie was baffled. 'What guys?'

Knowing every eye was on her Misty waved her hand in the air and stepped back. 'Just my old gob running away with me again . . .'

But Jackie wasn't letting her off the hook, no way. 'You've heard something haven't you?'

Misty kept it zipped until Schoolboy added, 'If you know anything you've got to let us know.'

Finally, with a long sigh Misty nodded. 'The thing is . . .' She had a think about what she wanted to say. 'I just got a call from Mickey.' They all knew who Mickey was, a solid friend of theirs who owned a few businesses under The Arches in Bethnal Green. 'Whispers are saying they know who the motor that hit the kids belonged to.'

Jackie stepped expectantly towards her friend. 'Who?'

Misty stared her straight back in the eye. 'Paul Bliss.'

six

A few miles away, twenty-five-year-old Paul Bliss pulled his hood down as he stepped out of his car. Rarely did anyone use his first name, he was just known as Bliss. And that's the way he liked it because calling him by his first name was too cosy, too friendly, and the world he'd chosen as his profession wasn't one where you came to make lifelong mates. What he didn't tell people was calling him Paul just reminded him of his alkie mum. He was lean, with muscles he developed in his home gym, hair gelled back with spikes on the top, blue eyes that many avoided looking into, legs like a dancer and, some claimed, was going to be the kingpin of London's underworld one day very soon.

He looked up at one of his many properties, a house in Limehouse. Four storeys high, plain brick, end of terrace in a pretty little Georgian Square. But he didn't have time to admire the house he'd picked up for a zilch as a dump years ago in a poker game and was now being touted as being part of a conservation area. His nerves were ready to pop as he took out a key from inside his pocket. Jammed it into the door. Stepped inside. He eased the door back quietly as he shouted, 'Sherry.'

She was his current number one, although he had a couple of other birds warming his slippers by the fire across different parts of town. They'd met at the funeral of her teenage sister, who'd been one of the workers in his drug factory in Leyton, but had got way too cosy with the merchandise and OD'd one night. Stupid girl. One minute Sherry had been laying flowers on her sister's grave, the next he'd had her black dress up and boobs out in his Bentley.

He called her name again. No response. Good. She must be out, most probably shopping. If there was one thing Sherry liked doing it was spending his cash as quickly as he gave it to her. He took the carpeted steps on the narrow staircase two at a time. Strode down the landing and stopped outside the door of the main bedroom, the last door at the end. Burst into the room and stopped dead.

There was his woman, who he paid exclusive rights for, going at it, doggy style, with some bloke. The couple moaned and groaned for all they were worth a good few seconds before Sherry realised someone else was in the room. She twisted her head around.

'Shit,' she cried, pushing her latest squeeze off.

The man stared at Bliss with terror in his eyes. He knew who Bliss was. What he could do.

'This ain't what it looks—' Sherry pleaded.

'Shut up.' She shook at his words. His gaze swung to the man. 'Get out of here before I scramble your balls and have them with a bit of kipper for brekkie.'

The guy didn't need any more prompting, grabbing his clothes and hightailing it for the door. Bliss let him go. He never forgot a face and this man's was no different. He'd deal with him later.

Sherry looked at him, her gloss-coated lips rubbing nervously together. Then her body language changed as she leaned back seductively, making sure her 38 double D implants were on full display. 'It didn't mean nothin' you know.' She ran her tongue slowly over her bottom lip. Her top lip. 'Just been a bit lonely waiting for you love.'

Bliss kept his blue eyes on her chest as he sauntered towards her. Smiled. She hitched herself forward as she eased towards him. His hand snapped out and grabbed her by the hair. She yelped in surprise and pain as his fingers tightened into her newly done blonde extensions at the back. He shoved his face into her space, breathing hotly against her skin. 'And you're forgetting that you mean nothin' to me. Just a handy pussy to poke when I'm in these parts, got it?'

Her face grew hard. She knew the score. He let her go as quickly as he'd grabbed her. His hand moved towards the bedside twin-drawer table and pulled out the top drawer where he knew she kept her stash of C. A minute later he was sniffing the three lines he'd cut on the tabletop. As the hit swung into his body he dropped onto the bed. Shit he needed this after what had happened this afternoon.

Sherry grinned as she got out of bed in her birthday suit and said, 'I know what you need.' As she moved across the room Bliss's mobile pinged. Text. He popped it out of his trouser pocket.

Ls kids dead. Word is u did it.

S

The words slammed into him as he read the message from his right-hand man, Sean. He knew who L was – Stan Lewis, the prick he'd learned to hate above everyone else.

'Your favourites,' Sherry said bringing him out of his thoughts. She held a box in her hand and he knew it was a packet of over-the-counter painkillers he loved to take to relax him even more when he was coked up. And he needed relaxing alright. He got up and moved towards her. She opened the packet and as soon as he got close to her popped a tab into his mouth. He twisted her around so that she faced the window onto the street below. He leaned her against the dressing table as he whispered into her ear, 'If anyone asks, I was with you until this afternoon.'

She nodded as he bent her over and unzipped his jeans. Her eyes caught the motor he'd parked outside. One she'd never seen him drive before.

'Paul Bliss.' Roxy picked up the name that Misty had said in a stunned voice.

Before anyone could utter anything else, Schoolboy dropped to his haunches and took Darius by the shoulder. He stared into eyes that were a mirror image of his own and saw his son's confusion. Darius didn't have a clue who Paul Bliss was, but Schoolboy knew who he was alright. One of London's most ruthless rising stars of the underworld. His name had been mentioned from drugs to prostitution, from robberies to murder. He wasn't attached to any of the well-known families, he was his own player which made him dangerous because he answered to no one but himself.

Schoolboy shoved his hand in his pocket and pulled out some loose change. He pushed it into Darius's palm. 'Go down to the vending machine at the end of the corridor and get yourself something nice.'

Darius didn't want to leave his mum or dad's side, but he could tell that his dad wasn't asking, he was telling. He nodded, picked up his Arsenal rucksack from the chair and moved down the hall.

Schoolboy stood and faced the others. 'Are you sure that's what you heard?'

Misty raised her hands in a helpless gesture. 'I'm only telling you what Mickey says he's hearing. It might be wrong. It might not have been Bliss behind the wheel even if it belonged to him. It might or might not have been a lot of things. That's why you ...' she turned her grey eyes onto Jackie, '... need to leave it to the cops, they'll find out. Don't get in over your head, especially with a man like Bliss.'

But Jackie being Jackie there was no way she could leave this one alone. 'Why would Bliss be driving his jeep like that outside a school at chucking out time? It doesn't make sense. The devil himself does 10mph outside a school.'

'If – and I mean if – it was Bliss,' Misty carried on, 'it could be anything. He likes a drink, he might have been pissed, it happens. Or maybe he's got a plan, I don't know.'

'A plan?' Jackie finally spoke again. The others kept quiet knowing this was between Misty, Jackie and Schoolboy. 'What, you think it was deliberate?' Jackie shook her head as if she couldn't take it in. 'No one's that evil, not even Bliss.'

By the look on Misty's face everyone could see she regretted opening her trap in the first place. 'If you think mowing kids down is beyond the likes of Mister Bliss, you're way out of touch. He's done worse things than that. People have been saying for years it's going to kick off between him and Stanley Lewis.' Seeing Jackie's mouth fly open Misty quickly answered her question before she asked it. 'What's going on between those two I don't know. Maybe this is his opening bid. I dunno – the only thing I do know is that you need to keep your trotters and your beak well out of it.'

'Misty's right,' Ollie calmly added, pushing her glasses up her nose. 'Jackie you need to be focusing on Preston. You should be thinking about how we all can help make him get better.'

Jackie scoffed. 'I'm not staying out of anything. If it's Bliss, he's dead. Simple.'

Suddenly Misty grabbed her arm and dragged her close, lifting Jackie on to her tiptoes. 'All that wax had better be out of your ears girl coz you need to listen good. This is Bliss we're chatting about. Bliss! Do you hear me? I heard that him and some of his crew like to "interview" girls for jobs in his clubs by inviting them to a party, slipping a mickey into their drinks and then taking turns with them. The ones who pass what they call the "Double P Test" are the ones they give the jobs to.' Jackie became pale. She felt like puking just thinking about what Misty was saying.

'That the kind of guy you think you can go up against?' Misty finished quietly. She eased the smaller woman to her feet. Let her go.

'She's right,' Schoolboy agreed.

'I don't care,' Jackie threw back defiantly, giving him a look that said she regretted ever kissing him for the first time thirteen years ago on the open-aired balcony outside her front door. 'The Bill won't catch Bliss. He's been getting away with it for years. He hasn't even had a parking fine, he's too clever. There's no point in waiting for the referee to red-card him, he has to be hacked down. And I can see none of you lot are going to support me.' Jackie wore her defiance hot and red like her hair. 'I don't give a fuck who Bliss is, I'm going to make him wish he'd stuck to drugging girls instead of killing innocent little kids.'

She stormed off towards the exit.

In another part of the hospital Marina Lewis stood terrified outside the door. The cut in her lip throbbed from where Stan had back-handed her, but it was nothing compared to the pain in her heart.

'Do you want me to come in?' the nurse beside her quietly asked.

Marina just stood, as if she hadn't heard, looking at the translucent doors that hid what was inside the room. As her fingers curled tightly into her palms she felt where some of her pink, artificial nails were missing. They'd broken off when she'd frantically whipped Minnie off the cold, grey ground. Minnie.

The nurse parted her lips as if to repeat the questions then clamped them shut. Instead she hooked her arm into Marina's and gently asked, 'Ready?'

Ready? What a fool thing to say, Marina thought bitterly. What parent would ever be ready for this?

'I'm alright,' Marina said, her voice distant.

She pulled in some air. Straightened her shoulders. Her hand came up. Stopped as it trembled and wavered for a second when it reached the door. With another huge breath she finally pushed the door. Stepped inside.

Marina's breath caught at what she saw. Two trolleys, close together with green sheets that hid what lay underneath. Oh God, she thought, as her legs trembled.

'I'm alright,' Marina said again.

She moved forward, the nurse keeping pace with her every step of the way. Finally they halted at the side of the trolley on the right. Marina's shaking hand came to the sheet. She touched it. Her hand leapt back as if she'd touched fire.

'I can't,' she let out, her head continually shaking. She tried but couldn't stop the movement of her head.

The nurse pulled the green sheet back. Marina sucked in her breath as she stared mournfully at the lifeless face of one of her beloved twin angels. The child's small face was chalk-white, her eyes closed and her blonde hair neatly arranged at the side. She could've been sleeping she looked that peaceful.

Marina's palm tenderly touched her daughter's face. 'That's Molly,' she said softly. 'Not many people can tell them apart you know. Even when she's sleeping Molly always has a tiny smile on her face. Can you see it?'

The nurse couldn't, but she just nodded knowing how important it was to reassure this woman who'd had her children so cruelly taken from her.

The swing doors flew open. Both women turned around. A huffing and puffing Stanley Lewis stood in the doorway. His face was red from either crying or anger. Ignoring both women he marched forward and stopped at the trolley. Looked down at his dead daughter. He didn't touch her. Didn't speak. Stood there for a good minute just looking down. Then, without any warning, he twisted around to his former wife. Tears streamed down his face. 'Are you happy now bitch?'

The nurse knew grief did terrible things to someone's mind but she wasn't putting up with this. She didn't care that he was the father.

'Hold on a minute—'

But he continued to spit out his venom as if she hadn't spoken. 'You were taking them away from me today. Trying to take my little girls away.' He took a menacing step towards his ex. She shuffled back. 'Well they're gone now for fucking good. I hope you're pleased with yourself? This is all your fault, you might as well have been behind the wheel.'

Marina started sobbing hysterically. The nurse immediately put her arms around the broken woman. 'Now you look here—'

Stan turned his fury onto the nurse. 'You keep your schnoz out of my business . . .'

Marina started screaming as if the devil himself was in the room. She started swaying, her legs starting to wobble. Then she fainted, her limp hand catching the green sheet on the other trolley. As she fell, the sheet fell with her, revealing the still body of Minnie Lewis.

As the nurse attended to Marina, Stan lifted the lifeless body of his daughter and held her in his arms. Sobbing he said, 'Goodbye baby. Daddy loves you.' His next words made the nurse shoot her gaze towards him. 'I'm going to find who did this. And by the end of the night it ain't gonna be just you who's lying on a slab.'

With that he replaced his daughter gently, ignored the crumpled figure of his ex-wife and stormed out of the room like a hurricane heading for land.

seven

Eighteen-year-old Ryan Jarvis walked out of the Gents of The Five Fingers Club in Bethnal Green with a big grin slapped on his face. He had fiery red hair that he'd inherited from his grandmother, a sparkle in his green eyes and was a similar height to the father he'd never known, a few inches off six foot. His smile slipped slightly as he thought of his mum. If she ever found out what he'd been up to in the toilets he was a dead man. He swaggered into the main room, chat and music blaring around him and approached the table where his girlfriend sat.

'Did you do it?' she whispered nervously at him when he reached the table.

His smile grew full blast again as he stared at Foxy Jones. Her real name was Frances but her professional name was Foxy. She'd been trying to break into the glamour modelling scene for the last year and Ryan knew she certainly had the necessary equipment to succeed. She was slim, tall, with a smooth peachy complexion that the camera loved, fly-away bleached-blonde hair and boobs that had been a 36 B last year and were now a 36 double E. Her low cut top and leopard-print Lycra miniskirt made the best of what she had on top and below her waistline.

Instead of answering he stretched out his hand towards her and said, 'Let's get out of here.' Hand-in-hand they hustled towards the exit. Stopped when the tough-looking man, wearing a suit, who stood near the door, gave them the once-over. Ryan swallowed, suddenly scared. What if this man knew what he'd been doing?

No, he convinced himself, no way could the geezer have sussed him out. He stared out the guy with a cheeky grin and a confident wink. The man stepped to the side, letting them pass. Soon they were in the daylight rushing up the stairs, towards the pavement, Foxy's leopard-print heels making a loud clacking sound against the concrete.

Foxy flashed her baby blues at him behind her thick, spiky fake eyelashes. 'Did you do it?' she repeated, with impatience this time.

But still he wouldn't answer. Instead he dragged her down the road until they reached his home, Herbert Morrison Tower, which lay behind Cambridge Heath Road. The block had once been council owned, but now was a private complex housing mainly City workers and artists from the growing Bethnal Green art scene. Like all the other mainly young residents, Ryan loved the spacious accommodation and the amazing views he had of London from his twelfth-floor two-bed flat. He'd only been living there for six months, a present on his eighteenth birthday from his mum and stepdad, Schoolboy. Where his mum and dad – he'd been calling Schoolboy dad since he was eight years old – got that kind of money from he did not know, and didn't care, all that mattered was he was a young lad about town with the world at his feet.

As soon as they got inside his home he dragged Foxy towards the cream sofa, threw her on it, then pushed his hand into his pocket and chucked a bundle of twenties onto her. She grinned wildly, showing her recently whitened teeth, as she scooped some of the notes into the air. Ryan collapsed next to her the same time his phone pinged with a text message. He ignored the message as he gathered Foxy into a bone-crushing hug.

'You're bloody right I did it.'

Foxy's blue eyes flashed at him. 'How much?'

'A oner.' His joy abruptly fell away as he gently eased her away from him and looked seriously at her. 'This is between me and you remember, no one else.'

'Of course babe.'

Five minutes later they were smoking blow and snorting a couple of lines of C. Dizzy with the drugs entering her bloodstream

Foxy started peeling her top off. Next her bra flew across the room. Giggling they got down and dirty on the tan-coloured laminate floor. Ryan's phone pinged again. This time he got it.

'Shit.' He bolted upright as he read.

'What's the matter?'

He swallowed as he looked at Foxy. 'It's my little brother. He's in the hospital.'

Sean McCarthy looked at the CCTV footage of the toilet in the club. He twisted his mouth in a face that could have been handsome if it wasn't for the deep knife scar across his chin. His slightly receding curly, dark brown hair was gelled back away from his stony white face. He leaned forward in his seat, inside the office at the back of the club, as he watched the drug deal that had gone down in the Gents fifteen minutes ago. The boss wasn't going to be happy about this. The only person who dealt in his club was him. Sean swept his harsh gaze away from the punter handing over his readies for a bag of crystal meth to the drug dealer. He memorised the dealer's face – white, freckles with red hair. Picked up the phone to call the boss.

Screw the lot of 'em.

Jackie sucked hard on a ciggie as she motored down Vallance Road, the Krays' old turf, and hit Bethnal Green Road. If her mates didn't want to help her find who did this to her Preston, then so be it. But Schoolboy? He should be here now by her side. Her mind batted angry thoughts backwards and forwards as she kept moving. Bliss fucking Bliss. Who would've thought it? The geezer must've been doing some heavy shit to commit such a terrible crime in broad daylight. Outside a school. What had the underworld come to? Even the underworld had its rules. Rule number one, never snitch, rule number two, never touch a kid. So why would Bliss try and break years of tradition? She just didn't get it, didn't get it at all. The smoke settled in her mouth as the questions rode like crazy in her brain.

She flicked the butt the same time she took a right turn into an area of Bethnal Green that people just called The Arches. Most of the businesses that were under the old railway bridge and spilled out onto the Victorian cobblestones were garages. She passed a business that had nothing to do with cars, an art gallery of all places. She'd heard that art galleries were springing up all over Bethnal Green. Who would've thought it? Yeah Bethnal Green like the rest of East London was undergoing a change.

She stopped outside Mickey's Steam Cleaning Service. A couple of guys who were looking inside the hood of a black cab nodded at her as she walked past them into the entrance of Mickey's business. The place was a good size displaying the original bricks of the Victorian walls and arched roof. A few men worked away on two vehicles. One was a jeep, which made Jackie shudder.

'Heard what happened.' Jackie turned to find Mickey lounging in the doorway of his office located in the right-hand corner near the entrance. Mickey wasn't the type to hug anyone, it just wasn't his way, but the way he felt about you was all in his eyes. And Jackie could see that his eyes were hard. He was well into his fifties now, but still kept himself fit and trim and still got his head profession-ally shaved every month.

Jackie walked steadily over to him. 'Misty said that you told her it was Bliss.'

'Let's go and have a brew,' Mickey said showing his gold teeth as he twisted back around towards his office. As soon as she was inside he pointed to a chair positioned in front of the wall where, higher up, there were framed photos of Princess Diana and Barack Obama, but she shook her head. She couldn't sit down while her boy was down the Royal London fighting for his life.

Mickey moved across to the waist-high fridge where a kettle and supplies for tea and coffee lay. She was that jumpy she couldn't wait for her drink. 'I need you to tell me where that scumbag lives.'

Mickey's hand came away from the kettle and he turned to her, his face full of concern. 'You don't want to know that.' His tone softened. 'You should be down the ozzie with your kid.'

That's what the others had said. She should be with Preston holding his hand; praying for him; doing everything on this earth to make him better. But the truth was she couldn't watch her boy with tubes coming out of every end of him while the bastard who did this was most probably having a jar and a giggle with his mates.

'You owe me,' Jackie said slowly. She swallowed, knowing her words bordered on a threat and no one, who was still living that was, trod on Mickey's toes. Before she lost her bottle she rushed on. 'You did say that because of what we did for Kimmie you'd always be in our debt.'

Kimmie was Mickey's youngest sister, the baby of the family. The one who started out as a sweet little girl and ended up as a crack whore somewhere in the back alleys of east London. Jackie and the others had taken Kimmie under their wing when Mickey had asked them to, gave her a job down at the club, but not even they could've saved her. Now Mickey had sole custody of her five-year-old son while Kimmie's only real love was a pipe full of crystal.

Jackie's heart hiccupped in her chest as she waited nervously. Mickey folded his arms across his barrel chest. 'You're right. I owe you. I know you and your friends loved Kimmie like you were her mum and I'll always appreciate that. But I'm going to be straight up with you, I don't like the payment that you're asking me for.'

She remained silent so he knew she hadn't changed her mind. He nodded. 'It's out Hornchurch way. Number 1 The Rookery.' Number 1. That figured, Jackie thought. The bastard thought he was the premier player. Mickey carried on, but this time there was real sorrow in his voice. 'My Kimmie told me she went there once. To one of Bliss's parties. She had all bruises down the side of her arm and around her throat.' Mickey swiftly turned to get his mug, but Jackie knew it was so that she wouldn't see his pain. But she wasn't finished with him yet. 'I need another favour?'

He twisted back around, his face composed this time. He just lifted his eyebrows. Jackie wet her lips. 'I need a gun.'

Mickey casually stood in the doorway as he watched Jackie melt into the evening that was taking over the daylight. As he continued to watch her he pulled out his mobile.

'She's just left. And she's packing a shooter . . .'

eight

Ryan Jarvis rushed into A&E, his green eyes wild with worry. Foxy's five-inch heels pinched her toes as she tried to keep up with him.

'I'm looking for Preston Campbell,' he asked the male receptionist, breathing hard.

The man calmly turned to his computer screen as Foxy rubbed her hand soothingly against Ryan's back. 'It's gonna be OK babe.'

But Ryan didn't really hear her. His little brothers meant the world to him. He'd never forget the day they were born, two little wriggling brown bodies that he had held gently with love.

The receptionist looked back at him. 'He's in intensive care.'

Ryan reeled back because he knew that was bad. 'Don't forget to disinfect your hands,' the man behind the desk added, pointing to a clear bottle on the wall. Once they'd followed his instructions they took the stairs to the intensive care ward. Ryan saw Schoolboy and his other brother, Darius, as soon as he turned the corner. His dad pulled him into a deep embrace as soon as he reached him. He loved this man as if he was his real father.

'What happened?' he asked.

Schoolboy told him quickly, making Ryan's legs wobble as the full impact of what had happened to his young brother sank in. He pulled Darius to his side, rubbing his hands over his head as he asked, 'Where's mum?'

Schoolboy sighed and said nothing. That's when Ryan noticed his aunts, Ollie, Roxy and Anna standing in the background. No Aunty Misty, which surprised him.

'Alright everyone,' Foxy said cheerfully, stepping forward. Ryan couldn't help but notice the way the other women and his dad ran their gazes over her clothes and heavy duty make-up. He knew that none of them had taken to Foxy, why he just didn't know. I mean, Foxy was fantastic, showing him a good time and was a total knockout in bed. Once they got to know her a bit better he was sure they would like her as much as he did.

Suddenly the drugs he'd taken earlier made his head swim. He rapidly blinked his eyes trying to steady himself.

'You alright?' his dad asked, catching his arm.

He turned to Schoolboy and nodded. Abruptly the other man tipped his chin up and looked into his eyes. Eyeballed him. Ryan tried to look away, but Schoolboy held his chin tight. 'You on something?' Schoolboy asked harshly.

Ryan rapidly shook his head, managing to get out of Schoolboy's grasp. 'No way dad. I ain't stupid.'

'Then why do your pupils look as big as the Blackwall Tunnel?'

'Just tired that's all. I've been studying hard for my exams. It's hard work being an art student.'

Schoolboy remained silent for awhile, then said, 'You just remember that your flat is in mine and your mum's name until you turn twenty-five. Any funny business and we'll have you back home before you can blink.'

Ryan nodded with relief. His dad carried on, 'I want you to take Darius and stay with him at our house.' He looked over at Foxy. 'On your own. I'll give you a bell later with news of Preston.'

A few minutes later Ryan, holding Darius's hand, stood at the lift, a grinning Foxy by his side. He thought she'd be spitting at the treatment from his family, like she usually was.

'What you grinning at?' he asked.

She tugged open her leopard-print shoulder bag. 'Coz I'm going to take all your troubles away later on with this.'

He peered into the bag and saw a bottle of the hospital's hand sanitiser fluid. 'You never nicked that?'

''Course I did. Pinched it off the wall. Mix a little bit of this with some vodka and you're singing "I'm Forever Blowing Bubbles" for the rest of the night, you get me?'

Laughing she stepped into the lift. That's the only problem he had with Foxy, she just thought about herself too much sometimes. He got in behind her, still clinging to his little brother's hand, his thoughts on his other brother who lay seriously injured in a hospital bed.

Marcus Lloyd, Marky-Boy to most people, knew he'd had a close escape this afternoon. Being caught shafting one of Bliss's birds was stupid. He grinned over his pint at the bar of The Diamond Rose boozer in Stepney. But he'd got away with it. And would get away with it if the rumours he was hearing about Bliss were true. Bliss would be too worried about being fingered for topping Stanley Lewis's kids to be worrying about what he'd been doing in Bliss's bed that afternoon. Maybe he should pay Stanley Lewis a visit and tell him what he had seen – Bliss turning up at his dolly bird's looking as white as a line of cocaine. Maybe if he did Stanley would give him a spot in his crew. He could picture himself now, wearing a designer suit with a shooter stuck in his back pocket. Hadn't he dreamt about being a real gangster since he was a little boy? Since he'd seen those two geezers give his dad the beating of his life for money he owed them. Oh yeah, he could see it all now.

Decision made he quickly finished his pint. Walked outside. Thought about the best route to Stanley's club on the Hackney Road. As he started walking towards the bus stop someone yelled out his name. He looked around to find two men, real hard-looking nuts, pulling up beside him in a black Jag.

'Yeah, who wants to know?' he called back, his tone full of arrogance, as if he was already part of Lewis's crew. Then he spoilt it with a sniff at the end.

The man in the passenger seat answered, 'We hear you're the man to do business with if we want some DVDs.'

They'd got that right. 'We're looking to invest a sizeable amount of dosh,' the man carried on.

Pound signs always got Marky-Boy excited. 'Yeah I can sort you out.'

The passenger door sprung open. 'Hop on in.'

His H supply had been running low so he did what they said. 'How many are you . . . ?' He started gabbing as soon as the engine ignited.

'Not here,' the man in the front cut over him. 'We've got a nice place to do business in.'

Thinking of the high life that was zipping his way Marky-Boy eased back and enjoyed the ride. Fifteen minutes later the car stopped outside a lock-up. He jumped out of the car as the two men in the front got out as well. Only when he saw the size of the blokes did he swallow. A shiver went down his spine but he followed them anyway. The man who'd done all the talking slid the door of the lock-up open with a bang. Marky-Boy peered inside. The place looked dark and didn't smell too good.

'You wanna make this deal or what?' the man said impatiently.

Marky-Boy ran his tongue over his lips as he stepped inside. His track marks on his arms itched. The lights flipped on. Seeing the handcuffs on chains hanging from a beam in the ceiling he realised he'd made a big mistake.

Get Bliss. Get Bliss.

That's all that kept Jackie going as she finally hit a leafy suburb just outside Hornchurch. The sky above was beginning to change from light to evening. She checked the blue satellite signal on the map on her mobile that tracked her movements. She was getting closer. Finally she stopped at the end of a street filled with big houses, the type that you either worked your fingers to the bone for years to get or the type you got from having your fingers in several dodgy pies. Some of the houses were gated and others weren't. If Bliss's was gated she wasn't sure what she was going to do.

A swift, painful image of Preston lying still in the hospital shot into her mind. She'd bloody climb the fence, that's what she was going to do. Whatever it took to get justice for her kid . . .

She reached the final house on the street and knew she'd found it. It wasn't what she was expecting. It looked respectable with its neat hedges and flower beds. Two motors were parked outside. One was a 4x4 and she wondered if it was the one that had run down her boy. She shook as she moved over to it. Her heart thundering, she checked it for damage. She couldn't see any, but all of sudden all she could see was Molly Lewis's legs scraping against the road as she was dragged to her death by the car.

She pulled out her phone. Called the hospital, suddenly needing to feel close to her child. Quickly she asked to be put through to the ward Preston was on. As soon as she heard one of the nurses she emotionally let out, 'How's my boy?'

No change. She shook her head. She so wanted to cry.

'What do you think you're doing?'

The pissed off cockney voice shattered her thoughts. Jackie twisted away from the car and faced the house. In the doorway stood a man. Young, cocky, well he looked cocky to her, wearing black jeans and an open-neck blue shirt. She finally had him. Now she needed to get him by the balls.

'What am I doing?' She advanced, shoving her mobile in her pocket without cutting the call, the fury puffing out her chest. 'I'll tell you what I'm doing.' Her hand dived into her pocket. Pulled back out.

'You're a dead man.' She thrust the nozzle of the gun deep into his face.

'Don't do anything stupid,' the man in front of Jackie squeaked.

'Stupid!' The pistol trembled in her hand. 'I think you're talking about yourself. Coz only a nutter would've killed those girls and hurt my kid.' Her voice ended on a sob.

'I don't know what you're talking about . . .'

She pushed the gun closer. Terrified he leaned back. Her voice croaked as she spat each word with the speed of automatic gunfire. 'My boy was going to be Confirmed in three weeks' time and now because of you he might not make it.' She saw his look of confusion when she mentioned Preston's Confirmation. Bloody heathen. Her finger tightened around the trigger. Suddenly her voice became calm. 'Those girls were lovely regardless of who their family were.

Innocent. And now they're dead you're going to pay the price Bliss.' Her finger tightened. 'This one's for Marina—'

'Paul Bliss?' He shouted. 'I'm not Mr Bliss.'

Her hand wavered. 'You what?' Her mouth twisted as her hand became steady again. 'Don't think you're having one over on me.'

'But he lives at Number 1.'

'This *is* Number 1,' she insisted.

'No this is Number 2. Mr Bliss's house is over there.' She followed the direction of his nod still keeping the gun on him. Spotted a house in the distance in a large expanse of grounds behind a high, black iron security fence.

His voice drew her back to him. 'Are you the mother of the boy who was hurt in the appalling incident outside the school today?' Even though his hands were still in the air she saw the pity flashing from his eyes towards her. Without another word she lowered the gun and turned away. Like a deflated balloon she walked aimlessly back out into the street. She shook her head a couple of times because all of a sudden she couldn't think straight. Jesus, Mother Mary and all the saints, she was losing her friggin' mind.

Jackie felt disorientated. Lost. The trees and the houses blurred past her as she drifted down the road, gun hanging limply by her side. What the fuck was she doing here? She should be at the ozzie at her son's bedside. Holding his hand, kissing his forehead, threading her fingers through his springboard locks.

'Get in.' Jackie jumped when she heard the voice.

She twisted to the side to find a car beside her. The passenger door was open. In the driver's seat sat one of the last people she'd expected to see.

The man at Number 2 got on the blower as soon as he got to his plush study on the ground floor.

'Get in,' Misty demanded for the second time from the driver's side of the car.

This time Jackie obeyed. As soon as she hit the seat Misty's mouth went into fifth gear. 'What the hell are you doing here?

Have you seen yourself, prancing around the street with a shooter in your hand as if you're holding a Cornetto or something? The Bill could've happened along at any moment . . .'

'How did you find me?' Jackie asked in a dead beat tone.

'Mickey who else? My bloody hairpiece nearly flew off when he says you're off to Bliss's like Calamity Jane.' Suddenly Misty grabbed the gun out of her hand. Opened the chamber. 'See.' She shoved the gun under Jackie's nose. 'No bloody bullets you stupid girl.' When she saw the amazement on Jackie's face she added, 'Mickey took 'em out when you weren't watching. He was frightened that you might hurt yourself or somebody else.' As quick as she'd started Misty stopped her ranting and raving. Her face softened. 'Do you want me to call your mum?'

Her mum, Nikki, was living *the life* in Switzerland. Respectable, married to a man with more cash than he knew what to do with and just plain flamin' happy. She needed the comfort of her mum's arms so much. But what if this all became dangerous? Stan Lewis and Paul Bliss? No, she didn't want her mum anywhere near any of that. God knew her mum deserved some happiness after all the crap she'd been through. But if anything happened to Preston she'd call her.

Preston. Mummy's little boy.

Jackie looked at Misty and opened her mouth as if she wanted to speak. But her mouth just flapped open like a fish, no words came out. And that's when she felt it, this tight wave of pain sweeping through her body. It stuck in her chest. Hurt like the devil. Kept pressing and pressing until she thought she was going to go bonkers. Misty opened her arms. Jackie fell into them. Then she started crying, horrible sobs that made the tears settle in the bottom of Misty's eyes.

'It hurts, it really hurts,' Jackie sobbed.

'I know,' Misty soothed. 'I know.'

Jackie lifted her tear-streaked face and gazed at Misty. 'What am I going to do if my beautiful boy dies?'

nine

The last time Stan Lewis had been refused entry to a club was when he was fourteen. The priest in charge of his local youth club had barred him for fighting, thieving and threatening. Stan had pointed his finger at the priest and warned him, 'You'd better get your dog collar fire-proofed mate – you know what I mean?'

On the way out he turned over a ping-pong table and dented a soft drinks machine. Now as he stood on Bethnal Green Road looking down at the entrance to the Five Fingers Club he knew he was going to throw more than a few tables around. He patted the blaster on his inside pocket. Yeah, when he got his hands on Bliss . . .

The Five Fingers was Bliss's main base. It was housed in the basement of a building that doubled up as a hairdressers on the ground floor and clothing wholesalers on the upper levels. Both businesses kept their beaks well out of anything that went on beneath them. Stan took the concrete steps two at a time until he stood in front of the steel reinforced door. He rang the bell and waited. Popped the pistol from his pocket, released the safety, pushed it back in again, before pulling it out once more and fiddling with the catch for no particular reason, he just loved playing with guns. By the time the door opened he had his gun levelled at the man who opened the door.

'I want to see Bliss.'

The horrified man was a heavy in a DJ and bow tie. 'Fuck me mate, take it easy.'

Stan pushed the shooter deep into his face. 'Don't tell me to fucking take it easy, you fucking dicksucker. I want to see Bliss, now go and get him.'

'He ain't in – please, come on, take it easy . . .'

The door began to swing as the guy in the bow tie retreated into the reception area. Stan kicked it open to be met in reception by more men in bow ties – Stan raised his gun and they stopped in their tracks, raising their hands. A stocky man, with a receding hairline, deep scar on his chin, tight set eyes and who appeared to be the chief bow tie hissed, 'What's this about Stan?'

Stan knew who the man was. Sean McCarthy, Bliss's right-hand gorilla. 'I want to see Bliss.' This time Stan's voice shook as his anger grew.

'He ain't in tonight.'

'You won't mind me coming in for a little look around then?'

Off to the left, another bow tie was gently trying to open the drawer of a desk. Keeping his gun trained on the others, Stan pulled a second gun out of his waistband with his spare hand and the reception shook and echoed to the thunder of a gunshot as bits of the desk blew and splintered around. Stan turned to the bow tie who'd been trying to retrieve a gun from the shattered desk and calmly whispered, 'They don't call me Stanley "2 Guns" Lewis for nothing.' He pointed both guns back at the main man. 'I just want a quick word with Bliss. You show me around and prove he's not here and I'll leave won't I? There's no need for any silliness now is there? I ain't a silly person, you know that.'

'Stan Lewis,' the man sneered as he twisted his mouth. 'You don't know what the hell you're starting—' But before he could finish Stan pulled back one of his guns and smashed him in the mouth with it.

The man stumbled back as his hand flew to his mouth. Stan quickly pointed the guns at the other men. 'No one try anything fucking funny alright?'

None of the men moved. He twisted his guns back onto the other man who raised his head, his fingers wiping the blood from his cut mouth. 'Inside and take me to your boss,' Stan ordered.

Sean straightened. 'Like I said—'

'Just do it.'

Sean held up his palm signalling to the others to stay in place. With a sigh he pushed through the double doors into the club. The place was packed with punters dressed to the eyeballs. The high-energy beat of one of the latest chart toppers cut over the deadly atmosphere. A few gasps went up when everyone spotted Stan's shooter. Stan pushed the man further into the room as he raked over the place hunting for Bliss. His rage fired up – he couldn't see his target anywhere.

He pushed one shooter back into his waistband and used his free hand to climb onto a snooker table. And shouted, 'When you see Bliss, tell him I've got a message for him . . .' He whipped the second shooter back out. Raised both pistols over his head and fired each in turn, three or four times into the ceiling to create a rolling thunderstorm of gunfire. Some of the women screamed as the punters took cover around the side of the room. When he finished the only sound was plaster and wood tumbling to the ground around him and the music system still whacking out top ten hits.

Stan jumped down and made his exit through the reception area, the bow ties watching him go. But when he was halfway up the steps outside he remembered he'd forgotten something. He ran back down, pushed his way back in and levelled his gun at the leg of the bow tie that had first opened the door to him. The man squealed in horror and pain as a gunshot blasted open his thigh, squeezing red juice from his veins over the men standing next to him.

'Don't ever, EVER, tell me to "take it easy" again.'

When he reached street level, the waiting car drove up at speed and Stan jumped in the back. The car took off and Stan watched the East End fly past through the tinted windows. The driver knew better than to ask him any questions. He leaned back still feeling the fury trembling throughout his body. He saw the image of his daughter's trainers lying in the road. He covered his mouth with his palm, scared that he was about to throw up. Breathing like a donkey going up a mountain he tried to steady the air shooting out of his mouth. As his breathing got easier his mobile went off.

'Son?' It was the big man himself; Kenny Lewis; his dad.

Stan gulped. 'Dad.' Then his voice wobbled. 'They're dead and that cunt . . .'

'Listen boy and listen good. You need to calm down, OK? Stay indoors and we'll sort everything out when we're in the picture, until then you keep quiet. Are you getting me, soft lad?'

Kenny could hear slipstream on the car down the phone as he spoke to his son. So, he was already out on the road, the little prick . . .

'Are you listening to me?'

'He's a dead man, and not a nice dead either.'

The kid was rambling. Kenny gritted his teeth. There were times, and this was one of them, when he regretted leaving his boy in charge while he was away. It was the first rule of their line of business, you stay cool, all the time, no matter what happened, you stayed cool, until you had all the facts and then, and only then, you started killing people.

Kenny had another go. 'Are you listening?'

'Yeah, I'm listening. I've got everything under control.'

'Stay strong son,' were his dad's parting words then the line went dead.

As Stan calmly eased his mobile back into his pocket he heard his dad's words: *Leave Bliss to me.* A nasty smile settled on his lips. His dad was inside and he was out here and he was the one now running this show. Leave Bliss alone? Not fucking likely. He still had one more surprise visit to make.

Jackie saw Schoolboy as soon as she got back to the intensive care ward. Misty had dropped her off and declined to come upstairs to give Jackie and her fella some space or as she put it 'A little bit of one-to-one.'

She held Schoolboy's eyes as she moved towards him. She was the first to look away, knowing he'd go ballistic if he knew what she'd been up to.

'Ryan turned up. He's taken Darius home.'

Jackie nodded. 'Any news?' He just shook his head. She wanted to touch him, reassure him, but didn't. They'd been so close once and now they needed to be more tight than ever they were miles apart. She never saw him much these days because he was always up at the restaurant. She knew he was working his bollocks off to give her and the boys a good life, but sometimes, just sometimes, she hated that restaurant like it was a bit of skirt he had on the side. All she wanted was her carefree, fast-talking, finger-up-to-the-world bloke back.

As if reading her mind he boldly stated, 'I don't know what's up between us, but it can't go on like this. Has it got anything to do with you having an ozzie appointment today?'

That shook her up. How the hell had he found out? Seeing her incredulous expression he added, 'Ollie let it slip.'

She covered her arms protectively over her chest. As much as she wanted to blame him for working all the hours that God sent in the restaurant she admitted that most of the bother between them was because of her, not him. Why she'd taken to sleeping in the spare room most nights. But she couldn't tell him why she had an appointment. Couldn't. Not now. They had enough troubles already.

'We used to be like this, me and you.' He wrapped two fingers together. 'I wanna know why you had an ozzie appointment,' he continued softly.

She was so tempted to tell him. So tempted. This was her Schoolboy for crying out loud. Her fella. He should know. She opened her mouth, but a voice behind her got there first.

'Jackie?'

Jackie twisted around to find a heavy-breathing Daisy Sullivan coming towards her. Jackie immediately wrapped her arms around the woman she'd taken into her home as a scared and grief-stricken fifteen-year-old kid ten years back. Daisy's dad had been Frankie Sullivan, one of the most feared villains around. A man Jackie had put at the top of her 'hate 'till I die' list. Jackie was so proud of Daisy because she'd cut all her links with her dad's past and forged a career as a lawyer, a bloody good one from all that Jackie heard. Mind you that had all nearly gone down the drain when Daisy's long-gone mum had reappeared in her life . . . Jackie might only be ten years older than Daisy but she always thought of her as her daughter, her girl. The only thing that Jackie didn't quite approve of about her was that she'd hooked up with a cop for her fella.

Daisy backed out of Jackie's embrace as she stared at her with her brilliant blue eyes, her long, black hair covering the left side of her face. 'I just found out that the other child involved in what happened this afternoon was Preston.' Jackie saw the pain imprinted on Daisy's gorgeous face. Daisy loved Jackie's boys like they were her own flesh and blood.

'I should've called you sooner, but I didn't want to worry—' But before Jackie could finish Daisy's face turned a nasty shade of green as she covered her hand with her mouth. 'Toilet,' Daisy frantically mumbled. Swiftly Jackie pointed down the corridor. Concerned, Jackie watched her rush away. Then she swung her troubled green-eyed gaze to Schoolboy. He nodded in the direction that Daisy had fled indicating that Jackie should follow her.

Jackie hesitated at the loo door, then entered. She found a sweating Daisy gripping one of the white sinks as she took deep breaths.

'You OK?' Jackie asked as she joined her. She caught Daisy's reflection in the long mirror on the wall in front of them and didn't like what she saw. Her adopted daughter's face was pasty with a thin sheen of sweat covering her forehead, the beauty spot at the corner of her mouth standing out against her stark pale skin.

'Yeah,' Daisy insisted, turning the tap on and splashing some water on her face. She drew in a long breath. Turned to Jackie and gave her a reassuring smile. 'Really. Must be something I ate last night.' Her voice trembled. 'How did this all happen? Ricky won't tell me much.' She lifted her eyebrows. 'Police business he says.'

Jackie's mouth tightened as she heard the name of Daisy's man. Ricky Smart. Detective Inspector Ricardo Smart. Just hearing his name made her think violent thoughts. He wasn't quite up there on her hate list with Daisy's dad, but she'd wanted someone safer for Daisy. Plus the guy was too bloody cocky for her liking.

Jackie sighed as Daisy turned to face her, the colour coming back into her cheeks. 'I was just outside the school with the boys at home time and out of nowhere this motor takes out Marina Lewis's kids. Then the car went around the corner and . . .' She couldn't say it.

'Oh Jackie,' Daisy said softly.

Jackie ran her fingers through her close-cropped red hair above her forehead. Her eyes blazed. 'But people are saying that the driver was Paul Bliss . . .'

'Paul Bliss,' Daisy threw back completely surprised.

'He ain't someone you know?'

Daisy avoided looking in Jackie's searching green eyes as she answered, 'No. But of course I've heard of him.'

Jackie didn't like the way the taller woman wouldn't look at her. 'If he did this I'm going to get him.'

Daisy got that pinched expression again hearing Jackie's deadly voice. 'If it's Paul Bliss let the police deal with him. I couldn't bear the thought of you getting hurt as well.'

Maybe Daisy was right. Maybe the others were right. Schoolboy was right. Maybe she should let the Plod sort this out and put all her energy into making sure her boy got well again. But she didn't trust the cops. Never had, most probably never would. They hadn't helped her and the others when they were fifteen and going through hell in that place the state had the flippin' cheek to call a *care* home.

Daisy took her hand and squeezed it. 'Can I see Preston?'

They left the loo still holding hands but stopped when they saw the backs of two suits talking low to Schoolboy. Jackie's hand fell from Daisy's and she quickly moved forward. Hearing her approach, the men turned around to face her and that's when she realised that one of them was a woman. Early thirties, short hair, caramel skin and a way of holding her body that said she didn't take dick from no one.

'Jackie Jarvis?' she asked, her almost-black eyes giving Jackie the once-over.

'Who wants to know?' The woman stepped forward. 'Inspector Sunita Begum.' She pulled out her badge and flashed it. 'We need you to accompany us to the station.'

That's when Jackie realised that Bliss's neighbour must've called the cops.

Daisy tried to take charge straight away. 'Right, you're going to need someone to represent you–'

But Jackie never let her finish. 'They ain't going to charge me with nothing.' Although Jackie suspected they would when she got to the nick. 'If I need you I'll give you a bell.'

Five minutes later Daisy anxiously watched the police car drive Jackie away as she stood with Schoolboy in the cooling night outside. As the car disappeared she turned to Schoolboy and said, 'She'll be fine. Why don't you find out if I can see Preston and I'll join you upstairs in a minute.'

As soon as Schoolboy was gone she pulled out her mobile. 'It's Daisy. I'm so glad I caught you before you went home. Do me a favour before you go, get Paul Bliss's file out and leave it on my desk please.'

ten

Interview Room 2.

It wasn't the first time she'd been in the cop shop and most probably wouldn't be the last. Jackie sat calmly in Unity Road police station in Hackney. A female cop stood stiff in her uniform in a corner keeping her gaze above Jackie's head. The two cops who'd driven her to the nick had explained that as part of their routine enquiries they were questioning all the witnesses, much to Jackie's relief. So the cops didn't know about her hunting Bliss with a shooter. Mind you she didn't understand why they couldn't have just done a quick and easy question and answer session at the ozzie. Why drag her here?

The door opened. The sight of the tall, black cop who walked into the room holding a folder made her groan. Bouncing bollocks. She slumped back into the chair. Of all the people why him? Why Ricky Smart? Her maybe, might-not-to-be future son-in-law.

'Jackie,' he greeted her as he took the seat opposite and settled the manila folder to the side. She nodded her head ever so slightly.

There wasn't a lot of love lost between them even though Ricky had been dating Daisy for almost two years now and Jackie had the funny feeling the relationship was headed straight down the aisle. She'd never approved of their relationship. Thought her Daisy was just too good for him. Besides the idea of having a cop in the family was way too creepy. But maybe she could turn this to her advantage and milk Ricky to find out what was going on.

Their eyes locked. He was the first to look away as he asked, 'How's Preston doing?'

She considered his question, not really wanting to talk, but she did. 'Touch and go.' She ran her fingertips through the short strands of her hair. 'The school ain't on your patch so what's your snout doing in this?'

'The higher-ups think I'm the best man for the job. Can I get you some tea? Some water?'

Jackie stared at him incredulously. Tea? Water? What did he think this was, some friggin' tea party? She leaned impatiently forward. 'Let's just get this over and done with so I can get back to my boy.'

He sighed as he leaned his forearms on the table. 'I know this is upsetting for you but I need to ask you exactly what you witnessed today.'

Her mouth felt dry and she wished she'd taken up the offer of some water. She swallowed. Spoke. 'I went to pick the boys up. I usually let them go home on their own but we had a few things we needed to do today. Then Stanley Lewis turns up—'

'Was he with anyone?'

Her mind raced back. 'Yeah. A couple of heavies, that's all. He sees his ex and they start having a real barney right there in front of the school. You know the usual, you shove me, I shove you shit. And out of nowhere this car comes belting up the road and goes straight into the Lewis girls—'

'And you think it was deliberate?'

That shook her up. Her green eyes danced with outrage. 'Of course it was deliberate.'

'There's no "of course" about it. Traditionally, the police do an investigation and then draw conclusions, not the other way around.'

'I was there.' She stabbed her finger at him. 'You weren't.'

'In a case like this, we tend to find a drunk or drugged-up driver is the culprit.'

She gazed at him as if he was a nut job. 'Bliss runs down Stan Lewis's kids and you think that makes an accident do you? No wonder you've never been able to catch him.'

With a flick of his dark eyes he held her gaze. 'Who mentioned Paul Bliss?'

That made her shove back into her seat. 'Oh, do me a favour.' She rolled her eyes. 'You boys might be a few days behind everyone else but even you must have heard that the jeep belonged to him.'

Ricky leaned back in his chair. 'OK, what would make you think the girls were the target and not their dad?'

She leaned forward again and asked ever so innocent like, 'You think someone was trying to kill Stanley Lewis?'

Ricky raised his eyebrows. 'I'm asking the questions Jackie not you.'

She shook her head. 'Their dad was quite a way from them. It just went straight for the girls.' She leaned back again. Tilted her head to the side. 'Why do you think someone would be after Stan?'

Ricky leaned back as well. 'I'm sure you know the stories about the Lewises as well as I do. There could be a million and one people who'd want to take him out.'

'Enough to kill his kids?'

Ricky pushed himself forward, his face deliberately in Jackie's space this time. 'You know I can't share that type of info with you.' Suddenly his eyes looked deep into hers. 'Are you being straight with me?'

That took her by surprise. Just for a moment. Then she reminded herself that no one, including Detective Inspector Ricky Smart, was getting in the way of her finding justice for her boy. So she kept her gaze steady with his. Answered in a light, easy tone. ''Cross my heart—'

'Hope to die?' He finished for her. 'Because that's what might happen if you're lying to me. This might prove dangerous.'

'Why the hell would I want to lie to you? I want *you* to find out who tried to hurt my son.'

'Do you?' His look put her in the spotlight. 'Or do you want to try and find out for yourself? Why don't I get that dumb Ricky Smart to tell me all that he knows?' He spread his palms against the table. 'That's why I wanted to get you down here because I know you. Know how you operate. I haven't forgotten that you held a gun in my face once.'

He was bang out of order to remind her about that incident. He knew she'd only done that to help her Daisy. She half lifted herself out of her seat. 'You don't know dick about me.'

Without warning he grabbed her wrist. Drew her close to him. He of all people knew that the only way sometimes to get through to Jackie was with a bit of force, although he understood how she must be feeling about her son in the ITC unit. 'This isn't ladies day at Ascot. This is the Lewis gang that we're talking about. Someone murders Stanley Lewis's daughters and there could be all kinds of stuff happening.'

The tension grew electric as they stared at each other, him still clinging on to her tight.

It was Jackie who broke the silence. 'I don't think Daisy's going to like the way you're mauling her mum at this minute.'

He let her go. She rubbed her wrist as she plonked herself back down.

'Where did you hear these rumours about Paul Bliss?'

She gave him one of her wide-eyed and innocent looks. 'Probably the same place you did?'

Ricky couldn't help it, he rolled his eyes in annoyance. 'Come on, you can tell me, this is private.'

'You're the cop – why don't you do your own investigating? I expect you've got a licence plate for him, look him up.'

He looked away from Jackie and nodded at his colleague stationed near the door. Without a word the policewoman left.

Ricky used a fingertip to drag the folder in front of him. Opened it. 'I want to give you a friendly warning. You're right, we are the police, so just in case you're planning to go vigilante in this case, let me give you a top ten run through of Bliss's rap sheet.' He started speaking and didn't leave much out.

Shoplifting aged 12.

Assault and battery aged 14.

Demanding money with menaces.

Living off immoral earnings.

Attempted murder, case dropped after the witness refused to talk.

Suspected of being one of London's major league drug dealers.

The list went on and on, until Jackie said, 'Alright I get the picture, he ain't no Gentleman Jim.'

'No, he's not. And that's just the tip of the iceberg.' He snapped the file closed. 'So don't do it Jackie. You keep all your energy for Preston because he needs you. Let us take care of the rest.'

'That it then?' was all she said as she absently threaded her fingers through her red hair.

Ricky folded his arms. 'Let's make a deal. I'll keep you informed with what I know as long as you do the same.'

She slipped her head to the side. 'Sure. Why not.'

As she moved to get up he placed his hand over hers. 'Mess with Bliss and you're dead. Mess with Stan Lewis and you're dead. Mess with both of them and you're deader than a Christmas single in January.'

'Guv, you're not going to like what I found out about the speed cameras near the school,' Detective Sunita Begum, who introduced herself as Sonny to most people, informed Ricky as he came out of the room. Sonny was tall and fit with eagerness brimming in her brandy-coloured eyes.

He didn't like her calling him Guv. Made him feel like he was play acting in an episode of *The Sweeney*. But he never said anything because she seemed to like it. Plus she was one of the only Bengali officers he knew on the force and he felt protective towards her. Knew that it wasn't always an easy road being a brown-skinned cop on the force.

'They didn't show anything?' he asked.

Sonny sighed. 'Worse than that, there weren't any films.'

Ricky frowned. 'What do you mean there weren't any? There are cameras at the corner of Claremont Road.'

'Might be cameras, sir, but no film in them. With this recession the council have had to make cuts. So the cameras are there just as a deterrent for any motorist pretending to be Lewis Hamilton.' Ricky swore violently.

Sonny carried on. 'But someone at the scene took down the number plates, so at least we've got that to go on.' Then she asked, 'She know anything Guv?' He knew Sonny was referring to Jackie.

'That little red stick of dynamite is my girlfriend's mum. Adoptive mum.' He saw the shock cover the younger woman's face. 'And if there's one person who knows what's happening in this corner of our fair city it's Jackie Jarvis.'

So Bliss's neighbour hadn't shopped her to the cops, Jackie thought as she hit the police station exit and the dark outside. She wondered why? She should really give Schoolboy a bell and let him know what's what. She fiddled inside her pocket, hunting for her mobile as she stepped outside. The light breeze tousled the front of her hair. Her hand stopped when she felt something that wasn't her phone. A folded piece of paper. She pulled it out as her steps slowed. Her own hospital appointment. That's why she'd gone to pick the boys up from school, so she could get to her appointment and take them out for a munch after. The appointment was long gone now and she knew she should make a new one. But just the thought of it did strange things to her tummy. It had taken her months to finally see her quack and he'd arranged the appointment as a matter of urgency. But she couldn't do it. Just couldn't do it. What if they said . . . ?

She turned a corner, head still down and ran right into a hard chest. She stumbled back as a hand caught her arm to steady her.

'You alright, love?'

Startled at the husky, Cockney voice she looked up to find a man standing in front of her. And what a man. She wolf whistled in her mind. A natural born heartbreaker, who could tempt a nun to drop her knickers. He was tall, lanky really, and despite the grey that threaded through his brown hair she judged him to be no more than in his late twenties. He wore a black, hip-length leather jacket, slimline jeans with a silver buckle belt and polished boots. He should've looked like some pretty boy, but he didn't. Maybe it was that cleft in his chin that made him look like a fella she would've gone after if she didn't have that gold band on her finger. Half his mouth was lifted into a cheeky, boyish grin that produced tiny wrinkles at the corners of his nut brown eyes. Schoolboy had smiled like that back in the days when he'd shown the world the finger and hadn't given two hoots about what Tom, Dick or Harry thought of him. Out of nowhere tears sprang to her eyes.

'Hey, hey,' Mr Gorgeous whispered. He gazed at her, his grin gone, his features stamped with gentle concern. 'Whoever has made a beautiful lady like you sob her eyes out needs shooting. Want me to sort them out?'

Something in his voice made Jackie realise he might just go and do it. Then she caught the mischievous twinkle in his eyes. Then he winked. She started laughing. God, that was the first laugh she'd cracked in a couple of days.

'That's more like it.' And before she knew what he was doing his fingers brushed over the freckles on her cheek. Now if any bloke other than Schoolboy had the brass balls to touch her with such intimacy they would have got a mouthful and maybe a swift kick in the family jewels for good measure as well. But for some reason she let his fingers glide over her skin. She wasn't sure how long she stood there letting some stranger touch her like that, but she only came back to reality when he stepped back. 'Don't let the world get you down little lady,' he said. The merriment dropped out of his face. 'They'll find who hurt your kid.'

Her mouth fell open in surprise. How did he know ...? But before she could question him he was walking towards the station entrance whistling 'Love Is In The Air'. As he reached the station door, Ricky and a female cop came belting out. The same female cop who had come to the hospital. Immediately she knew something was up. She rushed over to Ricky. Grabbed his arm. 'What's going on?'

He just stared back at her saying nothing.

'Is it Bliss?' Her fingers dug into his arm.

But he shook her hand off. Started running again until he reached his car. Jumped in and sped off. Shaken, Jackie stared after the disappearing car. Her mobile rang in her pocket. She jerked it out. Instantly stilled when she saw the name on the screen. Schoolboy. Her heart seized up. *Please no.*

'Is it ... ?'

'You need to get down here now.'

eleven

They didn't want any warnings they were coming, so there were no blues and twos ripping through the night. Ricky and Sonny reached their destination thirty-two minutes after leaving Unity Road nick. Abruptly Ricky stopped the car.

'Let's do it,' he told Sonny.

They got out of the car. Walked across the road. Stopped outside a respectable looking family home in Loughton, in Essex. Number 9 Mansfield Crescent. Nothing out of the ordinary.

'Check around the back,' Ricky ordered.

Sonny hesitated. 'But shouldn't we knock on—' Her words froze when she saw the expression on her superior's face. She'd seen it too many times to not know that he didn't need her questioning anything that he said. She did what he asked as he moved closer to the front of the house staring at the gravel in the drive. His face grew grim when he saw the tyre marks. Large and wide.

'I've found it,' Sonny called out without coming back around. Ricky moved to find Sonny standing beside a black jeep. Tinted windows. She was staring at its front. He knew exactly what she was looking at.

With a triumphant expression she lifted her face and looked at him. 'The number plates match.'

Jackie flew down the hospital corridor. A few of the nurses looked up at her, but no one tried to stop her. She reached her son's room. Punched the door open. Rushed inside. Her breath halted in her chest at what she saw.

Schoolboy leaning over Preston's body. She couldn't see her son's face, but what she could see of him was still. Too still. Sweet Jesus, Mother Mary and all the saints how could this have happened? She gulped and staggered backwards, her hand covering her heart. Hearing her, Schoolboy twisted around as he raised his head.

'Jackie?' He straightened.

But she squeezed her eyes tight, openly moaning, 'No, no, no . . .' She couldn't look at Preston. Wouldn't look at him. She knew what he'd look like, the two dead girls she'd already seen earlier today. She rammed her fingers into her hair and slumped against the wall. Suddenly she felt Schoolboy wrap his hand around her raised wrist. 'Jackie?' She just carried on shaking her head. 'Jackie!' This time his voice was louder. Rougher. Demanding. Slowly she opened her green, tear filled eyes.

'Look.'

First thing she noticed was his silly grin. Then his finger pointed towards the bed. She followed it. Merciful Lord Jesus and all his wonderful saints. There was Preston with his dark eyes looking straight back at her.

He didn't look like a child killer. In fact thirty-two-year-old Peter Bell didn't even look like a drunk driver, Ricky decided. What the man sitting on the sofa inside Number 9 Mansfield Crescent did look like was dead scared.

'We can sort this out Mr Bell very quickly if you can just answer some questions . . .'

'Sort what out? I don't know what you're talking about.' Bell tensed in his seat. 'What are those people doing with my car?'

Ricky looked out of the window. The forensic team, in white suits, were giving Mr Bell's jeep the once over. They should have towed it away and checked it back at the lab but Ricky was hoping for some quick results that would put Bell on the back foot and get the whole thing wrapped up.

Ricky left the window and walked across the room, past a stony-faced Sonny and popped himself on the edge of the single sofa opposite Bell. 'We're investigating a very serious offence Mr Bell.

Can you confirm that you're the owner of the vehicle at the back of this house?'

'Of course it's my car. How hard is it for you to check that? If I'd stolen it . . .' Bell tailed off as he wrapped his arms tightly over each other in his lap and slightly rocked. 'I want a lawyer. I'm supposed to have a lawyer. You can't come in my house and accuse me of stealing my own car.'

'I just need to confirm your ownership, I'm not accusing you of stealing it. Can you tell me where you were this afternoon at approximately 3.30 p.m.?'

Bell had gone very white and seemed to have shrunk by a couple of inches. 'I was auditing a customer's account in Southend-on-Sea and any discrepancies in their accounts you should take up with them, not with me.'

There was a quiet knock on the window. Ricky got up and went outside; one of his forensics boys was taking off his gloves and sighed. 'Given it the once over chief. I'd have to take it back to the lab but I'm pretty sure this isn't our target. It hasn't been washed for a week and that's the least you'd expect if the guy was covering something up. There's no marks on it to indicate any sort of collision at any time, nothing's been changed to hide any damage, the tyres haven't been swapped – well, you know what to expect if it had been in a vehicular homicide. Do you want me to take it in?'

Ricky shook his head. 'No, I don't think this is our man.'

As the man from forensics walked away Sonny took her place at Ricky's side. A few people from the houses opposite stood in the distance observing the proceedings.

'He's complaining his human rights are being abused,' she informed him.

Ricky nodded. 'Unfortunately, he's probably right.'

'Wrong car?'

'Looks like. That means the plates will have been ghosted and that means we've got a different sort of a problem because Joe Criminal doesn't go to the trouble of spoofing plates, so we must be talking about a serious player.'

'Bliss?'

Ricky thought for a bit as a few more of Bell's neighbours came outside. 'Dunno. But we can't arrest him because we've got no evidence.' He moved to the jeep and kicked one of the front tyres. Cursed beneath his breath. 'Somewhere out there is a 4x4 which murdered two kids today.' He looked troubled to her. 'If we don't find it soon Stanley Lewis will and God knows what will happen then.'

His gun tucked in the back of his trousers, Stan stepped out of his motor. The street was bathed in darkness, except for the solitary lamplight in the middle. He checked left. Checked right. Good, no one else in sight. He stared up at the house in front of him. And smiled. He pulled out his semi. Calmly walked up to the door and booted the front door in. Raised his gun and confidently stepped inside. He stopped when he found who he was after.

And there she was, on her feet, looking terrified as she stood distressed by the high-backed leather armchair. He pointed the gun at her. This time he didn't grin. She shifted back but her gaze didn't waiver from his. He had to give her credit. She was a cool bitch.

'What do you want?' Her voice was as cool as her look.

He stepped further in. Checked out the room. Chic, not over done, just the way Stan knew she would live. Nice and neat, everything in its place. Shame he had to stomp in and mess it all up.

'Nice gaff you've got here.'

She folded her arms across her middle as she quietly said, 'If you don't get out of here now I am calling the police.'

He laughed humourlessly. 'You ain't going to do that darling and we know why.'

Her look changed to one of fear. Yeah, the bitch didn't look so cool any more.

His next words turned the screw on her fear. 'I know what you and Bliss have been up to—'

'I don't know anyone called Bliss,' she sharply cut in.

Taking her by complete surprise he rushed forward and grasped her, one-handed, by the throat. She gasped as he dragged her forward and slammed her down on the sofa on their right side. Her legs dangled over the edge, her upper body pinned to the back. He leaned deep into her. Inhaled her expensive perfume into his nose. One of his hands grabbed the side of her grass green blouse and with a yank ripped it open. Her left breast popped out of her bra.

Her eyes radiated with terror. 'Please . . .'

His brown gaze lingered on her exposed flesh. His fingers found her nipple and with a grin he twisted it. She groaned. He jammed his legs between her thighs forcing her legs further apart. 'We could have such fun me and you.' He dramatically sniffed the side of her neck. Then he looked straight into her eyes. 'But then you ain't really my sort.' He shoved the nozzle of the gun into her face. Directly under her left eye. Her head jerked back as her legs twitched around him. 'If you and that cunt Bliss had anything to do with my kids—' His finger curled around the trigger. She panted in accelerated fear.

'You know I wouldn't ever harm any children,' she rushed out. 'Never.'

'What I do know is that you and that boyfriend of yours are trying to pull a fast one on me. Take over my turf.'

This time she didn't even bother denying she knew Bliss.

Suddenly he dipped his head and ran his tongue along her nipple like it was the most delicious lollipop he'd ever tasted. Her breathing jumped in her chest as she twisted her head away from him. Then he eased back. Stood up. 'You tell Bliss I know where his stash house is.' And with that he was gone.

She lay like that for a good few minutes, too shocked to do anything. *I know where his stash house is. I know where his stash house is.* If Stanley Lewis knew . . . She scrambled to her feet. Ran for the phone in the adjoining room. Picked it up. No, she shouldn't be making this call on her landline, she reasoned. She headed back to the lounge for her mobile. Jammed it to the side of her face as she nervously paced across the polished floorboards. 'It's me . . . Yes I know you said not to contact you . . . Lewis has been here. He knows about us . . . Stay calm?' She yelled. 'How can I . . . ?' But she was talking to thin air. She squeezed her eyes closed as her hand tightened painfully around the phone. She was in way over her head and she knew it. But Bliss would help her. Get this all sorted out. He loved her. Didn't he?

Despite the tubes coming out of him, Preston scrunched his face into a little-boy look of embarrassment as his mum covered his face with tiny baby kisses. Yuck! But Jackie didn't notice, all she could see was that her little man was back among the living.

'Mum,' he croaked softly, with just enough childish whine to let her know how he was feeling.

She gave him one last hug then pulled back, her gaze eating him alive. Then her face lit into a gigantic grin. 'I know, I know, big guy don't want his mum showing him up.'

Preston swallowed, then croaked, 'No one's got a smile like my mum.'

Jackie's heart lurched at the unexpected words. All she could do was nod her head because the lump in her throat was way too big to allow her to speak.

'Ms Jarvis.' She knew it was the doctor. She found Dr Ruth Brown standing next to Schoolboy in her white coat.

Immediately she got up and walked over. 'So is he alright now? When can we take him home.' The hope in her voice rushed out with her words.

The doctor's look was grave. 'Little Preston is definitely a fighter, you should be proud of him. We need to keep him in for further observations. The last thing you would want is for anything to happen to him if he went home.'

She nodded. 'But there's no lasting damage?' Her head flicked back to Preston.

Dr Brown smiled. 'If he continues to make progress within the next forty-eight hours, he should be fine.'

Jackie flung her arms around her and hugged tight. 'Can't thank you enough doc. Any time you want a free night out you come down to my club.' She let the other woman go and by the look of the doctor's face she knew she was making a right old tit of herself, but who cared when her son was back in her loving arms. The expression on the doctor's face suddenly changed as she asked,

'Can I have a . . . um . . . quiet word with you?' She looked at Schoolboy. 'On your own?'

'Sure.' Jackie moved to the side with the doctor as Schoolboy made his way back to their son.

'You are Jackie Jarvis?' And then she rattled out Jackie's address. Jackie frowned. 'Yeah.'

'I run the *clinic*.' The doctor emphasised the word clinic. 'Upstairs. I think you had an appointment with me this afternoon. At four.'

Jackie blushed. How could this be the same doctor? As if reading her mind the doctor gently explained, 'I sometimes do the emergency ward in the evenings. Of course with all this happening I understand why you missed the appointment, but I'm just checking that you will make another one. It's very urgent that you come to see me.'

Jackie's eyes skidded downwards. This was the last thing she wanted to chat about. This could wait. 'Yeah, sure.' But she didn't meet the doctor's eyes. And with that the other woman left. Jackie let out a hefty sigh.

'What did she want?'

Jackie turned at Schoolboy's question. She ran her fingers threw her red hair, punching up the strands over her forehead. 'Nothing much. Just wanted to make sure I was OK with everything.' His dark gaze remained steady on her. Instead of trying to meet his look she rushed to the other side of Preston's bed. Took the armchair. Pulled it close. She stared lovingly at her son. Gave him one of her special mummy smiles. Smoothed her hand over his hair. Suddenly she felt Schoolboy's hand cover hers. Her hand stopped moving. Then she laced her fingers through his. He pulled their clasped hands down onto the blanket covering their boy.

'Do you remember what happened?' she quietly asked Preston.

He swallowed. Nodded. Then opened his mouth. Tried to speak but nothing came out. Tried again, this time his voice came out in a small whisper. 'This car came at me.' He took another breath. 'I crossed the road proper mum at the lights.'

'I know son,' she reassured quietly.

'But it wouldn't stop.'

'Sh,' his dad soothed. 'That's enough for now.'

But Preston kept going, his voice getting stronger. 'I tried to move but it just kept coming at me. I saw . . .'

Jackie tensed. Leaned forward. 'What did you see?'

Preston's chest rose as his eyes blinked rapidly. 'I saw . . .' Suddenly Preston's eyes fluttered. Slammed shut as he slumped back on the bed. The lights on the monitor started to go crazy as a loud beeping noise ripped through the air. Schoolboy jumped up. Leaned over his son. Frantically he grabbed his shoulders and shook him. 'Preston? Preston?' But he didn't move and the noise didn't stop.

Jackie bolted for the door and yelled down the corridor. 'Help us. Please someone help us.' A nurse came running down the corridor and into the room. She took one look at Preston and ran for the door again. Shouted, 'Respiratory arrest. Call the crash team!'

twelve

Bliss stared at the contents of the wooden box in the back of the parked van, as if it were gold. Guns. All shapes and all sizes. The thrill went right through. He was soon going to be *the* man supplying most of the hardware on the street in this manor.

He turned to the solitary man by his side. He looked more like a geography teacher than a major league arms dealer. Said his name was Risikoff but Bliss expected that was a lie, just like he was telling porkies that he was called Harry Smith.

'My client would like to know if this is the type of merchandise that you're after?'

Before Bliss could answer a sound like an animal howling interrupted from the lock-up behind them. He twisted around and yelled at the lock-up's closed door, 'Keep the fucking noise down please, I'm trying to do some business here . . .'

He turned back noting the uneasy look now in Risikoff's close-set eyes. 'Yeah, that's what I'm after. You know I'm looking to do a major deal, so when can your boss sort me out?'

'Sort me out,' Risikoff said with a smile. 'I like your quaint English expressions.' Bliss didn't smile back. He got the feeling this man was taking him for some street virgin. So he placed his arms around the man's shoulder like they'd been mates for donkey's years and said, 'Let's do some more talking inside.' He walked Risikoff to the door of the lock-up ahead of them. Pulled his hand off Risikoff so he could slide the door back. Placed his arm back around his shoulder as they moved inside.

What Risikoff saw nearly made him run for his life.

Marky-Boy's body dangled from the handcuffs attached to the ceiling by chains. His body was a mass of deep slashes that dripped blood down his flesh onto the bloody pool beneath him. Sean stood next to him with a red stained knife in his hand. As his eyes caught Bliss, Marky-Boy moaned pitifully behind the metallic tape across his mouth. Sweat and saliva bubbled at the sides of the tape produced by his screams.

Bliss's arms tightened around Risikoff's shoulder. 'Just thought you might like to see something else very English.'

Sean grinned as he raised one of his victim's feet. Positioned the ankle in a certain way. He took the knife and carefully pushed into the flesh under the ankle bone. Marky-Boy's body rocked. Sean tore the skin slightly before pulling the blade back out. He had a second go which left a wound like a bloody mouth, grinning as it hung from the victim's foot.

Bliss said with pride, 'Tendons. That's Sean's speciality. Cutting them clean away from someone's muscle and bone. Learned that in his uncle's butcher's shop as a kid.'

Sean dropped his victim's foot and announced as if he was a lecturer with a bunch of first year students, 'The Achilles heel, now that's the toughest and strongest tendon of all. Watch.' He lifted Marky-Boy's other foot and repeated the knife action. The dangled man's body ripped and swayed with pain. Blood, fluid and sweat trickled from the gaping wound which exposed the white bone underneath but there was much less blood than before.

Risikoff gulped as Bliss turned him slowly around. In a hard voice he said, 'You better not be fucking me around . . .'

'No, of course not.'

'Good man.' Bliss patted him on the back. 'I want the big delivery to arrive next week—'

'That's not possible.' Marky-Boy's muffled scream ripped through the air. Risikoff flinched but stood his ground. 'We need to proceed very carefully.'

'So when?' Bliss was losing his patience.

'Three weeks today. But we need to be sure that you have a solid location, a place that is secure.'

Bliss laughed the same time a gunshot rang out from the lock-up. Marky-Boy didn't scream any more. 'My place is secure alright. Even the cops wouldn't ever guess where my stash house is.'

The medical team worked furiously on Preston as Schoolboy and Jackie clung to each other in a corner. Five minutes. Ten minutes. Half an hour. And all the time the medical team flung out terms that Preston's parents didn't understand. Finally the doctor who spoke to them earlier moved towards them. Jackie took one look at the doctor's face and tightened her arms around her husband.

'I'm sorry, but he's in a deep coma. He's unresponsive and not breathing on his own so we've had to connect him to a ventilator.'

Jackie felt her legs going, but Schoolboy kept her upright.

'I don't understand,' Schoolboy said.

'He seems to have had a relapse. We're not sure why . . .'

'But he was talking,' Jackie interrupted weakly, dazed, her head moving from side to side. 'He looked ready to come home.'

'Is he going to die?' Schoolboy said the dreaded words that were zooming around Jackie's mind.

Jackie and Schoolboy held their breath. 'As I said earlier,' the doctor continued softly, 'your son is a fighter. He'll be under 24-hour observation.' She nodded gravely and was gone.

I'm not going to cry, I'm not going to cry, I'm not going to cry, Jackie told herself. What was the point of crying? That wasn't going to help her boy. Instead she loosened her arms from Schoolboy and began walking towards Preston's bed. But she turned swiftly around when she realised that Schoolboy was headed for the door.

'Where you going?' she screamed.

But he didn't answer as he hit the corridor outside. Madly she rushed after him. Reached him and caught his arm. For an instant he halted as she shouted, 'You can't just go now.'

He violently threw her arm off making her stumble back. That's when she saw the tears leaking from his eyes. 'Don't you get it?' he cried, his locks flying around his shoulder with the force of his words. 'I thought I could do it, but I can't.' He shook his head. 'I can't just stay here and watch my son die.' Briskly he turned and got out of there as quickly as possible. He burst through the emergency exit doors. Jackie staggered back until she hit the wall. Finally her legs gave way and she slid towards the floor.

Stan Lewis righted himself as he watched the black geezer with the dreadlocks, who'd nearly knocked him over on the emergency stairs, take the steps two at a time. The bloke should thank his lucky stars that Stan had his own business to sort out or he would've knocked him flat on his back. No one stamped on Stanley Lewis and got away with it. In Stan's world, all slights were paid for, even if it wasn't by the culprit. He dismissed the incident from his mind as he clutched the bunch of red roses he held in his hand. Moved up the stairs towards the next floor. The ward was quiet. He moved towards the reception desk where a single nurse sat.

'I'm here to see Marina Lewis,' he announced.

'I'm sorry sir. But she's heavily sedated and won't be—'

Now he was going to get in a row with a nurse, it was turning out to be a bad day.

'Look love, I'm her husband, I'm sure you heard what happened to our girls today.'

The nurse consulted her notes. 'It says here the patient is divorced.'

Stan bit his lip. 'Married? Divorced? What's the difference? I'm the father, that gives me some rights don't it?'

She gave him a sympathetic look. Stan cashed in. 'I just wanted to make sure she's OK, alright? I won't even stay long.' He pushed the flowers forward. 'These are her favourites.'

The nurse looked at the flowers. Back at him. Gave him a gentle smile that said it was good to see a man treat a woman right. Then nodded. 'Room four. But only five minutes. She's had a traumatic day. I'm so sorry about your children.'

Stan shuffled his feet as he drew the flowers close to his chest. 'Yeah, so am I. She loved those girls from the bottom of her heart. I just need her to know that I'm here for her.'

He made his way along the corridor. Found the room. Entered. No other occupants, just Marina looking as fragile as a wilted flower in the bed. He walked over. Reached her side. Looked down at her with a soft expression on his face. He found a vase and filled it with water before spending several moments arranging the flowers. Then he set it on the bedside cabinet and he leaned over the display breathing in the scent. He sat on the side of the bed and gently ran his fingers through the blonde hair of his ex-wife.

He leaned over and whispered, 'You stupid bitch. This is all your doing. My girls are dead because of you. And I'm going to see that you pay, every day, you're going to pay.' Suddenly he ripped a petal off a rose and flung it in her face. Ripped another one and did the same. As he continued his hands moved in a frenzy. Finally the only things he was left holding in his shaking hands were the lonely stems. He dashed them onto the floor by his feet. Then he leaned close into her face. 'And then one day I'm going to fucking kill you.'

He spat in her face. Turned and left the room.

Marina's eyes flew open as soon as the door slammed. The drugs she'd been given had worn off ages ago, no doubt because her body was too used to the pills she popped all the time. With a trembling hand she wiped the spit and petals from her face as she pushed urgently out of the bed. Bastard. Bastard. Bastard. What did he mean it was her fault her girls were dead? He couldn't put the blame at her door, could he? It wasn't her fault what had happened.

One day I'm going to fucking kill you. The words of her ex kept running around her mind. She knew Stan, if he made a threat he meant to act on it. There was only one person she knew who could stop him.

She jumped off the bed. Looked crazily around for her handbag. Found it slung on the chair near the end of the bed. She rushed over, picked it up, fumbled inside. Pulled out her mobile.

Chest heaving she punched in the numbers she kept securely locked away in her head. She held the phone to her face. The line pulsed on. Kept ringing. No one picked up at the other end. Voicemail.

'It's me. He says he's going to top me. You've got to help me. I know you ain't taking my calls, but if you don't help me out I'm going to have to tell Stan the truth.'

thirteen

He was going to leave all of this to the boys one day. Schoolboy scanned his restaurant on Church Street in Stoke Newington as he stood at the window in his office on the first floor. The Melting Pot was jammed to capacity at ten thirty at night. People just didn't seem to be able to get enough of his nosh. And now it was one of the most sought after eating holes in the whole of London. He'd kept the décor simple, nothing flash or tarty, something for his lads to be proud of. Years back all he would've been able to leave them was a prison record and a ton of drug dealing contacts. With the help of Jackie and a few mates he'd ditched the gangster lifestyle and gone back to his first passion, cooking. Even he was gobsmacked at how well it had gone. And now some TV production company wanted him to front a show on the box about cooking. And one of his sons might never see him do that; might never reap the rewards of his years of hard work. Just thinking about it choked him up.

'Eli?' He didn't turn around immediately in response because he knew who it was. Only two people called him the shortened version of his given name, Elijah – his sister, Evie and his restaurant manager, Kelly. Couldn't be his sister, so he turned to face Kelly.

Kelly was as different from his Jackie as night was to day. While Jackie was a trousers and trainers girl, with a short cut that kept her hair out of the way, Kelly flaunted herself in gorgeous frocks, at least four-inch heels and golden, glossy hair that swayed just below her shoulder blades. He knew she'd been divorced for a couple of years, with money to burn from an inheritance. She'd been a regular punter, then they got chatting one night and before he knew it he'd agreed for her to play hostess to his owner.

Her heels clicked against the polished oak floorboards as she stepped inside. Schoolboy made his way to his desk and sat down. He stared at the framed photo on his desk. The twins together aged about six, with their big brother, Jackie's other son, Ryan, in between. All the boys were grinning like crazy.

'I didn't see you come in,' she said in that low voice of hers. She eased down into the soft, lilac sofa opposite the desk. Crossed her legs, giving him an eyeful of toned thigh.

'I came through the kitchen.' He let out a long wave of air. 'I just wanted to be alone for a bit.'

Kelly flicked the tip of her tongue against her cherry painted bottom lip before she asked, 'How's Preston?'

He tried to answer, but the emotion just stuck in his throat as he kept staring at the photo. He opened his mouth but still nothing came out. His face fell apart as he bowed his head. His shoulder shook as he tried to hold the emotions back.

That's when he felt Kelly's full embrace. He sank into her warmth, and light lemon scent. This was what he needed, a good dollop of comfort. The kind of comfort he hadn't gotten from Jackie in a long time. They remained like that until he could swallow properly again. Until he felt her long fingers begin to massage the tight muscles in his neck. That felt good, reeeal good. His hand tightened around her waist. Then his breathing caught when he felt her teeth nip his ear. He wasn't surprised. Knew she fancied the pants off him. He'd have to be missing both eyes not to see the come-on looks she sent his way. And with the way he was feeling it would be so easy to sink on to the floor and take what she was offering. And let's face it, back in the day he'd been pretty free with his favours. But not any more. There was only one girl for him.

Gently he unwound his hands and eased Kelly back. 'You know what I like about you?' He cupped his palms around her face. 'You always know what I want.'

'But you aren't going to take it?'

His dimples showed as he smiled. 'I'm a one-woman man—'

But before he could say anything else a voice called out, 'Schoolie?'

Kelly got to her feet as Schoolboy checked out the man he'd been expecting waiting in the doorway. The newcomer was large, with deep brown skin, muscular with a shaved head and the way he wore his designer suit made him look like a tough businessman or bouncer, either way it screamed don't fuck with me. The man stepped forward as Kelly said, 'Give Preston a kiss for me.' Then she blew him her own kiss and was gone.

'Not interrupting anything?' the man asked.

'And if you were Window you don't look sorry.'

Window made a huff sound. Window was married to his sister, but had once been Schoolboy's mentor back in the good old bad days and the eyes for a number of London's criminal crews. That's where he'd got his nickname Window from. But he'd left that life long behind, turned over his club, The Minus One, to Schoolboy, which was now his restaurant. He now lived in domesticated bliss with Evie and his two kids in a stunner of a house in Kent.

'Did you bring it?' Schoolboy carried on, the tone in his voice changing to serious.

Both men sat down. Window gave Schoolboy a grave look. 'You sure about this?'

'You know what Jackie called me today? A bloke missing a backbone. Said I didn't have the nuts to help her find out who did this to our son.'

Window considered his younger friend. 'Took a lot of *balls* for you to turn your back on that world man. I don't like the idea of you going back into it. Let the Babylon take care of it.' Window's use of the old-time black word for the cops took Schoolboy straight back into the world he'd been out of for years. It hadn't been easy for him to escape from that world. In his determination to kiss the underworld goodbye he'd nearly got his arse capped by two rival gangs. But he'd made it. Could he really afford to go back even for his boy? A shiver ran through him. Maybe Window was right, but still he didn't like the idea of being thought of as a man with a dick but nothing else. Not by the woman he was crazy about.

'Did you bring it?' Again he asked, harder this time.

Window dipped his hand into his pocket. Placed it on the table. Schoolboy's breath caught in his throat as he eyeballed it.

A handgun.

The large plasma screen TV in Jackie's sitting room showed the 10.40 local news, one of its reporters outside the school:

'The local community are understandably shocked at today's incident. The two dead girls are believed to be the daughters of the alleged London criminal Stanley Lewis. The parents of the boy who was also injured in the attack are not believed to have any connection with the Lewis family. Earlier we spoke to people on the street to find out their reactions to today's appalling incident.'

The image changed to show a young woman with a pram. She looked into the camera with a very angry face. 'This is awful. I really feel for the parents. Your kids are meant to be safe at school ain't they?'

The picture cut to show an elderly man and woman. The man spoke. 'Terrible, absolutely terrible. In my day they would've strung 'em up. I'd string 'em up myself if I got my hands on them.'

The news item flashed back to the reporter.

'As you can see feelings are running very high . . .'

Jackie pulled herself wearily off the sofa in her sitting room and turned the telly off. She'd wanted to stay at the hospital, but the Sister in charge of the ward had told her to go home and rest. She hadn't wanted to, but knew the other woman was right. She'd only left when Misty and the others had turned up and urged her to go. They would sit with Preston while she went home and got some kip. What a long, awful day and it wasn't over yet.

She pulled in a deep breath as she stood still. Then her eyes met the photographs mounted on the wall. Photos of her boys.

She smiled at the one of Ryan taken on his last day of secondary school. They'd bought this gorgeous house when the boys were young, deciding they needed more space than they had in her two-bed flat in Hackney. They'd decided to remain in East London because their roots were here; their histories. They'd played out their good and bad times on the streets of East London. They'd bought this particular house because Schoolboy had told her a story that when his dad had come to England from Grenada back in the early 60s he'd settled with his mates in the same house renting rooms from the landlord. Back then the Square had been almost on its last legs. Their landlord had asked the newly arrived immigrants if they'd wanted to buy it for a grand. But back then a grand had been a load of money. Besides, Schoolboy's dad and his mates said they were only passing through England, expecting that they would be back in Grenada soon enough. His dad had stayed in England for over thirty-odd years and his biggest regret was not buying a house that was now worth well over a million quid. So Schoolboy and Jackie had bought it. She knew some people raised their eyebrows about where they'd got that kind of dosh from, but that was a secret only her, Schoolboy, her three friends and Misty knew about. A diamond secret.

Jackie glanced away from the photos thinking she should maybe go back to the ozzie to check on Preston. She knew there would most probably be no change because the ozzie would've called her. But still she wanted to see her little boy's face.

Then she heard a sharp, high-pitched laugh coming from the kitchen. Foxy. She'd come home to find Ryan and his girlfriend snuggled on the sofa watching a DVD. Why oh why couldn't her son find a decent girl? As far as she was concerned Foxy was a brassy airhead who was leading her boy astray. Plus she was five years older than him for crying out loud. She didn't like the girl and she showed it. Plus she worried about Ryan. Worried that he wasn't mature enough yet to live on his own. Worried about that business that had happened at her wedding that they never talked about. What if he was still having nightmares about it like he used to when he was young? That's why he needed a decent woman beside him, someone to support him if the going got tough. She marched into the kitchen wanting that tarty piece out of her house.

Foxy was all over Ryan at the kitchen table. 'Oh, hello Jackie,' Foxy said as she untangled her arms from around Ryan.

Jackie hissed, 'It's Mrs Jarvis to you.'

Ryan threw her a disapproving look. She stared defiantly back at him. He could look at her all he wanted because she needed him to know that that girl wasn't good enough for him. She folded her arms. 'Thanks for staying with Darius. It's late so get yourselves off home.'

Ryan gave his mum a peck on the cheek. 'Let me know if anything changes.'

She nodded. 'I love you,' she said quietly.

'I know,' he replied, his face solemn.

After they had gone she wearily made her way up the stairs to the boys' room on the second floor. She eased the bedroom door back quietly so that she didn't wake Darius who was tucked up safe and sound asleep in the single bed against the right wall. The room was a typical lad's pad, posters on the wall of their favourite footie teams and popstars, a few items of clothing scattered on the floor and Preston's guitar propped up against the far wall. Her mouth twisted. How many times had she told the boys to put their clothes away? She inched inside and picked up Darius's Arsenal rucksack on the floor and popped it onto the computer chair. Silently she gathered the clothes on the floor and moved towards the wardrobe. Opened it. The first thing she saw was the navy suit and white shirt that Schoolboy had bought for Preston to wear to his Confirmation. She folded the clothes in her hands and placed them neatly on the shelves and then ran her hand lovingly over Preston's suit. She frowned when she noticed a wrinkle on his shirt. She smoothed her hand over it, but the wrinkle remained. She couldn't have that, the shirt needed to be ready for her boy to wear the day of his Confirmation. And he would be Confirmed, she vowed, he was getting out of that hospital. She pulled the shirt down and made her way outside.

Five minutes later she was ironing it with the cordless steam iron in the sitting room. The steam hissed from the iron as she picked it up the same time the knocker on the front door went. Bang. It made her jump, her heart pounding away. Shit, she didn't need any visitors right now, not this late at night. She'd already spent so much time on the blower today chatting to well-wishers concerned about Preston. Whoever it was she was going to keep it short and sweet. She placed the iron back on its cradle. Left the room and reached the door. Pulled it open. Her mouth fell open when she saw who it was.

Jackie froze in shock at the doorway. 'What do you want?'

Paul Bliss looked over her shoulder into the house. 'A word with you,' was all he said.

For a few seconds Jackie held on tight to the edge of the door and didn't respond. Then, with a strange calmness she said, 'You'd better come in then.'

She pulled the door back. Stepped to the side. Bliss took up her invitation and moved into the warmth of her home.

'Look I heard about—' Bliss started saying as he walked across the black and white floor tiles, but she cut over him, a shaky smile flitting across her face. 'Come into the sitting room.' He hesitated for a second or two. Then nodded. They entered a room that reminded him of a family life that he'd never really had.

'I heard about your son. What happened at his school,' Bliss launched into her as he faced her. 'And I know you came looking for me ready to blow my brains out.' Her face didn't even change expression with his revelation. But then he wasn't surprised, he knew all about Jackie Jarvis. A miniature tough nut who took lip from no one. And that business with Frankie Sullivan years back had told everyone she wasn't a woman to mess with. He'd even heard that she and the women who ran their club in Wapping took on the occasional job, nothing major, just lending a helping hand to those who didn't want to take their troubles to the cops.

'Why don't you park yourself down there.' She waved at an armchair. 'And I'll get us some brandy.' She left before he could say anything else. She hadn't even responded to what he'd said and who could blame her. Her kid was in the ozzie and she must be going out of her mind.

He took the seat, his eyes cruising the room. Comfy and cosy with family photos dotted around. He noticed the large framed one of a boy with red hair and freckles and knew it must be her eldest son. Nice place, not like that stinking hovel he'd grown up in. Just him and his mum. Mum? He felt like spitting when he thought of the woman who'd brought him into the world. All she'd ever loved was her bottle. So pissed out of her box most nights she didn't even know she had a son any more. And why? All because his dad had legged-it as soon as he knew she had a bun in the oven. Gone back to his missus. He'd despised her for letting someone control the rest of her life. Mind you he'd found his dad and now they were making plans.

He flipped out of his thoughts as Jackie came back with two glasses and a bottle on a tray. Without making eye contact she placed the tray on the oval glass table.

She stepped back. 'Help yourself and then we can talk.'

He could tell she was as nervous as hell because her hand was shaking. He leaned forward and grasped the bottle and started rabbiting away at the same time as he felt her walk behind him. 'I know what you've heard, but it ain't true. No fucking way. I would never, ever–' He wasn't sure what made him look up, but he did. Just as she came back to stand in front of him with a cordless steam iron heading straight for his face.

fourteen

As she plunged the iron straight at him Jackie pressed the steam button. Hiss. Skin-peeling steam puffed towards his face. Bliss's street fighting instincts kicked in as he threw his head to the side, but too late. He yelled with pain as the tip of the iron caught the skin on the side of his neck.

'You bastard,' Jackie screamed as she threw herself on top of him still clutching the iron. The air whooshed out of his body as her knees dug into his stomach. He tried to grab her arm, but the weight of the iron made her hand drop to the side. Somehow she regained the strength in her arm and swung the iron. She hit him a glancing blow to the side of his head. Dazed his head rocked back. His vision blurred. He snapped out of it when he heard the sizzle of steam. Felt the moist heat heading back towards his face. He ducked to the side. The iron slammed into the ruby red-coloured sofa knocking the wind from Jackie as she wobbled. Fell to the side. Bliss saw his chance and took it. He gripped her waist and toppled off the sofa. They landed on the soft, blue carpet. But still Jackie wouldn't let the iron go. Like a mad woman Jackie screamed abuse at him. 'Try to kill my boy ... Murdering two defenceless girls ... You scum. Scum. Scum!'

Bliss had forgotten about his own gun which might have come in handy in the circumstances but he wasn't sure even waving that was going to stop mad bird here. And he hated fighting women, they always fought so dirty. He didn't have time to suss her out now. He rolled her one more time. Managed to trap her beneath him.

That's when he saw the cold-blooded fury turning her face red. Turning her eyes a murky shade of green. He clamped his knees around her to hold her tightly into place. His hand skated down her arm until he found her wrist. He applied pressure as she threw every obscenity known to man in his face. He applied brute pressure, but she wouldn't let go of the iron. Pushed his words through his clenched teeth. 'I don't know what the fuck's going on here . . .'

Her face twisted in pain, but she wouldn't drop the iron. 'I'm going to fucking finish you off.'

He'd had enough of this. His skin beginning to burn like hell on his neck he pulled the shooter out of the inside pocket of his jacket. Held it point blank in her face.

'I ain't bloody scared of you,' she spat.

Before he could respond Bliss froze. Held his breath as he felt the nozzle of a gun touch the back of his head.

'Drop the piece.'

For a few seconds Bliss remained frozen as the gun remained at his head. But his blue eyes darted from side to side. The last time anyone had had the nerve to pull a shooter on him was when he was eighteen when one of the guys he'd done a post office job with didn't want to give him his cut. The guy wasn't around any more to tell his side of the story, Bliss had seen to that. He pushed his hand to the side and let go of his gun. He let out his breath, real slow, as the nozzle left his head. Slowly he turned his head as Jackie pinned her gaze over his shoulder.

Black guy with dreads looking like he wanted to take his fucking head off. Must be Jackie's old man. Jackie knew that by the way Schoolboy was holding his body he was no longer Schoolboy, successful businessman, but back to being the street hood he'd fought hard to leave behind.

Bliss finally broke the dreadful silence. 'One of my neighbours told me she came looking for me earlier. With a shooter.' Schoolboy sent Jackie a disbelieving look. 'So I came over here to calm things down. Pay my respects and she goes for me with an iron. I don't know what pills they gave her to help with her nerves but you need to take them back up the quack house and get a refund.'

Schoolboy didn't answer, instead he shifted his dark gaze again from his woman to Bliss. Finally he lowered the gun. Moved to Jackie. Leaned down and wrenched the iron from her hand. Flung it across the carpet. Turned his hot gaze to Bliss. 'Alright mate, get away from my girl.'

Jackie stared at him. Of all the stupid things for her to be thinking about while someone had a shooter in her face was that Schoolboy had called her *his girl*. Shit, he hadn't done that in ages. Bliss eased back to his knees. Grabbed his gun as he stood up. He shoved it back into his pocket. Jackie scrambled to her feet breathing heavily. She looked at him like she still wanted to put him six feet under.

'I'm Paul Bliss—' Bliss started to tell Schoolboy between quick breaths.

'I know who you are,' Schoolboy cut in. 'And I know what people say you did. So what the fuck are you doing coming round to my yard?'

'Like I told her I never done it,' Bliss shot back.

Jackie stepped threateningly forward. She stabbed her finger in the air at him. 'Turn it in Bliss, everyone knows you were behind the wheel of the motor that killed the Lewis kids. That car that ran my boy down . . .' she choked, '. . . and left my kid in a coma . . .'

'I ain't run no one over. That's not my style is it? Accidentally or otherwise . . .'

Yes, Jackie thought wildly, it most certainly is your style, accidentally or otherwise. She left her finger pointing menacingly in the air at him and snarled, 'I'm going to get you—'

'Be quiet,' Schoolboy hissed.

She stared at him with how-dare-you eyes. Who the fuck did he think he was talking to? Then she saw the expression on his face. Absolute, honest to God fury. She kept her mouth buttoned tight.

Schoolboy turned his attention back to Bliss. 'How did you expect my wife to react when you turn up on our doorstep after what we've been hearing on the street?'

Bliss's frustration showed on his face. 'Look, I don't do kids, everyone knows that, all my victims are of voting age. So, whoever has been putting it about is well out of order.' He pointed his finger at Schoolboy.

'So who did it?' Schoolboy asked.

'How the fuck should I know? I'm saying this once only to you mate, so listen good. I. Never. Done. It. And if I had done it why the fuck would I come here?' He gave Jackie one last look. 'You're lucky you're a grieving mum, coz anyone who pulled a stunt like that on me really would be getting run over.' He pulled the collar of his jacket more closely around himself. Pushed his hand once through his hair. Gave Jackie a final look and was gone.

Schoolboy turned an accusing look at Jackie. 'Are you off your face or something?'

'What did you want me to do? Make him crumpets and tea?' Only then did she realise that she was blubbing her eyes out. 'I had to do it for our son.'

'He's dangerous. Let it alone.' He turned away from her.

She rushed up to him and grabbed his arm furiously. Swung him around. 'Don't you dare turn your back on me for a second time today.'

They stared at each other, breathing hard, their fury beating between them. Suddenly Schoolboy waved the gun at her. 'Is that what you want Jackie? For me to follow Bliss right now and cap his arse in the street?'

Suddenly the look on Jackie's face became pinched as a groan of pain shot from her mouth and her hand rubbed at her chest. Schoolboy had his arms around her instantly, the gun flopping against her back. 'What is it Jackie? Did that prick hurt you?'

The last thing she wanted was him touching her when she was feeling like this. He might find out and then what? So she did what she always did, she thrust him away. Taken off guard by her movement he stumbled back. Suddenly he picked up the nearest thing to him – a vase – and threw it with force above the fireplace. With a crash it shattered against the wall. Jackie watched with disbelief. She was the one who usually found it hard to keep a hold of her emotions not Schoolboy. The uncomfortable silence tightened around them.

He finally broke the silence. 'Do you want me to move out?' He didn't look at her.

'I want you to help me find who damaged our son. And if that means you going out there now and cutting Bliss's nuts off in the street, then yeah.'

Now he looked at her. 'I can't do that. I was gonna use that shooter to hunt whoever the fucker was and blast them to kingdom come. But I can't.' His voice was loaded with pain. 'I can't go back into that world. And you need to leave it alone as well. I just want my boy back. If you need me I'll be at our son's bedside.'

Seconds later she was in the room on her own. Then came the slam of the front door. For a few seconds she remained fixed to the spot she stood in. So Bliss was claiming he didn't do it? Then where were all these rumours coming from? Why would someone put that around about him?

And if I had done it why the fuck would I come here? Bliss's words ran around her head. He was right, if he had it didn't make sense he would show up on your doorstep like that. What the hell was going on here?

She winced as the pain in her chest came back. She moved to the art deco mirror she'd bought in Portobello Road market that was above the fireplace. Raised her T-shirt. Stared at her right breast. Her fingers gingerly touched the lump inside it.

Darius's hand tightened on the stair rail as he sat on the second floor landing in his Arsenal jim-jams listening anxiously to his mum and dad going at each other's throats. Why couldn't they just stop? They were always having a ruck these days. Sometimes he didn't even wanna come home. He'd rather go around to Molly's and just hang out. Molly. Images of her being hit and dragged by the car grew large in his mind. He wished his big brother Ryan was here. Wished Preston wasn't lying in that bed in the hospital. Wished Molly . . . His shoulders hunched. The tears started streaming down his face. As he wiped the back of his hand across his cheek trying to scrub away the tears a door slammed downstairs. Quickly he bolted back to his bedroom before his mum or dad caught him. But he didn't get into bed. Instead he reached for his rucksack on the computer chair. Unzipped it. Shoved his small hand inside. Pulled something out. His and Molly's secret. He knew what it was. His mum would murder him on the spot if she found him with it. Him and Molly had found it when they should've been in the playground at lunchtime. That's what he'd loved about his mate Molly, they always got up to loads of naughties behind the grown-ups' backs. Mind you if they'd been caught it was an immediate trip to Mrs Moran's office for a mega telling-off. But they hadn't been caught. Now he wondered if Molly was dead and his brother was in hospital because of their secret. Maybe he should tell his mum and dad . . .

'It's our secret,' Molly had whispered, her blue eyes lighting up with mischief. No he couldn't tell them because he'd made a promise. Quickly he opened the wardrobe door. Found his Confirmation suit. Pushed his and Molly's secret into the pocket of the navy blue jacket.

Bliss was spitting nails by the time he got back to the car, where his right-hand man Sean waited for him in the driver's seat. Who was spreading all that shit about him? He got into the passenger seat. Looked at Sean. 'I think we've got a problem.' He told him quickly what had happened.

'Want me to go back in there and make the bitch and her fella understand who they're dealing with?' Sean asked, the muscle in his cheek twitching.

Bliss popped four painkillers. Closed his eyes as the drug shot to his bloodstream. Only when he was buzzing did he re-open his eyes and answer. 'Nah. I would've done the same thing in her shoes.'

Sean nodded, but quietly added, 'And did you do it? Kill Lewis's kids?'

Instead of answering Bliss sniffed a good-sized pinch of coke. Then he raised his head and said, 'Did you find out where this kid lives who was dealing in the club?'

Sean nodded. 'Bethnal Green way.'

'I think we need to pay him a visit.'

fifteen

Misty and Roxy stood outside the room where Preston lay fighting for his life. Inside sat Schoolboy. Anna and Ollie were downstairs in the canteen getting everyone some much-needed drinks.

Roxy yawned then looked sideways at Misty making her buttermilk bob move slightly. 'I'm worried about Jackie.'

Misty looked down at her plump friend, her grey gaze showing her concern. 'Yeah, so am I. The way she's behaving she'll end up doing something really stupid.'

Roxy moved away from the door, pulling out her asthma inhaler. She inhaled two quick hits. Then looked back at Misty who'd followed her. 'Can we do anything about it?'

Misty thought for a few seconds, her forehead creasing into a frown. 'I'm not sure. You know what Jackie's like once she's made up her mind.' Her tone changed as she continued, 'Do you know why she had an ozzie appointment today?'

Roxy shook her head. 'I think Ollie's the only one who knows that. Mind you it can't be anything serious or she would've told us.'

'I suppose so.'

Roxy shook her head back as she clutched her shoulder bag. 'I'm off to the loo. Be right back.' Before the other woman could answer she strode quickly down the corridor. As soon as she was inside the Ladies she quickly opened her bag. Pulled out a half bottle of vodka. The others would read her the riot act if they knew she was back on the booze. She unscrewed the lid and gulped. Not too much though, she couldn't afford to get pissed just yet, no, she'd leave that for later, behind closed doors. She closed her eyes briefly as the alcohol made her heart thump.

As Roxy pumped a breath freshener spray on her tongue, in the corridor Misty pulled out her mobile. Dialled a long-distance number.

'It's Misty. You need to get your arse here now . . .'

Sean McCarthy stopped his motor outside Herbert Morrison Tower minutes to midnight. He looked at his boss in the passenger seat. They didn't speak just nodded at each other. Bliss popped a couple of painkillers and then stepped outside. The men walked around to the back of the car. Sean popped the boot. Grinning they stared inside at their weapon of choice for tonight. Two twelve-inch scaffolding poles with a couple of inches of concrete inside at one end. The damage that both beauties could do to bones was amazing. As Sean leaned down to pick up a pole the screaming sound of cop cars belted around the corner onto the street.

'Shit,' Sean swore as he straightened up.

Bliss slammed the lid as two police cars screeched to a halt outside the block a few feet away from them.

'We need to—' rushed out of Sean's mouth but Bliss put a restraining hand onto his arm.

'Take it easy.'

They froze as five cops jumped out of the cars. They remained where they were, expecting the cops to come up to them. But instead the police ran past them towards the entrance of the building, one of them waving his arm for the concierge to let them in.

Both men let out easy breaths as they walked slowly back to the front of the car. Got in. As Sean twisted the ignition key, Bliss said, 'No. Let's wait and see what's going on.'

And so they waited. Five minutes. Ten. Fifteen. Almost twenty minutes later the cops reappeared, two of them holding the arms of a young man who stood handcuffed between them.

Sean snickered as they watched the scene. 'That is our toerag dealer. Never thought I'd live to see the day the Bill gave us a helping hand.'

Bliss leaned forward and peered hard through the windscreen trying to catch the dealer's face. The dealer turned his face around a few seconds before he was thrust into the back of the cop car. Bliss peered closer, the skin on his forehead creasing up. He knew that face . . . Bingo! He had it. He eased back into the seat as the Bill drove off.

Looked at Sean. 'You never guess who that kid is?'

Sean just stared at him, so he carried on, a small smile on his face. 'Jackie Jarvis's boy.'

'How do you know that?'

'I've just seen a happy family snap of him sitting pretty in her living room.'

Five minutes to one in the morning Jackie got the phone call from the one cop she could do without talking to again.

'What do you want?' she whispered, so that she didn't wake Darius who was sleeping sound in his bed. She'd been sitting by his side for God knows how long since Schoolboy had slammed out of the house. She stood up when she realised that he might have some more information about what had happened outside the school.

'Jackie I'm sorry to tell you this, but Ryan's been arrested.'

Jackie went back to Unity Road police station on her own. When she got Ryan she was going to . . . She ground her teeth together. As soon as she entered she saw Foxy Jones sitting anxiously in the reception area. The younger woman shot up as Jackie marched towards her.

Jackie pointed her finger in the taller woman's face. 'I want you out of here now.'

Foxy's manicured fingers fluttered in the air. 'It weren't my fault I swear.'

That made Jackie see red. 'My son would not be in a bit of bother if it weren't for you. He was a decent boy until he picked up with you.'

That made Foxy start booing very loudly. The desk sergeant and the two men sitting on the chairs in the reception looked over at both women.

'If I have to take one more friggin' step closer to you I'm going to wring your bloody neck, you got it?'

'I love him,' Foxy wailed. Strangely Jackie believed her, but that didn't make her like her any more. Foxy fled the station in tears.

'Jackie.'

On hearing her name Jackie twisted around to find Ricky standing behind her.

'I want to see my son.'

Ricky moved closer to her. 'Not before we have a chat.'

He took her to a small room near the reception. Anxiously she stared intently at him. 'He's a good boy,' she said finally.

Ricky nodded. 'I know he is. But the police raided his flat because one his neighbours reported that she thought he was dealing drugs.'

'Fuck off!' she exploded. 'My lad wouldn't touch the stuff.' She shook her head vigorously. 'He knows what will happen to him if he does.'

Ricky folded his fingers together. 'They found marijuana at his place.'

Jackie gasped seeing her boy going down for a long time. Ricky carried on in the same calm tone. 'But the amount found is classed as being for personal use.'

'Meaning?'

'He'll get off with a caution.' She let out a huge sigh of relief, but Ricky's next words rocked her again. 'But I think he's doing some other heavy shit. They didn't find anything else in his place, but I think you need to have a long chat with him.'

Slowly she stood up as fury started setting in. 'Chat? I'm going to bloody well string him up.'

But she didn't string him up, instead she sat him in her front room opposite her.

She hadn't allowed him to say a word on the ride back to hers. Now she had him where she wanted him she was ready.

'I'm really sorry mum.' Ryan kept his head down.

'Sorry!' Jackie shouted. Then she remembered Darius sleeping upstairs and lowered her voice. 'You look at me when I'm talking to you.' Her eldest son raised his head. Green eyes stared back at each other. Jackie took a deep breath. 'I'm going to tell you a story. When me and your aunts were young we got involved in the drugs business through no fault of our own.' She saw his startled expression but pressed on. 'Don't ask me why because I'm not going to tell you. What matters is we soon learned that it was a nasty, dirty business where people killed to get money. That's why I don't want you anywhere near it. I don't want my boy to see some of the things I had to. I ain't telling you this coz I read it in the *Daily Mail*. I've seen that life and as long as there's breath in my body you ain't going anywhere near it, you understand.'

'Mum, I'm sorry.' Then he was in her arms. She tightened her arms around him. Bloody hell, what a day. One son in the ozzie, another she'd had to collect from the nick.

Gently she eased him back from her and stared directly into his eyes. 'Are you acting like this because of what happened years ago at my wedding?' There, she'd finally said it. The one thing they never talked about.

He shifted his gaze away from her. 'I don't think about it much any more.'

Jackie's tummy seized up with pain. This was all her fault. If only . . .

Then he shocked her by looking directly into her eyes and saying, 'I'd do it all over again mum if it meant that I saved you like I did that day.'

That brought the tears to her eyes. Ryan gently wiped a tear from her face and gave her a big smacker on the cheek.

'Go upstairs and get some kip in the spare room.' She could've bitten the words back as soon as she'd said them. If Ryan went into the spare room he'd know that she was using it to sleep in and she didn't want him to realise that there were problems in her marriage.

But Ryan saved her from any embarrassment when he stood up and said, 'I'm going back to the hospital. Keep Schoolboy company.' He'd been like glue at Schoolboy's side when he was younger, loving the time spent with his new dad.

She nodded at him not able to speak. When he left she rubbed her hand over her right breast. Felt the lump inside.

On the way to the hospital Ryan took a detour to Whitechapel High Street. Banged on the door of someone he'd met the same time he'd moved into his new flat. As he waited for the door to open he thought back, wondering what if the cops had found all that meth he'd offloaded earlier in his place? Bollocks. If his mum ever found out . . . ?

The door opened cutting off his thoughts. He said, 'I'm looking to score.'

sixteen

'You did what?' Anna shrieked the following afternoon.

Anna stared at Jackie, her stunning brown face frozen in shock. Even her shoulder-length black hair seemed to be standing on end. They sat at the bar as some of the staff bustled around the Shim-Sham-Shimmy Club. The bar was their spot. They often sat on the kettle stools musing about life over a drink or two. Jackie had told her mate about Bliss turning up at her place and what she'd done.

'You off your nut girl?' Anna continued. 'If a man like that comes into your yard you don't try and iron out the bad creases in his life. '

Jackie let out a tired sigh. Boy was she fagged. Didn't even know how she was keeping her eyelids open. She'd been at the ozzie most of the morning. No change. Finally she'd listened to the ward staff and taken herself off for a lie down. Except she couldn't sleep. Every time she shut her eyes all she could hear was Bliss swear on his life that he hadn't done it. She kept seeing Ryan as he swore he'd never touch any of that filth again. She wasn't going to tell the others about Ryan. There was just stuff you didn't tell your mates. So she'd come to the club for some company.

'You saying you wouldn't have done the same thing?'

'An iron?' Anna wriggled her head with each word. 'No way girl, I would've tried to shove a few heated rollers up his backside.' They both looked at each other and burst out laughing. Oh, it felt sooo good to laugh again.

'Hello dears.'

They both turned to find a stylish older lady standing there. She wore an open, light black coat over a daisy-print sixties-style dress that billowed out at the bottom, just like that shot of Marilyn Monroe standing over the air vent, and Russell & Bromley soft leather two-inch shoes. But what caught both Anna and Jackie's eye was the blue-rinse beehive that seemed to go on forever.

Anna used her long legs to kick off the stool. 'Can I help you?'

But instead of answering, the newcomer twirled around running her gaze over the place. 'Oh, this is nice. I like it here. Reminds me of the Palais in its day.'

Jackie and Anna exchanged confused looks. Anna moved closer and started talking very slowly. 'Have . . . you . . . lost . . . your . . . way . . . ?'

The woman stared back with a twinkle in her eye. 'Don't think so. This is the shot-shat-shit club?' Both Anna and Jackie creased their lips together to stop them laughing out loud.

'The Shim-Sham-Shimmy,' Anna corrected.

The woman pointed to the glitter ball in the ceiling. 'Had a dress that used to sparkle just like that once.' Her lips spread into a dreamy smile. 'My Phil used to take me dancing in it.'

Jackie moved quickly to stand by Anna and whispered, 'She must've got out of that old people's home, the one by the river.' Jackie approached the woman. 'Shall I call someone for you?'

'Uh?' the woman answered looking slightly confused. 'Yeah. I need to see a Jackie and a Misty.'

That startled Jackie. She looked sideways at Anna. Anna shrugged her shoulders. But before Jackie could do anything else the woman continued, 'I've got something from my son for them.'

Her son?

'What?' Jackie said.

The woman clutched her handbag tight. 'Who are you?'

'I'm Jackie.'

'How's that little nipper of yours?'

Jackie was thrown. Now she was suspicious. Mind you she couldn't see Bliss sending some geriatric to do his dirty work, but then again you never know.

'What have you got for me?'

'I need this Misty to be here as well.'

Anna turned her head towards the metallic spiral staircase that ran up to a room with a glass front. And yelled, 'Mist–eee!'

'What?' roared back the answer.

'Someone down here to see you.'

'Tell them to come back in half hour.'

'No, now.'

The door upstairs flung open and Misty stood at the top of the stairs. She'd changed her hair from Paris Hilton to Jennifer Aniston and wore a plain, classic black dress with silver glitter around the scooped neckline. She looked down and spotted the woman. 'Who the blinkin' hell is that? I'm busy, I ain't got time to adopt a granny today.'

Jackie pushed herself forward. 'She's got something for both of us. Says it's from her son.'

'Christ in heaven,' Misty grumbled as she took the steps. The clear, spiked heels of her denim sneakers click-clacked against the metal steps. Finally she reached them.

The woman checked out Misty. 'You're a tall girl.' Then her dress. 'Nice figure.' She leaned into Misty and whispered. 'Is that a corset job?'

Misty smacked her lips together. 'What do you want?'

The woman rummaged in her bag. Pulled out an envelope. Passed it to Misty. Misty continued to look mystified. The woman's face became suddenly sad. 'Got to go to the dead house now. Need to bury my great-granbabies.' She drifted slowly out, her earlier sparkle gone as she left, her shoulders hunched over.

'Go on, open it,' Anna urged Misty.

Misty stuck her manicured fingernail through the envelope. Ripped it open. Two pieces of paper, one large, one small. She opened the smaller one first. A mobile number on it. Not a number she recognised. She turned her attention to the larger folded piece of paper. Read. Shook her head.

'What is it?' Jackie spoke this time as both she and Anna moved closer.

'It's a V.O.' Seeing the look of confusion on Anna's face she added, 'A visiting order. Someone wants me and Jackie to visit him next week in Her Majesty's big house South London way.'

'Where?'

'Oldgate prison.'

'Who?'

'Kenny Lewis.'

seventeen

Paul Maxwell Bliss.

D.I. Ricky Smart read the name scrawled in black ink on the front of the folder on his desk as a stream of afternoon sun shot through the window. Ricky looked liked he'd slept in his clothes. Wrinkled jacket, shirt half out, half in his trousers and his tie ... well he didn't know where that had got to. Instead of opening the folder he leaned back into his chair and sighed. Maybe he should piss off home, get some kip and dream about sinking into the sweet comfort of his woman. Daisy.

He smiled. What a lucky bastard he was to have found a woman like her. Lately she had a glow about her, a real sexy look. Mind you she'd been in a right state when she'd found out about what happened to Jackie's kid.

Jackie.

He thought back to their question and answer session yesterday. He knew she was holding out on him. Maybe he should have her followed. He considered it for a time. Then dismissed it. He couldn't see the boss upstairs giving him the go-ahead for that. Waste of resources no doubt he'd be told. Every department, including his, was under the cosh with this bloody recession as was most of the public sector. How the fuck was he meant to solve this one without the necessary back-up? Shiiit! This should be a slam-dunk case. Stanley Lewis's kids are mowed down outside their school and half of the world witnesses it and yet no one knows anything? Bloody typical East London. Trying to get people to talk was like finding free parking in Tower Hamlets.

He hitched himself forward again. Fixed back on the folder. Paul Bliss, Paul Bliss. Paul Bliss. How the heck was this scumbag involved in this? Finally he turned the pages. Checked Bliss's rap sheet out again. Sure it read like the top ten hit list of what to do to become a successful criminal, but nothing in it suggested that Bliss was a total headcase and you'd have to be to murder Stanley Lewis's kids in broad daylight. In fact it looked like Bliss played it pretty low-key. Got the job done without really showing his face. A knock at the door tore him away from his frustrated thoughts.

'Yeah?'

A head peeped around the corner. The desk sergeant. 'There's some woman at the desk who says she's got some info for you on the Lewis case.'

Finally a lead maybe. Now that made Ricky smile. 'Bring her in.'

But the sergeant hesitated. 'I should warn you sir that she's well known to the station. A bit of a timewaster.'

Ricky swore. 'Yeah still bring her in.'

A few minutes later the sergeant showed the woman into the room. The white T-shirt she wore had the slogan *Sexy Babe* scrawled across it, but she was anything but. Fast food had years ago got the better of her complexion and body shape. Her brown hair was so lank that it looked like she'd washed it in a sink full of chip frying oil. And there was just something about the way her small eyes kept squeezing together that made Ricky think that what should be written on her T-shirt was one word: *Nutter*.

'Miss,' Ricky said as he waved his hand at the chair on the other side of the desk.

'Mrs,' the woman snapped as she squeezed her weight into the chair. The excess flesh under her chin wobbled. 'I'm still that bastard's missus even though he did a runner five years back.'

Ricky caught the sergeant's look above her head and rolled his eyes. He turned his attention back to her with a forced smile frozen on his lips as the sergeant left them alone. 'I understand you have some information that may be useful to the investigation into the incident outside Parkhurst Primary School yesterday?'

She leaned forward pushing the nicotine scent around her closer to him. 'I see it all you know. From my window . . .'

Ricky picked up his pen poised to write. 'What did you see?'

Her mouth settled into a wriggle of disgust. 'Men. Loads of them. All of the time.'

'What? At the school that day? Where were these men?'

'Outside of the school of course—'

Ricky let the pen drop as he cut in. 'There were only children and their parents outside the school that day.'

'What day?' She threw back bewildered.

Ricky linked his fingers together and gave her his hardest stare. 'Do you realise that I could have you locked up for wasting police time?'

She snapped her neck back squashing her triple chin. 'I ain't wasting your time fella—'

Ricky pushed back out of his chair. Placed his palms flat on the desk. Leaned his considerable height over the desk. 'If I see you back here again I'm going to personally dump you in a cell, lock the door and the only way you're going to get out is with my say-so, got it?'

The woman cringed back in the chair, 'But I—'

But before she could finish Ricky's door burst open. An out-of-breath Detective Sonny Begum stood puffing in the door. 'Sorry sir, we've got a major incident.'

Ricky straightened. Stepped forward. 'What?'

'That bloke we interviewed with the 4x4 in Loughton yesterday, we need to get to his house now.'

'Why the flamin' hell would Kenny Lewis want to see us?' Jackie asked.

She stood with Misty and Anna on the balcony of Misty's office that overlooked the Thames. The river was grey, in one of its more lazy afternoon moods, its skin gently lulling in the summer wind. Jackie blew on a fag while Anna just stared straight ahead. Misty leaned heavily on the rail with her back to the river staring at the two other women.

'Who can tell where Mr Kenneth Lewis is concerned,' Misty answered.

Jackie cocked her head to the side as she pulled a lug from her ciggie. 'You know him then?'

Misty folded her arms and twisted her mouth. 'Let's just say we go way back.'

From the faraway look on her face Jackie suspected Misty was probably remembering those days before she'd become Misty. The days when she was Michael, one of the knuckle-busting brothers in the McKenzie gang. Hard to picture Misty punching someone's lights out.

'Maybe he just wanted to send his sympathies to Jackie about Preston,' Anna offered.

Misty thought for a bit as the grey shade of her eyes deepened. 'Nah, he could've given his mum a card. He wants us for something else.'

'What's he like?' Jackie asked as she flicked the butt over the rail.

Just then a longboat came along the river and tooted its horn. Misty twisted around and leaned back on the rail. Jackie and Anna joined her. Misty sucked in some river air before she spoke. 'He's an alright sort for a bad boy. An old-time villain, only has a problem with people who have a problem with him. And you know what old-time villains feel about hurting kids. So he's going to be wishing he were on the outside now tracking down whoever did this to his grandkids.' Misty shook her head. 'And I wouldn't want to be in their shoes if he ever finds them. So if it is Bliss and I was him, I'd want to be away on my toes.' Her voice dropped low and became soft. 'That man loves his family.'

'So what's he banged up for?' Jackie asked.

'Some bullion robbery six years ago. He weren't one of the crew that did it, but he was managing the operation, usual story.' Misty frowned. 'Funny thing was though he said he never done it. That someone had fitted him up.'

Anna laughed. 'Come on, he would say that. Don't they all?'

Misty shook her head. 'No, he might tell a story in the dock but he's honest enough off the record.'

Jackie threw her tuppence worth in. 'But who would want to do that?'

'A man like Kenny has got lots of enemies. Maybe someone wanted to get him out of the way.'

'So are you both going to go?' Jackie and Misty stared at Anna.

'Let's put it this way,' Misty said. 'If Kenny asks to see you, you better be there.' Suddenly she caught Anna's eye. Anna punched off the rail. 'Got things to do inside.' And she was gone.

'So how you and Schoolboy getting on?' Jackie realised that Misty's look had been telling Anna to do one so that they could be alone.

'Don't start,' she grumbled.

Misty gave Jackie a penetrating look. 'I was the one that was bang against you getting hitched to him because I didn't want my girl hooking up with no former drug dealer. But you know what, he's proved himself over the years. He's been a cracking dad not just to the twins but to your Ryan as well and he's one hell of a businessman . . .'

Jackie shot off the rail. 'I don't need this, not after having to keep seeing my boy in some hospital bed fighting for his life.'

'Then when are you going to deal with it?' Misty sprang off the rail as well, fists planted firmly on hips. 'You and him should be like that now.' She locked two fingers together. 'Close. For your son.' Her voice softened. 'He ain't got another bird has he? Coz if he has I'm going to—'

'No.' Jackie waved her small hand. 'It ain't him, it's me.' Her hand unconsciously touched her right breast. Of all the people she should be able to tell about her breast it should be Misty. But how do you tell someone you might have the big C? How do you deal with the look in their eyes? How was she going to face Schoolboy if she didn't have a breast any more? He might not fancy her. He . . .

The sound of Misty's resigned huff of air shoved between her painful thoughts. 'I'm here for you as I've always been so when you want to chat you let me know.'

But the last thing Jackie wanted to do was talk. 'I better get back to the ozzie.'

Just as she turned Misty called out, 'And Jackie?' What now? She didn't need another lecture, but she turned back around anyway. 'Don't go around trying to steam iron any more people babe.'

After Jackie had gone Misty returned to her office and pulled out the smaller piece of paper from the envelope and stared at the mobile number. She shoved herself into the large, padded black chair at her desk and kicked her shoes off. She eased her legs on to the desk and twisted her toes sticking out of her patterned footless tights trying to get rid of some of the stresses and strains of the day. She picked up the phone. Dialled the number.

The line clicked on and so did a voice. 'What's your answer?'

Misty recognised it instantly as the woman who had delivered the envelope. The woman she now knew to be Kenny's mum, Pinkie.

'We'll see him. What does he want?'

Pinkie hesitated. Then said, 'After my great-granbabies have been laid to rest he wants you and your mate to do a big job for him.'

'Kiddie killer out. Kiddie killer out . . .'

Ricky swore as he heard the manic chanting heaving from the twenty-strong crowd as he pulled the car to a halt outside the house in Loughton. It was hard to see the house because of the angry mob outside.

'How the fuck did this happen?' Ricky asked Sonny.

'Press must've got onto it. And as usual got the wrong end of the stick. Maybe some of his neighbours who were hovering around yesterday tipped them off.'

As soon as they slammed out of the car a camera crew and reporter were in their face.

'Is it true that the man responsible for the deaths of the children outside the Parkhurst School lives in that house?' the female reporter threw Ricky's way.

He gave the reporter a look but held his tongue. He'd been on the media-training course and he knew better than to answer back with the camera rolling. The Met was still reeling from that business involving former Commissioner Barbara Benton last year. Instead he elbowed past her and made his way towards the house. The crowd was like a starving animal baying for blood. Some of them waved cardboard placards with a range of slogans:

Kill Our Kids We Kill You

String Him Up

Castrate The Bastard

Ricky shook his head with disgust as he pushed his way through the angry crowd. What a total mess. Mind you he shouldn't be surprised. The murder of a child always made the community see red. Even, or especially, the kids of a gangster.

Abruptly he stopped when he reached the front of the mob and saw the graffiti painted in blood red paint on the front door:

Kiddie Killer
We're Gonna Get You

A cop in uniform was posted near the door beside the window which had been smashed by God knows what. 'Get these people outta here, now.'

As the policeman waved frantically at his colleagues to carry out the order Ricky knocked on the door. It was opened by a plain-clothes cop. Female, short hair, sporting a grave expression and of equal rank to Ricky.

'Where's the family?' Ricky asked as he stepped inside.

She pulled herself up tall. 'Is it true that you came to visit Mr Bell yesterday in connection with this case?'

Ricky wasn't in the mood for some internal mud slinging, but from the look on her face he knew it was coming his way anyway. 'Yes.' He kept his answer short and sweet.

'Then you should've kept us informed . . .'

'Look detective inspector . . .' His sentence hung in the air.

She told him her name. 'There was nothing to keep you informed about. Mr Bell was helping us with our enquiries. End of story. Now why don't you show me where he and his family are.'

She pressed her lips together considering her next move. 'Inside the front room,' she finally responded.

With a huge sigh and shake of his head he made his way inside to find the woman of the house huddled on a settee with two kids and Peter Bell pacing. As soon as the man saw Ricky he rushed over. 'I haven't done anything. I told you that—'

'I know. Just calm down and we'll get this sorted out.'

'My kids are terrified. I haven't done a thing.'

'Have you got somewhere else you can spend the night while we get this sorted.'

The man nodded. 'OK. My colleague here,' Ricky waved at D.I. Abbott, 'will escort you. Don't worry you'll be back in your home by tomorrow.'

Feeling furious Ricky headed back outside. The mob were moving back but slowly.

'Right everyone,' he shouted from the doorstep. The crowd grew quiet. 'Could we have some calm please. This man isn't even a suspect at this stage, much less been charged, he's merely helping us with our enquiries, so could you please all go home.'

The crowd mumbled and sneered but allowed themselves to be moved on. Ricky and Sonny watched the crowd disperse.

'Nothing like a bit of community involvement in a case, it's what we're always calling for,' Ricky said mockingly.

'Can't blame them I suppose,' Sonny added. 'People feel strongly about the death of any child.'

'They could make sure they've got the right bloke before they get into mob rule.'

'Maybe they have.'

And with that uncertainty hanging between them they drove back to the station. As they got out of the car Sonny's mobile went off. She took the call as they started walking towards the station entrance. She stopped as she listened to the caller. Ricky noticed that her face lost its colour. She swallowed hard as she pulled the phone away from her face. Looked nervously at her superior and said, 'I'll catch you inside Guv.'

For a moment Ricky didn't move. He hoped it wasn't bad news. She'd been getting a lot of personal calls recently. She twisted away from him as she put the mobile back to her ear. Ricky left her and walked into the station. He nodded his head at the desk sergeant as he made his way to the security door that accessed the rest of the station. As he punched the security code onto the keypad the phone on the sergeant's desk rang. Ricky pulled the door back. Got one foot inside the entrance when the desk sergeant called his name. He turned to find the sergeant holding out the phone receiver towards him. 'Call for you sir. Someone who says they have information on the incident outside the school.'

Ricky pulled the receiver urgently from the other man's hand. 'Detective Inspector Smart.'

Ricky waited. Then the voice came. Male, street rough, husky from inhaling too many fags a day. 'I know who stiffed those girls.'

Ricky tensed. 'I'm listening . . .'

'Check out the Mountjoy Estate. Lock-up number 5. You'll find the wheels you're looking for in there.'

'You said you knew who it was?'

'I said check out the lock-up, officer – are you deaf?'

'And do you care to give me your name and number? We might need to talk to you further.'

The man laughed. 'Yeah sure, and maybe you'd like some naked pictures of my missus while I'm at it?'

The caller rang off. Ricky knew better than to ask someone to trace it.

Just then, Sonny walked back into the station. Ricky pulled her over.

'Who bosses the Mountjoy these days? I've had a call saying our car is there.'

Sonny looked back at him excitedly. 'Paul Bliss.'

eighteen

Ryan should've been down the college at his fashion art course or even down the hospital but instead he did a line of C at his supplier Lurch's place. He raised his head as he inhaled again, eyes scanning the room. Lurch's sitting room was surprisingly clean and tidy, the only mess the foil and flecks of white powder on the smoked-glass table.

He caught Lurch's eye as the supplier sat opposite him on a rocking chair. He looked more like a Sunday school teacher than a dealer. Small round glasses, always decked in a suit and with the scent of lemon floating off his hands as if he cleaned them obsessively. Lurch's eyes kept glancing nervously at the door.

'How did you get the name Lurch?' Ryan asked easing back into the single sofa.

Lurch glanced at the door, back at Ryan. 'Ain't got a clue. The other kids just started calling me it at school.'

'Yeah, but–' But before Ryan could carry on there was a thump at the front door.

Lurch sprang to his feet. Looked at Ryan. 'Really sorry man.' Before Ryan could ask him what he meant Lurch was gone and at the door. Puzzled Ryan pushed himself straight. What did Lurch have to be sorry about? He started to ease out of the seat when a newcomer appeared at the door. Tall, with blue eyes and gelled spiky hair.

'Who are you?' Ryan asked, some sixth sense telling him to take a step to the side.

'I hear that you've been dealing gear in my place.'

That's when Ryan noticed the shortened scaffolding pole in his hand.

Beep. Beep. Beep.

At minutes after three the sound of the machine was the only noise in the room as Jackie sat next to the bed with her son in it. No change. He looked like he was sleeping. She smoothed her hand gently over his cheek.

'Mummy's here,' she whispered. 'And you're going to be back in my arms before you know it.' She felt the tears threatening to fall. But she sniffed them back. It wouldn't help Preston to hear his mum crying her heart out.

She heard the door open. Looked around. Schoolboy looking rougher than he'd looked years back when two rival gangs were after him. She knew he hadn't come home last night, most probably opting to spend the night kipping at the restaurant.

'How's my little man doing?' he asked softly as he stood at the foot of the bed.

She looked back at their boy. 'I just want him to come home.'

'That's what I keep telling myself about you,' he said startling her. She looked across at him. 'I just want us to be a family again. To get through this together.'

'What you saying, I ain't a proper mum? That it's my fault Ryan did a little bit of blow?'

'You're the best mum I know. But up here.' He touched the side of his head with a finger. 'You ain't with us. Darius needs you. Preston needs you. Ryan needs you.' He hesitated for a second. 'And I need you.'

Her mouth set into a stubborn line. 'You're asking me too much to let this go. Look at him.' Her head swiftly turned back to the bed. 'He should be playing with his mates. Or on his computer game. Or watching the footie on the box. Not lying here almost d—' She clamped her mouth shut. She couldn't say it, just couldn't let it out.

Her head dropped with the weight of her tormenting thoughts.

She never heard him move but felt him crouch down beside her. His finger touched the point of her chin. Lifted her head up to look at him. For a few seconds they said nothing as the love they felt for their son shone in their eyes.

Finally Schoolboy spoke, his words filled with pain. 'I wanted to take that shooter last night and tear this town apart until I found the murdering bastard who did this. But then I thought what if something happens to me? I would've left Jackie to deal with this on her own.' He shook his head and let out a shuddering breath. 'If you do this you might not come back. I can't lose you Jackie, I can't.' He laid his head in her lap.

She picked up her hand and let it hover over his head. Then she let it fall. She caressed his locks as she spoke. 'I ain't going nowhere babe, nowhere.'

'Promise?'

'You bet.'

Then she remembered the V.O. from Kenny Lewis. Should she tell him? No. She moved her fingers more deeply through his hair. What he didn't know wouldn't hurt him.

Jackie eased back from him. 'I need to get some fresh air.' He lifted his eyebrows knowing that was her way of saying she needed a ciggie. He didn't smoke these days, not even a bit of weed, the nicotine on his breath reminding him too much of the taste of the bad life he'd left behind.

'You should get some sleep girl,' he answered taking in the deep circles under her green eyes.

'I'm alright. Just need to clear my head.'

With one last look at her child she left the room. But she didn't go outside, instead she took the lift to the next floor. Briskly walked into the waiting room in the second corridor on the left. A few women waited on plastic, blue chairs and a flat-screen telly mounted on the wall flashed up sound and images from a 24-hour news channel. Jackie stopped at the reception desk where two women sat in front of computer screens. One of the women looked up.

'Yes?'

Jackie swallowed. Her voice shook. 'Name's Jackie Jarvis. I need to make an appointment for later today if you have one.'

Ryan knew he was in deep shit.

The man with the pole stepped forward. Ryan wanted to step back but he couldn't or he'd fall right over the sofa.

'Name's Bliss. You've been selling crap out of my patch? The Five Fingers Club.'

Now Ryan did step back and tumbled straight onto the sofa. He held his arms above his head to ward off a blow as he heard the man rushing towards him. He let out a wild yelp as the pole crashed down beside him on the sofa making the cushion jump. He peeped up at the man looming over him. Bliss braced his arms on either side of Ryan, the tendons straining against his skin, his hand and the pole sinking into the softness of the sofa.

Instead of hitting him, Bliss spoke, ever so softly. 'I would've thought your old man would've told you it's not a good idea to mix work like that with a bloke like me.'

There was a silence before Ryan shakily said, 'I've got a stepdad. I don't know who my real dad is.'

Bliss felt his chest tighten. He could understand where the kid was coming from, he hadn't known his dad until recently. He sighed, but leaned his face closer to the kid's.

'What's your mum going to say when she has to ID your body down the morgue?'

He raised the pole and slammed it down once more. Ryan cried out as he covered his head again.

'I'm talking to you boy,' Bliss yelled.

'I don't know,' Ryan mumbled back quickly.

'I'll tell you what she'd do. She'll bitch slap you until you don't have a mouth left to take any drugs, you get me?'

Ryan vigorously nodded. Then Bliss straightened and pulled himself back giving Ryan some space. When he next spoke his voice was calm. 'I want you to go to that hospital and sit with your mum while she sits holding your little brother's hand praying for him to get better.'

Startled, Ryan stared gobsmacked at him. 'How did you know . . . ?'

Bliss pointed the pole at him. 'You start being the kind of son Jackie deserves. Now get the fuck out of here.'

Ryan didn't need to be told twice. He scarpered. As Bliss watched him go he whispered, 'I must be going soft. What's the matter with me?'

Ricky and Sonny parked up the unmarked police car on a road opposite the Mountjoy Estate in Leyton, East London. Normally the only time the police appeared down that way was by the vanload. The estate had a long tradition of turning out London's worst. Bliss was elsewhere these days but he'd used it as a base at one time and still had soldiers and runners there. Chatter said that he ran drug-making factories and knocking shops on the top floor of the only tower block on the estate. It proved to be a lucrative business, punters going through one door for their chemical fix and another to practise their sexual tricks. Half of the residents were too scared to blab to the Bill and the other half were new to the country and didn't want any trouble. But the biggest reason that Ricky hated the estate with a passion was because it reminded him of the days he'd lived on the wrong side of the law.

They waited until the tow truck had caught up and pulled over then Ricky checked the paperwork: 'Right, our anonymous friend tells us what we're looking for is in lock-up number 5. Not that it matters, any lock-up we open here will have something inside to interest the law.' He looked at a plan of the estate. 'These garages – we drive in at the main entrance, turn left and then down to the end of the slip road. Have you got the bolt cutters?' She nodded. 'And your gun?'

She nodded again. Both of them had done their firearms training with authorisation to carry a firearm in what they deemed to be a potentially 'threatening' situation. And coming to the Mountjoy was always threatening.

Sonny held up the bolt cutters. Ricky nodded. 'OK, let's do it . . .'

'I still think we need some back-up.'

'Oh behave, it's 11 a.m. Gangstas don't get up till lunchtime – that's why you never see a probation officer in the morning . . .'

'You know this estate as well as I do Guv. Tupac Shakur would've applied for a transfer.'

Ricky looked up and along the rows of low-rise flats, bit his lip and then gently touched the car horn, the signal for the tow truck to follow. They drove onto the estate. Turned left, past the blood red graffiti that read,

Inform. Get Shot.

Drove down to the concrete block of lock-ups. On the right, the rows of balconies of the nearest block of flats loomed above them. Ricky pulled up outside the battered and buckled iron doors, got out and looked for number 5. It was an easy find; all the other doors had rusted chains and padlocks except one which had a fresh lock on. He checked the door and saw a faded and flaky 5 painted at the top.

Sonny got out and fitted the jaws of the bolt cutters around the lock. As she did so, Ricky noticed two small kids, wearing hoodies that were way too big for them, standing outside the flats. They were watching him closely.

Ricky whispered, 'Looks like Snow White's lost two of her dwarves.'

Sonny turned to look. 'It's not the dwarves you need to worry about, it's their older brothers and their big bad wolves. Not to mention Snow White herself, females round here tend to be worse than the boys.'

She turned back to the bolt cutter. Increased the pressure. The padlock clattered to the ground. Ricky slid the door upwards and the daylight revealed the back of a 4x4. Ricky smiled. 'Bingo!'

He went back to the unmarked car and pulled a torch out of the glove compartment. The boys had gone but on the balconies, just out of bed and in regulation gang clothes, groups of two or three youths had appeared. As he slammed the door shut, he heard someone above yelling, 'What do you think you're doing man?'

Ricky ignored the shout, switched on his torch and went into the lock-up. He examined the bumpers and got underneath the 4x4. He heard footsteps and looked up to see Sonny standing over him. Ricky got up to his feet.

'This is the car alright. They haven't even bothered to clean it up, there's still blood on the bodywork.'

Sonny anxiously glanced towards the open door. 'If you don't get a move on, there's going to be a lot more blood on the bodywork.'

Ricky eased up, keeping his movements calm and casual as he made his way to the doorway. Emerged into the daylight to find a load more kids on the balconies and a larger group who'd made their way down to ground level, some with dogs on leads. This group gathered menacingly a short distance around their two vehicles, hoods and caps down, bandanas covering their faces. There were shouts and taunts from around and above. Ricky didn't feel intimidated. He'd learned long ago that the day you showed crims that you were shitting it you were fucked. He pulled his warrant card and flashed it.

'Police. We don't want your drugs and we don't care about your summons, so can you stand well back please?'

Someone made a pig snorting noise as a large youth stepped forward. Grey tracksuit and hoodie, Union Jack bandana. He sneered, 'Five-O? You can't just come on here like this. You have to talk to people first, get permission. Where's your fucking manners man?'

I'll give you fucking manners, Ricky thought, but instead he ignored the youth and held up his hand signalling for the tow truck to come forward. It started to move. As it approached, some of the youths banged on its bodywork and its wing mirror was bashed sideways. The shouting grew louder and coarser. Out of nowhere a brick sailed from one of the balconies above and landed a couple of inches from Ricky's size-eleven feet. Ricky and Sonny stumbled back as more missiles, including eggs and bulging plastic bags, began to rain down around them. One splattered on the ground beside Sonny, bursting on impact, splattering her with a foul smelling liquid.

'Bollocks Guv, that wasn't champagne. We need to get back-up. Now.'

Bastards, Ricky thought. If there was one thing he loathed it was attacks on female officers. It might sound chauvinistic but that's just the way he thought about it. 'Too late for that now. Not to worry, I've brought some back-up of my own. You get that car hitched up while I take care of the audience.'

He reached into his jacket and pulled out a pistol and waved it at the youths. The taunts and missiles immediately stopped.

'Alright, back off boys, this has got nothing to do with you, just take it easy and no one's going to get hurt.'

The youths were unimpressed and started laughing.

'Woah! Tuff guy . . . Call that a gatt? I wouldn't shoot my dog with it . . . You want gun play? We'll give you gun play man . . .'

A gunshot ripped through the air. Shit, this was getting way out of hand. Ricky swiftly turned to find Sonny with her pistol out. She let one rip over the heads of the youths scattering the crowd. But the large youth who had given them a load of lip earlier surged forward. 'Come on then.' He waved his arms out to the side. 'Shoot me! Shoot me, you chicken-shit pussy . . .'

Ignoring the taunt, Ricky rushed backwards and shouted at Sonny, 'Let's get this hooked up.'

They pulled the chain of the hook on the tow truck and rushed inside the lock-up. Attached the hook to the 4x4. As they ran out of the lock-up a gunshot from the crowd rang out.

Ricky and Sonny ducked as a bullet slammed into the concrete wall of the lock-up above their heads. They dived back into the lock-up. Braced themselves against the wall and looked at each other breathing hard. Everything had gone a bit Wild West.

'Guv, we should—' Sonny let out between spurts of air. But her superior never let her finish. 'Just get to the car.'

She nodded. Popped off the wall. Then took off, her only defence her gun waving in the air. Ricky let out a huge sigh when he saw her reach the car. Now it was his turn to try and get out of Dodge with the jeep. His breathing calmed down as he listened. It sounded strangely quiet. He did a quick three count in his head. Dived out and belted straight to the tow truck's cab. The driver inside looked like he was having the worst day of his life. 'Let's move it,' he commanded. 'We'll cover you.'

The truck lurched forward as Ricky ran back to the car, got in and started the motor. The sound of the engine was echoed by another shot. Ricky careered the car backwards, wheels squealing. The daylight in the car flickered as the sunroof crashed in, showering the two cops with tinted glass. A dustbin tumbled down over the windscreen and off the bonnet while the youths surged forward punching and kicking the bodywork. Ricky reversed up onto the pavement and then accelerated forward after the truck. He swerved around an attempt to push wheelie bins into his path and sideswiped some bollards as they crashed their way off the estate.

'Jeepers creepers Guv,' Sonny let out a couple of minutes later. 'That was a bit much for early in the morning.'

'That's alright, we've got our evidence. Forensics will have a party with this and then we'll know who killed those girls.'

nineteen

Jackie almost did a runner when she was told they could see her in an hour. Someone had cancelled their appointment. Her fingers tapped nervously on her thighs as she waited. What if . . . ? No she was not going down that road again. She had to deal with this once and for all. She sat in a corner well away from everyone else. She wasn't in the mood for any chit-chat with anyone else. She was too young for this to be happening to her wasn't she? Just felt like the other day that she didn't have a care in the world with sickness someone else's problem.

'Jackie Jarvis.' She looked up to find a nurse, holding a piece of paper, standing near the reception desk.

Jackie stumbled up, her heart beating wildly. 'Yeah.' Her voice shook. She moved to join the nurse, passing the television mounted on the wall with the news on. The nurse smiled. 'This way please.'

Less than a minute later Jackie was inside a room with a trolley, a couple of machines she hadn't got a clue what they were for. And *the* Ruth Brown, the doctor who had been seeing to Preston.

'I'm glad you could come,' the doctor started softly. 'I've read your notes and what we want to do today is an ultrasound and a biopsy.'

'A bi what?' Jackie asked not liking the sound of the word one bit.

The doctor leaned forward with a reassuring smile. 'We'll need to draw some blood so we can do some tests. I won't lie to you and say that we can rule out anything more serious at this stage.' Jackie winced. 'But this is more likely to be a cyst.'

A cyst. That was good wasn't it? 'Will I get the results today?' Jackie asked.

'We'll contact you when we have the results. There's no need to worry—'

'But I might have cancer,' Jackie cut in.

'What we need to do is explore all possibilities.' Jackie nodded. 'Why don't you pop yourself on the trolley and take off your top.'

Jackie got up. This was it. She was finally going to find out what was wrong with her.

Twenty minutes later she was at the reception desk, feeling like she'd just done fifteen rounds with Mike Tyson, making another appointment for three weeks' time. The lump in her breast twitched. She took the appointment card from the receptionist and turned to leave. But stopped when she caught the news headline running across the bottom of the telly screen:

Breaking news: Car in hit-and-run child deaths outside school found.

Ricky waited anxiously outside the lab while the techie people did their thing. Finally one of the forensic team emerged. 'Prints . . . Loads of prints.'

'Including the steering wheel?' Ricky cut in hopefully.

'Yep. They haven't even given it the once-over with a damp cloth. Very careless.'

Ricky nodded. 'Put them through the system and get the results mailed over.'

He left the compound and made his way to his office. As soon as he entered the open-planned office, the office PA stood up looking flustered. 'Sir—'

'Not now,' he cut over her.

'But sir . . .' He ignored her and carried on to his office eager to discover who the fingerprints belonged to. As soon as he crashed inside he knew what his secretary was about to tell him. Sitting in his chair was his superior officer, Carl Bridges. He wore his usual sour face that made it look like happiness had never been part of his life. They had one of those bite me and I'll bite you back relationships: Bridges always wagging his finger in Ricky's face about not following the rule book, but Ricky getting off every time because he brought in results. And that's exactly what the Met needed at a time when the public were moaning and groaning about the effectiveness of the police ... results. And by the expression of fury on Bridges' face, Ricky knew he was about to get a mouthful. Shit.

'Smart, why didn't you report the discharge of firearms on the Mountjoy Estate?'

Ricky quietly closed the door knowing that everyone in the large office outside was earwigging. But they weren't getting a free show out of him. 'When it comes to the Mountjoy, I would have thought that a non-discharge of firearms should be reported? But obviously I'm going to file something, I just assumed the deaths of two youngsters would take priority – correct me if I've called that wrong.'

Bridges thumped his palms down on the desk. 'Why do you always flout the rules? I thought you would've learned your lesson after the incident last year.'

He knew what his superior was talking about; that business with the King gang; a business that had taken up a lot of current affairs space on the box.

Ricky knew that all he could do was hold his hands up and look like the sorry naughty boy he was. 'All I can do is apologise sir—'

Bridges shook his head, sweeping Ricky's apology aside. 'And do you know how long we've been trying to build up good community relations on the Mountjoy?'

Community relations on the Mountjoy? Tow it to Chelsea and sell the flats off was Ricky's view, but he knew when to keep his mouth shut. But the ping of his computer changed all that. The fingerprints.

He rushed around the side of the desk. 'Sir, out of the seat please,' he said with as much respect as possible.

'I beg your pardon?'

Ricky didn't have time for a polite exercise in manners. Instead he did the unforgivable. He grabbed Bridges under his arms and hauled him out of the chair. The older man staggered back totally shocked.

'You're done for Smart.'

Ignoring the threat of a disciplinary, Ricky slammed into the chair. Tapped into his inbox and drew up his emails. And there it was, the prints from the Forensic team.

'Smart I'm talking to you ...'

Ricky opened the mail. Saw the prints. Ran them immediately against the national database. Ping. A Match. Jeez-us. When he saw who the prints matched he nearly fell out of his chair.

'Smart ... ?'

Ricky turned to Bridges. 'I found out who killed the Lewis kids.'

That stopped his superior running his mouth. He moved towards Ricky. Leaned over his shoulder. Swore. 'Bring him in before Stanley Lewis finds out.'

Bliss did another line of Colombian Sherbet in the Bell Bar as the evening drew in. Then he gripped the head of the person sucking him off. A tiny smile tickled his lips as he closed his eyes. He got into the groove of the coke shooting into his bloodstream and the even more wicked sensation below his waistline. He was upstairs in a back room of one of his clubs. He could've owned more clubs, like that arsehole Stanley Lewis, but instead he'd put his money into as many houses as he could get his hands on. He didn't play it showy like Lewis. No, he liked to think of himself as a much more low-key kind of bloke. But when London's notorious King family had been wiped out a year or so back the club had come up for sale. He'd changed the name from The Pussy Hound to the Bell Bar, moved out the pole dancers and given it what he thought was a more gentle feel.

His head tipped back as he re-opened his eyes. His hand grew tighter on the head cupped between them. Fuck me, this feeling was going to blow his mind sky-high. His lips parted as he hit the edge. And with a groan he let go. He took some quick easy breaths to calm his heart rate. Looked down at the person knelt in front of him. What a kick that gave him, just seeing someone kneeling before him. Made him feel all powerful. Like he was the fucking king of London town. And if his plans all came right that's what he would be. The number one Face.

He stepped back the same time a small knock hit the door. Only one person would disturb him upstairs: Sean. His right-hand man came into the room. Half pushed the door behind him.

'Your *friend's* here.' Sean's voice was quiet.

He instantly knew who Sean meant. Bollocks, what the fuck was she doing here? He'd told her to stay put. Do some bloody knitting or whatever she did to calm herself down. It wouldn't do for him and the stupid tart to be seen together.

'She's chewing the carpet out here,' Sean continued, his eyebrows going up.

'Tell her I'll be there in a minute. Don't let her park her arse so she gets it that she won't be stopping long.'

His right-hand man left leaving Bliss to think about the woman he was about to see. He stepped over to the free-standing mirror in the corner. Ran his tongue over his top front teeth as he checked himself over. Then made his way into the adjoining room.

As soon as he saw her he knew she was going to ask the question that was on everyone else's lips. 'Did you kill those two girls?'

His mouth spread in a lazy smile as he sauntered towards her. He stopped in front of her, widening his stance as he settled into the scent of her expensive perfume. He gave her an innocent look. 'Me? Hurt anyone?' He held up his palms. 'You know how these feel all over your delicious body, babe. Think I could use them to murder someone?'

Her face flushed pink. She might like getting her leg over with him but he knew she hated talking about doing the dirty. Sex. He wasn't even sure she could say the word without choking.

'Tell me you didn't kill those children.' Her voice went higher. He hoped she wasn't going to flip out. He could do without that type of drama right now. 'Did you do it because you think Stanley Lewis knows where you hide your stuff?'

Now she was really peeing him off. He'd warned her never to talk about his stash house unless he was the one asking the questions.

'If anyone finds out that I let you . . . !' His features hardened. 'Thought I told you to stay put—'

Her breathing shuddered in her chest as she cut over him, voice tight and strained. 'I'm frightened that Stanley Lewis will come back. He held a gun in my face for Christ sake. He knows—'

'He don't know dick.'

'Then why did he come and see me? He said he *knew*.'

He tilted his head. Gazed in her face. His fingers came out and caressed, ever so slowly, against her chin. His tone dropped into the one he used when they were between the sheets. 'Don't worry about nothing sweetheart, nothing's going to happen to you while I'm around.'

She flung her arms around him. Pressed her body close. Her perfume circled him. 'I was so frightened. I thought he was going to kill me.'

He smoothed his hands over her back. 'Ain't I always taken care of you? Sorted things out?' He held back the irritation in his voice so that she didn't clock that the last thing he needed to deal with today was her crap.

'I love you.'

'Yeah, well I love you as well babe.' Love her? Was she out of her tree? He didn't love nobody. Stupid cow still didn't get it that he'd been using his dick and whispering sweet nothings in her ear to string her along. Did she really think he could fancy *her*?

Suddenly her body stiffened. She jerked back from him. He saw the shock in her eyes as she looked over his shoulder. He half twisted to find the person who'd been blowing him off standing in the doorway of the adjoining room. Slowly he turned back to her and watched as she ran her widening eyes over the newcomer's unbuttoned top, bare feet. Her nostrils flared as if she could smell the sex in the place. She knew what he'd been doing alright. He shrugged his shoulders because he knew her shock had nothing to do with her discovery that she wasn't his one and only, but had everything to do with who he'd been down and dirty with. A fella.

Johnny baby he called him. Gorgeous lad. Found him in a club one night. They'd been fucking, on and off, for about five weeks now. No big deal.

'Sorry,' Johnny baby said softly. 'Thought you were alone again.'

He could hear her breathing increase as her shock grew deeper. He decided to twist the knife a bit so she started to really understand her place in his life. So he gave Johnny baby a slow, sexy smile. 'Why don't you go back and warm up those sheets so you make it all nice and hot for me?'

As soon as Johnny baby was gone she blasted out, 'What's going on here?'

He turned his back on her. Strolled over to the bar. Picked up the nearest bottle to him. Brandy. Filled up a glass. Turned back to her.

'That was Johnny. He just sucked my cock.'

Her mouth fell open as one of her hands fluttered to her chest. 'So you don't love me? You've been gay all this time.'

He rolled his eyes. What was it with chicks and love? Like they needed to hear the word every two bloody seconds. Just like his mum who never got over his dad doing a runner back to his wife when she got knocked up. She'd lived the rest of her pitiful life on prescription tabs and bottles of gin mourning the loss of the love of her life. Stupid bitch. God he hated her so much sometimes. Hated his dad even more. Well that was until . . .

'Answer me.' Her tortured shrill bought him back into the room.

He held onto the glass as he leaned back onto the bar. 'I like blokes and birds, no big fucking deal.' He let out a little laugh. 'Come on girl, you had a good time. That pussy of yours hadn't been on a decent outing in years.'

She straightened her shoulders, trying to pull herself back into control. 'We're finished.'

Before she could even move he had her in a choke-hold, with one hand, slammed into the wall. He held her frightened stare as her chest pumped up and down. 'We're finished when I say we're finished. You just do what you're told and everything will be alright. You cross me and I'll make you understand that a bullet isn't the most horrible way to die.'

He let her up. Watched as she rubbed her throat and scarpered out the door. She'd keep her mouth shut. She was in way too deep.

He goes down, she goes down. Simple. And she had a lot more to lose than him.

Five minutes later Bliss was downstairs nodding and smiling at the clientele in the bar. It still gave him a thrill seeing all these people in his place. Abruptly his good feelings disappeared when he saw the revolving blue lights echoed in the mirror above the bar.

Bliss turned and vaulted the bar, pushing his way through the door marked 'staff only'. He ran down a corridor, leaned on the fire exit bar and emerged into the night. He was in a yard surrounded by a ten-foot brick wall. He turned to see the doorway at the end of the corridor filling with cops. He banged the fire exit shut and rolled two barrels in front of it. He ran at the wall, yelped as his fingers were cut on the broken glass that protected the top and then by force of will dragged himself upwards until he was crouching on the pointed shards. He yelled as he jumped down, tumbling onto the pavement below.

As he looked upwards, Bliss could see a figure running towards him.

'Stop! Police!'

On his back, Bliss raised his hands in surrender and offered his open hand to the cop so he could get up. The officer took it and Bliss gripped his hand tightly and then power kicked the guy's belly. Used his hand and foot to throw the cop upwards and over so that he somersaulted onto the bonnet of a parked car behind. He bolted up. As the cop slid off the car, Bliss punched and kicked him so he couldn't follow and then set off down the street.

The dripping blood from his fingers Bliss knew would give him away so he wrapped the wounds in tissue as he ran. To the right was an estate but that was too obvious a place to escape into and it would be too difficult to get one of his boys to pick him up. Off to the left were tidy, straight terraced streets where there were no people and not much cover, so that was no good for him either.

All around him he could hear sirens in the neighbouring streets. He ran on towards the high street where he could lose himself in the crowd. He passed a young traffic warden who was ambling along checking car windows. The warden was the right build and Bliss had an idea. He turned, approached the warden and said, 'Excuse me . . .'

'Yes?'

By way of explanation, Bliss punched him out and he collapsed onto the kerb scattering his tickets. Bliss dragged him between two cars, stripped him of his uniform, dressed himself in it and then bundled his own clothes together and dropped them into a dustbin.

He walked now rather than ran, inspecting car windows as he went. As he turned a corner he could see the high street at the end and despite himself he increased his pace. Behind him he could hear a car accelerating down the road, its brakes screeched and it drew to a halt beside him. Bliss didn't look round. A voice from the car called, 'Excuse me boss . . .'

Bliss turned. Shit, a cop car. He kept it cool. 'Yes?'

'Seen a guy in a designer suit running these streets, about your age and build?'

'Nope. Sorry.'

'OK.'

The car took off. Bliss kept walking.

As he hoped, the high street was crowded and busy but it also seemed half of London's police force was roaming the street with them. Making sure to keep his eyes on the windscreens of parked cars, Bliss walked carefully down the road. When he reached the Mile End Tube he realised the station had been closed and sealed off by the cops.

'Oi, I want a word with you!' Bliss turned to see an irate motorist waving a parking ticket at him. 'Five fucking minutes I was there . . . what's the fucking matter with you fucking people?'

The car driver was in his face and pushing him backwards with his outstretched hands. Bliss looked at the police posted outside the station who had a clear view of the parking incident that was developing. Bliss knew this could be disaster.

'I'm only doing my job.'

'What? Being a fucking cunt is your job is it?'

'Look mate—'

'Believe me you've got the wrong bloke,' a voice said calmly behind Bliss.

He turned to find a calm-looking, large black geezer standing behind him. No one needed to tell Bliss that he was a cop.

The man looked calmly at one of the cops behind him. 'Cuff him.'

twenty

Jackie groaned in pain as the lump in her breast throbbed. As she rubbed her hand over her chest, Schoolboy jumped up from the chair opposite her on the other side of their son's bed in the hospital. She groaned louder. Usually the pain let go but it wouldn't ease up this time.

'Jackie baby what is it?' her husband said anxiously as he put his arms around her.

Just tell him. Just tell him. But all of her doubts came flooding back. What if they had to take her breast and he didn't want her no more. What if he found another bird?

Suddenly the stabbing pain was gone. She folded her body back up. Looked into Schoolboy's face. He looked a wreck. Bloodshot eyes, shadows under his eyes and his locks, which he always kept so neat with pride, were hanging wildly about his face. No she couldn't tell him. Not now with their boy fighting for his life right before their very eyes.

'Just some indigestion. I ain't been eating right since this business.'

Abruptly he took her face between his hands. 'You ain't feeding me porkies are you? You'd let me know if you weren't well?'

'Me not well?' She let out a nervous laugh. 'I don't get sick you know that.' She pulled her head back and waved her hand dismissively. 'I just want our son to wake up.'

Before he could answer, the door opened and Misty came into the room. And by the sombre look on Misty's face they both knew something was up.

'Just thought I should let you both know.'

'What?' It was Schoolboy who spoke.

'The cops have arrested Bliss.'

Jackie jumped up. 'The bastard. I knew he did it. How could he do that to those kids? My boy?' She waved her arms around. 'If he was here in front of me I'd kill him.'

'No you wouldn't,' a gentle voice said from the door beside Misty. Jackie looked up. 'I bloody well would.'

Jackie ran into the arms of the one woman she needed right now. Her mum, Nikki Flynn.

Marina was in the dead house when she got the news. Pinkie Lewis stood beside her as she looked lovingly down at the face of Minnie. The funeral parlour had done a good job. Her little angel looked like she was sleeping. Her golden hair was combed neatly, not a strand out of place. If Marina didn't know she was dead she would swear that Minnie was going to pop her eyes open any moment and say 'Hello mum.'

But that wasn't going to happen. Her little girl wasn't coming back.

'We should let them have this,' Pinkie said as she held up the small black holdall bag she held. Inside were the clothes that Marina had picked out for the twins to wear at their funeral. She'd chosen the beautiful, white lace dresses they would have worn for their Confirmation. Just as she nodded at Stan's nan her mobile went. Numb she pulled it out. 'Alright Jackie.'

'They've pulled Bliss for killing the girls.'

She should've felt something then, but she didn't. It didn't matter who did it because her angels weren't ever coming back.

Kenny was reading his trial papers as the man with his head inside his cell toilet gagged. Kenny looked up briefly as his two big associates meted out some old style punishment to someone who'd tried to muscle in on his illicit distillery. The cheeky bastard had been brewing his own round the back of the gym and trying to sell it on under the counter while he served brekkie to the inmates. Did

he really think that Kenny wouldn't find out? If any of the prisoners wanted their own private happy hour after lights out they came
to him and no one else.

Kenny nodded his head sharply at one of the men. He grabbed
the choking man's hair. Yanked his head up and back. The man
shook as he gulped in air and pleaded, 'I didn't mean it Mr Lewis. I
won't do it again, I could work for you instead.' Kenny didn't even
reply just nodded again. The terrified man cried out as his head
was pushed back.

Kenny calmly went back to reading his trial papers looking for
clues. Clues to who may have fitted him up. He hadn't had nothing to do with that stolen bullion being found in his place. I mean,
come on, if he had he would never have left it sitting pretty in such
an obvious spot. No, someone had wanted him out of the way. But
who? As the question milled around his mind and his captive's
body began to jiggle more wildly his mobile kicked off. Getting a
mobile inside prison was easy. Some of the prisoners did a bit of
plugging – smuggling phones up their jacksie – and rented them
out or sold them on. All Kenny had organised was the importation
of a SIM card and not many men had refused him the use of their
mobile to slot his card into.

He took the call:

'Yeah?'

His mum. 'Bliss has been picked up. They say he did Minnie and
Molly.'

He cut the call as fury burst throughout his body. Bliss? He
jumped off the top bunk. Nodded to one of the men, who pulled
the man's head back for a second time. Without letting him take a
breath Kenny aimed a fist with all the rage he felt at his jaw.

*   *   *

She was leaving work when the news about Bliss finally reached
her. Two women who stood at the exit of her workplace chatted
non-stop and loudly so she couldn't fail to hear.

'The Bill have picked up the scumbag who did it?'

She knew what the woman meant by *it*. The death of Stanley Lewis's children. 'Who?' the other woman fired back.

'Someone called Paul Bliss . . .'

'You're kidding.'

'You sound like you know who he is.'

'Bloody right I know who the scrote is. Beat up one of my younger brothers once in a pub fight. Mind you that brother of mine was no good . . .'

She hurried past them, missing their greeting to her. Jesus, Bliss had been arrested for killing the girls. He'd sworn he hadn't done it. And now what was going to happen to his shipment, which would be arriving in three weeks' time? Why, oh why had she got involved in this in the first place? Whatever her reasons, she decided, she made a firm decision. This was the last time she was going to let him use the place to stash his guns.

Jackie watched as her mum dropped a soft kiss onto Preston's forehead. Despite being in her fifties Nikki Flynn was still a stunner. Slender, back-straight tall, with a face that still caught the eye, the same way it had when she was a stripper, and shoulder-length copper-red hair that still took the breath away. She eased away from her grandson and moved towards her daughter. And smiled. Jackie took after her father's people – not that Jackie had a clue who her dad was – small, freckles, determined face, even her hair wasn't naturally red it was brown. But she'd kept it red when Nikki had disappeared all those years ago as a way of hanging onto memories of her mum.

Nikki embraced Jackie in a tight hug. Jackie hesitated for a second, then leaned into her mum. She loved her mum to bits but when Nikki had reappeared in her life something had changed between them. Before that business they'd been as close as a mother and daughter could be, but then Jackie had had to do some quick growing up. On her own. Without her mum. And somehow it had created a distance between them.

'At least they've got the bastard who did this,' Nikki said as she gently eased Jackie away from her.

Jackie folded her arms around herself, her gaze darting away from her mum. 'Mum I still can't believe that my little boy is lying there. I just want him to wake up.'

Nikki stepped towards her and caressed her daughter's face. 'He will darling, he will.'

Jackie sniffed and said, 'How are things, mum?'

Nikki flicked her hair over her right shoulder as she answered. 'Not bad. Funny, I don't really miss London, thought I would.'

Jackie wasn't surprised that her mum didn't miss the place, not after all the bad memories it contained. She did wish that Nikki was nearer to her, but her mum deserved some happiness after the crap she'd been through.

'When Preston's better you'll have to come over to see us in Switzerland,' Nikki carried on.

Jackie twisted her lips at hearing the word *us*. Jackie didn't approve of who her mum had got hitched to. Besides, seeing him just made her own awful memories come flooding back.

Jackie looked up at her mum and gave her a tired smile. 'I'm just pleased you're here.'

'Anything I can do to help, you just let me know.' Then an expression came over her mum's face and Jackie could've sworn it was fear. 'Promise me Jackie that after those little girls' funeral you won't go anywhere near the Lewises.'

Startled by the forcefulness in Nikki's voice Jackie responded, 'Do you know them?'

Nikki's face half turned away. 'Let's just say I've heard all about their reputation.'

'Alright,' Jackie reassured her. There was no way she could let her mum know that her and Misty would be going to visit Kenny Lewis in prison.

Bliss wasn't saying dick and Ricky knew it. Ricky was back in interview room number two with Sonny by his side this time. Back in the same seat that he'd been in when he'd questioned Jackie yesterday. This time the suspect wasn't talking. Bliss stared defiantly back at him as his fingers idly pushed around the plastic ashtray on the table.

'Like I said before, soul brother.' His lip curled at his own humour. 'I ain't saying sweet FA until my brief gets here.'

Ricky relaxed back in his seat like he had all the time in the world. 'Think your brief's going to help you when you're locked down in with the pervs? I suppose we could dump you in with the general pop but that would be cruel coz you wouldn't last long. No one likes a child killer.'

Bliss just stared him out, so Ricky carried on twisting the screw. 'Kiddie fiddlers. Rapists. Grasses. Rotten cops. That's who you'll be waking up with; taking a piss with first thing in the morning; bedding down with at night.' He inched closer. 'And who knows, one of them rapists might just take a real shine to you . . .'

Bliss flew up, the force of his move knocking his chair backwards. Sonny shot out of her chair but Ricky shoved his hand in front of her. She eased back down, her attention never leaving Bliss. An ugly ripple went across Bliss's mouth. 'You going to charge me, then charge me . . .'

Calmly Ricky got up and rounded the table. Bliss kept his eyes on him all the way. Ricky moved behind him and picked the chair up. He stepped to the side. 'Sit back down.'

He was surprised when Bliss did exactly that. This time his suspect's pose had moved from bored and sulky to high alert. The veins in his throat throbbed. 'Like I said before, it's all crap, you know that . . .'

Ricky pushed one of the transparent packets next to him in front of Bliss. He swivelled it around, clockwise, to face him. 'Do you recognise this vehicle?'

A photo of the jeep.

Bliss's eyes flashed as he stared at the 4x4. 'Not my style. I'm a Merc man.'

Ricky inched the photo closer. 'Are you sure Bliss? Only we've got mile after mile of traffic camera footage that shows you at the wheel going back months. Are you sure you don't recognise it?'

Bliss sneered. 'You can do anything with film and a computer. I thought you people had cleaned your act up? Faking evidence? My legal team are going to piss all over this, you know that. I could be in line for compo here—'

Ricky cut over him as he leaned forward. 'The number plate matches one recorded by a camera-phone witness outside the school.' Ricky presented Bliss with the second transparent packet. 'This is a fingerprint. And do you know where we found it?'

Bliss tilted his head to the side and Ricky was sure he saw the colour drain away from the man's face. Finally he raised his head and gave Ricky one of his bollocks-to-you-mate stares. 'On the Queen's arse?'

Despite his jokey comeback Ricky could see the twitch in his veins beating harder.

'Do you know who this fingerprint belongs to?'

'I think Prince Philip is the man you're after mate.'

Ricky stated the obvious. 'This is your fingerprint. We can trace the 4x4 back to you. It's registered in one of your many false names and we can prove it's one you use. The vehicle was hidden in a lock-up on an estate you run and this is just one of the dozens of your fingerprints we found on the jeep. Be fair Bliss. What would you think?'

'I think you can fake fingerprints on anything, you should watch more cop shows. As for any 4x4 or lock-ups, I don't know what you're talking about—'

'We also found an empty bottle of Jack Daniels. More of your prints.'

Bliss said nothing. The vein under his chin beat stronger. Ricky pushed on. 'I tell you what I think happened. You got pissed and decided to take Lewis's kids down? Or was it all a tragic, if very coincidental, accident?'

Silence.

'I'm serious Bliss. Help yourself out.'

Bliss finally spoke through clenched teeth. 'I never fucking killed no bloody kids, you hear.'

The door came open. The desk sergeant popped his head around the door. 'What?' Ricky roared. Of all the times for there to be an interruption . . . He nearly had Bliss by the balls.

'Sir. Bliss's . . .' Before he could finish, another person barrelled past him.

'That's it,' the newcomer said. 'Interview over.'

Bliss shrugged his shoulders. Ricky groaned. A tall woman with long dark hair wearing a smart suit and accompanying briefcase came inside the room, her high heels clipping on the floor.

'Detective Inspector Smart.'

Ricky leaned back in his chair as he looked at her. Of all the lawyers out there why did it have to be her defending Bliss?

Wearily he answered, 'Miss Sullivan.'

The woman he adored, Daisy Sullivan, took the empty seat next to Bliss.

twenty-one

The tape recorder clicked on. The interview kicked off for a second time.

'My client is ready to make a statement.'

Ricky stared at a cool-as-cucumber Daisy. He'd shown her the evidence and given her twenty minutes alone with Bliss.

He folded his arms on the table. 'OK, let's hear it.'

Bliss ran his finger under his nose and sniffed. Then started talking. 'OK the jeep's mine and all the paperwork is fake. Or rather it was mine. So if you want to waste time booking me for that, fair enough, I'll pay a fine. But I wasn't the owner when it hit anyone and I certainly wasn't behind the wheel . . .'

Ricky and Daisy looked unconvinced. Even Bliss didn't seem too sure but he went on. 'I was down my club, The Five Fingers, the night before the stuff outside the school. I got into a card game with some flash bird.' Ricky raised his eyebrow at hearing Bliss say it was a woman, but let him carry on. 'And the stakes started mounting up. I was taking a bit of a hit so I told one of my people to go and get some dosh from the safe. I mean, I don't care do I? It's only money, a few grand here and there don't make no difference to me, I enjoy a game of cards. But Cool Hand Lucy asks me who the jeep outside belongs to. So I says it's mine and she says, "OK why don't you put that up, I've just totalled mine, I need a new one". So, I shrugged my shoulders. A couple of straights and a few flushes later and the cheeky bint has walked off with my car keys. To be honest, I admired her balls, coming in my club and clearing me out. But I always pay my debts. I'm well known for it.'

There was silence around the table. Even Bliss didn't look convinced. Then Ricky unwound his arms. Leaned forward. 'So that's your statement is it? You're planning to get in the witness stand with that?'

Daisy answered, the beauty spot above her mouth moving with each word. 'My client has answered you and informed you about what happened. It sounds to me like you need to be putting your resources into looking for this woman.'

Ricky ignored her and directed his statement at Bliss. 'So let me get this straight, the same car that belongs to you, the same car that kills a couple of children, the children of a well-known rival of yours, you just happened to lose it in a card game the night before to a woman who you'd never seen before?'

Bliss sneered. 'Finally, a copper who's listening to me.'

Ricky almost felt sorry for Bliss. 'Does your club have CCTV? Perhaps we can have a look at this mysterious deck-dealer?'

Bliss smiled at him. 'Oh yeah, 'course all my guests want to get caught on film don't they? Perhaps I should collect their prints on the way in too? You need to wise up mate; I've been set up. Even London's finest must be able to see that. Why don't you get out and do some real investigating for a change.' Bliss's smile turned into a smirk. 'Perhaps you're on the real culprit's books?'

Ignoring the implication that he was a dirty cop Ricky carried on. 'Where were you yesterday at approximately 3.30pm?'

Bliss smirked. 'Screwing my girl against the one grand dressing table I bought her.'

'Her name's Sherry Long,' Daisy added. 'I have the contact details if you need them.'

'Two women,' Ricky said. 'You are putting yourself about.'

Ricky had had enough. 'I think we can move on to some ID parades and from there it should be a smooth run in to the charges—'

'But my client has given you—'

'Nothing. Our evidence points to him having killed two children.'

Daisy butted in. 'My client's going to be looking for bail.'

'Anything your client's going to be looking for will have to be found in the confines of a cell. If he was fessing up, I might be able to help but if he's sticking to this "story", we'll oppose bail tooth and nail. And I'll tell you this – I'm doing him a favour. Even his rep wouldn't save a child killer from an angry public . . .'

'He didn't do it you know?'

Ricky stared back at Daisy sternly as they walked past a man entering the station on their way outside.

'You shouldn't be representing Bliss. You've got one too many other connections to this case—'

She snapped back at him before he could finish. 'You don't need to be worrying about who I should and shouldn't be representing—'

'And what do you think Jackie's going to say when she finds out?'

Daisy pinched her lip, making the beauty spot at the corner of her mouth move. 'Leave Jackie to me. All you need to know is that my client didn't do this.'

'Oh please, give me a break,' he simply answered as they moved to the unofficial smokers' corner around the back of the building. He pulled out a packet of cigarettes wishing it were a boxful of spliffs instead.

With an annoyed move of her hand Daisy flicked her long black hair off her shoulder. 'Look, I'm the first to admit that my client isn't Robin Hood.' Ricky grunted at that, then lit up. 'But it's precisely because he isn't that you know he didn't do it. The car would be at the bottom of the English Channel by now. If he had done this he would have gotten rid of every scrap of evidence. No way would he have left it sitting pretty, all nice and neat waiting for Her Majesty's finest to find it in a lock-up with a pink ribbon around it. Come on,' she pleaded as she waved away the plumes of smoke coming from him. 'Even you can see that.'

'Yeah, it's very careless, I agree with you. Maybe he gave the job of clearing up to the wrong guy. I don't know and I don't care.' Suddenly he flicked the half gone butt into the air. Pulled her into his arms. 'I suggest me and you find somewhere to get all nice and sloppy.'

She pushed herself out of his arms. 'I'm not joking Ricky, this is a set-up. You're being lazy.'

'My job is to deal with the evidence. Anyway, your boy has still got a chance, if the witnesses pick out a seven foot black guy with a twitch, I'll put my hands up–'

'And my job is to make sure that my client gets a fair–'

But she never finished the sentence because he gave her a huge smacker on the lips. He pushed his lips to her ear and whispered. 'What about me and you start celebrating two years together a couple of weeks early . . . ?'

'Ricky we can't . . .' But he was already dragging her away.

The man Ricky and Daisy passed on the way out stood at the sergeant's desk. The sergeant flicked his tired looking eyes up. 'Can I help you sir?'

'I've come from Miss Sullivan's office for Paul Bliss to sign some papers.'

The sergeant eyed him up. 'No can do. Only the brief sees the client.'

'It's all above board, I'm working with Miss Sullivan on the case. I just saw her go outside if you want to ask her.'

The sergeant checked him over. 'You'll need to show me some ID.'

Just as the man in front of him opened his mouth two policemen came in dragging in a man who was struggling, yelling and screaming. 'Sarge,' one of the cops shouted. 'Help us get this one to quieten down.'

As the desk sergeant moved, the man in front of him said, 'What about me?'

The sergeant looked back to his two colleagues who were now wrestling their suspect to the floor.

'Yeah, alright,' he quickly muttered to the man in front of him. He picked up the phone beside him on the counter and spoke briefly, then rushed to help the two other policemen.

The man at the desk waited patiently. A few minutes later another cop appeared, younger with red hair and nodded at the man. He escorted him down to the block of cells in the back of the building.

Stopped outside the second cell from the end on the right. Pulled out his keys and opened the cell. Shoved his head inside and called out, 'Your brief's here.'

The man stepped around the cop. And rushed inside the cell.

'What the fuck's he doing here?' Bliss yelled.

The man turned around and kicked the cop in the nuts. He advanced on Bliss, pulling out a hammer from under his jacket. 'Kill my kids did you? Well I'm going to batter you to death.'

Bliss stared eyes wide at the deranged Stanley Lewis, hammer raised in the air coming straight at him.

'I never touched your kids. It's a set-up you fuckwit. Ask around, you'll see.'

Stanley said nothing, just kept on moving forward. Bliss inched back.

The cop on his knees just managed to press the panic alarm the same time the first hammer blow came down. Bliss twisted to the side, but the hammer caught him in the shoulder. He yelped out in pain as he fell to his knees.

'You'll never touch anyone's kids again,' Stanley spat as he raised the hammer again.

He brought it down but this time his opponent flung his body to the side. Stanley stumbled as the hammer glanced off the concrete floor.

'Fucking help me,' Bliss cried out to the policeman. But the cop was still on the floor trying to fight waves of sick that rolled through his stomach.

'Ain't no one gonna fucking help you now,' Stanley snarled.

Bliss tried to slide away, but Stanley caught his foot and dragged him back. The hammer went up. Came down. This time Bliss's hand came up and grabbed Stanley's arm. Twisted it. But Stanley didn't let go of the deadly weapon. Instead he used his foot to kick him in the side. Bliss groaned but kept his hand tightly locked around the other man's arm. He was fucked if he was going to let Stanley Lewis batter him like a piece of sheet metal. Without another thought he hauled him forward. The surprise attack made Stanley totter. He wavered for a few seconds. Then his body tipped heavily onto Bliss's. Like a madman, Stanley threw his head back. Then forward. Nutted Bliss straight on the bridge of his nose. Blood poured from his face. Onto his shirt. Bliss blinked rapidly as the pain sliced through his head making him dizzy. Shit, all he could see were black, dancing dots.

'You're going to die, you cunt, you're going to die!'

Bliss's vision started to clear and what he saw nearly made him wet himself. The hammer was coming straight towards his face.

'Put it down!' Ricky shouted from the doorway.

Stanley wavered with the hammer still raised high. Bliss breathed hard, bloody and beaten, eyes never leaving the hammer.

'You heard me!' Ricky ordered, moving inside the cell.

'Gonna get you!' Stanley yelled at Bliss, then he stumbled to his feet and threw the hammer to the ground.

Ricky stormed over, grabbed his arms and cuffed him.

Kenny had never begged for anything in his life, but he was begging now. Begging the Number One to let him attend his grandkids' funeral in five days' time.

The Governor stared uncomfortably back at him as he carried on pleading. 'I swear I'll behave myself. All I want to do is see them laid to rest. I'm their Granddad for Christ's sake.'

The Governor leaned back in his seat as he continued to stare at one of the most dangerous inmates in the prison. If it was anyone else he might consider it, but not Kenneth Lewis. If he allowed him out and something went down it would be his head on the block and he'd spent years working his way up from a nobody screw on the wing to being the man in charge of the house.

He shook his head. 'Sorry, Kenny. Permission denied.'

Sherry Long, Bliss's girlfriend in Limehouse, had just locked the front of her house when she was grabbed from behind. A hand clamped over her mouth. The tips of her metallic stiletto heels scraped along the hard pavement as she was dragged backwards to a waiting car. She was shoved on her front across the back seat. Before she could right herself someone crammed in beside her. The doors slammed, shutting out the world beyond the tinted windows. As she raised her head up, something was shoved over it. A plastic bag. Her face moulded against the plastic.

A voice growled, 'If you don't want me to tighten this around your neck so you can't breathe, you'll shut up and enjoy the ride.'

Ricky entered the holding cell. Stanley Lewis flicked his head up at Ricky's entrance. His nostrils flared showing the anger he still felt. Ricky knew he should've had him taken to another nick, but what he was going to do wouldn't take long. Mind you Daisy had given him a mouthful about how she was going to write to his superior to find out how this mess had happened.

'I hope you've had time to cool off,' Ricky said.

Stan spat, his face becoming angry red. 'That fucker had it coming to him. He killed my girls.' His voice strained at the end, grief at the loss of his children stamped across his face.

Ricky didn't want to feel anything for this thug but he did. He knew what it felt like to grieve for someone you loved and this man had two people – two kids – who he was never going to see alive again. Jee-zuus, the weight of that must be more than most men could live with. But still that didn't give him the right to come in here and take the law into his own hands.

'I should charge you really. Attempted murder is at the more serious end of the spectrum, legal-wise. But I'm going to overlook it this time as long as you promise to leave it to us. Bliss isn't going anywhere and we're most probably going to charge him tomorrow and to be honest, him going into the prison system as a child killer is going to hurt him a lot more than any damage you could do with a hammer. So if I decide it's not in the public interest to charge a grieving father, you can decide it's not in the public interest to kill my suspects. OK?'

Stan cocked his head to the side and when he spoke his voice trembled. 'What would you do in my shoes? Let the cunt get away with it? My girls were ten years old. One liked strawberry ice-cream and the other liked vanilla. One loved to watch *Strictly Come Dancing* and the other the *X Factor*. One loved sleeping with her thumb stuck in her mouth and the other with a smile on her chops.' Stan's voice cracked as the breath staggered from his body. 'I ain't gonna apologise for coming in here and trying to take out the fucker who took all of that away from them and I ain't promising not to have another go. I know people, you can't keep him safe, no one can.' His voice echoed around the cell walls. 'Go on, charge me, you know why? Coz when Joe Public finds out, no jury will convict me. What dad wouldn't do what I did in my shoes?'

Ricky knew he was right. He didn't want his own face all over the tabloids. He knew that he was going to have to tread very carefully indeed. 'I'm going to let you go with a warning. Stay away from Bliss. Let us do our job. If he's guilty he's going down.'

Stan just stared up at him. 'Can I go?' As Ricky nodded he was stunned to see the tears in his eyes. 'See, the thing is I've got to get ready to bury my kids now.'

And with that Stan stood up and was gone.

Sherry didn't know how long she was driven with the carrier bag over her head. She was shitting herself. Couldn't think what she'd done, unless it was that Syrian drug dealer she and her dead sister had rolled over last year for a cool five big ones.

The car stopped. Her fear increased as she was dragged out of the motor. She didn't know where the heck she was but could smell the freshness of the air. A hand clamped around her arm.

'Move.' She stumbled along steered by the hand holding her. The ground beneath her feet made crunching sounds. A few minutes later they stopped. The carrier bag was whipped off her head. She drew in huge gulps of air as she stared at large trees around her and realised she was in some type of wood. Whoever was with her stood behind her. Shit, she knew what happened to people who were taken to woods.

Anxiously she twisted around to find Sean McCarthy in front of her. She knew who Sean was, Bliss's right-hand man. He gazed at her with those dead eyes of his, the sweat on his forehead shining in front of his receding hairline.

'I ain't done nothing,' she wailed.

He grabbed her by the arm and flung her forward. She stumbled as she stopped at the edge of a freshly dug grave. Breath whizzed inside her body as her hand clamped over her mouth in horror. Inside the grave was the battered body of Marky-Boy, the bloke Bliss had found screwing her brains out yesterday afternoon.

Sean started speaking, no emotion in his voice. 'The boss just wants to remind you what might happen if you don't tell the Bill he was with you yesterday afternoon.'

She thought she was going to throw-up. But instead she nodded her head furiously.

twenty-two

Four days later, the night before the funeral, Marina Lewis smiled because her girls were back with her. Just her and them. Alone. In her sitting room. She tipped the whisky bottle to her mouth as she looked at the two open coffins. They lay side by side the same way the girls had slept in their single beds in their room. Both coffins were white, not that nasty off-white, but the type of white Marina thought you only found in heaven. Pure and glowing. Minnie's coffin had her Barbie pillow on it and Molly's her Arsenal shirt. Stan had wanted to take the girls back to his but she'd told him where he could shove it. They might be dead but she still had custody of them. Dead. The word kept repeating in her mind. Her little girls weren't coming back. Marina swayed as she moved forward drinking from the bottle all the way. She ran her hand lovingly over each coffin. This was their last night all together. Tomorrow they were being laid to rest. Now the tears started to come as the bottle fell from her hand. She fell to her knees. She scrambled in her pocket for her mobile. Tears and spit dripped from her mouth as she sobbed into the phone, 'It's you who should be beside me at the funeral, not Stan . . .'

twenty-three

For most parents, July 10 was just another might-be, might-not-be-hot summer's day. For Marina and Stanley Lewis it was a day they would never forget. The day they buried their daughters. And, as it turned out, it was also a day that the rest of East London wasn't likely to forget for a long time either. There wasn't a seat to be had inside St John's Church in Mile End. Bottom and top pews were jam-packed with people. Packed with relatives and friends. And, of course, a who's who of London's most well-known Faces. Only one thing London's underworld liked doing more than killing each other was burying one of their own. Not that the girls had been part of any action, but they were Stanley Lewis's kids and it would've been seen as maximum disrespect to Kenny Lewis if certain people hadn't put in an appearance. And they'd come in their Beamers, Mercs, Jags, dressed in flowing coats despite the warm day and shades with their muscle accompanying them.

The only spot that was empty was the front-row pew because it was reserved for the Lewis family. Jackie and Misty sat in the middle row on the right. Jackie wore a simple black trouser suit, while Misty was dressed in a long black dress and low, flat heels. It was the first time in a long time Jackie had seen Misty without any make-up. Jackie held tight onto the funeral sheet, which had a heart-shaped colour photo of Minnie and Molly together smiling their little hearts out. Above the photo was written in fancy script:

In memory of the best girls in the world.

Jackie swallowed trying to hold back the emotions that were choking her up as she stared at the girls' laughing faces. If Preston didn't come out of his coma, this might be her soon. She shuddered at the terrible thought. At least she knew that Darius was safely at home with her mum.

'You alright, my girl?' Misty whispered as if she sensed Jackie's sad thoughts.

Jackie tore her eyes away from the photo and shook her head. 'How does any mum and dad deal with having to bury their kids?'

Misty took Jackie's hand and squeezed. Jackie looked up at her friend and was surprised at the tears she saw in her eyes. 'Don't really talk about this,' Misty said. 'Everyone thinks I was the youngest in my family but I weren't.' Jackie's eyebrows rose up in surprise. 'My little brother Connor was born four years after me.' Misty let out a quiet laugh as the memories took her. 'He was such a lovely little boy. Looked just like mum. Used to follow me around all the time. I weren't meant to be playing near the road, but we were. Playing catch with the new football dad had given me for Christmas. I chucked the ball at him. The ball went into the road. He didn't stand a chance. A black cab came round the corner and . . .'

Only then did Jackie realise that she was now the one giving her friend comfort by squeezing her hand. 'You don't have to say any more.'

But Misty went on anyway. 'I'll always remember my mum's face when she got the news. She looked like someone had told her that the devil himself was coming for tea. She never blamed me once for being near the road. On the morning of Connor's funeral, as she was knotting my black tie, she says to me that Connor's time was meant to be short on earth. He was one of them good boys who were sent to bring his family laughter and joy. And that's how she told me to remember him, with laughter and joy. And that's what the Lewis family are going to have to do, remember all the good times their girls had. Believe me if they don't they will kill themselves in the end.'

The sound of weeping coming from the back of the church cut short anything else they might have said. They turned around, like

everyone else, and what Jackie saw made the pain in her heart twist
some more. The church was silent as the girls' coffins were slowly
and solemnly carried down the aisle by four men. The coffins were
small, as white as an angel's wings with a golden cross on top.
Jackie's eyes swam with tears. Stan Lewis, dressed from head to
toe in black and sporting dark shades, followed, holding a large
wreath in his hands. A sobbing Marina staggered behind him with
Pinkie Lewis's arm around her shoulder. Pinkie's beehive was black
to match her clothes. Funny thing, Jackie thought, there they were
at the funeral of their kids and they looked like a proper family. A
real family united in grief. Pinkie Lewis walked stiffly, with not a
lick of emotion on her face as if going to funerals had always been
part of her life.

Jackie watched the procession as it passed the pew where
Detective Inspector Ricky Smart and his partner sat at the end;
bloody cops couldn't leave it alone for a minute. Past the pew
where Mrs Moran, the head teacher, and Scott Miller, the Chair of
Governors of the school were. The procession reached the front
of the altar where a beautiful arrangement of lilies lay. The priest
stood to the side, his black Bible in his hand, his eyes downcast.
A white and blue statue of the Virgin Mary looked down as the
coffins were laid out at the front of the church. Then Pinkie Lewis
gently guided the dead girls' grief-stricken mum to the front pew.
Stan didn't follow them straight away. Instead he just stood there,
as still as the statues of the Saints all around him, looking at the
coffins. Then he bent and laid the wreath of roses he held in front
of the coffins. He sniffed as he stood back up and stepped to the
side. Everyone, including Jackie and Misty, gasped with horror
when they finally saw his floral tribute to his daughters. Black
roses arranged into a single word:

Revenge.

A wave of shock swept the church.

'Nothing like a statement wreath is there,' Misty muttered. 'Can't
he just let his girls be buried in peace?'

Jackie didn't answer because if the truth be known she knew
exactly how he was feeling. Didn't she have revenge running

through her heart as her boy lay in the ozzie fighting for his life? No, she couldn't blame Stan for what he was feeling.

As Stan turned to take his place with his mum and ex, his eyes caught the lilies. Those flowers weren't a tribute from him or his family he knew that for sure. Who were they from? Instead of taking his seat he walked over to them. His body seemed to rock as he read the card attached to them. Suddenly he yanked the card from the flowers and twisted violently around.

'Deepest Condolences. Paul Bliss,' he read out in disbelief, his face turning scarlet. 'What the fuck are these doing there?'

The congregation gasped as Stan went ballistic. He grabbed the lilies and ripped them to shreds in a wild frenzy. When each petal lay in a mess at his feet in front of the altar, Stan bent over and did something that even the most hardened criminal would've thought twice about doing in a place of God. He spat on them.

He glowered at the mourners. 'Who's responsible for allowing this? So help me, I'm going to kill them.'

A camera flashed. The two huge men who stood at the back door rushed forward, trying to find the source of the camera. They found it, some young man desperately trying to shuffle his way out of a pew. But they found him. One hauled him by his jacket while the other grabbed the camera.

'Hang on fellas. I'm a journalist. I'm on Mr Lewis's side ...' But his words fell on deaf ears as he was dragged from the church.

'I'm going to get you Bliss,' Stan bellowed.

'Take it easy,' a strong voice called with stern authority from the back of the church.

Every head turned. Both Misty and Jackie's mouths flipped open in surprise at who they saw.

'Blimey,' Misty whispered. 'Get your tin hats on, now it'll all go down.'

There, in the doorway, with the sunshine beating down on him from the red and blue stained-glass window above, was the last person anyone had expected to see.

Kenny Lewis.

Two uniformed prison officers stood on either side of Kenny. He was dressed in a deep black designer suit, his appearance all neat and clean as if he'd just come back from the barbers not from inside one of Her Majesty's cells. But no one was looking at his clothes. They were looking at the black jacket covering his hands in front of his tummy no doubt hiding a pair of handcuffs. The crowd followed him step-by-step as he silently began to walk, escorted, down the aisle. They stopped when they reached a heavy-breathing Stan. Father looked at son. Son looked at father.

'I'm going to fix this,' Stan hissed. 'No one can stop me. Not even you.'

'Come here son,' Kenny replied.

Stan wrapped his arms around his dad. And cried. A tiny mutter swept through the church.

'Calm down boy,' Kenny whispered. 'You're here to bury our kids. OK? Don't put on a show. Show some dignity and show some respect. Yeah?' Stan pulled himself away, rubbing a hand under his shades as he nodded.

Stan looked down at the shattered flowers. 'But dad, Bliss—'

Kenny's expression turned nasty. 'Don't worry about it. We'll sort things out with Bliss. You just have to be patient. But leave it for today, OK?'

'I thought they weren't going to let you come,' Stan sniffed.

'I had another little chat with the Number One.'

Stan, Kenny and the guards moved to take their place on the front seats. Marina stared deeply at Kenny. He nodded once to her. The priest, who looked liked he wished he had a wedding to conduct, stood up and began the service.

No one noticed the tall man, with grey strands threaded through his brown hair and a dimple in his chin wearing a smart black suit, standing in a corner in the shadows at the back of the church. He dipped a finger in the font of holy water. Placed his finger on his forehead. Made the sign of the cross and left.

*

Minnie and Molly Lewis were finally laid to rest at the City of London Cemetery. The crowd around the graveside was much smaller than the one in the church. Jackie and Misty stood directly facing the Lewis family. Marina was crying horribly as the priest neared the end of the service. Pinkie and Stan stood still as the cool wind whipped around them, their faces expressionless but pale. Kenny remained with his escort, his head bowed as he stared into the grave. There was only one grave because Marina thought that if they were buried together the girls could always remain with each other forever: twins to the end.

Suddenly there was a ripple through the mourners at the back behind the Lewis family as someone made their way through. Jackie stared with open surprise at the person who emerged on the right-hand side of Marina. It was the same guy she'd bumped into coming out of the police station. Mr Gorgeous. Tall, dark and grey hair swept back from his face, lanky frame covered by a black overcoat, and this time his brown eyes weren't dancing with laughter.

'What do you think you're playing at?' Stan shouted when he saw the newcomer. He stepped right into the guy's face.

The newcomer didn't move. Didn't show that he was scared. 'I just came to pay my respects. I've got a right.' His tone was quiet and low.

'Respects? Rights? You?' Kenny Lewis snarled, his face getting redder by the minute. 'What next? Paul Bliss dropping by for a cuppa and a chinwag? You ain't wanted here. Now piss off.' He tried to take a step towards the newcomer but one of the prison guards laid their hand on his shoulder holding him back.

'They weren't only your flesh and blood,' Mr Gorgeous threw back.

'Look mate, don't rile us up. Not today of all days,' Kenny hissed. 'Now go for a walk, there's a good boy. Don't get any more on the wrong side of me than you have already. I've got a long reach, you know that.'

Jackie's green eyes flashed between Kenny and the man. And back again. What the heck was going on? Who *was* Mr Gorgeous?

'Kenny.' This time it was his mum, Pinkie, who spoke. 'Let him say what he's got to say and leave it at that, alright?'

The muscles around Kenny's mouth jumped, like he had plenty more to say. But he nodded at his mum and stayed quiet.

'Is it alright if I say a couple of words?'

The priest looked too frightened to refuse the newcomer, so he gave a short nod of his head.

The man pushed his hand into his jacket. His hand came out a fist wrapped around something small. He folded his arms in front of him. Stared down at the grave. The wind swept through the cemetery. Then the chill increased as the man started to speak:

'I was gutted when I heard about the girls. Thought it was some kind of joke. I weren't around when they were born, but I remembered them every June 9th, their birthday.' The side of his face lifted in a gentle smile. He pushed what was in his hand to the tips of his fingers. Jackie heard a hiss from across the grave. She looked up to see that Stan had sucked in his breath, as his skin went puce. She peered harder at the object in Mr Gorgeous's hand, but couldn't make it out. 'I want all of you to have love in your heart today when you think of those two little girls. Two girls, unspotted by the evils of life.'

'Quite the poet . . .' Jackie whispered.

The silence lengthened as his tribute came to an end. Whatever was in his hand he threw into the grave making Stan gasp. Stan jerked forward breaking through the silence with his rough, don't-play-me voice. 'Alright, that's enough, you've said what you've got to say, just leave us alone.'

And with that, the man, head still down, left just as a car came to a halt in the distance.

Jackie turned to Misty as the nervous priest rushed through to end the service. 'Who was *that*?' she whispered.

'Dunno.' Misty shrugged her shoulders.

A frown danced across Jackie's forehead. 'You don't know?' her voice was incredulous. 'But you know everyone—'

'Well I don't know who that was, alright?' Jackie's head reared back at her friend's abrupt response. But before she could say anything else a voice started yelling at the back of the mourners, 'Let me through.' Female voice, erratic and Cockney.

The congregation parted to reveal a brassy-looking young woman. All lipstick and no style. But no one was staring at her face, they were all glued to her midriff. Her belly was so big and round it looked like she was going to drop her baby any minute now. She sashayed over to Stan and tucked her arm into his. She settled a cocky expression onto her face and stared boldly at Marina across the grave. Marina was in no doubt who the father of the baby was.

twenty-four

Stan placed his hand proudly on the beaming woman's belly and maliciously pronounced, 'How's our little fella doing?'

'You bastard,' Marina stormed. She looked with disgust and pain at the woman who had once been her best mate. Tiffany Matthews. The slag. Slapper. She was going to have Stan's kid. The nerve of the bitch. While she was getting ready to bury her girls, Stan was already getting ready to play daddy in another family. She saw red. Jumped towards the woman. The crowd scattered back, including the priest and Jackie. Stan managed to get between them. He grabbed Marina's arms.

'You tart!' Marina yelled over his shoulder at her former friend who looked as scared as hell.

'Cool it!' Stan yelled.

But his words only inflamed her more. She let out a string of curses. Stan delivered a stinging slap to her cheek. Marina wobbled as her mouth started to bleed. Now Jackie saw red and took a step forward, but Misty's hand held her back.

'Just shut it you stupid cow!' Stan shouted.

'Stan–' his dad started to warn.

'Well I'm sick of it. Her carrying on like she's the best mum in the world.'

'You never wanted them in the first place!' Marina screamed. 'You wanted me to get rid of them.'

That stunned the crowd even more than his slap. The wind picked up speed around them.

'Why you—' Stan's grandmother stepped forward but she was too late. Stan grabbed his ex-missus with one hand and back-handed her with the other.

'Stan!' his dad roared, the same time Pinkie grabbed the back of Stan's jacket. This gave Marina the time she needed. She raised her bag and walloped Stan around the head. As he staggered back she delivered a swift kick to his shin. He groaned and fell onto her. Marina's balance went and she tottered backwards on the edge of the grave. Then she fell dragging Stan with her. They landed on the top coffin inside the grave. The crowd froze watching the drama as Kenny and Pinkie rushed towards the grave.

'You dickhead.' It wasn't Kenny who spoke but his grandmother. Even Pinkie looked shocked that she'd used a word she would've scrubbed out in felt-tip in one of her library books. 'Get off those girls. You're making a total show of the family. Now!'

Stan scrambled out, but not before giving his ex a lethal look. He got out, turned his back and marched with his family away from the grave. The crowd followed as sobs erupted from Marina, still on top of the coffin. Only Jackie remained. She couldn't desert Marina like everyone else was doing. She walked to the grave. Crouched down. Marina lay, clutching the coffin, sobbing her heart out.

'Marina,' Jackie called softly. 'Come on babe, let's go.'

Marina looked up at Jackie. She was a mess, hair all over the place, make-up trying to do a runner and dirt covering part of her face. 'I just want my little angels back.'

'I know,' Jackie responded soothingly. 'But they've gone to a better place now, alright?'

'I can't have no more babies you know.' Jackie looked at her, shocked. 'And now his tart is going to give him a new family.' Jackie felt for Marina. What a blow, to know you had lost your kids and were never going to have any more.

Jackie didn't know what to say. 'Come on.' She stretched out her hand. Marina turned back to the coffin. Ran her hand lovingly through the dirt on top of it. Then she took Jackie's hand. As Marina scrambled away from her dead daughters, Jackie scanned inside the grave trying to find what Mr Gorgeous had dropped into it. Then she saw it curled on the edge of the coffin. A gold chain medallion with a picture. She couldn't make out what the picture was.

Jackie watched Marina get into the black car as she stood with Misty by her own motor. Her gaze skidded to the side and stopped at the sight of Kenny being led back to the prison van. Suddenly he twisted his head and caught her staring at him. Held her gaze. And nodded. She knew what that meant; not to forget to visit him with Misty in prison tomorrow.

'When my time comes,' Misty said, making Jackie turn to her, 'just make sure you don't invite the Lewis clan to my funeral.'

'Who was that bloke?'

Misty didn't need to ask who she meant by *bloke*. Instead of answering Misty half turned as she said, 'Let's get out of here.'

But Jackie placed her hand gently on her arm. 'You know who Mr Gorgeous is don't you?' She saw the look of confusion in Misty's eyes at her use of the nickname for the man. 'I bumped into him the other day outside the nick.'

Misty huffed. 'The nick? Well, you wouldn't meet him running a marathon for charity, let's put it like that . . .'

'Who is he?' Jackie pressed on.

Misty just stood there, lips closed tight like she wasn't going to answer. Then she spoke. 'That, my girl, is the original black sheep of the family. And you can guess how dark a sheep that makes him. He's the eldest boy, Benjamin Lewis. But everyone called him Flick on account of how good he was with a knife.'

twenty-five

It was more like a rave than a wake, Jackie decided in disgust. It was being held in one of Kenny's 'gentlemen' clubs in Shoreditch, minus the pole dancers, strippers and dirty old blokes. People were roaring with laughter, guzzling away like fishes and chit-chatting at the top of their voices. But then that was East Enders for you, anything for a good ol' knees-up. If it wasn't for Marina she would've gone home ages ago, which is what Misty had done, but she felt bad deserting the woman who seemed to have no true friends. Right, she was going to give it a half hour then hightail it out of there.

She wandered around, holding tight to a G&T, checking out the crowd. Bloody freeloaders, she thought, knowing that most of the crowd would have long ago forgotten about the dead girls. She couldn't see Marina anywhere. Where was she?

'Oi,' a voice called out.

Jackie turned. Bollocks. Stanley was coming towards her with the speed of a hurricane. But bollocks, she weren't scared, no soddin' way. She'd dealt with tossers way bigger and more dangerous than good ol' Stanley Lewis. Calmly she stood her ground. When he reached her, through gritted teeth, he said, 'I want a word with you.' And before she had a chance to answer he grabbed her arm and dragged her outside.

He walked into the club hosting the wake using the back stairs. He'd known this place like the back of his hand years back. He stared around. Hadn't changed much. Still looked like the type of place a man went to find a bit of illicit brass for the night. He knew exactly which room he was looking for: second floor, third door on the right. Kenny Lewis's private room. He hesitated outside. Listened. Heard voices. A man and a woman. He placed his hand on the handle. Opened. Stepped inside.

And there he was, Kenny Lewis, minus his handcuffs, pants around his ankles, doing some bra-busting blonde on the table.

'See nothing much has changed, dad,' Flick Lewis said as he closed the door.

Kenny was hopping mad. Flick could see that a mile off, but he wasn't surprised. He knew that his dad wasn't going to welcome him into his loving embrace. Kenny pushed the blonde off and told her to 'Do one.' Quickly she straightened her clothing and tottered on her heels towards the door. She gave Flick a perky I'm all yours smile. He looked right through her. She got the message and left.

Kenny was back on his feet by the time his eldest looked in his direction. He sent his son a stone-cold stare. 'I told you never to show your face around here again.'

'Ain't you going to ask me what I've been doing since I got out?'

'Don't know, don't care. The only reason I'm giving you the time of day is coz of your nan.'

'Dear old Nan. Bet you were thinking about her as you were poking your bit of fluff?'

Kenny bolted over and raised his hand ready to give him a taste of something harsh. Flick didn't move an inch, staring defiantly back at his old man. 'Go on. Do it,' he dared. 'You've been wanting to do that for years, ever since that night.'

Kenny's hand rocked in the air as he fought for control. This was his boy. The one he'd *really* loved; the one he'd take to see the Arsenal play; the one he'd take to Ladbrokes to show him how to place a bet; the one he'd pinned all his hopes for the future of his business on. The one who'd almost broken his hard heart all those years ago. He dropped his hand and turned his back. 'If you know what's good for you, boy, you'll get out of here.'

'And if I don't?'

Kenny didn't bother to turn around. 'You won't live long enough to tell the tale.'

Only when he heard the door close did Kenny turn around. He stared at the door thinking about the son he'd loved to bits but had hoped never to set his eyes on again.

Jackie and Stan ended up by the wall near the café next door.

'How could you do that to Marina?' Jackie blasted between clenched teeth. 'Rub her face in it like that? Ain't it enough that she's lost her girls without seeing you already on your way to starting another family?'

Jackie knew she was taking a big risk mouthing off to a man like Stan with the tone she was using, but she was too disgusted to find another. And she was ready to use her tongue like fists on behalf of Marina. Someone needed to put Stan Lewis in his place. She held her breath waiting to see what he'd do. A young couple holding hands passed them, no doubt making their way to trendy Hoxton Square around the corner.

But instead of doing the whole *Who you effing talking to like that?* routine, Stan thrust his fingers through his hair and shook his head. 'You're right.'

'You what?' she said like she couldn't believe it.

He looked her straight in the eyes. 'I went too far. It was bad of me, there's a time and a place.' Grit entered his voice. 'But she makes me so mad sometimes.'

Jackie searched his face looking for fakery, but all she found was regret. Maybe Stan had a heart after all.

'Well it's done,' she added quietly. 'You said you wanted a word . . .'

'How's your boy doing?'

She swallowed. 'Still in intensive care.'

'Don't worry about it, I'll sort Bliss out. He'll pay, you'll see.'

'I've heard you had a go already.'

Stan shrugged. 'Yeah, I blew it. I wasn't thinking straight and I didn't get my act together properly but you have to take your chances when you get them. It's no problem, there'll be another time. I heard you tried to straighten him out with an iron!' Jackie stared at him shocked. How had he found out about that? He answered her. 'There ain't much I don't know about what happens in this town. All I'm saying is, Jackie, that you don't need to worry. I'll do all the sorting out.'

She didn't like Stan and that was a fact and knew what he was saying to her, but she didn't like the idea of him doing any favours for her; being in his debt.

'Thanks, Stan, but I can look after my own business.'

The expression in his face shifted. From nice bloke to you-better-watch-out. 'I don't think you're hearing me. I said I would take care of it.'

She just looked at him defiantly and then tried to move past him but he grabbed her arm tight. She saw the hard expression in his brown eyes and started to feel scared. Really scared.

He shoved his face so close to her that his alcohol-warmed breath rippled across her face. 'Look love, you're out of your depth. Now you listen and you listen good, no disrespect but this isn't about your kid, it's about my little girls, so you forget about Bliss and that way you won't get hurt.'

For a few seconds they just stared at each other. Then he let her arm go as he pulled a ciggie out of his pocket and made his way back to the wake. Jackie sagged against the wall as she rubbed her arm. She knew that Stan wasn't playing games. If she meddled in his business, he was telling her, point blank to her face, she was going to end up being the loser. But why would he care what she did? What was it to him? But before she could wrestle with her thoughts any more a voice quietly said, 'Nice people my family, ain't they?'

'What's a girl like you doing at a wake like this?'

Jackie stared at the man she now knew to be Flick Lewis. He was leaning in the café doorway with a half-gone cigar in his hand. Even in mourning black he looked like he was on the pull. Then she reminded herself that he was part of the Lewis family.

He hitched himself straight and moved towards her. Stopped so he wasn't crowding her too much.

'People call me Flick,' he said with a lopsided smile.

'So I've heard.' She pulled herself off the wall.

'He didn't hurt you did he? Coz I'll—'

'Work him over for me?' she finished, remembering what he'd said the day she met him with tears stinging her eyes. 'I know.'

He let out a small laugh. 'That all you going to say to me? "I know".' He mimicked her voice. 'And your name would be?'

She thought about saying 'Charlene' – she'd had enough grief from the Lewis family for one day but something about his smile made her feel it would be alright. So she told him.

'That the real colour of your hair?' Cheeky sod. That made her smile. He must've got all the charm in the family because God knows Stan didn't have none.

'I'm a mate of Marina's,' she added. Then she remembered their first encounter outside Unity Road cop shop. 'But you know what my name is, coz that time we met, you seemed to know all about my business.'

'Poor cow,' he answered, refusing to be drawn into any chat about their first encounter. 'It ain't been a great day for her, but then she should've known better than to marry into a family like this.'

'You slagging off your own people?'

'They ain't been my people for years. I'm a civilian, I ain't "involved". Although I can't claim the credit, the old man threw me out when I was fourteen years old.'

Wherever he'd gone when he'd been turfed out at such a young age must've been hard to turn his hair a premature grey. But then she looked at his expensively cut suit and hair, the gold watch on his wrist.

'So if you're not in the family business, how do you earn a living?'

He smiled. 'I'm a sportsman, you know, roulette, blackjack, poker – anything that helps keeps you fit. Although I'm a poacher turned gamekeeper these days, my last job was as a security officer at a casino in Spain. If anyone started winning heavily at a table, it was my job to stand in the background in a dickey-bow, making sure the bloke was legit. And if he was legit, of course I threw him out. There ain't much I don't know about cheating, although in a strictly professional way of course. And before that, I was teaching rich Arab kids how to play snooker in the Middle East, all the tricks of the trade. It was good money.'

'I'm sure the Lewis family would pay you more if you worked for them . . .'

He saw where she was going with her question and smiled. 'You're cute, I like you . . .' Without warning he traced his finger down one side of her cheek. Their eyes held as his finger stopped at the corner of her mouth. 'You need any help Miss Gorgeous, you come to me.'

'It's *Mrs* Gorgeous.' She stepped back so that his finger fell away.

She thought he'd laugh at that but he didn't. Instead his face remained dead serious as he said, 'Stan give you any more grief, you know whose door to come knocking at. He might frighten other people but he don't worry me, I know how to take care of plastic hard men like him.' He swaggered off, a new cigar in his mouth.

As with any chat with a member of the Lewis family, Flick Lewis had left her with more questions than answers. It wasn't like Kenny Lewis to ding out family members and it wasn't like Lewis family members to allow themselves to be dinged out, even if they were only fourteen. What on earth was that about? And now he was back. She decided to keep an eye on Flick Lewis and not just because he looked like trouble.

She shook her mind up. Right, she was out of here. A quick trip to the Ladies, then she was gone. As she made her way inside she pulled her mobile out to check with Schoolboy if he was at the ozzie. She pressed his number as she hit the loo door. Stepped inside. The line connected as she pushed one of the cubicle doors.

'You at the—?' But she never finished her sentence as she looked inside the cubicle.

The mobile nose-dived from her hand at what she saw.

'Jackie? Jackie? Jackie?' She heard Schoolboy screaming her name from the phone, but she couldn't move. She was frozen in shock. Marina was slumped on the floor with an empty pill bottle and whisky by her side.

twenty-six

If Jackie never saw the inside of a hospital again it wouldn't be a day too soon. She was the only person in the corridor anxiously awaiting news on Marina's condition. She shook her head, mind still reeling at the scene she'd found in the loo. She'd screamed, like a woman possessed, for help. And then everything had happened like some mad movie. Jackie had felt for a pulse in her neck. Barely found one, but it was there. Then she was riding in an ambulance with Marina headed for the ozzie. Stanley had refused point blank to accompany his ex.

'She got what was coming to her,' was all he said. Bastard.

A door opened flipping Jackie out of her thoughts. A female doctor walked towards her.

'How is she?'

'Alive.' The doctor shook her head. 'But she's in a very fragile condition. We need to keep her in overnight but she says she wants to go home.'

'Can I see her?'

The doctor nodded. Jackie took in a deep breath as she moved towards the room.

Marina sat on the edge of the bed looking like a wreck.

'Suppose you think I'm a stupid cow?'

'What I think you need is a slap.'

Marina's voice turned bitter. 'All I kept thinking about was him and that pregnant slut by his side. He's going to have more babies while my little'uns are dead. That ain't right. That just ain't right.'

'You've got to forget about him. If he wants to screw half the world and increase the population that's his business. And your business,' Jackie let her tone drop to soft understanding, 'is to get on with your life. Put the past way behind you. I know that ain't going to be easy, but you're going to have to do it.'

'Sorry.'

'You don't need to apologise to anyone. Ever. You've just lost the two people in the world that you love the most, so it's only natural that you're going to be looking over the edge for a while. But you can't go over it. You have to carry on living for your girls. And fuck Stanley Lewis. You hear me?'

They both looked up when the door opened. In the doorway stood Flick Lewis. Jackie got to her feet and eyed him suspiciously. What was he doing here?

As if reading her mind he remained in the doorway as he said, 'I heard what happened.' His brown gaze settled on Marina. 'Are you OK?' Now he stepped inside.

At first she bent her head, avoiding his probing eyes, most probably too ashamed. Then Jackie watched as he moved slowly across the room. For some reason she held her breath. He stopped in front of Marina. Hunkered down. Then placed the tip of his finger under Marina's chin, reminding Jackie of the time he'd done that to her near the cop shop. The pressure of his finger made Marina slowly raise her head and meet his concerned gaze. 'You haven't got anything to feel ashamed about. We all do stuff when we're under pressure. Your girls were my family, so you'll always be my family. You ever need to come to someone for help just ask for me at Nan's.'

He was good at this, Jackie thought, remembering how he'd calmed her outside the cop shop. And Marina must've thought the same because she just kept looking at him as if he'd waved a magic wand over her. Without waiting for a response he got to his feet, nodded at Jackie and left.

'Wow!' Marina said and for the first time Jackie saw some sparkle enter her eyes. 'I think I married the wrong brother.'

'I'm afraid there aren't any right brothers in that family. Why did he leave the family all those years ago?' Jackie asked as she sat back down.

Marina shrugged. 'Dunno. All I know is they never mention his name so whatever it is, must be really bad.' She turned to Jackie. 'Do you think he meant it? That I can go and see him?'

Immediately Jackie saw the wave of longing in her face. Marina was so starved for affection she'd even hang onto a member of the Lewis family. Jackie took her hand. 'If I was you I'd forget about anyone in that family. You've got to make your own way in the world now.'

For a few seconds Marina sat. Didn't answer. Then she sniffed and squeezed Jackie's hand. 'You're a good mate, you are.'

Jackie wondered if Marina would say that if she knew she was planning to visit her former father-in-law in prison tomorrow.

Thirty minutes later Jackie held another hand; her son's. She sat by his bed just watching him. As much as she'd wished it, he hadn't come out of the coma. Might never wake from the coma. She swallowed. Kept the tears held way back. She didn't hear the door open. Only saw Schoolboy on the other side of the bed a few seconds later. She watched as he took a seat. Took their son's other hand in his.

'Where's Darius?' she asked.

'Your mum and Ryan took him to the pictures.' His voice changed as he carried on speaking, but really softly. 'I shared this cell with this young guy once.' Jackie looked at him in surprise because her Schoolboy rarely spoke about his bad old days. 'He'd just been sent down from spending years in some borstal to do the rest of his stretch with us big boys. I never asked him but I heard on the grapevine that he got put away for killing two kids, cousins of his.' Jackie sucked her breath in at that. 'He never said he didn't do it, but I think there was more to his story than he was letting on. All I ever saw in his eyes was hate. Only time you didn't see it was when he dressed up for some of those plays they would put on. Who he hated I don't know, but I did know when he got out he was going to go gunning for them. I used to try playing games with him, dominoes, cards, you know, anything to try and make his hate go away; remind him that he was just a kid himself. I don't want that to happen to you Jackie babe. I don't want to see you filled with hate.'

Their gazes held. Then they both looked at their boy and prayed that he would wake up soon.

'Nan,' Flick said simply as he stood on Pinkie Lewis's doorstep.

She was in her jumbo curlers and lime green slippers. Her face split into a grin.

'Ben. Oh my boy.' She gave him a hug. His nan was the only person who ever used his birth name. Most people thought he'd got his nickname Flick because he was handy with a blade, but they were wrong. Her Ben had loved watching all those Bette Davis and Barbara Stanwyck black and white flicks with her when he was little. So the family had started calling him Flick. She pushed him back and stared at the premature grey in his brown hair. Trembling, she whispered, 'What did they do to you?'

He touched her cheek. 'I'm fine Nan.'

Pinkie sharply pulled in some air. She let her breath go as she shoved a shaky smile on her face. 'What you doing standing on the doorstep like a bottle of milk? Come on in.'

He stepped inside, his eyes immediately drawn to the closed door to a room on the right. A large palm shaped into a cross, the same ones people got from the priest on Palm Sunday, was fixed to the door. It had lost some its cream colour slightly like it had been there for years. Pinkie followed his gaze and swallowed. The silence grew as they both stared at the door. Stared at the palm. Then Pinkie let out a nervous laugh and grabbed his hand. 'Let's make you a nice brew.'

She drew him into the sitting room as she fluttered off to the kitchen. He looked around. Nan's place hadn't changed much. Still photos of the family around the room. His eyes were drawn to the one of his dad as a young boy with his younger sister, Glenda, beside him. He knew that his nan hadn't seen her daughter in years and it was all his fault.

'Can you believe it?' Pinkie said as she bustled into the room with a tray filled with a teapot covered with a red, gold and green-striped tea cosy and two mugs. 'People slugging it out at a grave.' She made a quick sign of the cross after she popped the tray on a coffee table. 'Bad luck that is, bad luck. Mind you, Stan should've known better than to let that bit of skirt he's with come anywhere near the funeral. And did you see her belly? Sticking out from here to Mile End. Thought I brought Stan up to be a gent.'

'Nan, can I kip here for a bit?'

Her face froze as her hands fluttered in front of her. 'I'm not sure. Your dad wouldn't like it . . .'

He smiled slightly, the dimple in his chin stretching. 'It's only for a couple of days until I sort out digs somewhere else.'

'You planning on staying?' Her question was incredulous.

'This is where I grew up. My mates are here. My family.'

She pulled a face. 'You ain't got no family and you ain't got no mates.'

He smiled. 'I've always got my grandmother though, eh?'

She frowned. 'I know I should've visited you—'

'Sh. That don't matter. What matters is you're here for me now.'

Pinkie touched one of the jumbo curlers in her hair as she thought about what she should do.

'Please Nan,' her grandson coaxed.

She stared at the dimple in his chin that he got from her Phil. 'Alright, son.'

He grinned as he grabbed his bag and followed her out of the room upstairs. They passed the closed room they'd been staring at earlier and entered the room next door. Small room with a single bed and plain dressing table. A wooden crucifix complete with Jesus was pinned to the wall over the bed.

He dumped his bag on the bed and gave her a gentle kiss on the cheek. 'Love you, Nan.'

Ten minutes later a tense Pinkie sat in her favourite armchair sipping her cough mixture with a book in her lap and a felt-tip pen. Benjamin was back. She did the sign of the cross quickly. She wondered if she'd gone too far. If Kenny found out Flick was dossing at her place, he wasn't going to see the funny side, that's for sure. OK, what had happened here years back was horrible, but everyone deserved a second chance. Didn't they? Especially her Flick. She was giving him one anyway. He used to be such a beautiful, gentle little boy. If only she hadn't fallen asleep that night. Hadn't taken all that cough medicine ... She shuddered as her mind slipped back ...

It was the scream that woke her. A girl's scream. Pinkie's eyes snapped open. What the hell was that? She looked around the room. Where the hell was she? Then she remembered she was in her sitting room. She felt drowsy from the cough mixture. Her tongue was all sweet and heavy. Slowly she remembered what she was meant to be doing – looking after her grandkids. She heard a noise from somewhere, but it wasn't a scream this time.

'What you lot doing?' she yelled as she forced herself straight. Her beehive slipped like a lopsided mini mountain on her head.

She pulled her skirt down as it had ridden up her thighs. Stumbled up and wobbled trying to get her balance. Someone started crying. What was going on with those kids? She'd told them to behave themselves; couldn't leave them alone for a minute without one of them putting their little mitts where it didn't belong. She staggered towards the door shouting out, 'You lot had better be behaving yourselves or you'll feel the back of my hand.'

She entered the passage. Used the palm of her hand against the wall to guide her to the room where the kids were, the large one with four bunk beds in.

She got to the room. The door was shut. Strange how silent it sounded now. Her hand circled round the door knob. Turned. Opened. That's when she saw the blood ...

Pinkie snapped out of the terrible memories as she tightened her hand desperately around her glass. If only she'd kept an eagle eye on them it might've never happened. But it had. And she'd lost Flick. Lost her daughter Glenda because of it. Lost her two other ...

That's when she heard it. The music that Flick started playing in the spare room. And her heart nearly stopped. Neil Sedaka's

'Breaking Up Is Hard To Do'. The same music that she'd been playing that long-ago night when she should've been looking after the
kids. The one song she vowed never to play ever again. Her heart
froze as Flick hiked up the volume. Her hand trembled as she put
the glass down. Picked up the book and black felt-tip pen in her
lap. Opened the book and started looking for words she would
never have wanted her great-grans to see if they were still alive.
But there was only one word that seemed to upset her every time
she read it.

Family.

She scrubbed furiously with the felt-tip every time she came
across it.

~~Family~~

~~Family~~

~~Family~~

She crossed out the fourth 'Family' as a chill settled over her as
the song came to an end. As she wondered, with horror, why Flick
had really come back.

twenty-seven

Stan watched the two men digging up the newly laid grave of his daughters. The dark was well set in and the temperature had dropped. He lifted the collar of his coat as he watched the two gravediggers work quickly. He had palmed them both five hundred each, no questions asked, and they were all his. His dad would do his nut if he knew what he was doing, but then his dad had his own problems to sort out being stuck away in Oldgate.

'Is this it?' one of the men asked, chest heaving, dragging Stan out of his thoughts.

He walked closer, peering at what the man held between two fingers. He nodded as he held out his hand. The man dropped the object into it.

Finished with them, Stan walked away leaving the men to refill the grave. Into his pocket he dropped the gold chain with the medallion of the Virgin Mary that Flick had thrown into the grave, and felt the same chain he wore around his own neck.

'I'll be honest, officer. I have got something concealed about my person. Let's see if you can find it,' Misty said cheekily the following afternoon.

The prison officer in front of Misty blushed. Jackie would've laughed her knickers off if they hadn't been standing inside the walls of Oldgate Prison. They had arrived with the rush of friends and relatives of other inmates waiting to see their nearest and dearest, while they had come to see Kenny Lewis. The prison officer's hands dropped away from Misty, realising that what her comment meant was she was no real lady (although Misty would no doubt argue with him till the cows came home that she was). The PO gave his head a single nod indicating that Misty's body search was over. She gave him a final grin with the flutter of her heavily mascaraed eyelashes and moved to join Jackie in the queue waiting to be admitted to the visiting room.

'We're meant to be keeping it low-key,' Jackie whispered. Her heart was beating like mad because if Kenny Lewis had more information about what had happened outside her boy's school that day she wanted to know about it.

Misty's grin broadened. 'Yeah, I know. Relax, it's only a prison . . .' Jackie's gaze flicked around. She'd heard tales about being in the slammer, not good ones, so she just wanted to get in and out of here as quickly as possible. 'Still can't figure out why Kenny Lewis would want to see us?'

They'd talked their way through that, along with Ollie, Anna and Roxy, for God knows how many hours last night and still hadn't come up with an answer.

Misty shrugged her shoulders as the smile died on her face. 'Well, I expect he's going to tell us.'

The inmate in their prison issues sat at tables in the large room. Two POs sat at a desk. Misty and Jackie spotted the head of the Lewis family almost immediately. Until the funeral yesterday it had been donkey's years since Misty had clocked Kenny. Last time she'd seen him had been at one of those 'community' events he liked to attend. In those days he'd liked to spread money around the estates to prove what a top bloke he was.

But it was difficult to square the man she remembered with the older guy on the other side of the visiting table. In those days he'd been a wiry looking 'face', in his trademark mohair suits, shades and cigars. Now he was plumper, greyer and looked more like a favourite uncle. But then the 'Hate' and 'War' tattooed across his knuckles and the nicks on his face reminded Misty there might still be some life in the old dog yet.

He looked up as they approached, gestured at the chairs on the other side of the table and relit his fag.

'Michael,' Kenny greeted Misty boldly, which surprised Jackie. No one, but no one, ever called Misty by her given name except her family, which must mean that the relationship between Kenny and Misty was close. But why hadn't Misty told her that before?

Jackie followed suit as Misty eased herself into a chair.

'And this is—' Misty started, looking at Jackie.

Kenny leaned back in his chair as he cut in, 'Yeah, I know. Jackie Jarvis. Her name's on the V.O. as well.'

Misty raised an eyebrow. 'Still got your ear to the ground I see.'

Kenny leaned forward as if he were telling a secret. 'You know what they say, best place to find out what's going on on the outside is on the inside.'

Misty laughed. 'You sign up for some poetry workshops in here or something?'

Misty and Kenny sniggered. Jackie's interested green eyes swung between them. These two definitely knew each other well. But how well?

Before another word could be exchanged another prisoner appeared with a tray of orange juice in plastic cups. Kenny nodded at him. He popped three cups on the table and left. To Jackie's surprise Misty slid one of the cups towards herself and straight off the table. What the heck was Misty doing? Misty opened her bag under the table and Jackie let out a startled breath as she watched Misty tip the neck of a bottle over the cup and began to fill it. The orange juice turned a deeper shade of orange. Whatever Misty was pouring she knew it wasn't Ribena. Blimey. Jackie's gaze darted towards the POs. Shit they were going to get caught. She didn't fancy spending a night inside the slammer. Calmly, Misty placed the cup back on the table and slid it towards a grinning Kenny.

'Thought you'd gone soft when you swapped your y-fronts for a pair of French frillies, but I can see I was wrong. You ain't lost your touch.' He picked the cup up and took a huge gulp. Placed it back down again as his tongue licked the corner of his lips. 'Remember that time me and you were both banged up in that place in the country and the screws used to get all misty-eyed at Christmas and let cons' families sling a bottle of something over the wall. While I got a bottle of hard liquor you got a bottle of Champers.'

'Look, Kenny,' Misty said. 'You haven't asked us in here for a trip down memory lane now have you? It's really not your style and you're far better informed about any "gossip" that's going on than we'll ever be. Now why don't you tell us what this is about?'

Kenny nodded as he took another swig of his drink. 'You're a straight talker, I've always liked that. I've got no room for bullshitters. Bullshit is time and time is money and money's what makes the world go round. You know what I mean?' He leaned across the table, 'I'll front up – I've got a business proposition. You know about my grandkids.' His brown gaze settled on Jackie. 'Sorry to hear your boy got hurt as well. Now, I know you take on the odd job every now and again with your mates. I'd like you to make some discreet enquiries about it. Talk to people, ask around, see what you can find out–'

Misty interrupted. 'You could save your money and spend it on a newspaper instead. It's all in there. There's no mysteries here Kenny. It wasn't Princess Di or Lee Harvey Oswald at the wheel; it was Paul Bliss. He's banged up. Case over.'

Kenny locked his hands together so tight that the blood drained away from them. 'See that's the thing. It weren't Bliss.'

Jackie almost jumped across the table, her heart beating with each word that stormed out of her mouth. 'What do you mean, he didn't do it?' If this man knew something different from the cops she wanted to know about it.

Jackie eased back when she felt the coolness of Misty's hand on her arm.

Kenny's voice dipped low as he continued. 'No way could it have been Bliss.'

Neither woman was able to respond at first. Then Jackie broke the silence leaning forward. 'But the cops must have some pretty kosher evidence to finger him.'

'Yeah, I'll bet they have. You see that's the problem here. Bliss is a psycho alright, but he isn't a stupid psycho.'

Jackie's mind zoomed back to the words Bliss had thrown at her after she'd tried to attack him with her iron: *And if I had done it why the fuck would I come here?* Now Kenny Lewis was piling more doubt in her mind.

'So you think someone's stitched him up?' Misty asked, pulling Jackie out of her tumbling thoughts.

'I'm saying I *know* but I ain't got proof.' Kenny unwrapped his hands and placed them flat on the table. 'Look, say it was me who did it, the fucking first thing I'd do is get rid of the motor. You know, get rid of the evidence.'

Jackie shook her head in confusion. 'Maybe he got careless. He's been in the game a long time.'

Kenny laughed, this time with not a lick of humour. 'He's not a careless psycho either. He'd be long gone if he was. He's a crafty bugger who runs his firm with an iron rod. So why would he just leave the motor for anyone to find? Then there's the whole thing in the round. Bliss runs down my kids by accident? That's quite a coincidence. He runs them down deliberately? Why would he do that? From what I hear he's a man on his way up so why do something as crazy as this in broad daylight?'

Jackie slumped back in her seat. What he was saying all made sense, but her mind was finding it hard to deal with. The idea that whoever hurt her boy, killed those girls, was still walking it large around London was enough to send her over the edge.

As if reading her thoughts Kenny looked directly at her. 'I loved those girls just like I know you love your boy. But how are *we both* going to feel years later if it comes out that Bliss never done it? That some other fucker managed to get away with it?'

That made Jackie sit back. 'What makes you so sure?'

Misty added, 'Maybe he did it for revenge. Stan and Bliss, from what I hear it was always going to kick off. They're constantly on each other's toes. So maybe Bliss just took some revenge.'

'That's true about Stan and Bliss. But killing kids isn't revenge. Flying a "Paul Bliss Done It" banner from your own car isn't revenge. That's a set-up, that is.'

'Maybe you should let the cops sort it.' Even Jackie gasped at Misty's comment.

Kenny shook his head. 'They've got someone already – you said yourself all the boxes have been ticked evidence-wise. I'm just asking you to snoop around and ask a few questions that's all.' His gaze settled on Jackie. 'You want to know for sure they've got the right bloke banged up. You want justice the same way I do.'

Jackie looked back at him, her breathing becoming unsteady. It had to be Bliss didn't it? The cops wouldn't have got it that wrong? But what if . . .

'Why don't you get Stan to do it?' Jackie shoved out, jumping out of her muddled thoughts. 'He's in charge while you're away, isn't he? He's got loads of soldiers on the streets? Why don't you get them on the case? Plus he warned me at the funeral to keep my nose well and truly out of it.'

He let out a long sigh. 'Ah yeah – my boy. Thing is, Stan's a bit urgent isn't he? He don't do discreet – he does punch ups and shootings. And of course, no one will want to say anything off-colour to him, what with him being the father and everything. This younger generation don't understand the old ways of the under-world. Always scrapping to get what they want rather than mending bridges over a pint. Plus which, people prefer talking to women don't they? It's the mother thing . . .'

Misty looked into his eyes. 'Why us?'

'Jackie needs answers the same way I do. Plus you know people don't you? You've got a contacts book. I hear you're smart and you're female. That's enough for me.' He leaned closer. 'So you up for it?'

'And all we've got to do is drop a question or two around and report back to you?' Misty asked.

'Yeah. That simple. I'll make it worth your while, I'm good for it, you know that. But if you take the job on, there's one thing you need to be clear about – the big thing here is "discreet", you know? I don't want anyone finding out that I'm paying the bills. Not the cops, not Bliss and definitely not my boy Stan. You get me?'

Jackie leaned forward. 'And if we find out that it ain't Bliss?'

Kenny just smiled as he drained the last of the 'orange' juice from his cup.

'So are we going to do it?'

Jackie's question hung in the air as she sat next to Misty on the Victoria Line train. It wasn't rush hour but the train was packed, no doubt with people heading for the summer sales on Oxford Street.

'We said so, didn't we. Anyway, if he's right, we've still got to find the driver who nearly killed your kid,' Misty snapped.

'Do you think he's right?'

'I don't know. You can't tell with old man Lewis, he juggles so many balls at a time, even he's not sure how many he's got up there. We need to be careful.'

Jackie rolled her eyes at her friend's response. As soon as they'd left the prison, Misty's mood had changed and she hadn't uttered a word to Jackie on the way back to the Tube.

'What's up?' Jackie finally asked.

Instead of answering Misty pulled out the bottle from her bag. A Lucozade bottle filled with dark brown liquid. She tipped the bottle to her mouth as Jackie's gaze settled on the 'no alcohol permitted' sign on the window opposite.

Misty shoved the bottle back in her bag as she finally spoke. 'Don't get me wrong, Kenny's an alright sort of bloke. But his family are fucking out of their tree. He should've sorted that bloody son of his out years ago.' Misty's grey gaze intensified as she looked at Jackie. 'I know you want to find out for sure if Bliss did it, but I'm not sure we should get mixed up with the Lewises.'

Jackie let her words settle over her. 'I know, but this might be my chance to find out what really happened to Preston. If that means I've got to hook up with Kenny Lewis, then that's the way it's going to be.'

They changed trains at Kings Cross and for the rest of the journey they didn't speak, just sank into their own thoughts. As they took the exit stairs at Whitechapel station, heading back to the hospital, Jackie's mobile pinged. Text message.

She checked it out as they hit ground level and entered the
bustle of Whitechapel market. She stopped dead after reading it.

'Who was it?'

Jackie looked up. 'Ricky Smart. He wants to see me down the
nick.'

'Right, I'll call the others and tell them to meet us at *Miss
Josephine*. Whatever Ricky wants make sure you pump him for as
much info as you can.'

twenty-eight

This time Ricky saw Jackie in his office. They both had a mug of strong coffee. Jackie had never been inside his office before. Because she didn't want her Daisy marrying him she'd convinced herself that his place of work would be a right old tip. But she was wrong. It was neat, everything in order.

'Ryan still keeping his fingernails clean?' Ricky asked.

She blushed. She still felt embarrassed about what Ryan had been nabbed for and knew she owed Ricky one. And she didn't like owing Ricky a thing. 'You didn't ask me down here to find out about my boy.'

Ricky cupped the warm mug. 'No, you're right I didn't. You wanted me to keep you informed of what was going on and I'm doing that because you're the parent of one of the other victims involved in this.'

Jackie smirked. 'Did Daisy tell you to be a bit nicer to me?'

Ricky didn't answer, but the slight twist of his lips told her she was right. 'Bliss is denying he had anything to do with it.'

'I'm sure he is,' Jackie answered. 'Bliss is from the "never complain, never explain" end of the underworld.'

'You don't like me do you?' His words steered their conversation into another direction, surprising her.

She could've lied to him for her adopted daughter's sake but she didn't. 'No. I don't. Is that a problem?'

His handsome brown face split into an easy smile. 'No. Is it just because I'm the law?'

'I ain't going to deny it, that's not helping.' But then she thought better of getting into the reasons why she didn't like him. 'So tell me, what's Bliss's story?'

Ricky's hands left the mug as he settled back in his seat and pulled the file on the desk in front of him. He opened it and scanned the contents. Looked back up at her. 'We found the car that did it in a garage on the Mountjoy Estate, which I'm sure you know everyone says Bliss controls. His prints were all over it. Short of having his name tattooed on the car he did it. There's ID evidence, although . . .' He didn't finish. '. . . It all adds up. I don't buy his alibi . . .'

The freckles on her face twitched as she frowned. 'Which is?'

'Claims to have lost the car in a card game . . .'

'Where?'

'Down his club.'

'His club?' The skin above her eyebrows wrinkled. 'Do you mean The Five Fingers?'

'I'm not telling you that. Look it up in the underworld section of the Yellow Pages.'

'Who won his car in the game?' Ricky just smiled at that. She ploughed on. 'Has he got any witnesses?'

'He gave us some names. Only a couple of them have given statements. The rest "can't remember". They obviously decided with lynch mobs running around, they'd take their chances with Bliss.'

'So he has got some witnesses?'

Ricky twisted his mouth. 'Yeah. And I expect Al Capone's accountant gave a statement on his tax return. They're Bliss's people, so they will back him up won't they? Don't worry about them, a decent brief will leave their bones in the witness stand. So there's no need for you to turn amateur detective here. He's guilty.'

But Jackie pressed on. 'What's the gossip at his club?'

Wearily he answered. 'Plain truth is, Jackie, the Met is suffering just like the rest of the public sector with all these budget cuts. So there's no cash, not even coppers, left in the till to pay overtime for my people to go and hang out listening to what his people are saying about what he's saying about it. Plus I don't care. If his legal team have got any actual evidence to support his case, they know where to find me.'

The door half opened and Sonny Begum popped her head around the corner. 'Sorry, Guv. Can I have a word?'

Ricky sighed as he stood up. 'I'll be back in a mo,' he told Jackie.

Jackie alone, her eyes fixed on the open file on Ricky's desk. She looked back at the door. Back at the file. Back at the door. Then leapt up and around the desk. Quickly she scanned down the sheet that Ricky had been reading, looking for the name of the club. Her gaze slammed to a halt when she found it. She'd been right, it *was* The Five Fingers, Bethnal Green Road. This was her chance to look through the rest of the file. Her head tipped up to look back at the door. She knew she was taking a chance. What if he walked back in on her? What if . . . ? Her fingers got stuck into the file as she flicked pages scanning for information. Stopped when she came across a name she knew:

Witness: Scott Miller.

Scott Miller? Scott Miller? Now where had she heard that name before? Her mind lit up when she remembered. Scott was the Chair of Governors at the school and had been there that day, calling the ambulance with his son by his side. Yeah, that was right, his son was in her boys' class. She carried on reading. Scott had been the witness who had taken down the car's number plate.

The door started opening. Jackie dashed towards the window. Relaxed her body as if she'd been looking outside.

'Sorry about that,' Ricky said.

Heart thumping like crazy Jackie casually twisted around. 'I suppose his brief will be looking into the club?' She knew she had to say something to distract him from the fact she was now standing up.

'I dunno if Daisy's . . .'

Jackie froze. No way, she couldn't have been hearing right. 'Daisy?'

'Shit.' The harshness of the word hit the room as Ricky shook his head.

'You ain't telling me that my Daisy is defending that scumbag?' Jackie moved forward angrily.

Ricky waved his hands at her. 'Look I thought she'd told you.'

Without another word she stormed out of the room. She bolted outside, her face red with fury. How could Daisy do that to her? Do that to Preston?

It took Jackie thirty minutes to get from Hackney to High Holborn. She entered the offices of Curtis and Hopkirk's law firm and pulled out her mobile. Tapped in a number.

'Get your arse down to the reception right now.' She cut the call and began pacing.

After a while she heard a voice call out, 'Can I help you?' She turned to find the smartly dressed receptionist looking at her with a frown on her face.

Mind your own sodding business was what she really wanted to say, but she didn't. Instead she shot the woman a tight smile and replied, 'Just waiting for someone, love.'

'It's OK,' a calm voice interrupted. Jackie and the receptionist both turned in the direction of the voice. Daisy stood by the lift, in a nicely fitted light blue skirt suit, her thick black hair hanging loose to her shoulders. Her heels clipped against the tiled floor as she walked towards her adoptive mum. She leaned over and kissed Jackie on the cheek. Then calmly said, 'I take it you've found out that I'm representing Paul Bliss.'

In a hurt voice Jackie responded, 'How can you do that to Preston?'

Daisy gently took Jackie's arm and led her to a couple of over-sized black easy chairs in a corner next to a large palm plant. Jackie was still hopping mad and didn't fancy sitting down but she did because she knew that Daisy had a reputation to keep and didn't want to make a show of her at work.

Daisy's intense blue eyes, which never failed to remind Jackie of her adopted daughter's long-dead gangster dad Frankie Sullivan, held her own. 'I know I should've told you but I thought you had enough on your plate already.'

Jackie sniffed. Bloody hell, she felt like booing. 'I don't want you anywhere near this case.'

Daisy stretched over and placed her palm on Jackie's knee. 'I know. That's one of the reasons I didn't tell you because I knew you would just worry yourself to death.'

'Can't you get one of the other briefs to do it?'

'I've been defending Bliss for a long time. He trusts me.' She removed her hand from Jackie's knee and meshed her lips together like she was carefully considering her next words. 'And I really believe that he didn't do it.'

'Why?'

Daisy shuffled to the edge of the seat. 'I know I need hard evidence but believe me, he's not stupid and he's not insane.'

Kenny had said the same thing, Jackie thought. Daisy carried on. 'There's loads more going on here and I intend to find out what it is.'

'The cops aren't making enquiries down the club, they've only done the minimum with the names Bliss put up.' Seeing the amazement in Daisy's face, Jackie added. 'Ricky just told me.'

Daisy's voice rose slightly. 'He shouldn't be doing that.'

Now it was Jackie's turn to place her hand on the younger woman's knee. As much as she didn't like Ricky she didn't want to cause trouble between them. Daisy had had enough trouble in her life to last anyone a lifetime. 'He wanted to fit me up with one of them family liaison officers but I wouldn't have it. Any information I wanted comes straight from him. So he's just telling me what he knows.'

Suddenly Daisy grinned. 'Sounds like you're starting to like him a bit more.'

'Yeah, when I'm in my grave, girl.' But Jackie grinned back.

Daisy's teeth pinched her lip as a wistful look covered her face. 'Well you better start getting to like him because . . .' She smiled. 'Jackie can you keep a secret?'

Why the hell was Daisy behaving so strangely? Shit, Jackie hoped she wasn't in trouble. Jackie's eyes darted around making sure no one was watching them. Then she whispered, 'You ain't in trouble?'

'Trouble.' Now Daisy openly laughed. 'Yes I think I'm in big trouble.'

Jackie grasped Daisy's hand tight. 'Tell me.'

Daisy's hand moved gently to her tummy. 'I think I'm pregnant.'

Jackie's jaw dropped. Pregnant? A baby? Her Daisy? Jackie just looked at her, incapable of speech. Then she remembered Daisy puking up her guts at the ozzie the first time she'd come to see Preston. Jackie wrapped her into a mother-lovin' hug. 'Oh my girl,' she whispered. 'Me a gran?'

Between fits of tiny laughter Daisy pulled away. 'I'm not sure yet, so just between me and you for now.'

Jackie nodded back. But Jackie couldn't help staring at Daisy. Who would've thought the sad girl who'd come to live with her when she was fifteen might now become a mum? Mind you, she knew that having a family had always been important to Daisy. As if it were her way of proving to the world that she had risen above being the daughter of one of London's once most dangerous men.

Suddenly, Daisy jumped to her feet when a young woman came into the building. 'That's one of my clients. Got to go.' She blew Jackie a kiss. 'Love you,' she mouthed.

Jackie watched her go, the sunny feelings inside her disappearing as she thought about Daisy being Bliss's brief. She already had one kid in hospital and now she had to worry about another. She prayed hard that defending Bliss wasn't going to bring a wagonload of grief to Daisy's door.

Darius knew he should be at school, but he wasn't. He'd done a bunk during afternoon playtime because he wanted to see his brother. He knew he would be missed at school by now and that there would be hell to pay but he didn't give two bollocks about what grown-ups thought about him any more. Not after one of them had killed his Molly. Done his brother. Plus all his mum and dad did these days was argue morning, noon and night. He hated them all. All he wanted to do was spend time with his twin.

Clutching his Arsenal rucksack he peeped his small head around the corner of the hospital ward checking who was around because he needed to get to Preston's room without anyone seeing him. He spotted a nurse at the desk laughing with a man in a white coat, who he figured must be a doctor, and some old guy moving slowly as he clutched tight to some metal-shaped frame in front of him. He jerked his head back. No way could he get to the room without being seen. His fingers twisted into the handle of his bag. What was he going to do? He shoved his head back. Almost danced with joy when he saw that the nurse and doctor were gone and only the old man remained. He skipped out of the corner and rushed down the corridor. Clipped the old man as he passed.

'Kids these days,' the man muttered. 'No bloody manners . . .' Grumpy old sod, Darius thought as the man's words drifted away in the distance and he hit Preston's room. He rushed inside and closed the door. His heart squeezed painfully when he looked at his twin. Tubes coming out of him and his eyes shut. Looked like he was a goner for sure. Darius walked slowly to the side of the bed as the tears rolled down his face. What was he going to do if Preston never opened his eyes again? Who was he going to play footie with? Who was he going to argue with who got to choose which cereal they ate in the morning? Who was he going to snuggle down with when he had those nightmares?

'Pressie?' he said softly, using the name only he ever called his brother. 'I brought your Arsenal scarf.' He couldn't believe that neither his mum nor dad had brought it to the ozzie. Didn't they know that Pressie slept with it every night under his pillow?

'The Gunners were shit last night,' he carried on softly as he pulled the scarf out of his bag. 'Got beat 3 nil by Man U.' He sniffed.

He wanted to put the scarf under Pressie's pillow, but he was frightened to touch him. Say something went wrong? So instead he moved to the foot of the bed and tied the scarf around the corner of the metal bed frame. Then he moved back and stared inside the open bag. Stared at his and Molly's secret. He looked heavenward, closed his eyes and prayed:

'I know you took Molly because of what me and her did. I know it was bad, God, but we were only playing. But Pressie never had anything to do with it. He never. I'll put it back if you wake him up. I swear I will . . .'

Abruptly he stopped speaking when he heard hard footsteps coming down the corridor. Quickly he dived under the bed. His heart beat like he was watching Arsenal score a goal. Then the door started to open.

twenty-nine

'It wasn't your fault you ended up forced to work in a brothel.'

Daisy's passionate statement hung in the air as she looked at the terrified young woman in her office. The same client who had arrived as she sat talking with Jackie downstairs. Small and fragile, with dull blue eyes that looked down most of the time and a long-sleeved sweatshirt, Daisy guessed to hide the scars she suspected she had on her arms. Scars that were from either self-harming or track marks, whichever they were this girl had been to hell and back. She said her name was Kate, but Daisy thought it was most probably really something like Katerina, a popular Ukrainian name. She'd run away from a brothel, ended up at a women's refuge battered and bleeding. She wouldn't go to the police. What she wanted Daisy to help her do was to be able to stay in this country legally. Daisy did a spot of work for the refuge free of charge, but she explained to Kate that she would be better able to help her with her application to remain in the country if she knew which brothel she'd been forced to work in. But Kate wasn't telling. So Daisy tried again now.

Kate just stared back, her eyes brimming with shame. That made Daisy angry, really angry. Sometimes she wondered if some men even thought about women as human beings. She'd met women who'd been forced into prostitution before and it wasn't a pretty sight. The things she'd heard had turned her stomach. Still turned her stomach. And now one of these poor women – no, girls – was sitting in front of her again too terrified to say where she'd been brutalised.

'I need to be able to present a good case for you being able to stay in this country. One of the best ways for me to do that is for me to know—'

Kate rapidly shook her head.

'OK, OK,' Daisy said repeatedly to put her back at ease. But it wasn't OK, and if it was the last thing she did she was going to find that brothel to make sure the men who ran it were punished. All she knew was that it was in East London somewhere and from the sounds of things it was one of those underground ones specialising in certain tastes with a very select clientele so no advertising itself in phone booths. It was going to be tough to find but she knew the exact women who could help her.

A knock at her door drew her out of her thoughts. The door opened showing one of her assistants. Lovely girl, black and eager to learn her trade well.

'Just to let you know that in about an hour I'm off to the . . .' She looked at Kate. 'You know.'

Yes, Daisy did know. Paul Bliss's club to check out his alibi.

She knew she should tell him. Pinkie Lewis's hand hovered over the phone. Her Kenny had a right to know that Flick was stopping with her. But she knew he'd go postal when she told him. No one, absolutely no one, he'd told the family years ago, was to mention Flick's name ever again. If they ever saw him coming down the street they were to cross the road. If he ever called them, slam the phone down. If he ever turned up on their doorstep they should shut the door in his face. She couldn't blame Kenny, what Flick had done was terrible, but he was still her favourite grandkid. Stan didn't have a patch on him. Growing up, Stan was always lying, keeping secrets, while Flick, well the girls loved him to bits, he always helped the old folks in her block carry their shopping. But most of all Flick loved to read. She'd take him down to Whitechapel library with her every month and that boy couldn't get enough of the books. *Treasure Island* had been his favourite written by that bloke . . . oh, what was his name, oh yeah, Stevenson. He'd make her laugh when he did his Long John Silver impression. 'Aye, aye, Captain.'

No, she loved that boy and if he wanted to stop with her that was her business. If Kenny wanted to blow off steam let him. Flick had been punished for what he'd done and now the slate should be clean.

Mind made up she stepped back from the phone and almost jumped out of her woolly socks when she saw Flick standing behind her. He stood there, the shirt he'd slept in open and his grey-brown hair topsy-turvy and it should've reminded her of the boy he'd once been. But there was something about the way he was bent over her, the way his eyes looked at her, that made her feel unsettled. Instinctively she stepped back and clutched her fingers into her silk dressing gown. For the first time she admitted to herself that she was frightened of her grandson.

Flick's gaze stopped on her fingers in her gown. He stepped back as he softly said, 'Nan, if you want me to find somewhere else to rest my weary head ...'

Her hand fell from her clothing. 'No. It's just ...' Her hands fluttered in the air. 'I'm worried what your dad's going to do if you stay with me.' She rushed on. 'I'm not worried for myself, it's you.'

His fingers touched her cheek. 'Don't fret about me Nan, I've been looking after myself for years now ...'

'We should've been the ones looking after you ...'

His fingers stopped moving as his eyes widened slightly. 'You never told anyone ...'

'No.'

'Let's keep it that way.'

'But we should've told the truth. I should've told Kenny the truth.'

For a moment there was silence. 'We did what we had to do. Now it's over with we need to look forward to the rest of our lives.' His huge smile suddenly sprang back to his lips. 'I'm off for a shower.' His head moved closer to her face and he whispered, 'Then I'm going to smell all nice like little boys should for their grandma.'

He left her standing as he laughed. She headed for the kitchen and found the cupboard that she kept her cough medicine in. Three bottles of cough mixture. She pulled down the first one she came to. Blackcurrant flavour. She didn't even look for a glass just tipped it back to her mouth. And swallowed. Ten minutes later she was singing her heart out as she cleaned around the place with her Henry Hoover feeling as happy as the vacuum cleaner's smiling painted-on face. She did the sitting room; her bedroom; Flick's bedroom and ... she nearly tumbled over her little round Henry when she got back to the passage. Flick was coming out of *the* room. The one she always kept locked. He stopped when he saw her.

'What you doing?' Her voice wobbled.

'Just thought I'd swap rooms.'

Henry's hose toppled from her hand. 'But you can't—'

She never finished because Flick turned back around and slammed the door, leaving her to stare in a daze at the cross-shaped palm on it. Shut her out. Then the music started behind the closed door – 'Breaking Up Is Hard To Do'.

Pinkie stood there in shock, with the Hoover's smiling face touching her leg as she stared at the door of the room no one had been inside for sixteen years.

Marina Lewis clutched the bloodstained picture her daughter had drawn with one hand and popped a happy pill with the other. She had a mega hangover from last night after she'd left the ozzie. So what, she'd tried to top herself, it weren't the first time. She hadn't even had a wash this morning and still wore the same clothes she'd been to the funeral in. Didn't have a clue how long she'd been sat in the sitting room. Could've been hours, might've been minutes. Who the frickin' hell knew? And who cared? Coz she didn't. Her babies were gone. Her little angels ...

The pain sliced through her. It felt like only yesterday that her little girls were being born and she was holding them snug and safe in her arms. And their dad had been beaming down at them with such pride. She looked at the picture Minnie had done as the happy pill began to smooth out her smashed-up nerves. She felt like screwing up the picture. And why? Because it was a drawing of him. Stan. She hadn't always felt that he was a class A prick. Oh no, back in the day when she'd first met him he'd been a complete gent, buying her flowers, taking her around town, snorting Charlie together. She'd been a pole dancer back then in one of his dad's clubs and yeah she was the first to admit that she'd seen a lot of life from the viewpoint of her back. But anything had been better than living with her mum and sister. She told most people that her mum was an alkie and her sister a crackhead, but the truth was much worse than that – they were religious nuts. Shoving the Bible down her throat every second they got; showing her up as they preached damnation down Petticoat Lane market. She'd cut out of there as soon as she'd hit sixteen. Found the one man who was going to be her salvation, but he'd turned his back on her after she'd given him her all. So she'd settled on Stan and what a total mistake that had been. Once he got his ring on her finger she'd found out about his string of tarts. She'd stood up to him a time or two and got a couple of black eyes for her troubles. Yeah, Stan had proved himself to be a total HERO. Bullying bastard.

Her mournful thoughts were interrupted by a knock at the front door. More like a pounding really. Who the heck? She hoped it weren't that ugly, old witch Pinkie Lewis. She'd had a bellyful of her yesterday, wagging her finger in her face reminding her of how us Lewises behave when they bury one of their own. The fist at the door banged away again. This time she got up. Placed Minnie's picture carefully on the low-level glass table in the middle of the room. As she moved, her head started thumping.

'Keep your thong on,' she yelled.

She opened the door to find the last person she wanted to see – Stan. Sporting his trademark D&G shades and a mean look on his face. Without a word he barged past her. She swayed. What the . . . ? He didn't have no right to come into her place. No fucking right at all.

'Get out!' she roared, not even bothering to shut the door. Let the whole fucking world hear, she didn't care.

'Stupid, stupid, stupid cow,' he slung back, remaining in the hallway. 'Look at you.' His eyes raked over her as his mouth curled in disgust. 'You're a friggin' mess. My girls would be alive if I'd got custody.' He'd been as pissed as hell, him and his dad, that the

Judge had given her the kids with him only having weekend visitation rights.

'Well if you hadn't knocked me around so much you might've stood a chance.'

'They were my kids . . .' She just laughed at that. A nasty laugh that almost pushed her former husband over the edge. But Stan kept a tight hold over his control because he'd come up here to make sure he had the last laugh.

He swaggered up to her. 'Just wanted to share my good news with you. Of course, I've known about it for months.' Marina stared back at him with bewildered eyes. He shoved his hand inside the top pocket of his jean jacket. Pulled something out and threw it on the floor. Looked like a photo.

He took a step closer as her eyes remained on the thing on the floor. 'It's the one thing you could never give me.' He shoved his face into her. 'A boy.' She pushed her head back as if his hot breath had left acid on her skin.

Then with a nasty laugh he brushed past her and was gone.

A boy? What the heck did he mean? She scrambled onto her knees and picked up the piece of paper. It was a photo but she couldn't make out what it was at first. It was all fuzzy, it didn't make sense. Then it hit her what it was. An ultrasound photo of Stan's and that trollop Tiffany's baby. A boy. She started sobbing as if she were going to die. She didn't think she could feel more pain but she did. Stan was going to have another family while the only family she would ever have she'd buried yesterday.

The Regents Canal near Vicky Park was silent except for the major ding-dong going on inside one of the houseboats.

'I say we don't go anywhere near this,' Anna growled.

'And *I* say we do.'

Jackie's reply shook the boat. *Miss Josephine* was Misty's old houseboat. The furnishings inside the cabin were cheery, with a few pot plants scattered around and a few knick-knacks that had seen better days but were filled with Misty's memories. The others loved the boat as well. Without *Miss Josephine* they didn't know what would have happened to them all those years ago when they did one from local authority care. *Miss Josephine* was also the place they ran their Ladybird 'cleaning' company from rather than the club.

Jackie stood, hands on hips, facing Anna. They looked like they were ready to slug it out in the ring. Misty and Ollie sat in comfy chairs while Roxy sat at her usual spot beside the wireless laptop.

'Ding, ding,' Misty interrupted dramatically. 'Both of you need to calm down and park your arses down.'

Anna flicked her hair back and walked her long legs with a huff back to the cane wicker chair opposite Misty's. She picked up her rum and coke. Jackie dropped down to the green fluffy rug and crossed her legs.

'Anna might have a point,' Roxy said in her squeaky voice. Her buttermilk bob looked slightly lifeless today and her plump, homely cheeks were stained red.

Jackie snorted. 'All he wants us to do is ask around about who might have done it. Nothing heavy. Just a question here and there. You're all forgetting that my son is also lying in a coma because of this.'

'But the Lewis gang are a crazy crew, aren't they Misty?' Roxy carried on.

The others all looked at the woman sat by the door that led to the small kitchen. Misty had kicked her heels off and wore one of those long, Gypsy-style, colourful patchwork skirts that had come back into fashion. She was a brunette today with just a touch of mauve eyeshadow that set off the lightness of her grey eyes. 'Yeah, Stan and his dad ain't the type of people you ask to head up a neighbourhood watch, but it don't matter what you think, Jackie gave Kenny her word and there ain't any way in hell she can go back on it.'

Anna reared forward, her brown face darkening in rage. 'You didn't have no right to do that before you ran it past the rest of us.'

Jackie's face grew pink. Anna was spot on. They never took on anything without a majority vote. 'Look, it's no big deal . . .'

'So what do you know about the Lewis family?' Roxy asked Misty.

Misty wriggled her toes. 'Me and my brothers knocked around with Kenny when we were growing up. Even did a couple of jobs together. I shared a cell with him one time years ago.' That raised everyone's eyebrows. 'Whereas my brothers went all legit, Kenny decided that he was going to become one of the hardest nuts around. The way I hear it there ain't much that he ain't into. And the family weren't none too pleased when Stan took up with Marina ...'

'How come?' It was Jackie who asked this time.

'Thought she was a bit of a slag. She was some sort of dancer when Stanley met her working at one of his dad's clubs.'

'Dancer?'

'Yeah, we're talking poles and I don't mean the sort of Poles who make very good plumbers either. They wouldn't have minded if he kept her as a bit of slap and tickle on the side, but to take her down the aisle was taking it too far. But Kenny loved those kids.'

'And Stanley?' Anna asked.

'Thug, pure and simple. The sort who thinks brains are for wimps. No one, not even his old man, can make him keep it under control. There was a story doing the rounds last year about some poor sod who accidentally ran over his daughters' puppy. Next thing ...' She raised her plucked eyebrows. 'He disappears ...'

'Jackie.' Anna swung her head from side to side. 'We ain't def doing this, you get me?'

'We've given our word and we can't go back,' Misty threw in. Anna swore, then finished the last of her drink. For a while there was silence, the only sounds the lapping water and kids screaming their heads off in Victoria Park.

'So,' Misty broke the silence. 'Did you find out anything from Ricky?'

Jackie swiped a couple of nibbles that Misty had put out on the table as she spoke. 'Ricky-boy is convinced Bliss did it. As far as he's concerned that's it, game over. While Kenny's saying it all smells like some set-up. Or maybe it's the other way round, you can never tell with them people. So what do you think?' She popped some nuts into her mouth and munched away.

'He might have a point,' Anna said leaning back in her chair. 'If you did something that bad, you'd "wear gloves" wouldn't you? A kid on his first burglary wouldn't be that careless.'

'Unless someone's playing a longer game here,' Jackie said.

'It'd have to be a fucking long game . . .' Misty added shaking her head.

'But what if he weren't thinking straight?' Roxy chipped in. 'What if all of a sudden he realises what he's done and he gets scared. Maybe he was drinking.' Her eyes dipped down. 'Back in the days when I used to have a glass or two, I couldn't remember what I'd done half of the time.'

They all remembered those days too. Roxy pissed out of her head trying to run away from the troubles in her life.

Misty unwound her legs from her soft chair and stretched them out in front of her. 'We don't need to dot the i's, all Kenny wants is some asking around, that's all.' She didn't include herself in this because the others knew she always said she was too old to run around town. Besides, she just liked being at the club. 'Then if no one knows nothing we just go back to him. Simple.'

'And what about you?' Anna looked up at Jackie. 'Think you can handle this?'

Jackie looked affronted. ''Course I can. Why wouldn't I?'

'No need to jump out of your three-wheeler pram babe,' Anna shot back. 'I'm just saying if we find out it was someone else you can't go around bashing them up with a steam iron, you get me?'

Jackie frowned. 'I know. That was a stupid thing to do, but I ain't saying this ain't personal because it is. That's my kid lying up there in Whitechapel and I'm going to do justice by him.'

'So where do we start?' Roxy asked.

Jackie leaned her elbows onto her knees as she sat forward. 'The Five Finger Club . . .'

But she got no further because Misty swore. 'You on LSD or what? We can't go there.'

'Why not?' It was Roxy this time.

'It's bloody dangerous that's why. That's where Bliss and his crew hang out. We can't go to that place. Piss someone off down there and you don't get chucked out on the street and banned, you turn up in the river instead. Or more likely several rivers.'

The women flinched, except for Ollie. Jackie stared at her suddenly realising that Ollie hadn't spoken a word. She wore black jeans, trainers and a turquoise T-Shirt, nothing flash, and her short afro was out of shape as if she'd run her fingers through it one too many times. She couldn't see her friend's eyes properly behind her thick-framed glasses but the way her mouth was fixed told Jackie that she was lost in her own thoughts.

'Ollie, you alright?' she asked gently.

She peered at Jackie, her dark face tinged with a touch of grey. 'Dealing with the death of children is never easy.'

They all knew, without having to ask, that she was thinking about her time as a child soldier in Africa. About the terrible things she had been made to do. Jackie got up and moved towards her. Dropped onto the arm of Ollie's chair and slid her arm around her. 'You don't have to do this,' Jackie said quietly.

'Yes I do. I have to make up for every child I killed.'

The others sucked in their breaths. Of all the people to answer it was Roxy, who was usually full of a lot of empty-headed chat. 'You've paid the price for something that wasn't your fault a long time ago. Where would all those refugee kids you help at your centres be now without you? Do this for those girls' mum. Do this for Jackie.'

Ollie punched her fingers through her short Afro. Then she nodded. Jackie gave her shoulder a gentle squeeze before she went back to her spot on the rug. She hit the cashew nuts again as she talked. 'I found out something else in Ricky's office. One of the dads at school, Scott Miller, who is also the chair of the school's governing body, was the one who took down the number plate and called the ambulance. I think I should pay him a visit, he might've seen something else.' They all nodded at that. 'And of course there's Flick?'

'Who?' Ollie finally joined in the discussion.

'Ben "Flick" Lewis. The black sheep. The eldest son. He left the family when he was fourteen. Something happened. What, I don't know.' She swung her eyes to Misty as she carried on. 'But I know someone who I think does.' Misty pressed her raspberry-painted lips together. 'Come on Misty, I know you ain't telling me all you know.'

Misty rubbed her lips together for a bit, then unlocked them. 'All I know is that something happened one night at Pinkie Lewis's place years back. After that no one saw Flick again until yesterday.'

'Do you know what happened?' Jackie pressed on.

Misty shrugged her shoulders. 'Nope. But whatever it was, was bad. Kenny loved that boy like you wouldn't believe and now . . .' She shook her head, her grey eyes sad. 'Now Kenny don't allow no one to mention Flick's name.'

'So what's he doing back now?' Anna chipped in.

'I don't know. But it won't be to look up old friends. He's still a Lewis.'

'Roxy,' Jackie said. 'Get Googling girl, see what you can find out, any stories linked to the Lewises. Something might pop up about Flick.' Suddenly she got to her feet. Tucked her hand in her pocket and pulled out a fag. Lit up. Took a couple of deep lugs of smoke into her lungs. Then she looked at the others and said, 'Alright, this is what we're going to do . . .' But before she could finish, her mobile went. She pulled it out. Took the call. 'What?' She started breathing hard. Her face was bright red when she finished the call.

'What's up?' Anna asked.

All Jackie said was, 'I'm going to murder him.'

thirty

The happiness fell from Roxy's face as soon as the others were gone. Her mates would be shocked to see her expression now, after all she was always the joy-jumping, life's-gonna-be-hunky-dory one. At least that's what they thought. She didn't touch the computer. Instead she just sat still, listening and waited a good minute before she moved. She dashed to the main window to check that the others were gone. With a sigh of relief she headed for her large black bag resting on the arm of the computer chair. As she pulled it off she sat down. Opened it and pulled out a large bottle of cherry-flavoured vodka she got from that new Polish shop on the high street near her home. The others, especially Jackie, would wring her neck if they saw her with it. She'd had a bad drink problem a few years back. Couldn't get out of bed until she had a slug from the bottle she'd kept hidden in the bedside cabinet. Couldn't get through a day with that bastard she'd once been married to who used his fists on her like it was his daily exercise routine. The others had helped sort out the screw-up she'd made of her life – get a divorce and sort her drinking out. Supported her through her trips to AA meetings until she hadn't had a drink for a good two years. Then the loneliness had got her. Coming home every day to an empty house, not even a dog or cat to greet her at the door. And when it got really bad she'd start thinking that even coming home to a faceful of her ex-husband's fist would be better than this killing loneliness. She had tried, really tried to stay dry. She'd tried everything – hypnosis, counselling, the three-step programme, the ten-step programme, every programme known to man, but she hadn't been able to stay away. Finally, on one of those lonely nights, with just *Coronation Street* for company, she'd hit the bottle again. Kept up her routine of being the dizzy, giggling, chatterbox of the group so the others didn't twig that anything was wrong.

Now she greedily tilted the bottle to her lips, her chin-cut hair bobbing around her face. She gulped, and gulped, and gulped. She leaned back in the chair, her body trembling. She waited until the shaking stopped. Until she didn't feel the loneliness any more. Then she turned her attention to the computer to try and find out why Flick Lewis had left all those years ago.

Stan heard a noise, a movement behind him, as he neared the front door of his house in Stepney Green. He pulled the gun out as he flipped around. Raised it as the person started walking towards him. His brother Flick.

'You gonna shoot me?' Flick said.

Stan kept the gun aimed high at Flick. Stan moved closer.

'You stupid bastard,' he said. Then he laughed loudly as he threw his arms around his brother. 'I've got something that belongs to you,' Stan whispered.

Five minutes later they were sat in Stan's games room next to the pool table both with a glass in their hand – Stan brandy and Flick fizzy water. With his free hand Stan took something from his pocket and threw it at Flick. His elder brother caught it with one hand. Sucked in his breath, the dimple in his chin moving, when he realised what he held – his Virgin Mary necklace. Their grandmother had given each of them the same necklace on the day of their Confirmation sixteen years ago. The same night that . . . But how had Stan got it? There was only one way. A chill went through him as he was once again, in his mind, standing in front of his nieces' grave. What was the point of asking Stan if it were true? Stan was a man who long ago did what he wanted and stuff the consequences.

He threaded the chain through his slim fingers. 'I wanted to give them something important.'

'Yeah well you should've chucked in some cash or shit.' From the way he bit out his words Flick knew that Stan was well pissed off. 'We made a vow years ago and you've got to keep it.'

They'd vowed to always wear them. Flick had until that night.

Softly he said, 'They took it off me. It was the only possession I had. I got it back when I left.' He kept it short and sweet because he didn't like talking about that time in his life.

He slipped the necklace into his pocket as Stan said, 'I nearly fell into the grave when you came to the funeral. I thought we had an arrangement. I told you to stay the hell away from the funeral.'

Flick shrugged. 'The girls were my flesh and blood as well. Anyway, people are going to know I'm back soon enough.'

Stan slammed down his glass. 'You need to remember who's running the show here mate. It's me, OK? If you want to work your passage back into the family business, you need to keep that in mind. So, don't cut up clever like that again.'

'Cut up clever? You've got some front haven't you?'

'Don't fucking answer me back, what's the matter with you?' Flick looked at his brother, he was losing his grip again as usual. Same old Stan. 'Two more weeks tops and then you'll be back. My right-hand man.'

'And what's Dad going to say when he finds out you've been seeing me all this time?'

Stan stood up and walked over to the pool table. Drained the remainder of his drink and placed the glass on the edge of the table. Picked up a cue and stretched across the table. As he aimed the cue at the black ball he said, 'Don't worry about Dad. I ain't scared of him, he's past it. He's gone soft.' He hit the black.

Flick stood up and walked up to the table. He topped his brother by a couple of inches. 'Those chains weren't the only things we took a vow about.'

Stan froze. Straightened up, the cue still in his hand. Fury burned in his eyes. 'You threatening me?'

A smile lit up Flick's cheeks. He moved to his brother and put his arm around his shoulder like they were best pals. "Course not.

You should take a leaf out of Dad's book. Keep it cool – that was the secret of his success.'

So quick, that Flick didn't even see it coming, Stan twisted him towards the table. Shoved the cue under his chin and bent him backwards across the table. Pressed down. Flick's face grew pale as his brother's heated up. 'Keep it cool? You ask around what happens to people who threaten me. I'm the boss now and you're working for me, not the other way round.'

Flick just lay back and took it without saying a word. Stan kept up the pressure of the stick for one second. Two. Three. Then he pulled it away and stepped back. Smiled. He pushed his hand towards Flick, who took it and straightened up, shaking out his grey-threaded brown hair. Stan was a bit peed off that Flick didn't even look scared. Didn't even have a grey hair out of place. That's what he'd always admired about his brother, his ability to stay cool. And he was right, it was the secret of his father's success.

Flick cocked his head to the side and watched his brother. 'What you going to do about Bliss?'

'Don't worry about that scumbag, he's going to get what's coming to him after what he did to my girls—'

'What you planning to do?'

Stan smirked. 'Let's just say I've organised a little move for him.'

Flick raised his eyebrows. 'He's been muscling in on your turf for way too long. Have you found out where his stash house is?'

'I've got a pretty good idea.'

'Where?' Flick threw at him eagerly.

'I'll let you know all in good time . . .'

'I could—'

Stan shook his head. 'No, you stay well back from it. Leave it to me. When I get the word, that's when we'll strike. Take him out.'

'What's he importing?'

Stan moved closer to his older brother as he placed the cue down. 'Guns. Plus I hear that he has a place where he gets girls to entertain his importers.'

'Where his stash house is?'

Stan nodded. He picked up the cue again. Stretched across the table with it. 'A little bird has told me when his next shipment is coming in. Shame Bliss is banged up and can't be there,' he added sarcastically. He savagely potted the black ball.

She was going to strangle him. With her bare hands. Very slowly. Jackie took brisk steps along the school corridor past the 'No running please' sign heading towards head teacher Mrs Moran's office. The walls were busy with displays of children's work, notices for parents and the achievement targets for the school.

'Hello,' someone said in an accented voice. She looked up to find one of the new Polish teaching assistants coming towards her. The woman was a real beauty. Slim and elegant with brunette hair that bounced off her shoulders and legs that really should've been insured. The school had recently employed a number of teaching assistants from Poland. The new wave of migrants had grown so much that the local education authority had decided to try and recruit more Polish teaching assistants. Mrs Moran had targeted her own recruitment drive within the new community personally, well that's what Jackie had heard. Jackie couldn't remember the teaching assistant's name, but she worked in her boys' class. Jackie gave her a tight, polite smile but kept walking – she had other things on her mind, like reminding her son who was the Mum in the family.

She saw Darius as soon as she hit the reception area outside Mrs Moran's office. He was sitting in a bright red chair, his Arsenal rucksack on the floor, head bowed under the display of the monthly attendance figures. To the side of him was the automated TV screen that was currently advertising the adult literacy class held in the former school keeper's house. As if sensing his mum's presence he lifted his head and started to squirm in his seat. And he was right to feel anxious because at that moment she could've done him black and blue. Not that she was one to belt her kids. After she'd witnessed first hand what happened to children in Britain's so-called care system she'd vowed never to lay a finger on her own flesh and blood. But sometimes, just sometimes, she wondered if a tiny little pinch might be in order or a swift cuff behind the ear.

'What naughties have you been up to now?' She stood over him with vengeance blazing in her green eyes.

Instead of looking sorry he plastered a sulky expression on his face and he kept his mouth zipped. Her hands curled at her sides. 'I asked you a question.' Still he said nothing, but this time a spark of defiance crept into his stare. Her fingers began to twitch. She wasn't putting up with that, not from someone she'd given birth to. She'd show him bloody defiance. She began to mentally roll up her sleeves. Leaned over him. Stretched out her hand . . .

'Mrs Campbell?' a high female voice behind her enquired.

She turned to find Mrs Moran's admin manager standing there. Another one of Mrs Moran's Polish recruits and another stunner, except she was petite with curves in all the right places.

'Ms Jarvis,' Jackie automatically corrected.

The woman smiled. 'Mrs Moran is expecting you. Why don't I let her know you're here?' Quickly the other woman headed for her desk and picked up the phone. Jackie twisted her head sideways and caught her son's eyes and sent him an if-you-think-you're-off-the-hook-matey-think-again stare.

The door to Mrs Moran's office opened capturing her attention. The head teacher stepped into the corridor. She wasn't a head teacher like the last one the school had had with her punky silver hair, Doc Martins and four earrings in one ear. No, Mrs Moran looked like what everyone in the community wanted their kid's headmistress to look like. She wore a bottle green skirt suit, with the skirt falling well below her knees, a pair of black flats and a string of black beads around her neck. Her red-gold hair was tied back into a bun and her glasses were pushed not quite to the top of the bridge of her nose. There weren't many people in this life who Jackie respected, but Mrs Moran was somewhere near the top of the list. This woman had done so much for the school. When she'd taken over, Parkhurst Primary had been heading downhill fast, especially after that incident where one of the kids had tried to set fire to the toilets, but within a couple of years she'd sorted the place out. Now parents were queuing around the block to get their kids in. The woman was remarkable. Even last year when the education cuts had been so bad - it looked like Mrs Moran was going to have to lay some staff off, but she'd managed to get the money, through applying for grants and selling the school keeper's house, Jackie had heard, to keep the school running.

'Ms Jarvis?' She greeted Jackie. 'Please.' She stepped back and waved her hand inside her room.

Jackie gulped. Her hand tightened on her shoulder bag as she took up the invitation. As soon as she got inside her nerves began to ping. Brought back memories of her own school days. She'd been no angel. Been inside Sister Mary Margaret's office so many times it felt like she'd been inside it more times than the chippie she and her mates would go to after school.

The office was both professional and comfy, with shelves of folders and books, a large old-style desk just in front of the window with a view of the housing estate across the road. In the middle were three, soft lilac chairs around a low rectangular table that gave the room the feel of being more like part of someone's sitting room. Mrs Moran waved her hand at one of the soft chairs, the one underneath the large framed photo of Mrs Moran receiving the Head Teacher of The Year Award a few years back. Jackie licked her lips nervously as she took the seat. As the other woman took the chair opposite her, she settled her bag into her lap.

'Would you like some tea? Maybe a coffee?'

Bloody hell, Jackie knew whatever Darius had done was bad. Mrs Moran only ever offered a drink if she was telling a parent good news or really bad news. Jackie knew this was a bad news situation.

She shook her head. 'So what's he done this time?'

Mrs Moran folded one of her long legs over the other and for the first time Jackie realised that her son's head teacher had quite a pair of legs on her. Her skirt shifted slightly higher. She folded her hands in her lap as she started speaking ever so softly. 'I know that life has been very difficult for you with Preston in hospital.' She sighed. 'And believe me I feel very guilty because it happened at my school—'

'But you couldn't do anything. It weren't your fault.' Jackie hated to see one of the best teachers she'd ever known beating herself up like this.

'I know.' She pulled her neck straight settling a regal and poised air about her. 'But it still happened in front of my school gate. We have been campaigning for such a long time to get humps put outside the school and now maybe the council will listen to us.'

'So what's *he* done?'

Mrs Moran used the point of a finger to push her glasses to the top of her nose. 'I'm afraid that he absconded from school today.'

Jackie stared at her horrified. 'Did a bunk?' Her hands dug into the soft leather of her bag.

'He went missing sometime during morning play,' Mrs Moran carried on. 'He—'

'Oh my Lord,' Jackie interrupted, her hand covering her racing heart. Just the thought of Darius on the street, far away from home, was enough to make her fall flat on her face.

The other woman leaned forward in concern. 'Are you OK?'

'Yeah.' Jackie took a deep breath. And another. 'Yeah. Just makes me feel sick to think of him out there on his own, you know, what with the pervs there are around.' Her breathing steadied. 'So where did you find him?'

'We were about to call the police when the Royal London Hospital contacted us. He went to visit his brother. Apparently he wanted to give Preston his Arsenal scarf which he sleeps with every night.'

'Oh,' was all Jackie could say. Preston did sleep with it at night. He didn't think that she knew that he kept it under his pillow but Mum knows everything. Mind you that still didn't give Darius the right to do one from school.

'And I'm sorry to add,' Mrs Moran's voice grew grave, 'that when we got him back to school and his teacher tried to talk with him he told one of the teaching assistants to . . .' She cleared her throat. 'Fuck off.'

'He did what?' Jackie's heart hardened. 'That kid is dead.'

Her son had just handed himself a sentence of immediate grounding once she got him back indoors. Going to visit his brother in the ozzie she could deal with but cursing a teacher out . . . ? No, her kids knew better than to cross that line.

'I asked him why he would do something like that,' Mrs Moran carried on. 'But he wouldn't say.'

'Don't worry, just bring his little misbehaving self in here and I'll have it out of him in two seconds flat.'

The other woman unlocked her legs and placed her glasses carefully back on. 'This is a very traumatic time for him as I know it is for all your family. He must be finding it incredibly hard to deal with this situation. And Preston is not just his brother, he's also his twin and in my experience twins really do bond together. The Lewis girls were the same.' She stopped pressing her lips together as if carefully considering her next words. 'Before the incident, both myself and his teacher had noticed that he and Molly Lewis were getting into a lot more trouble at school. I had to speak with both of them on a number of occasions to remind them about the school rules. Forgive me for asking but are there any other issues at home that you might think it useful for me to know about?'

Issues? Did she mean problems? Jackie immediately got on the defensive. She didn't like anyone beaking about in her private business. Troubles indoors should stay exactly there, indoors. Reading the expression in Jackie's eyes and body language the other woman plastered a sympathetic look on her face. 'In my experience, sometimes if things are not right at home children begin to act up and sometimes behave in a way they don't usually. And I fully understand that this is not the best time for you or your family. I even hesitated about calling you in but in this situation I had no alternative.'

Jackie swallowed. 'Both me and my husband live busy lives . . .'

'Yes.' Mrs Moran smiled. 'I hear that Darius's father has got a very profitable restaurant business. I even had the pleasure of eating there myself. He cooks a mean hot pepper sauce spaghetti Bolognese.'

Jackie shifted nervously because she started to feel like Schoolboy was occupying the empty third chair. 'Look,' Jackie said. 'We're going through a bit of a patch at the moment. Nothing major or that, but we're a family like any other with their ups and downs.' Mrs Moran nodded with understanding. 'But I've brought my kids up to be proper and they know better than to run their mouth at an adult. And what's happened to his brother is no excuse.'

'Have you considered counselling for him?'

Jackie's eyes widened. Counselling? For her boy? No way. If you were from the East End you didn't go to a counsellor for crying out loud, you just sorta pulled yourself together didn't ya?

As if reading her thoughts the other woman quickly added, 'It's just something to think about. I can put you in touch with someone . . .' She left the offer hanging in the air. 'But I'm sure that you can understand that I can't have my staff being spoken to in such a manner.'

Jackie nodded. Mrs Moran's hard-line approach was one of the reasons she'd chosen the school for her boys. She'd wanted her kids at a school where the unwritten mission statement was 'Keep your mouth shut, your hands to yourself and your eyes on your book.'

'This offence is usually an immediate five-day exclusion, but we both know that this is a very unusual situation. Darius is having a hard time dealing with what's happened to his brother and his friend's death, so why don't you take him home for the rest of the day, bring him back tomorrow and he can apologise to Miss Karska.' Jackie suddenly remembered that that was the name of the Polish teaching assistant she'd just passed in the corridor.

Jackie let out a huge sigh. 'I can't thank you enough Mrs Moran—'

But the other woman waved her hands as she got up. 'No need for that. Just bring back the old Darius with you tomorrow. He's a lovely boy, bright and inquisitive, maybe a bit too inquisitive sometimes.' She let out a little laugh, startling Jackie. That was the first time she'd ever heard Mrs Moran laugh.

They headed for the door. Just as Jackie reached it Mrs Moran asked, 'How's Marina Lewis doing?' Seeing the surprised look on Jackie's face she quickly added, 'It's just that you were the only parent who seemed to talk to her. And I heard what she tried to do after the funeral.'

Jackie had forgotten all about Mrs Moran being at the funeral. She wasn't about to blab about Marina's private business with anyone. 'I suppose she feels like any parent would after her kids have been taken away from her like that.'

'Yes . . . Quite.'

But Jackie said not a word more. When she was investigating a case she kept everything close to her chest.

*   *   *

Doris Hunter munched a family-sized bag of cheese and onion crisps as she stared at Jackie Jarvis and her son from her window as they walked past the former school keeper's house that now ran adult classes for the community. She wore the same T-shirt she had on when she went to see that nig-nog copper Ricardo Smart. She lived on the seventh floor of Meridian House, an eighteen-storey high-rise that had been up for modernisation this year but the council had scrapped it all. More cutbacks. As well as having great views on the street below she also had an eagle-eye view of some of the rooms inside the school. The head teacher's office, the nursery, the top floor of the old school keeper's house and the two top classrooms, including the Year 5 class where that bitch of a Paki teacher had always been having a go at her Marcus before she'd taken him out of the school and sent him to St Patrick's around the corner. She'd been sitting at her window that day the stuff had happened on the street. Seen the car. Seen it plough into those beautiful girls. She'd seen it all.

And that wasn't all she'd seen from her window.

thirty-one

'You listen to me young man,' Jackie said hard and fast, her hand twisted into the collar of Darius's school jumper. 'You don't go to school to show me up.' She shook him with every word. 'You go to put your head down and learn, got it?'

She let go of his collar. Darius stumbled back, his eyes looking up terrified at his mum. That look made her feel like pure crap. She hated using any type of strong-armed tactics on her kids.

Darius turned his head and gazed fretfully down the street. She followed his stare and knew what he was looking at. The spot where Molly's body had lain, dead forever, in the road.

'Oh, baby,' she whispered. Darius threw himself into his mum's body and started sobbing. 'Why did she have to go away, mum?'

Jackie shook her head. What did you say to a kid at a time like this? How did you explain why someone had killed his friend? 'She's somewhere nice and peaceful where God can look after her.' His sobs grew as she smoothed her palm over his back. 'But the next time you want to go to the ozzie we'll go together, alright?' She clung on to him tight just hoping his pain would go away. She'd tried so hard to keep this type of pain away from her children's lives. Tried so hard for her boys not to go through the pain she'd known as a kid.

'Excuse me,' a slightly accented voice said. Jackie looked up to find the teaching assistant from Darius's class – Miss Karska, that was it – behind them, trying to get past.

Jackie's cheeks got all hot and bothered as she remembered that her son had cussed this woman off. 'Look I'm really sorry—' Jackie started.

But the other woman cut her off with a small smile and quietly said, 'We will all talk tomorrow.' Then she reached across and caressed Darius's head still cuddled against his mum's body. She nodded at Jackie and walked away towards a shop at the end of the road. What a nice woman, Jackie thought. If some kid had cursed her out she wouldn't be stroking his head. No, she'd be doing something else with her hand.

She took her son's hand gently and led him down the street.

'Jackie Jarvis?' an urgent, out of breath voice called from somewhere behind them as they reached the shop the teaching assistant had gone into. She twisted around loosening her grip on her son. A woman. She'd seen this woman somewhere before, but where?

'Who wants to know?' she finally answered.

The woman scooted close to her. 'I seen it all you know. That business. Your other boy.'

That got Jackie's attention. She dug into her bag locating her car keys. Tucked them into her son's hand. 'Wait for me in the motor.' She pointed to where the car was parked down the road. As a sniffing Darius walked off she gave her full attention to the woman.

The other woman scurried closer, to Jackie's mind like a rat that had just got out of its hole. 'Name's Doris—'

Suddenly Jackie knew who she was. Doris someone or other. Her kids had been at the school, the eldest a year younger than her twins. She was always up at the school shooting her mouth off about something or other. The rumour mill said that her old man had run off with some bloke and that she was a dedicated member of the JSA crew – job seeker's allowance. That wasn't the only thing that people said. Most of the other parents had her pegged as being weird and stayed well away from her, including Jackie.

'Look, I'm sort of busy . . .'

Doris took another step closer. The smell of fags hit Jackie full in the face. She took a step back. Furtively, Doris looked over Jackie's shoulder. Then to the side as if she thought someone was spying on her. Finally she turned her beady eyes back to Jackie. And whispered, 'I could tell you stuff what happens on this street that would make your eyes pop clean out of your head.' The only thing Jackie did with her eyes was roll them. 'I see it all you see. All those men.' Doris touched the corner of her eye. 'That cop didn't even let me finish what I had to tell him.' Her mouth twisted. 'Mind you, what do you expect from a darkie?'

So is my son, Jackie wanted to throw back, but she didn't. If this woman had info she was just going to have to bite her tongue.

Doris's mouth was still going like the clappers. 'Even though I told him about all those men he treated me like I was total shit under his shoes. Like I was a mad woman or something. Alright, so my Rodney did a bunk but that don't mean—'

'What did you see?' Jackie cut over her ravings.

'Can't tell you now. Got to be at the quack's. I've got a bunion as big as a balloon on one of me trotters.'

'But—'

'Come up to mine at five tomorrow.' She mumbled her address to Jackie. Then before Jackie could say another word she had scurried past her, mumbling on her way. Halfway down the street she halted. Turned. Called out, 'Yeah, you ain't going to believe what I've got to tell you.'

Click. Click. The shutter of the large zoom camera took another couple of quick shots of Jackie and Doris Hunter. The person holding the camera pulled it back from the window as Jackie began to power walk down the street. They watched as she got back to her car. When she took off a few minutes later they followed.

'I want to know what's going on, Misty,' Nikki said.

Misty slowly turned her grey gaze to Jackie's mum as they sat at the bar inside the Shim-Sham-Shimmy Club. In front of Nikki was an untouched Lurve Monkey cocktail.

Misty sipped her trademark G&T before she answered. She could give a load of BS to many people but not Nikki Flynn. They went too far back for that. They had met back in the days Nikki was

a stripper at some dive in Bethnal Green. Back in the days when
Misty had been Michael. Michael and his brothers had been provid-
ing 'security' for the club and he'd been the main guy manning
the doors. And he'd been the part alright, no one in those days had
dared to take him for a pussy. One night while Nikki was shaking
her thang on stage, he'd sneaked into the dressing room intent on
trying on Nikki's lippy. Of course she'd caught him red-handed but
instead of reading him the riot act she'd taken him off to Jezebel's,
a salon that specialised in sorting out women like him. And so
Misty McKenzie had been born. If it weren't for Nikki, he would've
never become the woman he was today.

So he didn't bullshit her when he replied, 'Jackie just wants to
make sure that it was Bliss who hurt Preston.'

'And how's she doing that?' Nikki asked, running her fingers
through her copper-red hair in a fretful motion.

Misty glanced away from her friend. Took refuge in her drink
before answering, 'Oh, you know, nothing much . . .'

Nikki folded her arms. 'Just spit out whatever it is that you
ain't telling me.' Despite years away from this part of the world
Nikki hadn't lost her cockney accent. Now it was hard and
forceful.

Misty drained the bottom of her glass. 'Stan's old man don't
think that Bliss did it.'

'And what's that got to do with my daughter?' For the first time
Nikki sipped her cocktail.

'He just wants us to ask around for him just in case there's more
going on here.'

Nikki said nothing for a few seconds, her long fingers tightening
around her glass. 'Jackie's more close to you now Misty—'

Misty waved a hand. 'That ain't true—'

But Nikki cut over her hard. 'Yeah it is. We might be mum
and daughter but we lost something all those years ago when I
should've been there for her.' Nikki dipped her head down, her
hair falling around her face. 'All I'm asking is whatever she's
doing for Kenny Lewis you look after her, like you did when I
weren't there.'

Misty grabbed Nikki's hand and squeezed. Nikki looked up at her. 'Like I promised you years ago, I'll always look after your little girl.'

Bliss's secret female associate shook as she listened. The person speaking to her finished, turned and left her alone in the room. What was she going to do? What was she going to do? She began to pace as she thought this one through. If she'd realised how much violence she was getting herself into she would never have got involved in this. Never. But she had and now she had a decision to make. She didn't want to do this but she had no alternative.

She pulled out her mobile from her bag.

'Is this Sean?'

Sean McCarthy, Bliss's right-hand man, answered roughly. 'Thought Bliss told you to stay low?'

'I need to speak to him.'

'Bliss ain't in a position to speak to you, you know that. Now he's banged up I'm looking after the business side of things.'

'This could mess up the arrival of the shipment in a week's time if you don't listen to me.'

Sean's tone changed from get-off-my-back-girl to high tension. 'Has something happened?'

'No. Not yet anyway, but I think it will if we don't deal with a problem I've just found out about . . .'

The doorman at The Five Fingers Club opened the door. The club didn't have a sign, no flashing lights, in fact it was located well out of sight in the basement of a shop on Bethnal Green Road. And if you didn't have an invite you shouldn't come anywhere near the door. And the woman standing looking at him didn't have an invite. He gave her the once-over. Modest blue skirt suit, no make-up just lip gloss, hair tied back and a black briefcase in her hand. And she was black. They didn't get many black birds here. But he liked her legs. Oh yeah he liked her legs a lot.

He raised his eyes to her face. Didn't move from his spot. Just said, 'Yeah?'

'I'm here to speak to a Mr Sean McCarthy.' Her voice was dead posh and deep.

Now he did move slightly back. 'No one here of that name love. You've got the wrong place.'

The woman took two determined steps forward. 'I need to speak to him about—'

Abruptly the man moved outside. His tone became more threatening. 'You a plod or something?' He didn't give her time to respond. 'Piss off.'

But she wouldn't move. In fact she straightened her shoulders like she was up for a fight. 'I'm here to see Sean McCarthy on behalf of his solicitor, Daisy Sullivan.' She pulled out a business card from her top pocket and handed it to him. 'You can contact my firm if you want to.'

He kept the card in his hand as he stepped back inside. Without a word he pulled the door back.

'Thank you,' she said calmly and followed him inside the foyer that was dominated by the flame-red colour of the walls.

He slammed the door behind her. She followed as he marched past her. They stopped beside a door. But instead of opening it he swung around making her rear back. Pushed his face close to her ear. 'You better not be pissing about because people who piss about don't come back out.' She held her ground and didn't answer him. Now he opened the door. 'Sean's at the bar.'

She moved inside. The booty-bouncing beat of Beyonce's latest chart topper filled a room that looked more like the replica of a pub than a club. The door slammed behind her. This time she jumped.

thirty-two

She watched the man behind the bar as she made her way across the room to him. Solid-built man, the slight curls in his black hair held back by gel, with a thin scar that ran across his chin.

'Yeah?' he asked.

'My name is Miranda Murdoch.' She let out a little cough as she laid her business card on the bar. 'I've been sent by Mr Bliss's solicitor, Daisy Sullivan, to make some enquiries concerning the loss of Mr Bliss's car. I understand he lost it in a card game.'

Sean leaned slowly onto the bar. Looked her over. 'I ain't never seen you with his brief before.' His voice dipped menacingly low. 'Maybe I'll give your firm a ring just to make sure.' He straightened and moved to the black phone at the end of the bar.

As he picked up the receiver she calmly said, 'When you get through ask for Daisy Sullivan. She's the lawyer representing Mr Bliss.'

His gaze flicked onto her as his finger hovered over the phone. They stayed like that, eyes locked. The music changed to another high-energy number. Someone laughed wildly in the background. The legs of a chair scraped against the hardwood floor.

'I'll trust you. You look like the reliable sort ...' he suddenly said, his hand falling to his side.

'Only the best for Mr Bliss.' She smiled.

He left the phone and stepped around the bar. His arm waved at a table with three chairs in a shadowed corner of the room.

'So what's your business?' he asked as soon as they sat down.

But instead of answering she popped her briefcase onto her lap and opened it. She jumped when she felt his hand wrap tightly around her wrist. Startled she looked up at him and the look she found on his face scared the shit out of her. Except for the music all the noise around them stopped as every eye turned to them. 'I'm just going to take some notes,' she explained shakily.

The pressure of his fingers grew. The pain he was causing her she kept locked inside. 'Notes? Please! You'll be asking for my inside leg measurement next. I'm sure a clever girl like you has got a good memory.'

His fingers unlocked from her wrist one by one. As soon as her arm was free she closed her briefcase and propped it by her chair on the floor. The noise of the other people started up again as they went back to loving their drinks and their secretive chats.

'Mr Bliss is claiming that the night before the incident at the school he was playing poker and that he subsequently lost his car in this card game. So I'm looking into whether anyone can fill out some of the details.' She lifted her eyebrows. 'Tell me in your own words, from beginning to end.'

And that's what he did. 'Bliss had some people in from out of town. They were playing a hand, nothing serious like, just for some yucks. Then this bird turns up.'

Miranda's eyes widened. 'A woman?'

'Yeah. A bit brassy. You know the type. No one saw her come and no one saw her go. She must've been on the guest list or she couldn't have got in. Bit odd though.'

'What did she look like?'

His mouth twisted. 'Blonde wig, slight figure. She was wearing a suit, lots of make-up. A pair of boots. No one took too much notice because she wasn't a looker or anything.'

'So she joined the game?'

He nodded. 'She was hanging around Bliss's chair. She noticed him about to play a card and she put her hand on his shoulder and shook her head. So she suggested a card and he humoured her. Before we knew it, she was playing his hand for him and she cleaned up. So Bliss suggests she pull up a chair and join in herself.

He's always admired someone who's useful with a deck of cards and him and his mates thought it was a big joke to have a skirt around the table. At least they did to start with until she started having the shirts off their backs.'

His eyes almost sparkled as if he were back there that night. 'One by one Bliss's friends decided they'd had enough until it was just Bliss and his mysterious lady friend. You know what Bliss is like, he's like a dog with a bone and he wouldn't give up. I reckon he'd have bet the firm if it had come to it. But it didn't come to that. She suggested he put his car up because she needed one. And then she proceeded to win that as well.'

The sound of raised voices from a neighbouring table tore over their conversation. Miranda and Sean looked over to find two men throwing verbal punches at each other. Sean sent them a wave of dirty looks. One of the men caught his eye and quietened it down instantly. He turned back to Miranda and picked up his story. 'Of course it all got a bit tense then. Some of boss's people decided it must have been a scam. Some of them were feeling their jackets, if you know what I mean. Bliss just sits there stony-faced. Then he puts his hand in his pocket and everyone holds his breath because they're thinking "bye-bye missy". Instead he pulls out his keys and hands them over. And he smiles and says, "well played". She winks at him and then starts stuffing the money into her handbag, she picks up the keys and says, "pleasure doing business with you . . ."' 'But as she goes, Bliss grabs her wrist and pulls her back and says, "I don't think we were ever introduced . . ." She says – and you had to admire her front – "My name's Betty. Is there a problem?" Then Bliss looks at her for a long time and finally he lets her wrist drop and says, "No, there's no problem." And then she left. But fair play to Bliss, he always settles up. So then Bliss turns to no one in particular and says "Can anyone give me a lift home?" and we all start to laugh our heads off. And—'

Once again he was interrupted by a shout from the neighbouring table. This time both men were on their feet and one swung an almighty punch at the other. Sean jumped up, his face stormy. 'Leave. It. Out.' Both men looked at him still in their fighting positions. 'You know the rules. Bliss don't like no one fucking about inside his house. Keep it up boys and I'll look after it.' Both men remained fixed in their positions for a few seconds. Then one of them swore as he sat back down. The other reluctantly did the same.

He returned to his seat. 'Sorry about that, some of the customers get a bit excited sometimes.'

'Her name was Betty?'

He laughed. ''Course her name wasn't "Betty" but I don't know what the real one is. This ain't the job centre, we don't ask for details when people come through the door.' Before he could say anything else the doorman from outside appeared at the table. He leaned down and whispered in Sean's ear. He looked at Miranda and said, 'Excuse me a minute, babe.' And with that he stood up and followed the doorman outside.

Miranda fidgeted in her seat as if she wasn't sure whether to leave or stay. But the decision was taken away from her when Sean plonked himself back into his seat.

He smiled at her, but she didn't like the smile. He leaned forward. 'There's a visitor outside. Guess where she says she's from?'

Miranda swallowed, so he continued. 'Says she's from that Daisy Sullivan with a couple of questions for me. Now she's either pulling my plonker or you are?' Before Miranda could move, his hand shot across the table and grabbed her throat. And squeezed. As she made choking noises he yanked her across the table. 'You're dead.'

A gunshot flashed through the air. Screaming filled the room. Still holding Miranda, Sean twisted around to see one of the men at the other table with a shooter in his hand aimed at the other guy. But he had managed to duck. Charged the other man. Got his arms around him. They staggered towards Miranda and Sean's table and hit it. The table tipped over. The noise inside the room was deafening like the bass at a rave. Another shot flashed through the air. More tables turned over this time as people fought to get out of the line of fire. Stunned and dazed, Sean's hand slackened around Miranda's neck.

She took her chance and made a run for it. She looked across the chaos of the room, her head swinging this way, that way. Which way to go? Which way to go?

She ran towards the bar as the music track stuck and played the same riff. She scrambled over the bar not looking back in case Sean was on her heels. Her right foot twisted in her high heels as another gunshot flashed. She groaned in pain but knew she didn't have time to stop. Limping she pushed open a door that led into a corridor with cardboard boxes strewn over it. She kicked the boxes out of the way with her good foot and ran into another room.

'Oi' was all she heard someone yell in the distance. The room was kitted out like an office. Her gaze swung around. Stopped when she noticed the high, half-opened window. She ran across. Shit it was too high. She heard the clap of feet in the corridor outside. With crazy eyes she looked around. Saw a chair at the desk. Dragged it across and under the window. Leapt onto it. Stretched her arms out and managed to hook them over the windowsill. The warm summer air outside stroked the part of her arm that was outside. With a deep breath and a groan she heaved herself up the wall, wriggling towards the window. Keep going, keep going. Her eyes came level with the open window. She was almost there.

She yelped as something clamped around the ankle of her injured foot. She looked down. Almost toppled down with fear when she saw Sean with a hand around her ankle like a chain and a gun in his other hand.

'You better get your arse back down here bitch before you go on the missing persons file.'

He kept the gun steady on her, never taking his eyes from her face. His mistake. She jacked her other leg full into his face with almighty force. He screamed out when the heel of her shoe scraped across just below his eye. He dropped the gun, let go of her leg as he clutched at his face. She twisted back to the window. The shoe slipped from her foot. She heaved herself. Higher. Higher. Until she was half in and out of the window. There was a drop but nothing too much.

'When I get you . . .' Sean roared from inside.

She knew she shouldn't do it but she couldn't help herself. She twisted around, looked down at him and mockingly sang the title line from Whitney Houston's 'Saving All My Love For You'. Then she twisted back around and let go. Landed, knees bent, on her feet. Pain pulsed through her injured foot. But she didn't have time to think about that. She scarpered down the deserted alley. Skidded onto the main street.

That's when she heard the feet running after her. She knew she shouldn't do it, but she couldn't help it. She looked around. The doorman and some other beefy bloke were coming after her. Other people began to look at her as she stormed off down the street. The feet were getting closer. And closer.

Shit they were going to crucify her and nail her to the pavement if they caught her. Suddenly the engine of a car burned up the air. It was coming straight at her. The men were getting closer to her. The car kept coming. And coming. The footsteps were getting closer. And closer.

The car stormed past a tall man, who stood to the side. His head did a double take as if he knew the person in the car. The car reached her first. Skidded to a stop in front of her. One of the back doors swung open. She dived inside.

As soon as she got inside, the car's engine died.

'Bloody hell,' Jackie Jarvis swore. She tried the engine again but the car just made that awful noise that said it wasn't going anywhere anytime soon.

'We need to get out of here. Now,' Anna screeched from the back seat as she scrambled into a sitting position.

'I know that!' Jackie yelled back, glancing in panic through the rear window. Bollocks. The men chasing Anna were getting closer. She tried the engine again, but it just wouldn't go. She almost jumped out of her skin when the driver's door flew open.

The tall man Jackie's car had just passed propelled himself inside shouting, 'Scoot over.'

Flick Lewis. She didn't even think, just dived into the passenger seat. Flick leapt into the driver's seat, hands already reaching for the steering wheel. He didn't bother to close the door. He kept trying the ignition and trying as the men got closer. Suddenly the engine burned up the air. The car stuttered forward. Wheels screeching, he swung it into a mad one-eighty as one of the men reached the back of the car. He slammed the pedal to the metal. The car careered off, driver's door still swinging open, their pursuers yelling abuse as they disappeared down the road.

thirty-three

Anna drank her third rum and coke on the trot inside *Miss Josephine*'s main cabin. Her heart was still going like the clappers. She winced as Roxy placed a towel filled with ice against her ankle.

'Does anyone want to tell me what's happening here?' Flick asked coolly.

He sat on the seat beside the computer as Jackie paced anxiously.

'No,' all the women shouted back together.

'Where did you spring up from?' Jackie added, stopping her pacing and looking at him.

He shrugged. 'I was just in the area when I saw your friend here.' He fixed his gaze onto Anna. 'Running like the devil himself was after her.' He switched his gaze back to Jackie. 'Then I noticed you at the wheel of the car and I did a double take. That's when I realised you must be in some kind of trouble.' He smiled. 'Now I'm not the kind of man who will leave a lady in the lurch.'

Jackie just looked at him for a couple of seconds. Then muttered, 'Thanks.'

His smile became a wide grin. 'Anytime, sweetheart. Anytime.'

'Who the bloody hell is he?' Anna gritted her teeth as Roxy applied pressure to her ankle with the towel.

'Flick Lewis. Here to help.'

Both Roxy and Anna, eyes growing wide, looked at him as if he'd just grown two heads. Then they turned to Jackie. She knew exactly what they were thinking.

'Anyone going to give me a drink or something?' Flick said cheekily as if the women had invited him over for afternoon tea. Abruptly the charm dropped from his voice. 'Or explain why you were running for your lives not far from The Five Fingers Club?'

None of them answered him, so he carried on. 'I don't know what the story is here, but you're playing a dangerous game. When Bliss hears, and he will hear, that some crazy black bird—'

'Oi.' Anna pulled herself straight. 'Less of the bird bit, thank you very much. I think you mean black *diva.*'

'Crazy black bird,' he continued, ignoring her. 'And that's how you're going to be described by his goons when they report back to him who was inside his place asking this and asking that. It ain't going to take him long to track you down.' Silence greeted his words. 'You need to leave this alone. Bliss is inside and Her Majesty's justice will make sure he gets what's coming to him.'

Finally Jackie spoke. 'Flick, let's have a word outside.'

He followed her out. Instead of going to the side rail of the boat she headed for a small ladder that led to the roof.

'Where we going?' he asked. But she didn't answer him, just climbed. He continued to follow. The top of the boat had four life-belt rings. Jackie stepped around the first one and plonked herself inside the second. 'Park yourself in that.' She pointed to the first ring. Flick's eyebrows went up as if he was looking at a disease. Then he did what she asked and did his best to fit himself inside it.

Jackie laughed at the awkward way his body looked. 'You don't look so flash any more Flick. Flash. Flick.' Her shoulders shook as she giggled. 'I like it.'

He shot her a mock-stern stare. 'If my arse gets stuck in this you're going to pay.'

Her giggles faded but there was still a smile in her voice as she looked around, sniffed the air and said, 'Me and my mates used to sit up here when we were younger. This is my ring I'm sitting in, and that one . . .' she pointed to the ring he was in, 'is Roxy's.' She stretched her arms behind her and placed her palms on the roof and leaned back. 'In the summer we would sit up here and chat and just watch the couples kissing in the park, the families having their picnics and the kids rushing around like a bunch of loony tunes. That's what a kid's life should be, full of chatting, laughing, just having a bollocks of a good time. Funny thing was even after the stuff we'd all been through we still knew how to be kids.'

He crossed his legs. 'What stuff? What happened to you?'

The lightness in her voice disappeared. 'Believe me you don't want to know.' She looked at him from under her eyelashes. 'Most probably freak you out anyway.'

'You won't believe what life tips I picked up as a kid.' His voice was quiet, but she could hear the bitterness in it.

She wanted to ask him about his past but she knew he wouldn't speak about it just as she wouldn't speak about her own. No worries, she'd find out about his past soon enough.

She swivelled her body around to fully face him. 'I always wanted my boys to have a happy childhood. No way did I want them to go through anything like I did. Some people might think this is a joke but family is still important to me. My kids are still important to me. I'd do anything for them, anything. Even find out who tried to murder one of them.'

Now it was his turn to fully face her. 'Stay out of it. Leave it to the law.'

'That's what your brother said.'

'Yeah? Well, my brother is a pretty good judge of these things. I'd take his advice.'

'Can't you understand I want justice for my kid—'

'Justice?' Her heart lurched as she saw the naked emotion on his face. She could've sworn that was pain. 'I know all about wanting justice believe me. I lived and breathed it for the last sixteen years. I wake up with it. I walk with it. I go to bed with it at night . . .' His mouth clamped shut as if he realised he'd said too much.

Why would Flick want justice? Had someone done something to him when he was a kid? Who? Watching him was like looking at one of her own kids in pain. She popped out of her ring and crawled over to him. He stared at her and she stared back. She stroked his arm and quietly asked, 'What happened?'

He ran his brown eyes over her for a few seconds. Then took her face in his hands. Even without his touch she knew there was a bond between them. Then he shocked her by popping his mouth onto hers, just like that. She knew she shouldn't do it, but she did. She dived headlong into that kiss. It took her back to the first time she'd ever snogged Schoolboy. Happened right on her door-step in front of that nosey neighbour of hers, Mrs Beech, who'd complained to anyone with an ear about the number of foreign-ers coming into the country. Seeing a white woman and black bloke going at it had nearly pushed her over the balcony. Her and Schoolboy had laughed their heads off when she'd slammed her door. Her and Schoolboy. What the fuck was she doing?

She wrenched her lips away from Flick's. She opened her mouth but he got there before her. 'Yeah, yeah, I know you're already taken.' He just smiled at her as he stood up. 'I meant it when I said that if you ever need anyone, come to me.' Then he turned his back and was gone.

Jackie swivelled back around to face the council block. Touched her lips with a single finger. Then she remembered she needed to find out what Anna had discovered at the club. She scrambled off the roof, but thoughts of Flick still remained with her.

The person parked in the car took another snap as Jackie climbed off the top of the boat. They pulled the camera onto their lap and flicked back through the photos they had taken earlier. Reeled forward again and stopped at the one with Jackie and Flick in a clincher. The snapper wondered what the boss would think about that?

'So what did you find out?' Jackie asked Anna, all thoughts of Flick safely out of her mind.

Anna had her foot hitched up on another chair close to Roxy, who was in her seat by the computer. 'Bliss's story checks out. Some woman—'

'A woman?' Jackie tensed in her seat as she frowned. Now she knew what Ricky had been holding back on her about what Bliss had said had happened to him that night at his club.

'That's exactly what I thought when that guy Sean told me. Some woman comes in there as cool as you please on foot and then leaves again by car. Bliss's car, together with a medium-sized lottery win in her handbag. And before you ask, the guy didn't know who she was.' Anna then ran down a physical description of the woman.

'I still don't get it,' Jackie said as she shook her head. 'Why would Bliss give up his motor? He don't come across as a bloke who gives up much.'

'Honour among card players apparently. If only he was the same in the rest of his business, he'd be quite the gentleman.'

'Pretty cool then, this young woman,' Roxy said slowly, then whistled.

Jackie stood up and started to pace as if getting her brain into gear. 'Alright, so we can tell Kenny that the word is that Bliss did lose his car. And in the frame is a woman who no one has got a clue about. Who she's connected to we don't know. Unless it's Bliss of course just playing at pulling the wool over everyone's eyes.'

Anna shook her head. 'Nah. Def sounded like he didn't know her from Eve.'

'After I left the school . . .' The skin on Jackie's forehead crinkled as she remembered Doris Hunter. Her nose twitched as if she could smell the woman's fag-gagging scent in the cabin. 'This woman, who used to have kids in the school said she knew something.' Both Anna and Roxy leaned forward. 'I wouldn't hold your breath, she's a bit of a nutter. But I'm going to see her today.' She switched her gaze to Roxy. 'Did you find anything about Flick on the Internet?'

'Not a dickie bird. In fact there wasn't much on the Net about the Lewises. A few news reports about Kenneth Lewis's appearances in court. He got off quite a few charges and there were suggestions about jury tampering. But he went down the last time and a couple of reports say that his lawyer said he didn't do it.'

'What about enemies?'

'Not too many stories again, although there may or may not have been some incidents between Stanley Lewis and Bliss over the last year. Bliss is supposed to have confronted Stan or Stan's

supposed to have confronted him in a club, argument about terri-
tory or boundaries. Or it may never have happened, it could just be
gossip. But there's some bad blood there.'

'Bad blood over what?' Anna asked.

'No one really knows. Could be anything. Maybe they don't even
know.' Roxy shrugged her shoulders.

Jackie retook her seat with a heavy sigh. 'So there's bad blood
between Bliss and Stan. If Stan thinks Bliss killed his kids because
of some hazy dispute there's going to be hell to pay because Stan
won't leave it alone until Bliss is on a slab.'

They all remained silent as they soaked up this information.
Then Jackie said, 'I don't know what happened to Flick in the
past but he let it slip that he's after justice. Sixteen years' worth
of justice. What over I don't know. But it seems he is holding a
grudge.'

Anna dropped her leg gingerly to the floor as she spoke. 'So
maybe it was him and this woman. Maybe he drove the car to get
back at his dad or brother in some way.'

'No,' Jackie responded. 'He loved those girls like they were his
own.'

'You were up there a long time with him.' Roxy lifted her well-
shaped eyebrows.

Jackie couldn't stop the blush that crept onto her cheeks. 'I had to
get him yakking to try and find out what he might be doing didn't
I?' Shit. She wished her voice didn't sound so high. 'Besides if it
weren't for him, me and Anna might never have got away today.'

Anna and Roxy looked at each other. Looked back at Jackie.
'What?' She held her hands up pretending not to know what their
collective look was getting at. But before the other two could
answer the door swung open.

A pissed off Daisy slammed the door as she stepped inside the
cabin. Her gaze swung between her adoptive mum and surrogate
aunts. 'It was you lot in Bliss's club today wasn't it?'

Every striking feature she had stood out as her anger grew; her
thick, free-flowing black hair; the beauty spot at the corner of

her mouth; those intense blue eyes that people didn't forget once they'd stared deep inside them. She marched into the middle of the cabin. 'I'm right, aren't I?' Then she noticed the towel covering Aunty Anna's ankle. She gasped. 'Did you hurt yourself?' Then a stubborn look took hold of her face. 'Well it serves you right. What the hell did you think you were doing?'

'Watch your mouth young lady,' Jackie cut in, stabbing her finger at Daisy. 'You ain't too big for me to turn over my knee.'

'I've got a job to do, which is to represent my client.' Jackie let out a snort when she heard the word client. Daisy ignored her. 'And today you all got in my way.' They all appeared slightly guilty at that. They knew how hard Daisy had worked to become a lawyer with a reputation that was growing each day. How hard she'd worked for people to see her as more than villain Frankie Sullivan's daughter.

'What did you find out because the person I sent to the club came over all scared and took off.' None of them would answer at first. 'Come on, you owe me.'

'Alright,' Jackie finally said waving her hands around. 'This is what we know . . .' So she told her. Triumphantly, Daisy said, 'I knew it. Bliss didn't do it, but Ricky won't believe me. Right that's it I'm going to try to find this woman–'

'Oh no you ain't.' Jackie jumped to her feet. 'You've got a baby to think about . . .'

'A what?' Both Roxy and Anna spoke in unison, their eyes drifting to Daisy's tummy.

'Bollocks,' Jackie said realising that she'd just let out their secret.

But Daisy beamed. 'It doesn't matter.' Her hand pressed gently against her tummy. 'I just got it confirmed. I'm two months gone.'

The women all swam protectively around her, umming and ahhing. They'd been protecting her since she was fifteen years old. She finally managed to shush them with, 'I don't want anyone to tell Ricky. I want it to be a surprise over our we've-been-together second anniversary dinner next week.'

'He gonna make an honest woman of you now?' Jackie said.

'I can get all the invites done,' Roxy chipped in happily.

'We can hold a mega reception at the club—' Anna added.

'Hang on a minute,' Daisy interrupted, her head spinning. 'If Ricky ever asks me to go down the aisle you'll be the first to know.' Her face suddenly turned serious. 'I came here for another reason as well.' Having got their attention she carried on. 'I've got this other client, a girl who I think is from eastern Europe. Usual story, came here expecting work as a waitress and was forced on the game. She managed to get away and wants me to try and get immigration to let her stay. But she won't tell me which brothel it was and it's important for me to know because it will make her case stronger. The problem is I can't find this brothel. I understand that some of these places are underground and only certain people are in the know.'

'So you want us to help you find it?' Jackie asked. Daisy nodded.

'I've got a few contacts,' Anna said. 'Me and Roxy can do it, while Jackie and Ollie are . . .' She clamped her mouth shut realising what she'd nearly let slip.

'Jackie and Ollie are doing what?' Daisy swung her blue eyes between them suspiciously. 'I hope you're not going to do what I think you're planning to do. Bliss is my client but he's dangerous. So are the Lewises. Leave it alone.'

Jackie heard her warning but ignored it. She was going to do everything she had to do to find out who'd hurt her Preston and if that meant playing dirty then so be it.

Suddenly the soppy theme tune from the film *Titanic* filled the air. Roxy's mobile. She plucked up her bag on the end of the computer chair and took the call. 'What?' she said startled. 'We're coming right now.' Anxiously she turned to the others. 'That was Misty. There's a bit of bother at the club.'

thirty-four

Jackie rushed into the Shim-Sham-Shimmy Club. At first she couldn't see any evidence of trouble. Nothing funny had been going on near the entrance and the foyer looked the same as ever. Only problem she could think of was that she couldn't see any of the staff around getting the club ready for later. As soon as she hit the main room she saw what the trouble was. No wonder she couldn't see any of the staff in the foyer, they were all gathered looking up at the stage. Jackie looked up as well. And there the problem was, making a total prat of herself – Marina Lewis.

Mic in hand, she was halfway through belting out an out of tune version of 'I Will Survive'. And from the way her body swayed to an unsteady beat Jackie knew she was completely pissed out of her head. A wave of sympathy hit Jackie when she realised that Marina was still wearing the same clothes she'd had on at the funeral. That woman must be going through pure hell. Two weeks ago she'd taken her kids to school and now ... well now they were dead.

'I should've sicced the bouncers on her, but I didn't have the heart to.' Jackie flicked her head to the side to find Misty next to her. 'We've had Amy Winehouse, Queen and now she's doing her disco turn as bloody Gloria Gaynor,' Misty went on. 'You're her mate, ain't gonna survive if you don't get her off that stage. As much as I feel for her, we can't afford to get a reputation for running a third-rate karaoke outfit.'

As Jackie weaved her way through the gobsmacked workers, Misty yelled out, 'Alright you lot, you've had your fun now back on the job.' The staff got to it quickly. When Misty issued an order they jumped.

Jackie reached the front of the stage. 'Marina, babe, why don't you come with me?'

The other woman stumbled as she screeched the word 'survive' and gazed down at Jackie. Her features lit up into a wonky smile. 'Hey, Jackie,' she called back as if she hadn't seen her in years. 'Get up here and sing along.' She waved her arm around like she was having the time of her life. Jackie shook her head. Time of her life? Not likely. She looked like the most tragic figure Jackie had seen in her life. Poor cow.

'Come on,' Marina said almost falling over as she took a step forward.

Never taking her eyes off her, Jackie got up on the stage using the small stairs to the side. She reached her, her nose wrinkled at the strong smell of booze mixed with sadness pouring off the other woman. She gently circled an arm around Marina's waist. 'Let's get out of here,' she whispered softly.

'What? You don't wanna sing?' Marina fluttered her false eyelashes.

Jackie didn't answer. Instead she tried to gently lead Marina away, but the other woman shook her off. Jackie pursed her lips. She was getting fed up with this. Marina pulled the microphone back to her lips making Jackie think she was about to assault everyone's eardrums again with another pop classic. But she didn't sing. Instead she spoke, her words amplifying across the room.

'I know who done it?'

'Done what?' Jackie stopped in her tracks.

Marina's voice trembled. 'I know who killed my babies.'

As Jackie gently led a hysterical Marina off the stage Anna pulled Ollie to the side as if she didn't want anyone else to hear. 'Me and Roxy are going to hit the streets and try and find out where this brothel Daisy's looking for is. But I want you to do something.'

Ollie looked at her with her dark eyes. 'What?'

Anna pulled her closer. 'Jackie can't know about this, alright. Well not yet anyway.'

The skin on Ollie's forehead tightened into a frown. Anna knew she wouldn't like going behind Jackie's back, but it had to be done. So she plunged on. 'I want you to follow Flick Lewis the first chance you get and find out what he's up to.'

Jackie and Ollie got Marina home and tried to sober her up. They stuck her in the shower, brushed her hair and kitted her out with some clean clothes. Once they had pumped some tea down her Jackie popped the question she'd been wanting to ask for ages.

'You said you knew who killed your girls.'

White-faced Marina nodded. 'It weren't that Bliss bloke, let me tell you now.'

Jackie nodded her head gently in understanding, clearly seeing that Marina was a woman on the edge. 'Who do you think did?'

Marina pushed herself straight. Put her cuppa down. Looked Jackie in the eye. 'It was me,' she whimpered.

Jackie and Ollie exchanged bewildered looks.

'But it couldn't have been you.' It was Ollie who spoke because she could see from Jackie's fly-catching, wide-open mouth that she was incapable of speech.

Marina glanced at Ollie, her eyes nervously assessing her. 'If I'd taken my babies away from here years ago none of this would've happened.' Her eyes grew as big as saucers. 'I was taking them away that day for good. If only I'd got there earlier.'

Jackie finally found her tongue. 'No one could've loved her kids more than you did yours. You would've never harmed a hair on their head on purpose or otherwise.'

'Then why couldn't I save them?' Marina shouted with all the conviction of someone inside the witness box up at court.

Jackie just kept her sad eyes on the younger woman. It was just grief talking. Marina's question was the same one that echoed in her own mind about Preston. Why couldn't she have saved him? Have got to him a minute earlier? Told him, point blank, that he weren't going for no ice-cream?

'Why don't you put your head down for a bit,' Jackie coaxed.

'You don't believe me do you?' Marina's voice was small. Jackie bit into her lower lip, her eyes growing sadder, but she wasn't going to lie to the other woman.

Suddenly Marina shoved out of her chair and with angry, wide strides disappeared into the kitchen.

'Maybe we should go,' Ollie whispered to Jackie.

Before Jackie could respond Marina was back with something in her hand. She thrust whatever it was towards Jackie. Jackie took it. A screwed-up piece of paper. She straightened it out and looked at it, but couldn't make out what it was.

'You know what that is?' Marina's voice rose to hysterical levels with each word. 'That's his fucking kid that he's having with that tart. A boy.' Realisation dawned on Jackie's face at what she held; one of those blurred photos of a baby, snug and safe in the womb. What an evil thing for Stan to do. 'Why's he allowed to have more kids when mine are dead and I can't have no more?' Marina's voice ended on a sob.

What a bloody total mess Jackie thought. She stood up and placed her arms around the bawling woman. Led her back to her seat. She crouched down by Marina and laid her palms gently on the other woman's knee. 'Have you got any family that you can stay with?'

Marina looked at her, her nose and eyes red. 'I've got a family alright but I ain't going anywhere near them. All they bloody chat about is Jesus this and Jesus that. Well you tell me where this Jesus was when some car's dragging my girl to her death down the road? Where's this Jesus when all your Preston wanted was an ice-cream and he's left with his head smashed in the gutter?'

Crippling pain shot through Jackie. She'd asked herself that question so many times, but she'd always come to the same conclusion, it had nothing to do with Jesus. It had everything to do with some scumbag in a car who might or might not have been Bliss. 'Marina, babe, maybe the ozzie was right and you should go back and see a psychiatrist—'

Marina slammed over her. 'Just coz I tried to top myself don't mean I'm bonkers. All I wanted to do was be with my girls.'

Jackie knew that Schoolboy would go stir crazy if he heard what she was going to say next, but she had to do it because she feared for Marina's sanity. 'Why don't you come and kip with me for a bit?'

'No.' Marina stood up. 'I can't leave my girls' stuff here on its own.' Jackie eased to her feet never taking her eyes off Marina. 'Besides I want to put this up in a frame.' Marina moved to the low-level table and picked up a large piece of paper.

She swivelled around and said, 'Where do you think I should put this?'

Jackie looked at Ollie with confusion. They didn't know what Marina was holding in her hand. They looked away from each other when Marina marched to the wall by the window. She carefully pinned what she held in her hand against the wall. 'Do you think this will look nice here?'

Jackie and Ollie stared with horror as they finally realised what Marina was showing them: the bloodstained drawing little Minnie had done of her dad.

As soon as the other women were gone, Marina went for the phone. Her fingers trembled as she punched in the numbers.

'I need you,' she sobbed.

'I told you not to call me. Ever.'

'Please. I need to see you.'

The other voice got hard. 'Well that ain't gonna happen. Don't ever call this number—'

'I'll blab to Stan I will.'

'You what?'

'If you don't let me see you I'll tell Stan everything and what do you think is gonna happen then?'

'You threatening me, you bitch?'

Marina's whole body shook. 'I just want to see you.'

Silence. Finally the other person spoke. 'Alright.'

A minute later Marina put the phone down. And for the first time since she'd laid her girls to rest she smiled.

thirty-five

'Do you know how many dead children I saw before I was fifteen?'

Ollie's shocking words settled in Jackie's motor as they sat in the front. Jackie was still reeling from seeing Marina with that drawing in her hand. What mother in her right mind would want that, bloodstains and all, hanging on her wall? Marina was slowly going over the edge and there was nothing she could do about it.

Jackie lifted an eyebrow in surprise at Ollie's question knowing exactly what her mate was referring to – her time as a child soldier in Africa. What surprised Jackie was not what she said but that she was saying it at all. Rarely did Ollie speak of her time in the rebel army. All Jackie and the others knew was that by the time she joined them in the care home when they were all fifteen, as an unaccompanied minor, she knew more about guns than Rambo and a bare-knuckle fighter could take lessons from her about dirty tricks to use with his fists.

Ollie spoke before Jackie could answer. 'So many I lost count, but I always remember this one boy. He was about ten or nine. We stormed into the village in the dead of the night. Looting and shooting like mad people. Our orders were clear, no one was to be left alive. His mother was raped and shot first, then his father and finally him. And you know who was ordered to shoot him?' Jackie ached for her friend already knowing the answer.

'Oh, Ollie.'

'He wasn't the first I killed or the last, but for some reason it's his face out of all of them that haunts me still at night. Just like these girls are starting to haunt me.' Her voice cracked. 'You don't know the things I had to do.'

Jackie felt Ollie's pain. Of all her four mates she was closest to Ollie. Ollie didn't talk much, liked to remain in the shadows, but if Jackie ever needed her she was there for her. Her protector.

'You don't have to be involved in this you know,' Jackie finally said quietly.

'I know.' Ollie took a deep breath. 'Maybe Anna was right and we should have just let this one go?'

'You know why I can't do that.'

Jackie wanted to switch the conversation. She just couldn't talk about this right now, not with Preston up in the hospital with all those tubes coming out of him. 'And talking about leads, I think we need to go and see Scott Miller, the chair of the school's governors who gave the number plate to the cops. He might have seen something.'

'But wouldn't he have told the police everything he knows?'

Jackie started the engine. 'Maybe. But it won't hurt us to ask him some more questions just in case he forgot something.'

The car hit the road and they drove in silence. Ten minutes or so later the car stopped outside a large house in a street more near Bow than Mile End. It was a four-storey, beautifully kept white Victorian house with a stained-glass panel in the front door and multicoloured pretty flowers sprinkled at the front. It looked like what it was, a well-loved family home.

Ollie checked the time on the dashboard clock. 'He might not be back from work yet.'

'That's good. It will give us a chance to have a chat with his missus if she's at home.'

They got out of the car and headed for the front door. Banged the ornate black knocker. Jackie flicked her fingers through the short strands of hair above her forehead just before the door was pulled open.

A woman with long blonde hair pushed herself half out of the doorway.

Jackie spoke. 'Excuse me—' But she got no further because the woman's face creased into a worried look as she stared at Jackie and said, 'I'm so pleased you've come around. I've been so wanting to speak with you.'

The voice was what Jackie called posh. Middle class, upper class, Jackie didn't see the difference, they all sounded *posh* to her. Jackie looked at her puzzled. Why would she want to speak to her?

The woman opened the door fully to welcome them in. 'There's something you should know.'

The inside of the house didn't disappoint. Wide hallway with Victorian-style patterned tiles on the floor, an old-style wooden stand with a small mirror for hanging hats, coats and umbrellas, and a cream-carpeted staircase that swept to the upper floors. It had a cosy, fresh feel that Jackie instantly liked.

The woman led Ollie and Jackie into a huge lounge room with French doors to the well-kept garden in the back, a modern fireplace and comfy sofas and a Turkish rug on the hardwood floor.

'Please.' The woman waved her hands at one of the sofas. 'Take a seat.'

'You said you had something to tell me,' Jackie said as soon as she was sat down.

The woman perched on a leather-backed chair facing them. 'Yes.' Jackie waited with bated breath, fingers crossed, hoping it was some information. 'I'm Belinda Miller and the chair of the school's PTA. Well, I'm sure you know that my husband is the Chair of Governors, so you can imagine our shock at what happened . . .'

Hurry it along love, Jackie wanted to say. But she didn't, instead she sat there patiently waiting. 'I wanted to express my condolences—'

Jackie stiffened. 'My boy ain't dead.'

'I know,' Belinda Miller uttered quickly. 'But still, myself and the other members of the PTA wanted to let you know how sorry we are.'

'Is that what you had to tell me?'

'Yes.'

'Look, I'm grateful.' And Jackie was. 'But I really wanted to talk to your husband because I understand that he was the one that gave the cops the number of the car.'

Jackie could see how Belinda lifted her eyebrow when she said the word cop. Suddenly Belinda pulled the edges of her cardigan together. 'He gave the . . .' She let out a little noise from her throat. 'Cops.' She said it as if she was in a foreign language class. Then smiled like she'd got a gold star. 'All the information he had.'

'But do you know if he clocked anything else?'

'Clocked?' She looked at Jackie bewildered. 'Oh, you mean saw.' She smiled again. 'I don't think so. I'm sure if he had he would have told the . . .' That little noise again. 'Cops.'

Jackie couldn't help smiling back. There was something about this Belinda that she liked. 'So what did your husband say he saw.'

Belinda shuffled closer to the edge of her seat. 'He um . . .' this time there was no little noise, 'clocked this 4x4 coming down the road as James, that's our son, was playing with his new mobile phone. And apparently it was just terrible. All Scott could do was grab James and get out of the way. I mean it might have been James.'

Suddenly Ollie joined in. 'Did you say your son was playing with his mobile phone?'

Belinda nodded. Ollie carried on. 'Will it be OK if we talked to your son, only for a minute or two?'

Abruptly Belinda's body tensed. 'I don't know. I'm not sure that Scott would—'

'We'd only talk for a few moments.'

Belinda shifted uncomfortably. 'He's having counselling, like some of the other children at the school. I don't want him to—'

'I know about the counselling,' Jackie cut in softly. 'Mrs Moran told me. We won't keep him long I promise.' She finished with a reassuring smile.

Belinda got up and left the room. Jackie twisted to Ollie. 'What are you thinking?'

'If he was playing with his mobile he might have—' But she didn't finish because Belinda was back with a fair-haired boy of about nine who was the spitting image of his mum. Belinda had her hands on the tops of his shoulders. 'This is Preston's mum.' The boy looked shyly at Jackie. 'She just wants to ask you a few things.' She walked him towards Jackie.

'You alright, son?' He nodded. 'I know this is awful and I don't want to bring it up but you were outside the school with your dad when my little boy got run over.' Again he nodded, his grey eyes growing slightly wider this time. 'Your mum said you were playing with your mobile phone. Is that right?'

Again he nodded, but this time he spoke in a sweet, well-mannered voice. 'Yes. I got it all on my phone.' Jackie sucked in her breath long enough for Ollie to jump in. 'Were you playing with the video.'

'Yes. I was just trying it out.'

'James why didn't you tell us that before?' his mother asked.

'Dad told me that he would talk to Five-O—'

'Five-O?' his mum asked puzzled.

'The police, mum. It's what all the other children at school call them.' He turned to Ollie. 'Do you want to see what I've got on my phone?'

Five minutes later they were huddled around a computer in a room kitted out like an office, further down the hall. James had hooked his phone to the computer. Jackie watched carefully as the moving image from the phone flashed up on the flat screen.

Children's and adults' voices played in the background as the film showed the quiet street outside the school. Then the film swerved sideways moving to another scene. This time showing Stan and Marina Lewis going at each other's throats.

'Good grief,' Belinda whispered in horror.

Then the scene skidded at an angle again. This time the 4x4 was rocketing down the road. Adults' and children's screams rose in the background. The image tilted at an angle.

'That's when dad told me to get out of the way, so I had to move the phone.'

'Didn't your dad grab you?'

He shook his head. 'He was near Minnie and Molly—'

'What is going on here?' a voice bellowed behind them.

*

Forty-two-year-old Scott Miller was not a happy man. When he'd found them all around the computer he'd demanded, no, flippin' shouted, that they turn it off.

And his mouth was still going. 'What were you thinking?' he threw at his trembling wife. 'James is seeing a counsellor and all this is doing is bringing it all back.'

Jackie jumped in. 'All we want to do is—'

'I'm sorry, but I'm going to have to ask you to leave. I'm really sorry about your son, but I'm not going to put my boy through this.'

Jackie looked at him and thought he was jumpy, way too jumpy. What was really happening here?

'But—' Jackie tried again.

'I need you to leave now or I will be calling the police.' Jackie was narked. That was way over the top. What was he so upset about?

'Please.' Belinda shook as she spoke. 'Just do what he says.'

Less than a minute later the front door was slammed behind them. As they started to walk away they heard it. A swift, brutal slap against skin. A woman inside the house screamed with pain. Then another slap. And another. This time a child's tiny cries could be heard coming from another part of the house.

Angrily Jackie swung back to the front door. She raised her fist to hammer against it but Ollie caught her hand. 'Leave it.'

'I can't let him do that to her.'

'You can't go around saving everyone.'

Jackie reluctantly let her arm fall. She knew Ollie was right. As they walked away she looked back up at the house and this time she noticed the wasps buzzing away in the flowers at the front. No, the house didn't look like such a pretty place any more. And inside was a man, she could swear, who was hiding something.

Ten minutes later, the sound of his wife weeping somewhere in the house, a sweating Scott Miller pulled out his mobile in the garden. A wasp whizzed by him as he spoke. 'They are on to me.'

'What do you mean?'

He used his free hand to furiously swat away the persistent insect. 'The child in the hospital, his mother was here asking questions.'

'What did you tell her?'

'What do you think I told her?' he bit out. 'Nothing of course.'

'If you didn't say anything they don't know anything. Stay calm.' Then the line went dead.

Calm? He breathed heavily as he felt anything but.

'Scott?' He turned when he heard the weedy voice behind him. He turned to find his wife standing between the French doors. He winced when he saw the purple bruise beneath her eye. He hadn't been thinking straight or he would've made sure he hit her in a place that didn't show, like he always did. He moved towards her and took her into his arms as he always did. Said the words that he always did. 'Sorry honey. I won't do it again.' She relaxed into his arms, but he wasn't thinking about her. All he could think about was if anyone found out what he'd been up to he'd be ruined.

thirty-six

'How are things with the shipment going?' Bliss said into the mobile phone.

He sat on his bunk in New Field Prison's remand unit. Getting his hands on a mobile had been easy. 'We're still on schedule,' Sean, the man he trusted with everything, answered.

'I want to be there when the deal's being done.' He still couldn't believe that the cops were holding him. He desperately needed to be on the outside.

'How you going to do that?'

He shook his head. 'Dunno. How's our little friend holding up?'

'She called me up to say we might have a bit of bother but I've taken care of it—'

Before Sean could finish, Bliss heard the rattle of keys behind the cell door. Without saying another word he cut the call and quickly shoved the phone in its hiding place. He relaxed onto the bunk as the door pushed open. Two POs stood in the doorway.

'Up!' one of them ordered.

Lazily he did what he was told. Both men moved over to him. One twisted him around and ordered, 'Hands behind your back.'

He knew what was coming next. He didn't even wince as the cuffs clicked around his arms. Then they escorted him out of the remand unit the back way. As soon as he saw the prison van he knew what was happening – he was being transferred. Shit, he hadn't anticipated this happening or he would've taken his phone. Finding another mobile was going to slow him down because he needed instant recall about what was happening with the shipment. He stepped into the van. The door slammed. The van started to move as he wondered which prison they were taking him to.

She didn't like it. That's what Jackie decided about Meridian Towers, where Doris Hunter lived. Didn't like the dirty floor, the peeling paint and the smell; she tried to hold her breath. It smelt like rubbish that had been left to ripen in the sun. She quickly approached the lift. Swore when she saw that the doors were jammed. She took the flight of stairs to the seventh floor. Only stopped when she reached the fourth and ran into a group of teenage boys on the block chatting and joking in a corner. They didn't pay any attention to her and she didn't pay any attention to them. Finally she reached the floor she needed and pulled the landing door back. The overpowering odour of cats hit her in the face. The square landing, in another life, could well have done as a cell. Dark, dank and impersonal. She checked out the doors until she found the one she was after: number 28.

She couldn't see a bell or a knocker so she used her fist to pound on the navy blue door twice. She hoped this Doris wasn't pissing her about because she could do without this trip to bleaksville. She heard the pitter-patter of small feet inside. The door was opened by a young boy, maybe the same age as her twins, with grey eyes that were already growing hard despite his young age.

'Your mum in?' she asked.

He held onto the door like he didn't want to let her in and she didn't blame him. She could be some nut. 'I ain't seen you before.'

She smiled gently at him. 'Name's Jackie. Your mum's expecting me.'

He looked her over again, then pulled the door back. She stepped inside and was surprised at what she saw. She'd thought that Doris Hunter's home would be a hovel; uncared for with stuff all over the place. But it wasn't. It was neat, clean and the wallpaper in the passage was pastel green printed with tiny leaves and bamboo shoots.

The boy shut the door, turned and said, 'Mum's in bed.' What, at this time of the day, Jackie wanted to ask, but instead replied, 'Can you let her know that I'm here.'

He didn't move, just looked at her, the hardness in his eyes unnerving her. 'Mum don't like us to get her up. She was already in bed when we got back from school.' So he was a latchkey kid Jackie thought. Well his mum was going to have to get her arse up that was for sure.

She gave him another cheek-popping smile. 'I'll get her, just tell me which room she's in.' He pointed at a closed door on the left-hand side and then left her to go back into the main room. Jackie sighed as she approached the door. Knocked. Waited. No answer. She knocked again, this time with more force. Still no answer. For crying out loud. She reached for the handle and slowly opened the door calling, 'Doris.' No response. She stepped inside a room that was dark because the curtains were drawn. The furniture in the room was simple; a bog standard Ikea-style wardrobe, a white dressing table and a double bed. As she moved closer she could make out Doris's outline in the bed. She couldn't see her face because the navy blue duvet was drawn completely over her. The laughter of children from the other room floated into their mum's bedroom. Jackie kept on moving until she reached the side of the bed.

'Doris,' she said again, this time with a wagonload of irritation. Bloody hell she hoped this woman wasn't out cold on sauce. She called out the name again this time with enough power to wake the dead. Still no response. Tutting she reached out and shook the woman. 'Doris, it's Jackie Jarvis. Get up.'

Still no movement. She'd had enough of this. She grabbed the duvet at the top and swept it back. And jumped back at what she saw. The bed was covered in blood. Doris Hunter had been slashed all over her body. Jackie slammed her hand over her mouth in horror when she saw the pink thing lying on Doris's stomach. Someone had cut out her tongue.

thirty-seven

Ollie watched Parkview Garden reflected in the rear-view mirror of her beaten-up red Mini and waited patiently for any sign of Flick at his grandmother's. She had no idea whether Flick was inside or not, but it was the only starting point she had for where he might be. She'd already been waiting for a good forty-five minutes and still no sign of him. She eased more snugly back into the driver's seat trying to get rid of some of the tension that stiffened her back. She'd been tense since she'd heard about the two girls' deaths; since she'd seen Jackie's son lying in a hospital bed. It had awakened every nightmare memory she had of what she'd done as a child – killed people. Held a gun and pulled the trigger. She squeezed her eyes shut as every painful memory came at her full blast in the face.

Blood. Bodies. Blood. Bodies.

Men, women, mothers, fathers, uncles, aunts.

And children.

It didn't matter how many times people told her it wasn't her fault, that she hadn't had any control, it was still the children she couldn't forgive herself for. She should've refused to do it; should've thrown down her gun. But she hadn't because of the fear. The fear that she would end up as another faceless corpse lying rotting in the African sun.

Ollie's hand dived desperately into her pocket as shivers shook her until she found what she was after. She pulled it out with trembling fingers. Her trusted bottle of Prozac. She popped a couple until the shaking stopped; until the memories passed; until the pleading in every child's eyes she had killed left her in peace. Well, peace for now. She pushed herself slightly forward as her attention settled back on the reflection of the tower block. The entrance door was pushed open and Flick Lewis stepped out. She was surprised to see that he held a bunch of flowers. She couldn't tell which variety but they were pretty and bright against the concrete grimness of the building he was striding away from. She flicked on the engine as soon as he got into a Ford Escort. Followed him for the next hour until he drove through some gates. The gates of the City of London cemetery.

Bliss felt the van slow down. Then it stopped. He rounded the tension out of his shoulders as the door was opened. One of the POs had a huge grin on his chops. Bliss wondered what that was all about. He soon found out once he stood in the yard outside. Shit. His heart almost stopped. It couldn't be . . . ? They wouldn't . . . ?

He got his answer when the prison officer, who was still grinning like it was his birthday, whispered in his ear, 'Welcome to Oldgate.'

The photos were slapped on the table in front of Jackie as she sat shaking inside interview room number two at Unity Road police station. Shock still ran through her at finding Doris Hunter's dead body. She'd called the cops straight away. She wasn't surprised that it was Ricky who turned up with a bunch of uniforms. He'd got one of the cops to escort her to Unity Road to wait for him. And now he turned up, the first thing he did was to put these photos in front of her.

Her mouth fell open because she was in every shot.

Going into Daisy's office.

Driving the car towards Anna, hightailing it away from The Five Fingers Club.

Her, Anna and Flick rushing aboard *Miss Josephine*.

Flick.

Shit.

Her heart rate pumped up before her gaze reached the next snap. Please don't let this show her and Flick on the roof of *Miss Josephine*. Kissing. Hands all over each other. She stared into the picture. Thank fuck for that. It showed her with Doris Hunter.

'And that.' Ricky stabbed his finger onto the photo of her and Doris. 'Literally puts you in the frame with a dead woman.'

She looked up at him astonished. 'How did you get all of this?'

He smiled smugly. 'My detective followed you the last time you were here. I deliberately left our investigation file on Bliss on the desk because I knew you weren't going to be able to resist sticking that,' he touched his nose, 'into it. And after that it was easy. You became like my adopted detective. We follow you and hopefully more of the pieces of the investigation start falling into place. And you didn't disappoint me.'

Jackie leaned across the table and hissed. 'That's why I don't want my Daisy involved with the likes of you. You ain't trustworthy, you set people up. After the life she's had she deserves just an ordinary fella.'

'Ouch,' Ricky responded in mock-hurt. Then his face became dead serious. 'Now, why don't you tell me why you were seeing Doris Hunter?'

'It was the other way around. She came to see me. Caught me as I was coming out of the school. All she said was she'd been to see your lot but you'd told her to sling her hook. So she says she's got some information for me.'

'What did she say exactly?'

Jackie racked her brains trying to remember. 'That she'd seen it all, what had happened on the street. She saw lots of men—'

'She said that to me. What men?'

Jackie just waved her hand helplessly in the air. Ricky carried on. 'When she came to see me she claimed to have been there that day.'

Jackie shrugged. 'I don't remember seeing her, but she must've been, I mean how else would she have seen it all happen?'

'So who knew you were seeing Ms Hunter?'

Jackie shook her head. 'How the fuck should I know? Someone must've been following me.'

'And now thanks to you one of our major witnesses is dead. Cutting out someone's tongue is a classic punishment for saying you should've kept your mouth shut.'

Jackie shuddered but she stabbed her finger on the table in irritation. 'I think you mean thanks to you. You had her in the palm of your hand and told her to piss off. You had your chance and you messed up.'

Ricky leaned back. He knew she was right. Shit. Shit. 'And what's going on with you and Flick Lewis?'

She paled and grew still. 'Am I a suspect all of a sudden?'

Ricky ignored her question. 'What was Flick Lewis doing helping you after Anna scarpered from the club, and at Misty's boat?'

Jackie let out a slow, easy breath. His detective hadn't seen them then on the roof of the boat. 'He just happened to be in the right place at the right time and helped us. I think you'd approve of him because he keeps telling me to keep my beak well and truly out of it.'

'Stay. Away. From. Him.' Ricky's voice was slow and firm.

Jackie saw her chance for more information and took it. 'You know *why* he left all those years ago?'

He just stared her out. Then stood up. 'I'll be in touch if I need you.'

She stood up as well, but cheekily whispered, nudge-nudge-wink-wink style, 'You could always leave his file on the desk.'

In a long-suffering tone he replied, 'Bye, Jackie.'

Jackie sauntered towards the door. But instead of reaching for the handle she twisted back around. 'You might want to think about this.' Ricky just stared back at her. 'As far as me and you know there was only one person following me. Your detective. You might want to sit her in this chair and start drilling her as a suspect.'

His mouth fell half open at that. What did she mean? Was she accusing Sonny of having gone bad? But before he could ask she was gone. He plonked himself down in the seat and opened the top drawer. Pulled out the file on top. Flick Lewis. A chill went through him as he read. If Jackie ever found out about this . . .

He flipped the file closed and looked back to the open drawer. Stared at the photo that the file had sat on top of. Jackie snogging the face off Flick Lewis. He could've shown her it but he didn't. Jackie might not believe it but he liked her. Liked her toughness. Liked the fact that she'd taken Daisy into her home when she was a confused kid and never threw into her face who her old man had been. Mind you, he admired Schoolboy even more. A black man who had become tired of being a crime statistic and had made something out of his life. Yeah, Ricky admired that because he'd been there himself and if he ever got to the heights of success that Schoolboy had, he'd be a proud man. Schoolboy had done right by his family and what was his old lady doing? Smooching with someone else. Well that just wasn't right was it? He deserved to know didn't he? Ricky placed the photo back and closed the drawer.

As he raised his head Sonny Begum opened his office door. Jackie's words came back to him: *There was only one person following me. Your detective.* He ran his gaze over his right-hand woman as the seeds planted by Jackie's words began to grow. No way did he believe Jackie was right about Sonny, but his mantra for success was 'Always explore every lead'.

'How did it go Guv?' Sonny asked as she stepped into the room. Suddenly she winced in pain.

He looked at her concerned. 'You OK?'

She stretched. 'Yeah. Just hurt my back the other day?' For some reason she shifted her gaze away from him. That made him stand up and move towards her. 'You sure you're alright? I came looking for you the other night to have that drink—'

'Oh.' She waved her hand, but still didn't look him in the face. 'I was tired, so I got an early night. What did she say?' Now she looked up at him.

He considered her for a while. What the hell was going on with Sonny? She'd been acting strange since the beginning of this investigation. 'You know if there's a problem you can always come to me. Right?'

Sonny just nodded, but kept flicking her eyes away from him. She was nervous, but about what? He didn't for a minute believe a word of what Jackie was implying but decided then and there to keep an extra eye on Sonny. He relaxed back in the chair and filled her in on what had happened with Jackie.

'I'll carry on following her,' she said swiftly as she turned back to the door.

'No.' His abrupt command stopped her. She turned back and looked at him in surprise. 'There's no point doing that.' Ricky let out a weary sigh. 'Kids. You bring them into this world and try and protect them. But sometimes that just isn't enough.'

A few minutes later as Sonny was moving down the corridor on her own her mobile went. She paled when she saw who the caller was. She banged into the Ladies so she could take the call in private.

'Yeah?' She listened, her face showing her panic. 'I'll be there.'

When she left the loo she never noticed her superior officer, Ricky Smart, watching her.

Flick stared at the single grave. At the single white headstone. But there wasn't just one name on it, but two. And for the first time in years Flick felt like crying. Felt he was back to being fourteen years old. Back to having cuffs clamped around his wrists as he screamed for his dad. 'Dad! Dad! Dad! Don't let them take me. Dad!'

His long fingers tightened like barbed wire around the bouquet he held, almost crushing it, as the memories almost buried him. As a magpie suddenly screamed nearby he gently bent and placed the flowers on the grave. He would've said a prayer if he believed in God, but he didn't. Hadn't really ever, even though his nan had taken him to church often enough; got him to do his Holy Communion; had just done his Confirmation on the day of . . .

He slowly lifted his head as the wind strengthened its hold on the graveyard. And stared at the headstone. 'I love you,' he whispered.

His head jerked to the side as he felt the warmth of someone pass him by. He couldn't see who it was because their head was down, their shoulders hunched over like their grief was too much to bear. He continued to watch the person until they reached a grave four down from the one he bent at. The person knelt and bowed their head. Then came the soft weeping. A woman. Suddenly the feeling of grief, loss, deep sadness all around him started to suffocate him. He needed to get out of here so that he could start breathing again. But before he did he looked at the grave one last time and said, the same time the magpie screamed its heart out again, 'And I'm going to make them pay, every last one of them.'

* * *

The woman at the nearby grave stopped pretending to cry. Lifted her head. Ollie. She gazed at Flick's disappearing figure, the tap-tap of his shoes becoming fainter.

And I'm going to make them pay, every last one of them. His words had whispered to her on the wind sending a shiver through her. Did it mean he was another Lewis out to avenge the death of his nieces? Oh what were their names again . . . ? A lightbulb pinged on in Ollie's mind as she remembered – Molly and Minnie. Whatever, the man obviously loved those girls.

'I love you.' The sweetness in his voice had been unmistakable. Maybe her following him was a waste of time and he was a genuine kind of guy. But she also couldn't help remembering that look in his eyes when she'd met him on *Miss Josephine*. The others wouldn't have recognised it, but she did because she looked at it every day in her own eyes in the mirror every morning. The haunted reflection of having been up close to death too many times. Whose death haunted him? His nieces? Someone else's? The possibility of his own?

She should really go after him and keep following him, but something kept pulling her towards Molly and Minnie Lewis's graves. She eased to her feet and made her way to the girls' resting place. But when she got there, it dawned on her. She'd read the situation all wrong. Totally wrong. This wasn't the grave of Minnie or Molly Lewis. Heart jumping, confused, she read the words on the single headstone:

DONNA HILL
AGED 10
1984–1994
WE WILL LOVE YOU FOREVER
MARTIN HILL
AGED 9
1985–1994
THE BEST SON A MAN COULD HAVE

This was the resting place of two other dead children.

thirty-eight

'I wanna see my brief!' Bliss yelled through the cell door.

But no one was listening to him. The prison authorities just didn't want to know. Surprisingly they hadn't put him in with the nonces, but in the general population and that made him tense.

'Better keep it down mate coz no one gives a shit.' Bliss turned around to look at the geezer he was shacked up with. Old-timer. Seen better days and looked liked he was just worried about where his next illegal drink was coming from. Bliss stared back at him hard. Who the fuck did this geriatric cunt think he was? Talking to him like he was some green pussy. The cell might be a small space but the other man needed to know who ran the kingdom, so Bliss growled, 'You know who I am?'

The other man stared back with beady, bloodshot eyes. 'I know who you are alright. So does Kenny Lewis. Why do you think you're bunking with the rest of us and not in seg?' He let out a little tickle of a laugh. 'They're taking bets on the wing whether you'll be getting back door parole before grub time tomorrow morning.'

Back door parole. He knew what that meant. Cons who got out alright because they were D. E. A. D.

Dead.

Ollie took what she had found out to the one person she thought could help her – Misty. The former drag queen was in a right flap when she entered the Shim-Sham-Shimmy, issuing orders left, right and centre like she was expecting the arrival of royalty.

'Not there, you cloth head,' Misty screeched as she pointed at a bewildered waitress carrying a couple of pink labelled bottles of Veuve Cliquot. 'On the bloody table not the stage.' She threw her hands into the air. 'I blinkin' well give up.' She stopped when she spotted Ollie in the doorway. 'I ain't got time to chat,' was her terse greeting.

Ollie wasn't put off, she'd seen Misty in one of her don't-mess-with-me moods before. 'Something special going on tonight?' Ollie said calmly as she made her way to the older woman.

Misty threw her head back and shook her hair. 'One of them Russian big shots has hired the place for the night to celebrate his daughter's twenty-first. He's putting up a wagonload of dosh so this has got to be alright or . . .' She let out another screech as her eyes caught what another member of staff was doing. 'Who ordered those bloody tablecloths? I said white, not flamin' pretty girl pink. What is wrong with you lot?'

Ollie laid her hand gently on Misty's arm. 'Why don't we go to your office for a drink?' Before Misty could protest Ollie tugged her arm and led her up the spiral staircase. When they reached the top Misty swung around, leaned over the side and yelled at the staff below. 'I want this place sorted in one hour flat. If it ain't done I'm gonna kick each of your arses outta the door.' And with that she pranced into the office with Ollie.

Immediately she opened the drawer of her desk and pulled out a good-sized bottle of gin. Uncorked the lid and tipped it to her mouth. After two strong swallows she eased herself into her seat, clutching the bottle to her chest and kicked her midnight blue heels off. Slammed her bare feet with their painted electric blue nails on the desk. Ollie took the seat opposite. 'Want me to ring down for a drink for you?' Misty offered.

Ollie shook her head. Of all her four girls, Ollie was the one she knew least of all and the one she worried about the most. Ollie might show the world that she was the calm one but Misty knew different. Not that Ollie had ever said anything to her but she just knew that this girl was still fighting her demons from the past. But she wouldn't open up, wouldn't let anyone in and until she did there wasn't much that Misty could do for her.

Ollie's next words made her freeze. 'I followed Flick Lewis today.'

Misty placed the bottle on the desk and leaned forward. 'What did you do that for?'

'We think he knows more than he's telling. But we didn't tell Jackie.'

'Why not?'

Ollie pushed her glasses further up her nose as she considered her answer. 'We think she's too close to him?'

Abruptly, Misty dropped her feet to the floor. 'What do you mean *close* to him? Did you find her in the sack with him?'

'No . . .'

'Then what the heck are you going on about?'

Ollie spread her palms against her thighs. 'We think there's . . .' She struggled to find the right words. 'An attraction between them.'

Misty laughed sharply and quick. 'Get lost. The only bloke Jackie fancies is Schoolboy. She'd never do the dirty on him in a million years.'

'You know that things haven't been right between Jackie and Schoolboy for a while. She's vulnerable right now . . .'

Misty used her feet and arms to propel the wheels of her high-back director's style chair towards Ollie. She stopped when their knees were touching. She looked deep into the younger woman's dark eyes. 'Vulnerable? Jackie don't do vulnerable.' Pushed her face closer. 'What are you holding back on me about Jackie?'

Ollie held her gaze. 'It's not for me to tell.' Before Misty could press her with more questions she asked one of her own. 'Have you ever heard of Donna and Martin Hill?'

'Who?'

Ollie quickly filled her in on what she'd seen at the cemetery. Misty wheeled her chair slightly back as she thought. 'Hill? . . . Hill? That name sounds familiar.' She ran the pad of a long finger across her bottom lip. Then shook her head. 'Donna and Martin Hill don't ring a bell.'

'He made a vow when he was looking at their grave. A vow to make them all pay.'

Misty wheeled herself close again. 'Who? Pay for what?'

'It must have something to do with why Flick Lewis went away all those years ago.'

Misty pushed herself to her feet and with a heavy sigh moved to stand near the floor-to-ceiling window and stared at the easy moving river outside. 'All I know about Flick leaving town was that it had something to do with something happening up at his nan's place. What that was I don't know and I have to say I don't want to know. And there ain't no point asking Kenny because no one in his family talks about it and the way I hear it he don't like anyone mentioning Flick's name either.'

Ollie came to stand by the window and shivered as if she was back in the graveyard. 'The key to what Flick is doing back here lies with two other dead children.'

Misty tipped her head sideways to look at her. 'That still doesn't mean that he had anything to do with the death of his nieces.'

'The only way we're going to find out what happened outside that school is to fit all the pieces of this puzzle together. And one of those pieces is called Donna and Martin Hill.'

Misty twisted away from the window and moved to her desk. Picked up the blower. 'It's Misty. How you doing?' She listened for a bit as she popped herself into the chair. 'Got some time for me to pop on over? . . . Tomorrow bright and early is fine. Wanna ask you some questions about a family called Hill.'

Jackie outlined the information they had gathered so far to the others as they sat on the roof of *Miss Josephine* in the darkening evening light. They each sat in the same lifebelt they would sit in when they lived on the boat when they were fifteen. Jackie sat in the first one, Anna in the next, Roxy in the third and Ollie in the last one. Vicky Park to the right was eerily quiet. High-grade R 'n' B music pumped from the council block on the other side.

Jackie took a sip from the small brandy bottle in her hand before she continued to speak. 'Biggest bit of info we have so far is that Bliss has got a wagonload of witnesses who are saying that they saw him lose his motor in a card game.' She passed the bottle onto

Anna. She wiped her mouth with the back of her hand. 'And that he lost it to some woman and no one has got a clue who she is.'

'So it looks like maybe Bliss was set up,' Anna chipped in as she passed the bottle to Roxy. Roxy swiftly gave the bottle to Ollie.

'Or,' Roxy added, 'he wanted it to look like he was set up.'

Jackie braced her arms behind herself as she soaked up the still, warm air in an attempt to recharge her batteries. 'And the only reason we can find that he might want some revenge on Stanley Lewis is that Stan knifed him up a few years back. But is that enough to kill his kids in broad daylight?'

'But maybe killing them in front of a large crowd was his way of saying "I'm the boss man".'

'No.' Ollie shook her head. 'When I was in the army I learned that the best way to exact revenge against an enemy was under the cover of darkness. Rarely in the dark is your enemy prepared or ready to fight back.'

'OK,' Jackie said as the bottle made its way back to her. 'Let's say that Bliss didn't do it. That he was set up. Who else have we got in the frame?'

'Flick Lewis,' Anna said. She frowned. 'Alright, he rescued Jackie and me, but we haven't been asking a real right-in-your-face question.'

'Which is?' Jackie supplied.

'What was he doing near The Five Fingers Club in the first place?'

They all thought about that one. Finally Ollie tried to supply the answer. 'Maybe he was playing the grieving uncle and on his way to the club to seek revenge against Bliss?'

Jackie snorted. 'That don't sound like Flick. He's really gentle.' She realised she'd said the wrong thing when she saw the way the others were looking at her. Like she'd been caught with her hand in someone else's safe-deposit box.

Anna was the one who voiced the others' concerns. 'What happened with you and *gentleman* Flick up here, girl?'

Astonished she looked at them. 'Give me a break puh-leeze! I'm a happily married woman.'

'Married. Not sure about the happy bit,' Roxy mumbled.

'You what?' Jackie stormed, shoving herself straight.

Usually Roxy got quite intimidated by one of Jackie's rants and would keep it buttoned just for the sake of peace. But not today. 'All I'm saying is he's a member of the Lewis family. We don't know anything about him. What we do know is that he turns up after years away and Stan's girls are murdered. Is there a connection, that's what we need to be asking? You yourself said he wants justice. Justice against who? What did someone do to him?'

Ollie looked directly at Jackie. 'I followed Flick today.'

'What?' Jackie's incredulous question slammed around them. She shifted her head and caught each of her friend's eyes. They sheepishly looked back at her. 'What is going on here? Why didn't I know that Ollie was going to be breathing up his arse?' Jackie's gaze shifted back to Ollie and remained there.

Ollie kept her answer calm. 'Because we knew that if we told you, you'd be carrying on like this.'

'Like what?' She shook her face at Ollie, spreading her arms wide.

'Like you care for him more than you should.'

'Give me a bloody break.' She snorted as the sun drew out the ripe redness of her pixie cut hair. 'The guy's been alright with us. Like I said before, he saved our bacon.' Anna kissed her teeth as she twisted her mouth. 'You got something to say?' Jackie flashed furiously at her.

'I followed him to the cemetery,' Ollie quietly cut in. 'He stood by the graves of two children. Donna and Martin Hill.'

'Who?' the others all chorused together.

'I don't know.' Ollie shook her head. She pushed her thick framed glasses up her nose. 'As he stood there he said that he was going to make them all pay—'

'Pay?' It was Roxy who interrupted this time. 'Pay for what? Sounds like this is linked to this justice he wants to get.'

'Maybe,' Ollie said. 'Misty's going to do some digging.' She turned to Jackie and spoke as softly as the summer breeze flitting around them. 'He reminds me of me when I escaped from the army – dead inside.'

Jackie blushed. Maybe they were right about him. Her mind wandered back to the last time she'd been pulled in by Ricky. 'I think that Flick has got a record because when I asked Ricky if he knew anything about him he didn't say yes, he didn't say no.'

'Maybe we can get Daisy to get it out off him,' Roxy suggested.

'No.' Jackie shook her head. 'I don't want Daisy any more involved in this than she has to be. Plus she's got a young'un to think about now.' They all grinned at that. 'We'll have to find out another way. So we've got Flick and who else?'

'Why would someone want to kill Doris Hunter? Did she see something that day?' Ollie asked.

'All I know,' Jackie answered, 'is she kept talking about what she'd seen on the street. Seeing loads of men—'

'What men?' Ollie cut softly in. Jackie shrugged.

'Maybe we should go up to her place and check it out when the cops have gone,' Anna suggested. They all nodded.

'There is one other person.' They all looked at Jackie. 'The Chair of Governors at the school, Scott Miller, who gave the cops the car's number. He was really angry when he found me and Ollie at his place talking to his missus. In fact as soon as we left he gave her a couple of slaps.'

Ollie cut in, 'Have you thought that maybe we've been looking at this all wrong?'

'What do you mean?' Anna asked.

'What if the car was never meant to hit the girls?' The others looked at her stunned. 'What if its target was never Lewis's children but someone else? Someone like Scott Miller?'

thirty-nine

The shower block fell silent as soon as Bliss entered the following morning, a threadbare towel wrapped around his waist. Every eye turned to him. And stayed on him. His body tensed. He was going to have to watch his back. The worst thing you could do was to make the other cons see you were ready to poo your pants. Do that and you were likely to become someone's booty boy. He stiffened his shoulders. It was time that he reminded all these losers why most people didn't use his first name.

He swaggered into the middle of the room marking every face as he went. Then he stopped, widened his stance and growled, 'If anyone wants to take a pop shot at me, come on then.' He waved his hands in a cocky bring-it-on motion. He shifted his head from side to side, looking every man in the eye. 'What you waiting for?' No one moved. He almost laughed. The fuckers did well to remember he was one of the big time Faces around. He twisted his mouth. Dismissed them and turned his back. As soon as he moved the talking started. He was so cocksure that he even whistled when he got in the shower. Daisy Sullivan would sort him out and get him out of this hellhole, it was all just a matter of time.

He was so lost in his thoughts that he never heard the voices of the other cons fade away and then there was silence. When he felt the quiet around him he quickly turned. But he wasn't on his own. In the middle of the room stood Kenny Lewis. The older man looked strong and tough, ready for a fight. Bliss stood frozen, the water dripping down his body. Kenny Lewis moved towards him.

His arms came up. Bliss shot forward. He threw his arms around the other man. Kenny's arms whipped around his back and held onto him tight.

Bliss whispered, 'You know I would never do nothin' like that.' He pushed his face back so the older man could see it. 'You know I wouldn't lie to you – not my own father.'

Misty's grass green stilettos clicked along the cobblestones as she made her way to Mickey's Steam Cleaning business under The Arches in Bethnal Green. A couple of guys working on a black taxi looked up at her as she walked past.

'Alright lads,' she said and winked. 'The man of the house about?'

They nodded giving her the once-over and one of them pointed inside. They continued to watch her as she strolled inside. She spotted Mickey as soon as she got inside. He wiped his greasy hands on a towel, smiled as soon as he saw her.

'Let's take this to my office,' he said when he reached her.

A few seconds later they were inside his office. Misty plonked herself opposite him across the cluttered desk. Mickey pulled open the top drawer and placed a well-used bottle of Cockspur golden brown rum and two shot glasses on the desk. As he poured he asked, 'So how's tricks?'

Misty relaxed into the wooden chair. 'Wish I could say it was the same old same old, but I can't, not with Jackie's kid still in hospital. Talking of sons, how you getting on with Kimmie's boy Mitch?'

A sad smile pulled the corner's of Mickey's mouth. Any mention of his much younger junkie sister always had that effect on him.

'A nice boy. He's getting on great. My missus loves him like he was her own.' The smile fell from his lips. 'He used to ask about his mum a lot back in the first days with us, but he don't ask no more.'

'So she don't come around?'

He picked up his glass and knocked the whole lot back. 'Oh she comes around alright, but just to ask for a handout. Won't give her dick coz I know she'll shoot it up her arm. Mind you, I ain't seen her in about six months.'

Misty could see that he was hurting so she got down to business. 'So what do you know about any people called Hill?'

Mickey leaned back in his seat. 'Only know one family called Hill and no way are they involved in anything dodgy. Always lived on the right side of the law, know what I mean?'

'What about two kids called Donna and Martin. Died years back when they were young'uns?'

Mickey frowned as he whispered, 'Donna and Martin. Donna and Martin. Sounds familiar but I can't quite place them. Look, let me ask around some more, but I just know I've heard those names before somewhere.'

'You don't think I did it?' Bliss once again asked Kenny the same question he'd asked him a couple of hours earlier. They sat in Kenny's cell, the door shut, keeping all prying eyes out.

'No way did you do that, son.'

Son. Bliss let out a steady breath. He still couldn't believe it sometimes that he was Kenny Lewis's boy. He would never forget the day he'd found out that this underworld legend was his dad. The man he'd hated with a passion for abandoning him as a kid. It was after his mum's death. He'd gone a bit crazy, trying to prove to the world that he was going to be the next big I Am of the criminal world. That was until he got pulled up by the Bill for a post office job. He'd thought he was going away for years. Then someone posted bail for him. He'd gone home, tail between his legs and never understood why, but he'd started sorting through his mum's stuff. That's when he'd found the snaps, in her dressing table. Of her and Kenny Lewis. His mum had looked like a glamour doll back in the days when she'd worked in nightclubs. There were pictures of her with her arms wrapped around Kenny; on his lap; her lips all over his face. And from the glowing look in his mum's baby blues he could tell she was in love. And that's how he'd known who Kenny was. His dad. The bastard. The man who had turned his back on him. He'd got mad; got tooled up, ready to take Kenny out of this world. He'd hunted him all over London and finally found him at one of his clubs in Hoxton. It hadn't been easy to get close to Kenny but he'd managed it. Stuck a shooter in his face, his youthful anger pumping through his trigger finger ready to take his old man's head off. And what had Kenny done? Just looked at him with a big grin on his chops and said, 'Took you long enough to get here, son.'

Son. Just the sound of the word had nearly made him pull his finger. But he hadn't. The unmistakable power of the man sitting in front of him, as cool as they come, had stopped him. Calmly, Kenny had ordered everyone from the room. With Bliss still holding the gun Kenny had told him to park his bum. So he had.

'Didn't you want me?' he'd asked, hating the pathetic pleading he'd heard in his voice.

And that's when Kenny had explained about him and his mum. How Mo Bliss had worked at his place in Bow as one of his hostesses. He'd been married and Bliss's mum knew the score. But she'd got up the duff deliberately to force his hand. But there was no way in hell he was leaving his missus and his kids. He'd look after his kid though but she hadn't wanted to know. Wouldn't let him anywhere near his son. She'd done a runner and re-surfaced back in London when Bliss was seven. Kenny had tracked her down but she still wouldn't let him see his boy, but she'd take his money, he suspected to keep her love affair with the bottle going. It was Kenny who had stumped up the bail money each time Bliss ended up in the shit. Knobbled a couple of jurors every time to make sure that Bliss got off. That's what made Bliss eventually pull the gun out of his dad's face. His dad might not have been there physically for him but he'd looked out for him. And that's what dads did for their sons, looked after them. This East End legend was his dad, not some faceless pisshead as he'd imagined all these years. There wasn't much that his mum had got right in her life, but choosing Kenny as the father of her son she had.

'You stick with me boy and I'll make something out of you.'

And that's what he'd done, learned the rules of being a bad boy from the master himself. They'd kept their secret, but that was all about to change.

'You think Stan's got wind of what's going down?' Bliss asked as he looked into his dad's squinting eyes. Bliss's one regret was that

he didn't look like Kenny – no his pretty-boy features came cour-
tesy of his mum. The bitch. God how he'd hated her. Her drinking,
her whining, how she'd bad-mouthed his dad without using his
name once.

'She weren't all bad you know,' Kenny answered as if reading
his thoughts. Bliss gazed back at him surprised. 'She was a real
stunner in her day. Pretty blue eyes and legs that were made for
dancing. All the punters loved her.' Kenny let out a little tickle of a
laugh. 'But that was her problem, she was always looking for love.'

Bliss never felt comfortable chatting about his mum with this
man. Sure he understood why Kenny could never be the man seen
on her arm but it still hurt that his dad weren't really there for
him when he was a young'un. He heaved himself off the bunk and
walked over to stare at the picture of Miss Whiplash 1990 stuck
on the wall. With his back to his dad he said, 'Well she's gone and
we're here and what I want to know is does Stan know about us?'

Kenny's booming laugh made him twist around. His dad's head
was thrown back but the expression on his face was as hard as the
concrete walls surrounding them. "Course he don't. Hurts my heart
to say this but Stan's way too thick. Know how old he was before
he could tie his shoelaces?' Kenny stood up. 'Bloody nine years
old.' He shook his head and strolled over to his youngest son. 'By
the time he figures it all out it's gonna be too late.'

'But he's figured out where our stash house is.'

Kenny shook his head. 'He only thinks he knows—'

'But he's been giving my contact the third degree—'

'As long as she keeps her gob well and truly shut he don't know
dick.'

Bliss's face became dead serious. 'Are you sure about this?'

Kenny tilted his head to the side. 'Sure about you taking over
the business? 'Course I am. I can't let that doughnut run the outfit.
He's made a total tit of it all since I've been in here. Only one son
I want running things when I'm gone.' He leaned over and cupped
his rough palm behind Bliss's neck with a proud daddy smile licking at his lips. 'And that's you.'

'What about Flick?'

Kenny's hand jerked from Bliss's neck as if the younger man's skin was red hot. 'How do you know about Flick?' From the hardness in Kenny's voice Bliss knew he wasn't happy.

Bliss's Adam's apple bobbed as he swallowed. He weren't scared of dick on this earth, except his old man. But he kept his tone casual as he answered. 'I heard on the grapevine that he's back.'

'Back?' Kenny exploded. 'What do you mean back? You know where he's been or something?'

Bliss quickly grabbed his arm. 'Dad keep it down or people are gonna hear what we're rabbiting on about. Remember we want everyone to think that I'm your boot boy.'

That's what they'd dreamed up so that none of the other cons realised who they really were to each other. Kenny had put it about that he was going to make Bliss lick the floor he walked on to punish him for what he'd done to his grandkids.

'I don't know nothing about Flick except that he's back. You might get all pally with him and decide he should be the one running the show.'

'No fucking way.' Kenny shook his head in disgust. 'That boy's dead to me.'

Bliss smiled. 'I need to be there when the shipment comes in.'

'But you can't coz you're banged up in here.'

'I need to be there.' His words were furious. 'And one way or the other that's what's going to happen.'

Before Kenny could say anything else the cell door was pushed back. One of the POs stood in the doorway. 'You got a visitor, Bliss.'

Fifteen minutes later Bliss sauntered into the visitors' room and moved towards the table his visitor was sat at. A man. Head down. Couldn't see who he was. But from the colour of the dark, slicked-back hair he clocked that it must be Sean. His stride grew longer with his urgent thoughts about all the stuff he needed to get Sean to do to get the next shipment sorted. But he still didn't know how he was going to get out of the slammer. Plus his bail hearing was tomorrow and the judge wasn't likely to let him walk. Maybe Sean could figure a way out for him. He scraped the chair back. Plonked himself down and started, 'Sean, my man, just the fella—'

But he never finished because the man raised his head. And he wasn't Sean McCarthy. The blood drained away from Bliss's face.

Flick Lewis.

forty

Jackie and Ollie followed Scott Miller. They had parked Jackie's motor bright and early that morning on his street waiting for him to appear. He'd left his house, dressed in a business suit and carrying a black rucksack, at minutes to eight. Jumped in his shining black sports car and took off. They followed. They kept a discreet distance, but close enough not to get lost in the growing traffic of Londoners heading for work. Finally he parked the car outside a tall building with huge, gleaming glass windows in the City. They watched as he left his car and went into the building.

'That must be where he works,' Jackie said, peering through the windscreen.

'That car he's driving cost a lot of money,' Ollie observed.

Jackie looked at her. 'You think he's involved in something dodgy?'

Ollie's glasses slid down her nose. 'What if he earned that money on the wrong side of the law? What if he's fallen out with the people he's doing business with?'

'And now they want him out of the way?'

Ollie remained silent for a while. Then, 'I don't know. But if we keep following him we might find out.'

And so they waited. An hour. Two. Then their target appeared again on the street, this time talking away on his mobile. And from the look on his face and the way his lips were furiously moving he wasn't the happiest man in the world. He pushed the mobile back into his jacket, found his car and hit the road again. Jackie and Ollie followed.

Just over thirty minutes later Scott parked his motor on a side street off Oxford Street. He got out and started walking.

'I'm going to follow him,' Jackie said opening her shoulder bag. She pulled out a navy blue baseball cap. Jammed it on her head, pulling it down over her forehead. Then she hit the street. Quickened her pace to keep up with him, weaving through the crowd of tourists and shoppers. He stopped at a crossing on Oxford Street. She held back. Suddenly he looked around him as if he were nervous. His darting eyes looked in her direction. Quickly she dipped her head so he didn't recognise her. She moved across to the nearest shop and pretended to look in the window display of latest high street fashion. The window reflected the street. Reflected him. She kept her gaze on his reflection until he finally looked away. She twisted around to find him and other pedestrians crossing the street and followed close behind him. He cut over Oxford Street and headed down Dean Street into Soho. Soho was one of the trendiest parts of London, full of watering holes and clubs, a place where people hung out on the street from morning to dark. But Jackie also knew that behind all the smiles and the drinks, Soho still had a reputation as a place where bad boys and girls came to meet. And as she followed Scott Miller she wondered if he was part of the bad boys' club. He slapped his wife around didn't he, so maybe he was stepping out of line in other ways? Hopefully she was about to find out.

Her target darted into a narrow side street. Walked halfway up and then pushed inside a building. Jackie slowly moved towards it. Stopped. Looked up. A neat-fronted café. No chairs or tables outside. She pushed her cap more securely over her face and stepped inside. The bell on the door tinkled. The warmth and the smell of a good old-fashioned fry-up embraced her. The place was small and the only customers she could see at first were a couple of guys, with their heads almost touching like two lovebirds. She kept her own down, but her eyes furtively scanned around. Bingo. She clocked him seated at a table with a free chair. Was he waiting for somebody?

'Can I help you?' Jackie twisted around when she heard the voice. A woman, somewhere in her mid-twenties with carefully styled, fluffy bronze hair, a nose ring and a mouth smeared with a shade of red lipstick that Hollywood starlets once wore.

'Just a coffee,' Jackie mumbled absently and without waiting for a response she headed for a table in a corner. Good enough to see her target, but keeping her hidden at the same time.

'What type of coffee?' Jackie looked up and realised that the waitress had followed her.

'What?'

'The type of coffee?' the young woman replied slowly as if she were talking to an idiot. 'Do you want a latte? Mocha? Espresso? Cappuccino? Americano ... ?'

'Look love, all I want is a coffee.' Her tone ground deep into sarcasm. 'You know, a spoonful of beans, some hot water and milk. No sugar.' Jackie stopped when she realised the two blokes on the nearby table were eyeing her up. Shit, she was meant to be playing it low-key. Her gaze skidded to Scott Miller's table. She heaved a sigh of relief when she saw that he was too busy looking at his watch.

'Just a glass of fizzy water, alright,' she amended quietly.

Now all she had to do was wait. She clocked her target checking his watch again. He was definitely waiting for someone. Five minutes later her glass of water arrived and still Miller was on his own. Ten minutes. Eleven. Twelve. On thirteen he scraped back his chair and got up. Jackie dipped her head down. The bell tinkled as the door opened. Jackie slowly lifted her head and was surprised to see him looking with relief at the door. He eased back down as Jackie dipped her head again. Someone moved past her table leaving a sweet perfume scent behind. Jackie gave it a couple of seconds. Then lifted her head. Looked back at his table. Her jaw dropped when she saw who joined him.

'What the fuck are you doing here?' Bliss looked nervously around the visiting room. His gaze darted back to a very relaxed-looking Flick.

'Chill,' Flick responded lightly. He leaned forward, his arms folded on top of each other on the small table. 'It ain't like anyone's going to recognise me now, is it?'

Flick was right about that. He looked like a completely different person. His hair was dyed a black that obviously came out of a bottle, not a grey hair in sight and his body bulked-up, and the stubble and bushy eyebrows Bliss was sure were make-up. He even wore a pair of jet black contact lenses.

'Where did you get the get-up from?' Flick said nothing and just smiled. Cocky bastard, Bliss thought, but then again that's what he liked about his brother, nothing seemed to faze him. Mind you, Flick didn't know that he *was* his brother. Half-brother. No, Bliss was holding that one back until the right time.

Bliss continued as he leaned forward. 'What if Dad . . . I mean your dad . . .' Shit. He'd slipped up there but there was no change to Flick's expression. '. . . was in here?'

Flick lazily scanned the room. Drew his new eyes back to Bliss. 'Well he ain't.'

'You're taking way too many risks.' If there was one thing Bliss hated it was surprises. 'The deal is you work for me not the other way around, so what are you doing here? You report to Sean and he reports to me.'

'There are some things that you don't tell the guy in the middle, know what I mean? Mind you, if you don't want to know what Stan's up to . . .' He braced his hands on the table ready to get up and leave.

'Pop yourself back down,' Bliss said in a rush.

Flick wavered. Then, with a crooked grin, did what the other man asked. He laced his fingers together as he started speaking. 'Stan's getting ready to make a move.'

Bliss's heart started beating like crazy. 'What do you mean?'

'You know what Stan's like, big mouth, little brain. He's going around telling the whole world and their mum that he's getting ready to take over your patch while you're inside.'

Bliss growled, teeth bared. 'That ain't going to happen. That cock—'

"Course it ain't.' Flick cut in swiftly. 'Not while I'm watching your business interests for you while you're doing bird. I've got a leash around Stan's neck and I'm pulling him this way and that and he don't even get it. You don't need to worry about my brother while I'm around.'

'Then if I don't need to worry, what are you doing here now?'

Now it was Flick's turn to lean forward. 'It's obvious that Stan knows where your stash house is.'

Bliss jerked back and jeered. 'He don't know nothin'.'

'That ain't the way he's telling it. He knows alright and it's only a matter of time before he makes his move. And you know what? No one's going to blame him. And you know why? Coz you're the geezer who killed his kids . . .'

Bliss's nostrils flared. 'I didn't kill those girls.'

'That ain't what the cops are letting the whole world know. And the way I hear it, Stan's already put a price on your head for anyone who has the balls to do you while you're inside.'

That made the blood drain back from Bliss's face. 'Twenty big ones,' Flick continued. The breath hissed out of Bliss's mouth. Flick's voice dropped low. 'Hearing that kind of money being offered can turn a man crazy. You'll have every nutter in here out for a slice of your arse.'

Bliss looked nervously around again, but this time it was like he was checking each man as if he'd never seen them before. 'Now if you tell me where your stash house is I can make Stan think it's somewhere else.' Flick's voice drew Bliss back to the table. 'I can divert him, make him forget all about taking you out.'

'That cunt can't fucking touch me.'

'You sure about that?' Flick tilted his head. 'I've lived at Her Majesty's pleasure. Know what happens. All you've got to do is turn your back, in the shower, in the yard, away from your cellie, that's all it takes to turn you into a dead man.'

Fucking hell. Bliss knew he was right. Even Kenny couldn't hold his hand twenty-four-seven. 'Get Sean to put it about that I'm offering ten grand more than Stan to anyone who watches my back while I'm inside.'

Flick leaned back and nodded. 'But it would be a lot better if you told me where this stash house—'

Bliss cut over him, suspicion brimming in his eyes. 'That ain't gonna happen so forget it.'

Flick shrugged his shoulders as one of the POs shouted that visiting was over. Before Flick eased to his feet he whispered, 'Let's hope the next time I see you it ain't laid out in a pine box.' Then he was gone.

Bliss stared at his disappearing back as he let out a puff of angry air. Fucking Stan Lewis. Why couldn't he just roll over like his brother was doing? Your brother, a tiny voice inside his head reminded him. His brothers. And when he got out of here he was going to make sure that he was the only son that Kenny Lewis had left. But he had to get out of here first. He got up and walked towards one of the screws.

'I want to see my brief.'

As he left the prison and stepped out into the outskirts of South London, Flick started whistling the intro to 'Breaking Up Is Hard To Do'. He shoved his hand into his jacket pocket as his whistle swayed in the breeze. Pulled out a photograph. Stopped as he studied the people in it. His dad and nan inside one of Kenny's clubs years back. And in the background, holding a champagne glass, was Paul Bliss's mum.

The screw entered Kenny's cell just as Kenny was in the middle of a Tai Chi routine. The screw closed the cell door.

'So who was his visitor?' Kenny asked as he took a deep breath and brought his arms out to the side.

'Never seen him before in my life. Young guy, sort of pretty like.'

Kenny nodded as he brought his arms to rest by his thighs. He inhaled. Exhaled. Did it again. Turned around to face the prison officer. 'Go and see my mum and she'll sort you out.'

Instead of leaving, the screw said, 'Your visitor is here.'

Kenny tensed. Seeing him stiffen the screw reassured, 'Don't worry, I've sorted out a nice private spot for you.'

The private spot turned out to be a room next to the small library. Kenny entered leaving the screw outside. The person waiting for him sprang up from the flimsy, white-topped table and rushed over to him. Flung their arms around him in a deep hug. Kenny did not put his arms around his former daughter-in-law, Marina.

forty-one

She tried to kiss his mouth but Kenny jerked his head back. Way back. Then he pushed her gently away from him, not hard but with enough force to show her he wasn't pleased. She stared back at him with hurt brimming in her blue eyes, eyes that reminded him of her children. Her dead children. She was done up like she was going out on a Saturday night: make-up plastered to her hairline, hair fluffed back and more flesh showing than clothes. He twisted his mouth. She looked like what he'd always thought she was, a total tart.

He finally spoke, keeping his voice quiet so that the screw outside didn't hear. 'Told you not to contact me.'

Her false eyelashes flickered nervously. 'I had to see you.' She used that little girl voice that he hated. The one she thought always turned him on. Bollocks, how had he got himself into this mess? Your dick, that's how, his mind shot back. If you had kept it locked up in your pants years back you wouldn't be standing here now with your son's former other half.

'We ain't got nothin' to chat about,' he answered hard.

But she said nothing. Instead she yanked off the crop top that she wore. Before he could do anything her boobs were on display. He took in a sharp breath. His dick started to wake up. Shit, it had been a long time since he'd had a bit. She waltzed over to him, boobs bouncing in the air. When she reached him she cupped her tits in her palms and pushed them into his face. 'Remember how you liked these for brekkie in the morning?' Her voice soft as the heat from her breath caressed his cheek. 'One nipple at a time, that's how you liked it.' Her hands shifted and started twisting her nipples with a finger and thumb. And God help him but he couldn't take his eyes off them. Looked like strawberries just waiting for him to gobble them up.

'Don't tell me you've become a back door merchant since you've been inside,' she taunted.

She got the result she was after. He grabbed her by the hips and strong-armed her towards the table. Threw her backwards over it. Had her skirt up in a flash. She wasn't wearing any knickers so the next bit was easy, he just jammed himself into her. Banged and grunted away like a man at his final meal. She started squealing so he covered her mouth with his hand. The table started squeaking and trembling. Kept on squeaking and trembling until Kenny thought his mind was going to blow. Then it did. He slumped onto her breathing hard. She rubbed her hand over his back and that's what broke the spell for him. He'd just fucked the woman who'd once been the wife of his son.

With disgust he pushed up from her and did up his trousers. She lay back on the table, legs still apart giving him the eye. 'You know what I like about you, Kenny?' He could've sworn she opened her legs wider. 'You know how to show a lady a good time.'

'What lady? You're a dirty, little slut.'

She pushed up from the table with anger. 'Yeah and who made me into one?' She yanked her mini-skirt down. 'I'd hardly been with a geezer until I bumped into you that night at the club. As fresh as a spring day I was. Seventeen years old. 'Course I lost my spring-clean look once this dirty old man fucked my brains out that night.'

Kenny didn't want to remember but he did. It had happened eleven years back. He'd walked into his club in Stepney Green, The Squeeze, and there she had been, laughing and chatting with some mates at the bar. She'd caught his eye as she lifted her head, a fluorescent pink straw in her mouth sipping a sea blue cocktail. Then one of her friends had whispered in her ear and from the eye-popping expression she sent him he knew that her mate had told

her who he was. So he'd gone over. Bought her a bottle of the best
fizz in the house. And yeah, she was right, after that he'd fucked
her brains out. He should have let her go then, with a nice double
pat on the arse, a few quid tucked in her toosh, but he hadn't. Got
her a job at his place in Hoxton showing all her bits and pieces off
to the punters. She showed him a good time at night and he got her
a job, a fair exchange. Then she started chatting on about 'love';
wanting him to leave his missus, the usual, whiney female clap-
trap. He'd been in that situation before and told her point blank,
to her face, to get lost.

She'd got lost alright. Straight into the arms of his idiot of a
son. And before he could do anything about it she was the newest
member of his clan. 'Course he hadn't touched her after that, no
fucking way, but the damage had already been done. Stan was still
in the dark about the whole sorry affair and Kenny was going to
keep it that way. If Stan ever found out . . .

Kenny's anger began to rise as he marched towards her. He
grabbed her arm and swung her towards him. His face settled in her
space and for the first time he could smell the fear coming off her.
'You listen up, slag. You ain't a member of this family any more.
Only reason I kept the door open for you was because of those
beautiful girls.' His heart caught in his chest as he thought about
Molly and Minnie. 'Now they've gone, the door's shut, understand?'

He could feel her shaking, but she wasn't done with him yet. 'I
really loved you Kenny.'

'You loved *the life*. The freebies I chucked your way, the money,
the humping behind my missus's back. And when I kicked you to
the kerb you just crawled to my boy to get one over me. To—'

'I'm going to tell Stan.'

He yanked her closer making her squeal in pain as his fingers bit
into her arm. 'You do and you're a dead girl.'

She tore away from him. Staggered back. 'You know what Kenny,
since my girls have gone I feel like I'm dead anyway.' With shaking
fingers she pulled her top back down and hit the door.

He stood there for a while in the empty silence. She weren't
going to say fuck all to anyone. And if she did . . . He meant it

alright, she'd be a goner. He only had two more months in this shithole left to do and when he got out she was going to be at the top of his to do list.

He turned around when the door opened. With surprise he saw that it wasn't the screw that came in but the Number Two, Mr Clarkson.

'Sorry, Kenny,' he said.

From the tight look on the man's face he knew he was about to tell him something he didn't want to hear. 'What is it?'

'You're on the move. Pack your gear. You're being transferred.'

Ollie knew something was up as soon as she saw Jackie's face. Pale making her freckles stand out.

'Did Miller meet someone?' Ollie asked as Jackie got into the driver's seat.

Jackie turned to her. 'Yeah!'

'Who?' Ollie pressed on.

'Miss Karska.'

'Who?'

'One of the new Polish teaching assistants from the school.'

Ollie showed her confusion. 'Why would he be meeting her?'

'Simple. She must be his bit of skirt on the side.' Jackie shook her head. 'I thought she was a really nice sort. She works in my boys' class and is really good. And helps out at the adult literacy class run in the old school keeper's house.'

Ollie settled back in her seat. 'So maybe he was a bit edgy yesterday because he thought we might find out about his affair with someone who works in the school. So he comes home to find us talking to his wife and thinks we might know and tell her.'

'Dirty bastard,' Jackie said between her teeth. 'At home he's slapping his missus around and once he's out of the door he's getting his leg over with a bit of European totty.' She gave a small shake of her head again. 'Mind you, I don't know why I'm surprised, that's men all over for you.' But not her Schoolboy, never her Schoolboy. Then she thought of Flick Lewis and blushed. No, she was the one with the wandering eye.

'Sounds like Scott Miller is a dead end.'

'Which brings us full circle back to the Lewis girls being the probable target. So we've got two dead girls, my son fighting for his life and one of the witnesses, Doris Hunter, is dead.'

'And if it weren't Bliss,' Ollie quickly added, 'there's only one other name in the frame. Flick Lewis. A man who maybe has got a grudge with his family. We need to find out what his grudge is.'

'And I know who might just be able to help us with that.' Jackie saw the unspoken question in Ollie's eye. 'Pinkie Lewis.'

forty-two

A stunned Kenny looked up at the building in front of him. It looked like one of them posh manor houses he'd seen on the box with a neatly kept multicoloured garden.

'Has the Queen invited me for tea or to look out for her corgis?' he asked one of the POs who'd escorted him from the back of the prison van.

'You've struck gold for the last couple of months of your sentence. This is Bronswick Centre . . .'

Suddenly Kenny understood where he was. 'An open prison?'

He'd had a mate in here once who told all about life at the Bronswick Centre. The place prepared prisoners for their release back into society and even arranged for inmates to do part-time jobs in the daytime outside and back to their cell come evening. His mate had even told how he'd been allowed to drive a visitor back to the nearby railway station. Now that had made Kenny laugh his bollocks off.

The PO chatted away as he led him to the main entrance. 'Yeah. The Governor got a bit nervous with you and Bliss in the same house. Apparently Bliss's brief was shooting her mouth off about it. Thought there might be trouble.'

Kenny stopped. 'No, I need to go back to Oldgate.' What was going to happen to Bliss if he wasn't there? What if someone stuck him one in the back?

'No-can-do,' was the firm answer. 'They don't call you prisoners in here but residents.' Kenny scoffed at that. 'You're going to enjoy it here. Get your own cell. They even let you go out and about to stretch your legs. If I had my way–'

Kenny turned on him swiftly and snarled. 'You'd what?'

The man next to him went pale. He'd forgotten who he was chatting away to. 'Just saying, Kenny, that's all.'

'What do I have to give you to get back into Oldgate?'

The PO shook his head. 'Can't be done.'

Fuck. Fuck. What was going to happen to his son if he weren't there to watch his back? And then what would happen to the shipment coming in tomorrow night?

Prison is a dangerous place for men with a contract out on them and Bliss knew full well that with his dad out of the way he needed to take precautions. He spoke to a couple of the boys in the know on his wing and they gave him a steer – talk to Haig, they said, he'll sort you out.

It wasn't hard to find Prison Officer Haig, he didn't move around much. Bliss caught up with him in the gym sitting on a stool eating a sandwich, his cap hanging on the armrest of an exercise machine. Bliss pulled up a stool and whispered, 'I hear you're the guy to speak to about security.' Haig ate his sandwich and said nothing. Bliss stared at men thumping punch bags. 'There'll be a drink in it for you obviously . . .' Haig finished his sarnie. 'I don't know what you're talking about–'

Bliss wasn't in the mood. 'Oh fuck off, Haig. If you weren't on the take, you'd get off your lardy backside and report me for trying to corrupt a prison officer. Now stop fucking about and tell me what services you provide and what we're looking at price-wise. I'm good for it, you know that.'

Haig lowered his head and spoke to his shoes. 'Who's after you?'

'You know full well who's after me – you read the papers don't you?'

'But Lewis has gone.'

'But his gorillas are still in town.'

Haig shook his head and tutted like a mechanic with bad news for a car owner. 'That's gonna be very difficult and it's gonna cost. You know Lewis, he likes to get his way–'

'That's your problem, I'm a paying customer and I expect a deluxe service. I'm a deluxe kind of a guy.'

Haig pulled an orange from his pocket and began to peel it. 'OK, I might be able to help you out. The Governor's got his hands on some private cash so the prison's renovating a block on another wing, the cells there are alright but they're empty at the moment while they're being refitted. I could put you in one of those, there's no access for the other prisoners so you'll be safe, the only time you need see anyone else is during exercise and I or one of my colleagues can keep an eye on you then.'

Bliss had a think as the citrus zing of the orange scented the air. 'What about the guys who are doing the block up? How can I be sure Johnny Ukrainian isn't going to put a chisel through my skull while I'm having a nap?'

'They're all east Europeans, how are they going to know who you are? I don't think your rep stretches that far, does it? And no one else will know you're there.'

Bliss didn't like it. But he didn't have any other options. They fixed a price and Haig said, 'I'll show you where it is so you can check it out.'

He followed Haig out of the gym, along the landing and then through a series of corridors to the new block that smelt of paint, wood shavings and newly cut metal. Pots and machinery were scattered around outside the cells. About halfway down a row of cells, Haig stopped, looked both ways to make sure they were alone and then whispered to Bliss. 'This is it. Keep your head down.'

Bliss stepped inside, but almost dived back when he saw the four men waiting for him inside. Four prison officers each holding bulging socks.

Bliss knew that something was up. He whirled to face Haig. 'What's going on?'

Haig calmly pulled out another orange from his pocket. Waved it around as he answered, 'It ain't just Lewis who wants your nuts. We prison officers take a real dim view of kiddie killers.' Gobsmacked, Bliss watched as Haig threw the orange at one of the other men, who caught it and then dropped it inside the sock he held. That's when Bliss knew what they were going to do. Beat him black and blue with oranges inside socks which would leave less bruising but some internal damage.

'You've got thirty seconds lads . . .'

Bliss took a swing at Haig but he was so angry he couldn't punch straight and his arms were grabbed before he made contact. Haig shook his head as he left.

'Drop him off at the hospital wing when you're finished lads.'

The first blow tore into the meat of his stomach. He cried out the same time another blow struck the flesh of his forearm. The pain was razor sharp as the impact tore through the tissue of his arm. As he crumpled to the floor, socks swinging at him from all angles, he knew that tomorrow when he went up before the judge he'd be a dead man if he walked back through the gates of this shithole.

Jackie knocked on Pinkie Lewis's door at twenty minutes past nine at night. The older woman opened the door wearing sky blue curlers under a hair net and a little-girl pink dressing gown.

'Mrs Lewis?' Jackie asked.

Despite looking tired, Pinkie replied in a chirpy voice, 'Well I ain't Mother Christmas.' She peered at Jackie. 'I know who you are. You're that little boy's mum. Marina's mate.' She pulled the door back. 'Come on in then.'

Jackie took up the invitation and stepped inside. The hallway was neat and tidy with a splash of lemon scent in the air as if the place had had a good clean recently. She took a step forward. 'Not that way,' Pinkie almost shouted, her voice bordering on hysterical. That stopped Jackie in her tracks. She noticed that the old woman had her eyes glued to one of the closed doors. Jackie remembered Misty's words about something happening in this woman's home years ago. I wonder if it happened in that room, Jackie thought.

'Come on,' Pinkie said, her voice back to normal. Jackie tore her interested green eyes away from the closed door and followed Pinkie into the kitchen. 'Park yourself there.' Pinkie pointed to the white table. Jackie pulled back a chair and sat down. Her gaze immediately went to the open book and she frowned when she noticed words scrubbed out in the book with thick blue pen.

'Fancy a brew?' Jackie flipped her gaze to Pinkie and shook her head.

'I'm not stopping long. Kenny wanted me and Misty to look you up, every now and again, to make sure you were alright.'

Pinkie shifted her face into a proud mummy expression. 'Good boy my Kenny. Always helping people. Don't believe none of that rubbish the Bill say. He got fitted up good and proper, that's why he's banged up.'

Jackie just lifted her own eyebrows at that. If this woman wanted to believe her son was Saint Kenny who was Jackie to put her straight. Suddenly, Pinkie stopped chatting away as she stared at the wall, the one with all the photos of her family on them. 'That's funny,' she muttered pointing to a space on the wall. 'One of me snaps has gone walkabouts. The one with me and Kenny at his place years back.' She shook her head and turned back to Jackie. And smiled. 'Look at me rabbiting away. Let's get you that cup of Rosie Lee. Why don't you find yourself a pew and I'll be back in a jiffy.'

As soon as the older woman left, Jackie knew this was her chance. She hit the corridor. Rushed over to the room with the palm cross on the door. Twisted the handle. Pushed open the door.

Jackie hadn't known what she was expecting but it wasn't what she saw. The walls were filled with framed photos of Flick and Stan as youngsters, some black and white, others colour, and pictures of two other children. A girl and a boy. She stepped closer to the photo of the girl on her own. Deep, rich brown eyes shone out of a chubby face and a gap-toothed wide smile. Her dark blonde hair was styled in two pigtails and she wore a green school uniform. Donna Hill? Jackie switched to a solitary snap of the boy. He was older than the girl maybe by a few years, with a face that put him squarely in the Lewis family gene pool. Martin Hill?

If he was a Lewis what relation was he to Pinkie? Maybe she'd had a couple of kids before? No, Jackie dismissed that, didn't fit in

with the dates on the tombstones Ollie had reported. Maybe they
were . . .

The door slammed. Jackie jumped, and twisted around to find
Flick standing behind her.

forty-three

The fun lovin' Flick Jackie had previously met was nowhere to be seen. His brown-eyed stare was hard and pierced her to the core. She recovered quickly.

'I was just looking for the little girls' room,' she said breezily, taking a step towards him.

'What are you doing in here?' From his tone she suspected he didn't believe a word she said.

But she kept up her game. 'My mate Misty wanted your dad's number so I came up to see if your nan might have it.'

She tried to move past him, but stopped when he laid his hand on her arm. 'They ain't allowed mobiles in the slammer, so what makes you think my old man's got one?' Jackie swallowed. 'What are you doing in this room.' She opened her mouth but he carried on before she could speak. 'And don't say that it was open coz Nan always keeps it shut.'

'And why does she do that?' His head moved slightly back surprised by her question. Her voice dipped low. 'What happened here? Did it have something to do with Donna and Martin?'

She heard the air catch in his throat. She pressed on. 'All I want to know is does this have something to do with my kid ending up in the hospital?'

'Where are you?' Pinkie's voice, somewhere in the corridor.

'She's with me Nan,' Flick answered, but his disturbed gaze never left Jackie.

'With you?' The sound of Pinkie's shuffling feet stopped outside the door. 'In there?' she shrilly added.

'It's alright, Nan, we'll be out soon. Ain't that programme on? The one where they reunite families?'

'Blimey, you're right.' The sound of her disappearing feet went into the distance leaving Jackie and Flick alone.

'This ain't your business Jackie.'

'It is if it has touched my boy.'

Silence. Neither of them moved an inch. The tension grew electric as she repeated, 'Does it have something to do with Donna and Martin?'

The blood drained away from his face as his hand dropped away from her. 'Donna and who? Never heard of them.'

She lied to test out her theory. 'Funny that because I'm sure those are pictures of them on the wall.' Jackie looked deep into his eyes. 'You can tell me,' she whispered. 'I won't tell another living soul.'

Such a tortured look came over his face that Jackie almost wished she'd left this alone. Then he began talking with such an ache in his tone that Jackie couldn't help but feel for him. 'Sometimes we do things as kids that change our lives forever.' She could understand that, she'd been in the same position when she was fifteen years old. 'Then everything that you ever loved is gone. The people you love are gone. And it don't matter how hard you cry yourself to sleep at night those things ain't coming back.' An image of herself crying for her mum while she was in the care system swiftly passed through her mind. And she started hurting all over again. He shook his head. 'And that's why I can't tell you because I ain't never going back to being that boy bawling his eyes out all over again.'

She couldn't help it, she just reached for him. Folded him into her embrace. 'I know what that feels like,' she whispered. 'Coz I've been there. But you know what, I felt ten times better when I told someone about it. You shouldn't keep those things locked inside because you're the only person who gets hurt in the end.'

His mouth touched the corner of her ear. 'It ain't me that's gonna get hurt this time.'

Then before she could ask him what he meant his lips were against hers. She didn't even think of Schoolboy just got deep into the kiss. This time he used his tongue so did she. He moved until her back was against the wall, never breaking the kiss. Her heart did flip-flops. She didn't know what it was about this man but he made her feel sixteen all over again. Days when her kid weren't lying in hospital; days when she didn't have to think about a lump being in her breast.

Then her mobile went, dragging her back to where she was, a room where she knew something terrible had happened. His mouth travelled to her neck as she pulled the mobile from her pocket. With a tiny groan of pleasure she put it to her ear.

'Jackie? It's Schoolboy.'

Her face flamed. Shit, that was her fella and she was in the arms of some other man.

Instantly she pushed Flick off. Turned away from him as she spoke. 'Yeah?' Bollocks her voice sounded out of breath.

'You need to get down here now.' Her heart galloped as she heard the emotion in his voice. 'It's Preston.' Now she could hear the tears in his voice. 'They don't think he'll make it through the night.'

Anna took a deep breath. For the second night on the trot she entered Speedball Central looking for her contact who might be able to help her find this brothel Daisy was after. Of course the area wasn't officially called Speedball Central, but those in the know name-checked it that because night and day, especially night, you could get most drugs just like that. H, C, rocks, crystal, uppers, downers, you name it, Speedball Central was pushing it. And along with the drug pushers came the crack whores selling their bodies. And it was a crack whore that Anna was after tonight. Not that she called those poor women whores, no way. That was just massive disrespect to womanhood all over the world. They were to be pitied not mocked. Sad souls who found that the only way to keep their doomed love affair with crack going was to sell themselves.

Anna was glad that Roxy hadn't come along because her mate didn't feel comfortable in a place like this late at night. So Anna had left her at the computer on *Miss Josephine* and come on her own. She carried on walking, the strands of her black hair blowing in the breeze, knowing that men in the passing cars were eyeing her up. Dirty bastards. They could look all they wanted, she was a woman's woman in the deepest sense of the word since she'd snogged another girl outside the school disco when she was fourteen.

The Toms were out in good number. Thin and lost. None of the other women made eye contact. She looked at each one trying to locate the person she was after. Bollocks, she couldn't see her anywhere. Just then a car screeched to a halt by the kerb a couple of metres from the train station. The passenger door was flung open. A female voice from inside yelled, 'I ain't going nowhere until you cough up what you owe for playing kissy-kissy with your dick.'

Then a long leg shot out, wearing stockings and black stiletto heels. Anna inched closer. Stopped when she saw a man and woman engaged in a mad struggle in the front of the car. It was clear that the man wanted the woman gone. Maybe she should help? No. She'd come here for her own business and should mind her own. With a violent push the man managed to heave the woman from the car. As she tumbled into the road the car sped off. Now Anna quickly moved. A car beeped furiously as it swerved around the woman. Before Anna could reach her she heaved herself to her feet and began cursing at full blast down the road. 'Bastard. Wanker . . .'

Suddenly she turned. Clocked Anna. 'What you doing here?'

Anna had found who she was after. Kimberley, Mickey's kid sister. She'd once worked in the club. Anna and Jackie had employed her as a favour to Mickey. Back in those days Kimmie had looked terrific, a real feast for the male eye. Slim, healthy peachy skin and glossy blonde hair that was always bouncing off her shoulders because she used to laugh so much. But Kimmie, as everyone called her, hadn't lasted long in the club. Her head had been turned, like so many other women throughout the years, by a bloke. Now she looked like an anorexic, shoulders slightly hunched and you couldn't even tell what colour her hair was any more. A man who had promised her the world and instead put her on the game. The addiction to drugs had soon followed. Her brother rarely talked about her because every time he did it almost brought him to tears.

Anna swallowed the lump in her throat, the one she got every time she saw this girl. What a waste. She cleared her throat and answered in a jolly manner. 'Well it ain't to welcome in the New Year that's for sure,' she said as Kimmie walked towards her. 'I've come looking for you.'

'Has something happened to my Mitch?' Mitch was her five-year-old son. Most thought his father was some Turkish Face, who'd been found knifed to death a few years back. Her son lived permanently with her brother.

Anna shook her head. 'He's doing good the last time I saw him. Look, maybe we should go for a drink?'

'No can do. I've got to find some punters, know what I mean?' Kimmie's eyes drifted to Anna's bag. 'Got any cash?'

On principle Anna didn't want to give her dick knowing what the money would be spent on, but she did need some info. She pulled out her purse and passed over a couple of twenties. Kimmie quickly tucked them into her push-up bra.

'So what you after?'

'I'm looking for this knocking shop—'

Kimmie laughed. 'What, you looking to earn some extra dosh by joining my club?'

Anna just shook her head. 'It's one of them underground places. Might specialise in bondage and other extreme shit. I think it might be Mile End way, but no one seems to know what it's called.'

Kimmie rubbed her painted lips together as she thought for a bit. 'I did hear there was some new place, but they wouldn't want someone like me. Not clean enough. Been on the streets way too long for your more exclusive punter.'

Anna's heart went out to her. 'Why don't you—?'

'Look I know what you're gonna say,' Kimmie jumped in, her tone bored. 'Why don't I leave this all behind and just go home and start being a mum to my kid? Well this is my home. And I don't want my kid anywhere near it.'

The silence settled between them as Kimmie pulled out a fag, displaying the tiny rose tattoo on the back of her hand, and started smoking furiously. As she let out a puff she said, 'I don't know the name of this place, but one of the girls who works here knows all the ins and outs. If she don't know, it don't exist believe me. She should be out later. Once I've had a chat with her I'll get back to you.'

Anna said a grateful, 'Thanks, babe. If your mate gives you anything useful give me a bell or drop by Misty's boat. It's down by Vicky Park.' Then she thought she might as well see if Kimmie knew anything about Bliss and Stanley Lewis. 'Who's running the drugs patch around here?'

Kimmie stiffened. Her eyes darted around as if she was afraid someone was watching her. 'I shouldn't be talking to you.'

'It's alright, I ain't working with the cops or nothing. Just need a little info.'

Kimmie took a quick couple of puffs. 'A year ago that was easy to answer. I would've said Stanley Lewis. But it ain't him any more.'

'Who?'

'Bliss. A right old argy-bargy it was too. Bliss just came in out of the blue trying to steal the action. And did it alright because his gear's cheaper than Lewis's. Punters don't want to pay through the nose if they can help it. 'Course it didn't go down too well.'

'So is Bliss still the main man?'

'As far as I know, although everyone says that's going to change now he's banged up for Lewis's kids' murder.' She shook her head. 'I mean fancy killing those kids. He must've been doing some serious shit. Nutter.' Her expression became shuttered as if she knew she'd said too much. 'Look, I've got to get back to work.'

Anna's hand went back into her purse. Pulled out a tenner. 'Get yourself some food.'

As Anna handed the money over, Kimmie grabbed her hand. And held tight. 'You give that to my boy the next time you see him. And a big hug and kiss from mummy, yeah?' Anna nodded. But Kimmie still didn't let go. 'Tell Mickey to stop worrying about me.'

Finally she let her go. Sadly Anna nodded. What she would do to just pick Kimmie up and take her home to her brother. But there was no point to it, because Kimmie would only be back in Speedball by tomorrow night. Kimmie straightened and rushed across the road when she saw a car stop. For a moment Anna watched her chatting up the punter in the half-opened driver's window. That might've been her once if the others hadn't taken her drug habit in hand all those years ago. She shook off the worries of the world and started walking away – she might not have any info on Daisy's brothel yet, but at least she knew a bit more about the bad blood between Stanley and this Bliss. But was it enough for Bliss to take out Stan's kids?

'Alright girl?' a voice asked behind Kimmie as she watched Anna being swallowed up in the shadows of the night. She twisted around to find her mate Tanya standing behind her. Tanya was Bengali, flash and a real favourite with the punters. As well as having a nasty H habit she'd developed as a schoolgirl in Tower Hamlets, she also kept her ear well and truly to the ground.

Kimmie pulled her aside so that they were hidden in a shop doorway. 'Some punter's just been asking me about some hanky-panky joint that might be a bit exclusive. You know, whips and shit, somewhere where he can get his rocks well and truly going. Meant to be in Mile End I hear.'

Tanya's face became closed. 'I don't know nothin'.' She moved to go but Kimmie blocked her way.

Kimmie patted her bag. 'There's a bit of dosh in it for you.' Kimmie flashed the money and it soon disappeared into Tanya's hand.

Tanya started speaking. 'I only know this coz someone started chatting away as I was nearby . . .' What she said next made Kimmie gasp and there wasn't much that shocked her any more. She let Tanya go still reeling from what she'd heard. She needed to hit the road and let Anna know. Her mind reeled back as she remembered where Anna had told her to meet her, some boat Vicky Park way. As she stepped out of the doorway one of her regular punters drove up. He liked her to sit on his lap and pretend she was a cat and say meow, meow as he stroked her bangers. Easy money. But shouldn't she go after Anna? Easy money or Anna?

She got into the motor. She'd see Anna after she'd made enough money to buy a couple more rocks. But Anna would be gobsmacked at what she had to tell her.

forty-four

Jackie was in a real state by the time they arrived at the hospital. She'd been trembling so much that Flick wouldn't let her drive. He killed the motor outside the entrance. Jackie flew out without looking at him. He called out to her but she didn't hear. She kept running, the lump in her breast throbbing along with her heart. Her boy was going to die. Her boy was going to die, that's all that pumped inside her mind as she took the stairs to Intensive Care. She spotted Schoolboy pacing in the corridor as soon as she got there.

'Please tell me he's not ...' She couldn't finish as she gazed at him with pain-filled eyes. Then her legs went weak and he caught her. He managed to get her to one of the plastic chairs.

He held onto her as he said dully, 'He's still with us. But there's a massive blood clot.' He took a shuddering breath. 'They're working on him now.' Then he buried his head in her neck and cried. She'd never seen her Schoolboy cry before. Never. Even throughout all the bad times in his life before they'd married she'd never seen him like this. He'd needed her and she'd been wrapped in some other bloke's arms. What kind of wife was she?

'Jackie?' They both looked up at the sound of someone calling her name. Flick. He stood there hesitantly, not looking at her but at Schoolboy. Schoolboy stared back at him, eyes wide, as he straightened away from Jackie. It was like Jackie didn't exist any more for both of the men.

Flick broke the spell. 'Sorry to intrude. You forgot these.' He dangled her car keys in his fingers. Stepped forward and placed them on the chair next to her. 'Sorry to hear about your boy,' he said quietly. Then without another word he was gone.

'What was he doing with your keys?' Schoolboy's bloodshot eyes held hers tight.

She could've lied, but didn't. He deserved the truth, well some of it at least. 'When you called I was at Pinkie Lewis's place—'

Schoolboy shot out of the chair as he rapidly shook his head, his locks swinging this way and that. 'I told you to stay away from that family.' She tried to butt in but he wasn't having it. 'Oh no, but Jackie Jarvis has to do what she wants. Never listens to anyone else. Fuck it that her man might be worried about her. Fuck it that her other son can't sleep properly at night because all he keeps dreaming about is kids being killed. Fuck it that her boy is lying in the hospital dying.'

No, that wasn't fair. She wasn't taking that. She jumped to her feet. 'No, you hold on a minute, mister.' She stabbed her finger at him. 'I've been out there, running around, trying to find justice for our kid. So don't you dare!' she screamed. 'Dare accuse me of not caring.' Abruptly she covered her hands over her face and sobbed.

She felt his arms go around her. He pressed against the lump in her breast and she winced. 'What am I going to do if he dies?' Then she realised where all of his anger was coming from, he was frightened.

Suddenly she realised that she had to be the strong one. She shuffled her upper body back so that she could see his face. There was so much pain there it really hurt her. 'If he goes the only thing we can do is stay strong.'

He inched away from her, his face becoming like stone, and said with steely determination, 'Believe me if our boy dies it will be me on the street hunting down the bastard.'

That shocked her. She knew that look on his face, he meant it. But hadn't this been what she'd wanted? Her fella beside her helping her to find out the truth?

'No.' She stepped towards him. 'You ain't going to do that and you know why? Coz I ain't going to let you. You were right, there isn't any way you're getting back involved in the gangster life. I'm not going to lose you as well.'

But he just turned his back on her and started power walking away. She rushed after him and gripped the back of his jacket. He tried to move but she wouldn't let go. With all her might she flung him around. 'What are you planning to do? Go home and get that shooter?' His nostrils flared but he wouldn't answer her. 'I'm not letting you do that, no fucking way.' Then she added, voice quivering. 'If anyone would've told me that the man of my dreams was going to be some fast-chatting drug hustler I would've told them to piss off out of here. Me? With a geezer like that? You must be bonkers.' Tears shimmered in her eyes. 'Well I must be mad then because you've been the best man, the best father, I could've ever wished for.'

Before he could respond a voice called, 'Mr and Mrs Campbell.' Jackie turned to see her son's doctor. This is it, she thought. This is where I've got to learn to be strong. She straightened her back. Took a breath.

The doctor reached them. 'Preston is still hanging on. He's a real fighter. We think he developed a blood clot in the veins of his legs and a CT scan confirms that the clot has travelled up to his lungs.' Just hearing it all made Jackie shake. 'We've tried to make the clot disintegrate with certain types of drugs, but he's still deteriorating.' The doctor saw the desperate hope in their eyes. 'I don't think we've got any alternative but to try surgery—'

'What are the odds?' Schoolboy cut in harshly.

'There's a forty per cent success rate.' Jackie gasped. The doctor carried on. 'But if you consent to this we will have to operate straight away.'

'Can we see him?' Jackie asked in a tiny voice.

They followed the doctor to Preston's room. Jackie's knees went weak when she saw him. There were so many tubes coming out of him she could barely see his small body. And his brown skin looked grey. They approached his bedside, hand in hand. The solitary nurse in the room moved to give them some privacy. Jackie watched his little chest rise and fall.

'What did you say the odds were again?' Jackie asked.

'Forty per cent,' the doctor repeated.

She looked up at Schoolboy. He turned to the doctor and said, 'Do it.'

The doctor nodded. 'This procedure is very delicate, so will take some time.' Jackie sucked in her breath thinking of her little boy under the knife for so long. She looked up when she felt Schoolboy squeeze her arm. She tried to send him a grateful smile but her lips just quivered. The doctor continued. 'Instead of staying here and worrying why don't you take some time out and get away from the hospital for a while?'

Jackie shook her head violently. There was no way in hell she was leaving her son. She opened her mouth but Schoolboy got there before her. 'We'll do that. You've got our number when you need to call us?' The doctor nodded.

Before they left both Jackie and Schoolboy went to their son. Schoolboy pushed his fingers tenderly through Preston's springboard locks and Jackie gave him a sweet good luck kiss on the lips. And whispered, 'You're going to pull through, you're going to pull through.'

As Flick moved away from the hospital entrance he pulled his mobile out. 'It's me. Jackie Jarvis has been at Nan's asking for dad's number . . .'

Roxy stared at the computer screen, her mouth feeling dry. She needed a slug of something. Vodka was her usual poison but she'd already downed the bottle in her bag. No, she told herself strongly. She wasn't going to have any more. She wasn't going to do it. She hit the keyboard, looked up at the screen but that feeling just wouldn't go away. She twitched as her skin started crawling. Abruptly her fingers slammed down on the keyboard. She couldn't do without it. Just one more that's all she needed.

Decision made, her tongue flicked over her bottom lip as she got up and headed for the kitchen. She opened the cupboard on the left side of the cooker and snatched the bottle of Jack Daniels inside. Hands trembling she opened it. Tilted it to her mouth and gulped. The fiery liquid burned in her throat as her nerve endings began to calm down. She pushed the bottle away from her mouth as she made her way back to the main room. Plonked herself in a chair as she stared at the bottle like it was a long-lost friend. Just one more. Just one more. The bottle was back at her mouth. The alcohol streaming back down her throat. Just one more. Just one more. She kept it up until her eyelids started drooping. Until her hand became slack and the bottle tipped onto the sofa. Until she left the loneliness behind and drifted into sleep.

'I told her to keep her beak out of my business,' Stan stormed.

He paced up and down in the sitting room of his house as Flick lounged back on the puffed-up black leather settee. The fucking nerve of the bitch. Sure her boy had been hurt as well but he'd told her to leave it alone. And when Stan gave an order he expected it to be carried out. He twisted to the table where a line of coke lay. Bent and sniffed. As he straightened, the hit shot through him.

'You should knock that shit on the head,' Flick said quietly.

Stan turned slowly and looked at his older brother. He moved his finger under his shirt and twisted it in his Virgin Mary chain that hung from his neck. 'I would've come and seen you if dad had let me.'

Flick remained relaxed. 'Don't worry about it. I'm back now and that's all that matters.'

'Yeah but if it weren't for me—'

Flick stopped him with a soft, 'Sh.' He sprang up and walked over to his younger brother. Ruffled his fingers through his hair like he used to do when they were young. 'Thinking about you was one of the only things that kept me sane.'

'Really?' The vulnerability burned so bright in Stan's eyes that if members of his crew saw him they wouldn't believe it was the same man who could kill someone in the blink of an eye.

'I'll always protect you, Stan, you know that. I did when we were boys and I'll do it now we're men.' His voice dipped low into the softest whisper. 'Anything you want you just tell me.'

'Why do you think Jackie wanted dad's number?'

Flick stepped back and ran his fingers through his own hair this time. 'Dunno. Want me to find out?'

Stan stepped back from the table. 'Yeah. Butter her up and get her to talk. Be careful coz I hear her old man was a bit of a bad boy in his day.'

Flick smiled. 'Don't worry about Schoolboy–'

'How do you know the name of her fella?'

Flick tapped the side of his nose. 'I might've been away but I've still got my ear to the ground. You leave Jackie Jarvis to me you hear? Don't do nothing crazy.'

Stan remained silent. Then said, 'Alright. I'll let you deal with her.'

'I mean it, Stan.' He walked over to his brother and gripped his head gently between his hands. 'Promise me.'

Stan gave him a cold, hard look. Then nodded. 'I promise.'

Five minutes later, Flick was back hitting the streets. He pulled his mobile out. 'Tell Bliss I've got some more info for him.'

forty-five

He needed to be quiet and quick. He checked that no one saw him as he silently boarded *Miss Josephine*. Rushed forward until he leaned against the outer wall of the main cabin. Waited. Heard no noise. Slithered down the wall and stared at what he held in his glove-covered hand – a large can of petrol. He undid the lid. The strong fumes soaked into the air as he again waited. No noise. Bent over, he started to move, angling the can and splashing the lethal liquid as he went. It took him less than a minute to cover Misty's beloved boat in a circle of petrol. He pulled out a lighter. That's when he heard the noise.

Dazed, Roxy woke up. She knew something was wrong. She jumped to her feet . . .

Bang, bang, bang. Someone was beating against the window he was crouched under. He popped up to find a woman's terrified face staring at him from behind the glass. Their eyes locked on each other. She beat her fists against the window. Suddenly the glass shattered under the impact of her moving fists.

'Help!' she screamed.

He ignored her. Bent back down. Moved his thumb against the lighter. Ignited the flame. Placed it against the petrol. The petrol lit up into a quick moving snake of orange flame around the boat. The man quickly jumped back onto land. He didn't look back at the screaming woman trapped inside.

*

Jackie and Schoolboy entered his restaurant still waiting for news about their boy. The place was packed with diners, their voices creating a good-natured buzz in the air. Schoolboy took his wife's arm as they pushed through the line of people waiting for a table. At any other time Schoolboy would have been strutting around as flash as a peacock at the popularity of his place, but not tonight. Not while his boy was fighting for his life. Some people at the tables looked up at him and nodded as he passed. As they reached the middle of the room Kelly appeared. Instead of smiling she had a frown on her face. 'I thought you were at the hospital?' She directed her question at Schoolboy her gaze lingering on him.

Jackie caught the way the other woman was looking at her man, like she wanted to rip his clothes off and then get down and dirty with him, well that's what it looked like to Jackie at least. She stiffened and linked her other arm possessively around Schoolboy's waist. Then she uttered in a tight, tough tone, 'As you can see, we're not – so why don't you show us to a table, love.'

Kelly stared back at Jackie, clearly surprised by her tone. Jackie eye-balled her back with a you-might-have-the-longest-legs-in-town-but-I've-got-the-guy-on-my-arm look.

Schoolboy broke the tension with, 'Somewhere quiet.'

Kelly drew her gaze away from Jackie and turned her hazel eyes back to her boss. 'I've got just the place.' She smiled at him and Jackie swore that if Schoolboy didn't have his hand on her arm she would've decked the cow. Flirting with her fella in front of her . . . As if reading her mind, Schoolboy pulled Jackie closer to his side.

As soon as they were seated at a small, round table in a corner Schoolboy snapped, 'What is wrong with you?'

Jackie didn't pretend not to know what he was going on about. She thrust her face forward. 'I tell you what's up with me, our lad is down in Whitechapel having the toughest battle of his life and you and posh bitch over there are making gooey-eyes at each other.'

Schoolboy kissed his teeth in maximum irritation. 'You know what, sometimes I do wish there was something going on between me and Kelly because at least she'd hold me at night without turning her back on me.'

Jackie went pale. That hurt. Really hurt. Maybe she should just tell him that she didn't want him touching her in case he found the lump? Maybe this was the moment to get it off her chest? Get it off her chest . . . what a laugh, except she wasn't laughing.

Suddenly Schoolboy's hand crept across the table and took her smaller one in his. 'I didn't mean that. You're the only woman for me. I know there's something wrong and when you're ready you'll tell.' He stopped speaking as he creased his lips together for a moment. Then his eyes sparkled. 'Remember that time that crew were chasing me and I come beating on your door, bleeding like a pig, looking for somewhere to hide. Instead of panicking all you said to me was—'

'Stop bleeding on my Bermuda Beech floor,' she finished for him. They both started laughing. 'Come on, I'd only had that floor put down for a couple of weeks.'

'That's what I love about you, girl – you're different. Understand me. Don't ask too many questions.' He stared directly into her green eyes. 'And you believed in me like no one else ever did. You gave me a chance when most people just wrote me off as a hood who was going to spend the rest of his days as a jailbird.' He swallowed as the pain swept into his voice. 'And you gave me a family. Two little boys who look up to me. And Ryan may not be my blood, but he's my son alright.'

Jackie tightened her fingers around his. 'And you know why they look up to you? Coz you're the best dad there ever is.'

'Jackie what am I going to do if he dies?'

But before she could answer, they heard a sharp, piercing scream from downstairs. Jackie and Schoolboy scrambled up from the table and looked over the balcony. They both froze. Just inside the entrance stood a man dressed all in black, wearing a balaclava. And carrying an Uzi. As another scream tore up the air he started to spray the place full of lead. Shouts and screams erupted as the diners and staff hit the deck, knocking tables and chairs over in their frantic bid to find cover.

'Ohmygod,' Jackie said, stunned. Schoolboy yanked her below the balcony rail. 'What's going on?' The sound of glass breaking mixed with furniture falling over and a wave of screams shattered the air.

'Stay put!' Without waiting for Jackie to respond Schoolboy moved, but she grabbed his arm like a lifeline. 'You ain't going down there!' she yelled back desperately.

But he shook her hand off and crept along the balcony towards the stairs. Not believing her eyes she watched him stand up. No! Get down, she wanted to shout. The shooting abruptly stopped. Jackie peeped over the rail and what she saw made her heart almost stop. The gunman had his shooter pointed at Schoolboy who calmly walked down the stairs. The diners cowered in corners, on the floor and behind overturned tables. And as cool as they come Schoolboy walked to within a metre of the gunman. Stopped. Said, 'What's the problem?'

Everything was still in the awful silence that followed. Then the masked man shifted his gun so it pointed straight at Schoolboy's head.

When Anna reached the canal she saw the crowd first. What the hell? Looked like everyone was having an open-air rave without the music. Then she saw the fire engines. Two of them. Looking back, she would never understand what had started to make her move fast. Really fast. She reached the edge of the crowd. Elbowed her way through. People shot her dirty looks but she took no notice. She got to the front. She drew in a huge breath and covered her mouth when she saw it. A fire crew battled with the fire still belching from *Miss Josephine*.

'Heard there was someone inside.' That made her head snap around.

'Someone inside?' she cried weakly.

The person next to her spoke, a small woman with a bobble hat on her head who Anna thought lived on one of the neighbouring boats. The woman tutted. 'Some woman. Couldn't get her out. No point now she'll be dead from the fumes.'

Woman inside? Anna scanned the crowd like crazy looking for Roxy. Left, right, behind. No Roxy. She'd left her mate working at the computer in *Miss Josephine*. Frantically she moved forward, but someone grabbed her arm. 'You can't go there, love.' But she was having none of it. She fought with them trying to break free. Trying to get to Roxy. More hands joined the ones already holding her back. She froze when two paramedics emerged from what was left of Misty's houseboat with a trolley. On it was a body covered, from top to toe, by a green sheet. She sagged, overwhelmed by her shock and screamed; 'Roxy! Roxy! Roxy!'

'Yeah, what's the problem?'

Schoolboy's heart nearly dived out of his body when he heard Jackie's voice behind him. Bollocks. He'd told her to stay put, bloody crazy woman. He kept his eyes on the gun pointed at him as he heard Jackie moving towards him. She stopped by his side and said, 'Did we overcharge you or something the last time you were here?'

Schoolboy sucked in his breath. Was Jackie out of her tree trying to joke at a time like this? Then he realised what she was doing – making the gorilla understand that she wasn't frightened of him. That was his Jackie, scared of nothing or nobody. Standing by his side, just like in the old days, her and him against the world.

Taking courage from his woman beside him, Schoolboy said, 'If you want the takings have them. They're in the till and there's a safe upstairs. Then I'd really appreciate it if you did one so that my customers can get back on with their meal.'

Silence. No one moved. The gunman didn't move. Then he swung the shooter from Schoolboy and aimed it at Jackie. Before Schoolboy could move to shield her the gunman aimed the shooter down and let off a spray of bullets in front of Jackie's feet. Jackie didn't even bat an eyelid, she just stood her ground. A few more screams pulsed in the air. Then as quick as it started, the shooting stopped. The gunman whirled around and rushed out of the restaurant.

Schoolboy took Jackie into his arms and yelled at Kelly, who was crouched in a corner, 'Call the cops. Ask for Detective Inspector Ricky Smart.'

forty-six

The pumping, loud music from the dance floor downstairs seeped into Misty's office as she stared at the old photograph in her hand. She kicked off her heels and stretched her long legs onto her desk. She wiggled the stiffness from her toes as she took a swift lug from the G&T in her hand. She often caught five minutes by herself when the club was rammed, just to re-charge her batteries. She popped the glass back on the table as she looked at the photo. It was of her four girls – Jackie, Ollie, Anna and Roxy. Except they hadn't been called those names back then, when they were fifteen. Jade, Grace, Amber and Ruby. Four fifteen-year-old girls running for their lives. Misty had looked after them on *Miss Josephine*. And that's where the picture had been taken, on board her beloved boat. The girls were all beaming as they sat on the roof in the summer on the Regent's Canal in King's Cross. They looked so different back then. Jackie was as plump as a pudding with long brown hair tied back in a ponytail; Ollie wore that baseball cap she never let go of and kept it so low as if she didn't want the world to see what emotions were hidden in her eyes; Roxy had been way thinner, looking shyly into the lens; and Anna, well she had long, plaited extensions then, but still stared into the camera as if she were loving the attention. Misty shook her head. Her girls had come such a long way. But she still worried about them. That business with Jackie's kid at the school made Misty feel sick. No wonder Jackie was trying to move heaven and earth to find out who did it. Even linking up with Kenny Lewis. Misty still wasn't sure whether that was a good idea; whether Kenny was playing straight with them. But he did seem to be genuinely blown away by what had happened to his grandkids.

She tipped the gin to her mouth as her thoughts turned to Roxy. There was something going on with that girl, but Misty couldn't quite pin down what it was. Maybe it was the way that Roxy laughed a bit too loudly, told one too many jokes that made Misty think something was up. When this business with Jackie and the Lewises was sorted she was going to sit Roxy down and get the truth, even if she had to squeeze it from her.

Misty stretched as the tune playing downstairs changed to some girl band number that all the young kids were humming these days; enough bass to make the girls want to shake their booty and forget about the naff lyrics. As she shoved her feet onto the floor and reached for her heels the phone went. Lazily she reached for it, fitting her feet back into her shoes at the same time.

'Yeah, yeah,' she said with a sunny tone. Then her happy mood vanished when she heard Anna talking frenetically. 'Hold up lady, I can't understand a word you're saying. Slow down.' Anna managed to compose herself and what Misty heard next made her shoot to her full six-one height. '*Miss Josephine?*' Her voice came out in a squeak. 'You're talking bollocks, no one would do that to my Josephine.' Anna's next words had Misty tumbling back into the chair. 'Roxy?' The blood drained away from her face.

'No one touch a thing,' Ricky announced as he strolled into the restaurant.

The people inside froze – Jackie and Schoolboy, near the bar, and a few members of staff scattered around. Sonny Begum and a forensic team followed behind him. Ricky quickly instructed the forensic team to start their work. The place looked like World War Three had just started.

'Hope this isn't one of your new menus,' Ricky said as he reached Jackie and Schoolboy.

Jackie twisted her mouth at him and Schoolboy nodded at him. Ricky nodded back. He'd always liked Schoolboy, admired him for pulling himself out of a life of crime. Ricky turned and surveyed the damage. And whistled. He turned back to them. 'So what's going on here?'

Jackie and Schoolboy caught each other's gazes for a few seconds, then Schoolboy answered. 'The usual bang the place up business. A geezer walks in and sprayed the place up.'

'Was it a robbery? Did he take anything?'

Schoolboy shook his head wearily. Ricky frowned. 'So if they didn't take anything why did they do it?' Once again the couple near him looked at each other. The wrinkled skin on Ricky's forehead deepened. 'Jackie, has this got something to do with the Lewis case?'

'I don't know,' Jackie rushed out breathlessly. Just the thought of her treading where she was told not to go, making all this happen, sickened her. Schoolboy's beautiful restaurant didn't look so hot any more.

Ricky grunted with disgust. 'I told you to stay well away from this. Why can't you understand that we've got our man? Bliss. Did. It. End of story.' Ricky waved his hand around. 'Someone could've got killed here tonight. How would you have felt about that?'

'Alright, that's enough.' Schoolboy stepped in, seeing Jackie's face grow pale. 'No one got hurt here. The hood rat most probably got the wrong place—'

But Ricky was having none of it and savagely cut in. 'Then you tell me why *Miss Josephine* went up in a ball of fire tonight as well?'

'What?' Schoolboy and Jackie said together, stunned.

'Didn't you know?' From their faces Ricky already had his answer. 'Happened about an hour ago.'

'Ohmygod,' Jackie exclaimed. Then another devastating thought occurred to her. 'Was anyone hurt?'

'Bollocks,' Ricky said softly. 'Why don't we go into Schoolboy's office and sit down.'

Jackie shook her head. 'No. Just fucking tell me.'

Ricky whispered his reply. 'I didn't go to the scene, but from what I hear there was a woman inside.' Ricky considered his next words carefully. 'No ID has been made yet.'

'What, you mean she's dead?' Jackie's emotional voice made everyone else in the room stop what they were doing and look at her. But she didn't see them, all she saw were her four mates. 'Who was it?' She stepped close to Ricky.

He shifted his eyes away from her. 'I don't know.'

But she wasn't letting him off the hook. She grabbed the collar of his jacket and twisted her hands around the material. 'Tell me!' Now she was shouting, her voice shaking.

Ricky could see the tears brimming in the bottom of her pleading eyes. 'They think it might be Roxy.' His arms moved quickly to catch her as Jackie's hands fell away from him and she fainted dead away.

'Are you sure it was Roxy?' Misty asked as she stared with disbelief at the remains of her treasured boat.

Beside her, a shaking Anna said in a choked-up voice, 'Must've been her. I left her on the boat before I hit Speedball Central.'

Misty continued to stare at the wreck of one of the best friends she'd ever had – *Miss Josephine*. She stepped closer to the edge of the canal and looked at the smouldering, blackened remains. A lump developed in her throat, not because she wanted to cry but because she was so flippin' angry. How could someone do this to her beautiful boat? Do that to Roxy? When she got her hands on them . . .

She felt Anna's cold hand on her shoulder. 'What are we going to do without Roxy?' She sniffed back a wave of emotion. 'I never forget the day you lot and Roxy first came to me on *Miss Josephine*.' She shook her head. 'Me and *Miss Josephine* have been together since I was twenty-five years old,' Misty said softly. She just kept staring at her lost friend. 'I was pissed off with life back then because every time I walked down the road in my clobber people kept staring at me as if I was some kind of friggin' freak. Back then I didn't have the front that I have now. I was scared, still weren't sure if I was doing the right thing. I just wanted to get away from it all. Spend some time on my own to figure out who I really was.' A tiny, sad smile flickered across her face. 'And that's

how we met, one bright summer's day on the banks of the River
Lea near Springfield Park. There was this for sale sign outside this
clapped out boat. She was a total mess, you couldn't even see what
her name was any more. She belonged to this old-time queen who
wanted to go off and live in Amsterdam. So I just did it, I bought
her. Got my brothers to help me get her into shape and I sailed off
in her.' Misty let out a puff of air filled with nostalgic delight. 'Two
lost women who needed a friend. I didn't think I could do it, but I
stayed on her the first time for a good six months, just us two, on
the water, in our own world. She gave me the confidence I needed
to become the person that I am. Without *Miss Josephine* I would
be nothing.' Now the tears pricked her grey eyes as she turned to
Anna.

But before Anna could answer, one of the cops near by walked
over to them. He addressed Anna. 'I believe you may have known
the woman who was on the boat?'

Anna nodded. He continued, 'Would you be willing to identify
the body?'

Anna looked grief stricken at Misty. Misty pushed her shoulders
straight and took Anna's hand in hers. 'Is there much left to ID?'

The cop nodded. 'Yes. She was curled up in a corner, but looks
like she died from smoke inhalation.'

Misty swallowed as Anna started sobbing. 'Yeah, I'll do it.'

Jackie came around on the sofa in Schoolboy's office. He was
kneeling on the floor next to her, his brown face filled with
concern. What the heck was she doing in his office? And why
was he looking at her as if someone had died? She froze as a mad
movie of the events of the night flashed though her mind: Preston
being operated on; the gunman shooting up Schoolboy's place;
Miss Josephine going down in a fire; Roxy . . .

She bolted upright. Schoolboy's arms came out to hold her
steady. 'Easy, girl.'

'Roxy.' It was a painful whisper.

Schoolboy took her into his arms. 'They don't know for sure if
it's her.'

She pushed away from him. 'This is all my fault. If I'd just left it all alone Roxy wouldn't be dead now.'

Schoolboy cupped her chin. 'You can't blame yourself—'

'Yes I bloody well can. *Miss Josephine* going up in smoke and bullets around this place are a warning. A warning for me to keep my fat nose out of it.'

'A warning from who?'

She shook her head. 'I don't know. All I do know is the more I find out for Kenny the more twisted this all gets.'

'What do you mean Kenny?' Jackie realised she'd dropped the big one in front of Schoolboy. Shit he was going to go bonkers. 'Tell me you ain't working for Kenny Lewis?'

She knew the time for telling porkies was gone. 'He ain't convinced that Bliss done it. And from what people are saying he might be right.' Jackie winced at the wounded look on Schoolboy's face. She shouldn't have hidden this from him, just like she should've told him ages ago about the lump in her boob. 'I need to find out who did this to our boy, and if that meant hooking up with Kenny Lewis then yeah, I was going to do it.'

Before he could answer, someone walked into the room. They looked up to find Kelly standing there. The woman still looking bloody cool, Jackie thought, even after the place had been shot up. Jackie felt a tiny spark of admiration for her. Kelly hesitated and then stepped forward. Her expression was grim. 'That was the hospital. They said you need to go back.'

The last time Misty had to ID a body was twenty-odd years back. Her mate Bluebelle, drag name The Mouth From Romford, had been beaten to death by someone who didn't like that she wore women's clothes. When she'd seen Bluebelle on that slab that had been the first time she'd ever seen her without her slapper on. An image that had never left her. And she knew that when she saw Roxy she was going to have another face to add to her nightmares.

She turned to Anna who stood beside her outside the door in the mortuary. 'You don't have to do this.'

Anna shivered. 'Yeah I do. I owe it to her. We fought like cats and dogs sometimes but that was just our way. I loved her and I need to be the one to tell her mum.'

From the emotion in Anna's voice Misty knew she was at breaking point. Seeing Roxy's dead body might tip her over the edge and Misty was worried what would happen to Anna. People dealt with grief in different ways and Misty remembered how Anna had tried to deal with what she thought was the loss of her mum by getting deep into drugs. She couldn't let that happen again. She'd taken a vow to look after her four girls years ago and that's what she was going to do.

'I'm doing it on my own,' Misty stated in her I've-made-my-mind-up voice.

'I have to do this,' Anna shot back with anguish.

'What you have to do is remember Roxy the way she was. Bubbly and bright and sometimes completely off her head. If you see her now you won't be able to do that.' The torment grew on Anna's face but she said nothing. Misty patted her on the arm. 'You wait here, yeah?'

Anna nodded. As Misty swept around, Anna caught her arm. 'Make sure her hair's tucked under. She always liked her bob to be bouncy.' That made Misty almost start booing her heart out, but she didn't. She had to stay strong for Anna and the others.

Misty turned to the female cop who stood near the door. And nodded. They entered a room that felt to Misty as if it were below zero. She shivered as she looked at the trolley in the middle of the room. The outline of a body moulded against the green cover. Oh God, oh God, oh God. How was she going to do this? As she carried on walking she thought back to the photograph of the girls she'd been looking at earlier. Roxy had been Ruby then, a quiet, shy thing, wearing thick glasses and always holding tight onto her asthma pump. That's what she was going to do, remember the face of Roxy as a young girl, when they made her look at her face now. Remember those lively grey eyes, that sweet smile.

The mortuary attendant gripped the sheet. She held her breath. Remember – lively eyes, sweet smile.

The cover was pulled back.

Lively eyes. Sweet smile.

The face was revealed. It was burnt beyond recognition. Misty stayed calm as the sheet was rolled back. That's when she saw it, a tiny rose tattoo still visible on one of the hands. Misty staggered back, her chest heaving. She slammed her gaze into the cop. 'That's not Roxy.'

Without another word Misty rushed out of the room. Anna immediately saw something was wrong.

'What is it?' she cried out when Misty reached her.

'It weren't her.'

'What?'

Relief started to flood Misty. 'The face was all gone, but there was this small rose tattoo—'

Anna staggered back. 'Oh no.'

'Do you know who it is?'

Anna nodded. 'This is all my fault. I told her to come and see me on the boat if she had—'

'Who?'

'Mickey's sister . . . Kimmie.'

forty-seven

Schoolboy and Jackie rushed along the corridor of the hospital ward. Abruptly they both stopped when they saw the doctor. She didn't look too happy.

'I need you to both come with me.' Before either Jackie or Schoolboy could say a word she moved ahead of them. Jackie's heart galloped. This wasn't good, wasn't good at all. The doc was most probably taking them into a room to break the bad news. How could she deal with Preston's death as well as Roxy's? They stopped outside a room. The doctor pushed the door back and said, 'After you.' They stepped inside.

'Sweet Jesus, Mary and all the saints,' Jackie let out as she stared into the open eyes of her son. She rushed over to him. Preston looked wiped out, his brown face still pale. He smiled at her but said nothing. She just nodded reassuringly at him and took his small hand in hers.

'It looks as if the operation was a success,' the doctor contin-ued. 'We managed to remove the clot, but we need to monitor his condition. He's tired so leave the talking until tomorrow.'

'When can we take him home?' Schoolboy asked, his eyes flick-ing to Jackie who just grinned like an idiot at their boy.

'Hopefully soon, but let's see how he gets on first.'

Jackie rushed across the room and threw her arms around the doctor. 'I can't thank you enough.' Then she let go, feeling a bit silly. The doctor must think she was a total prat behaving like this. 'Thank you.'

'You should both go home.'

But instead she pulled up a seat and sat down. 'I'm staying. I'm not taking my eyes off my boy this time.'

The doctor left them alone. Schoolboy looked dead on his feet though so she said, 'Go home and get some kip.'

He rubbed the back of his neck. 'Yeah, I might do that.'

But before he could leave, Jackie's mobile pinged. She pulled it out. Text:

Not Roxy. M

She breathed a huge, happy sigh and looked up at Schoolboy. 'The body on the boat wasn't Roxy.'

Once Schoolboy had left, she gave it ten minutes, enough time for Schoolboy to be well gone. Then she leaned over and kissed her son and as she straightened, her fury about the night's events began to grow. She was going to find out what happened tonight and she knew the person who might just be able to help her.

'Roxy!' Anna yelled as she whacked her fist against the front door. She'd raced across town to Roxy's home in Greenwich. She lived in a good-sized 1930s terrace in a tree-lined street. Roxy had enough of a pile to buy one of those monster-sized Victorian houses down the road, but they'd all agreed long ago not to be too flash with their cash. They didn't want anyone to find out where it had come from. Anna shifted from one foot to the other and hugged her arms around herself against the rapidly cooling night air.

'Roxy!' Anna went at it again.

She'd told Anna she'd be on the boat waiting for her. So where was she?

Anna peered through the window of the sitting room looking to catch any movement of the light coming through the drawn curtains. Finally she swore as she stepped back and yelled, 'Roxy, get your big, fat butt out here now girl!'

Anna let out a huge sigh of relief when a light popped on somewhere upstairs. Then she heard the patter of feet running down the stairs. She shuffled closer to the main door as the swift, hard movement of a bolt and lock sounded and the door opened.

A tousle-haired and red-eyed Roxy stared back at her in surprise. 'What's going on?'

Instead of answering, Anna flung her arms around her startled friend. 'I thought you were gone.'

'Gone?' Roxy whispered. She hitched herself away from the embrace. 'Of course I was gone, I went home. Decided to do a bit of work on the computer here instead of at the boat.'

'I thought you were doing your fifteen minutes of flame,' Anna rushed on. Seeing the confusion still in the smaller woman's face she snapped on. 'You know, got your ticket for the boneyard bonanza—'

Roxy's red-rimmed eyes ran over her, still lost. 'Why would I be dead?'

'Let's take this inside,' and without waiting for a reply Anna barged past Roxy into the house. She took no notice of the spacious and neat hallway as she headed for the lounge.

'Hang on a minute,' Roxy shot out flustered. 'You can't go in—' But it was too late, Anna was already inside the brightly lit room. Her nose twitched immediately. She knew that smell. She inhaled. Jack Daniels. Then she saw the empty bottle lying on the table. Oh no. Not Roxy. Not again.

She swung around to face Roxy, disbelief on her face. 'Tell me you ain't turned into a booze bitch again?'

Roxy wiped her fingers across her mouth as if she needed that drink badly right now. When she spoke her voice sounded dead. 'I tried, I really did.' Her head dipped down. 'But I got lonely. I'm not like you.' She looked up at Anna. 'I don't make mates, *real* mates, that easy. People will have a chat with me because they know I'm good for a giggle and a laugh – good ol' Roxy who looks like a dumpling and is as warm-hearted as a chicken chasseur casserole on a winter's night.' Anna winced at the pain laced in her voice. 'The last time I had it off was two years ago. Two years.' Now the tears started to fall. Her shoulders started to shake. 'I went to this escort agency and I had to pay for it. Pay for a bit of company.' Her hand thrust into her dressing gown pocket and she pulled out her inhaler. Sucked hard.

'Oh Roxy,' Anna replied softly, feeling every ounce of pain from her friend. 'Why didn't you come to us? Come to me?'

'Because I'm Roxy, the bubbly, bouncing bubblehead? Roxy doesn't have any problems because she's always the life and soul of the party. I didn't want to disappoint you lot.' She took another deep lug from her inhaler. 'That's why I wasn't at *Miss Josephine* because I decided to work at the computer at home instead. And then one thing led to another and I'm drinking like a fish in heaven. Finally, just nodded off. I did wake up at some stage and when I saw the clock I realised that something was wrong. Then it clicked I said I'd meet you on the boat, but I was too sauced so I went back to sleep.'

Anna walked towards her. 'I never thought I'd say this but the booze saved your life. If you'd come back to *Miss Josephine*—'

'What happened?'

They sat down and Roxy gasped as Anna took her through the events of the night. She covered her mouth when she heard what had happened at Schoolboy's restaurant.

'Who would do this?' she asked.

Anna shrugged. 'Dunno yet. But someone's trying to warn us off.'

'Whose body did they find?'

'Kimberley. I told her to come to the boat if she had any info about this brothel that Daisy wants finding. She must've come and couldn't get out.'

'What do you think she was going to tell you?'

'She did send me a text. I only realised I had it after we got to see her body.'

'What did it say?'

'50 Claremont Road. Must be the address of the brothel.'

'But if she told you the address why did she need to see you?'

Anna couldn't answer because she didn't know. But Claremont Road sounded familiar. Where had she heard it before?

*

A couple of hoodie-wearing youths, lounging beside the busted entrance door, eyed Jackie up as she strode towards Parkview Garden.

'Fancy a ride on my love handle Granny?' one of the boys let out as she nearly reached them. The youth laughed and high-fived one of his giggling friends.

She'd already taken a wagonload of stick tonight and she weren't in the mood to take any more. She turned her lethal, green eyes on him. 'You don't look old enough to know where to put it sonny. When you grow a dick come knocking on my door then.'

They just stared back, stunned. Little pricks most probably thought she'd be pissing herself with fear. The day she was scared shitless by a bunch of wannabe hood rats was the day she was six feet under. She swept past them into the communal reception. Hit the lift. Then she focused her mind on the one person she was gunning after – Flick Lewis. She just knew that he would have info on what had happened tonight. And if he was keeping it well and truly closed she would just have to turn those baby greens of hers on him. Flick wanted to get into her knickers alright and she might just let him have a touch if he was willing to talk.

She pressed the lift again in frustration but the red button remained on floor 10. It must be as broken as the entrance door, so she took the stairs. Breathing heavily she reached the fingerprint-smeared transparent door that led to the enclosed landing leading to Pinkie Lewis's door. As she pushed her hand against the glass Pinkie's door opened. She stopped. A man came out with his back to her followed by Flick. She darted around the corner. Gave it a few seconds, then sneaked a peak. The man with Flick threw his arms around him in a deep hug. Whoever it was knew Flick well. The man stepped back. Turned around. Gobsmacked, Jackie saw who it was.

Schoolboy.

In shock, she belted down the stairs.

forty-eight

The man in the balaclava took it off just before he got out of his motor. He stuffed it into his pocket as he walked up to the front door of the house in Stepney Green. Knocked. The door was opened by Stan Lewis a minute later.

Stan grinned when he saw who it was. Ushered him in.

'Who's that?' Tiffany screamed from upstairs.

'Mind your own,' Stan yelled back. He turned his attention onto the man in front of him. Didn't invite him into the main room, they didn't have that type of relationship.

The man spoke. 'I got it done.'

'Think you put enough frighteners on the bitches?'

The man laughed. 'They ain't gonna be no trouble any more. I came to tell you that the shipment will be in tonight. Dead on eight.'

'Good man.' Stan was feeling on top of the world. Tomorrow he was going to put Bliss out of business for good. Show the East End who the real number one Face was.

The other man's face hardened. 'You owe me big time so I expect my cut. If anyone finds out what we did—'

'They ain't going to unless you tell. Me and you are the only ones who know.'

'What about your brother Flick? What about if he figures out where Bliss's stash house is?'

'Don't worry about him, he's too busy trying to worm his way back into the family.' Stan didn't like the expression he saw on the other man's face, like he wasn't telling him something. Maybe about Flick? 'You know something I should know?'

The expression disappeared from the man's face. 'No. Be there tomorrow night.'

Then the man was gone.

Misty caught Mickey just as he was leaving his place under The Arches.

'Misty,' he greeted her. 'I'm glad you popped over because I—'

'Kimmie's gone,' Misty cut over him starkly.

Mickey froze, but he didn't look shattered. 'What happened?' So she told him.

Mickey looked into the dark night and shook his head. 'Funny thing is my Kimmie's been gone for a long time. I knew this would happen some day.'

'Do you want me to—'

He shook his head again this time turning to her. 'No. I need to get home and tell her Mitch.'

Misty began to retreat but he stopped her. 'Remember that info you wanted, about someone called Hill?' Misty nodded. 'I knew I'd heard the name somewhere. Kenny had an older sister called Glenda and she got hitched to a fella called Stuart Hill. Respectable, and Glenda never had nothin' to do with the family business.' He saw her next unspoken question in her eyes. 'Donna and Martin were Glenda and Stuart's kids.'

Misty's mouth fell open. Then she said, 'So those two kids were Flick and Stan's first cousins.'

The house was silent. Jackie quietly and quickly entered her home. She leaned against the inside of the front door still reeling from seeing Schoolboy with Flick. Schoolboy with Flick. In her mind she saw them embracing, talking. She'd walked around in a daze before coming back home, trying to fit it all together. What the fuck was going on?

'Baby?' Jackie looked up to find her mum standing at the bottom of the stairs, her arms wrapped around herself. The hall light above

Nikki's head shone on her hair, giving it a rich, red glow. She stepped closer, her face stamped with concern. 'It's not Preston again is it? Schoolboy said he's OK.'

Jackie shook her head. 'He's fine. He should be home soon.'

Before Jackie could breathe, her mum had her in her arms. They held on tight to each other as if the nightmare was finally over. School and Flick flashed in Jackie's mind. She knew it was far from over.

'Mum, do me a favour?' Puzzled, Nikki gazed back at her. 'Whatever you hear going on downstairs just stay put with Darius for me.'

'What's going on, Jackie?' Her mum's voice was soft and hard at the same time.

'Let's just say that me and—' But before she could finish, the sitting room door opened. Schoolboy stood in the doorway.

Nikki looked between them, nodded at her daughter and left them alone.

'Babe?' Schoolboy asked. Then one of his dimple popping smiles spread across his face. She didn't smile back. 'Come in here.' Then his head shot back inside the room. Finally she moved to join him. She found him standing next to the music system, still wearing that silly grin. He laughed as he reached over and switched the CD player on. 'Remember this?' he asked as he turned back to her.

Frowning, she waited for the music to start. Kool and The Gang's 'Get Down On It' grooved into the room. She couldn't help but smile. It was their song. The first song they'd ever danced to at their first date down at the Fuzzy Wuzzy, a club in Hackney that had long since been knocked down to make way for the new East London Line extension. She remembered how cautious they'd been around each other that night. They'd both been dealt some hard kicks by life and just weren't sure about how to deal with the feelings they'd had for each other. She'd been a single mum, bringing up a seven-year-old and he'd been a former drug dealer hoping that his love of cooking would keep his fingernails clean. But as soon as they'd touched, hand to hand, hip to hip, moving around

the dance floor, they'd known they were made for each other. The
memories drew her smile out even more.

Suddenly Schoolboy started clicking his fingers and moving like
he was James Brown. That's the Schoolboy she loved and remembered; a guy who was up for a laugh and a giggle any time of the
day.

'We need to talk—' she started.

But he wasn't listening to her as he did a three-sixty spin. She
couldn't help it, she laughed out loud. 'Jackie, don't you get it?
Our boy's alright. He's coming home. Nothing else matters.' Still
moving his body like he was in an old black and white Motown
video, he boogied on over to her holding out his hands. He took
her hands in his. 'What are you doing?' she cried out as he fixed
his hips to hers.

'Come on, babe – you remember the moves.' He shifted his hips
to the left. To the right. Left. Right. She couldn't help it, she began
to move along with him. And it was like they were back at the
Fuzzy Wuzzy all over again. Soon her feet were joining the beat
and he was swinging her around the room.

'That's it girl, let it go.'

'You're bloody nuts you are,' she answered between shots of
laughter.

He smiled into her eyes. 'Remember how instead of singing, "Get
down on it," we used to sing, "Get down on it/Does she want it/Get
down on it/Fuck she wants it."' She laughed again as she remembered exactly what the *it* in their version of the song was referring
to. And that's what they did, began to sing their version of the
song as they whirled and twirled around the room. And for just a
short time they forgot everything else except that their little boy
was coming home. Coming home so that they could be a family
again.

Then out of the blue he whispered, his lips brushing her neck, 'I
love you.'

She drew back from him and stared directly into his eyes. 'If
that's true, tell me why I saw you with Flick Lewis?'

*

There was no music any more. No Kool and The Gang. Jackie and Schoolboy just stared at each other, a few steps separating them, the ground under their feet no longer feeling like a dance floor but the canvas of a boxing ring. Her question hung in the air between them.

'You gonna answer me or what?' she finally broke the silence with her soft question.

She saw him flick his tongue out and lick his bottom lip and she knew what that meant, he was desperately trying to dream up a story. 'Don't bullshit me,' she added, shoving her balled hands on her hips.

He tilted his head to the side, his locks swaying as he let out a heavy-duty sigh. 'Can't we chat about this tomorrow? For tonight can't we just pretend we really are a family?'

The skin on her forehead screwed up furiously. 'What do you mean pretend?'

He shook his locks back as he straightened his head. 'You don't even sleep with me any more. Won't let me touch me. Any other bloke would've found someone else by now.'

She took a mad step towards him. Now he was overstepping the mark. 'Is that's what's been happening? You and posh bird Kelly been getting it on behind the dessert trolley?' She was almost afraid of him answering.

'And if I had, would anyone blame me?' His next words shocked her. 'I knew Flick when I was banged up.'

'But you ain't been in the slammer for donkey's years and you must be a good many years older than Flick.' But she saw from the expression on his face that he was telling the truth. 'Why didn't you say nothing to me before? You made out like you didn't know the Lewises.'

Schoolboy drew in a deep breath as he cupped his hand over his mouth. Let it out as his hand fell away. 'And I don't know them and don't want to either. But I don't think of Flick as one of them. When I see him I just see this scared kid who was pushed into the big boys' house after transferring from some youth offenders' craphole. The only thing that made him laugh was dressing up and doing parts in those plays.'

Her mind started ticking away. Back to the time they were sitting by Preston's bed in the hospital and he'd told her about this kid who he'd shared a cell with. Who had . . .

Her breathing broke painfully in her chest, making the lump in her breast twitch. 'Is Flick the kid who—'

'Murdered his two cousins? Yeah.'

forty-nine

'Breaking Up Is Hard To Do' played for the third time as Flick sat alone in the dark in the bedroom. The room where it had all happened. The reason why he'd come back. Why he was going to make sure it all ended tomorrow night. As Neil Sedaka's voice pulsed around, his mind shot back ...

Fourteen-year-old Flick grinned as he lay on the bed watching Stan, Donna and Martin have a massive pillow fight. Him and Stan were still in the suits they'd worn to make their Confirmation earlier that day. After having a bit of a bash at their house all the grown-ups had taken off to the boozer, so Nan was looking after them at hers. Nan was playing that old-style tune – something about hearts getting broken – in the sitting room. He could hear her singing and knew that she was dancing away. She always danced – The Twist was her favourite – after she drank that thick stuff she had in her glass. Looked bloody yucky to him. He weren't going to drink none of that booze when he got older. Nah, he was gonna grow up to be like his old man, tough and someone that everyone respected.

'Ouch,' Donna yelped after a massive wallop Stan had given her with the pillow.

Flick eased off the bed. 'Oi,' he told his younger brother. 'Take it easy. She's a baby compared to you.'

Stan threw him a stubborn look. 'But she hit me first.'

'It's meant to be a game,' Flick reasoned.

'Dad said if someone slugs you one you gotta show 'em who's boss.'

Flick pulled Stan back by the collar of his fancy jacket. 'Dad don't mean your cousin—' Before he could finish Donna and Martin bashed Stan over the head at the same time. Now it was Stan's turn to let out a shout of pain. Flick shook his head. Every time his cousins came over and they started play fighting it would always end up in a serious ruck.

Suddenly Stan started crying. He pointed his finger at his cousins. 'I'm gonna fucking get you two.' His cousins just laughed at him.

'Oi,' Flick shot at Stan. 'None of that bad language in here or Nan will take her belt to you.'

'Cry baby. Cry baby. Cry baby.' The cousins started taunting Stan, who started crying harder.

'You two.' Flick pointed at them. 'Leave it out.' He liked his cousins but sometimes they got right on his nerves. They had a nasty, mean streak in them that his Aunty Glenda just couldn't see. As far as she was concerned they were her little angels. Couldn't put a foot wrong.

'Look what Nan bought us,' Stan said, his tears drying up as suddenly as they'd come. He opened the top of his shirt and showed his gawping cousins the gold chain with the Virgin Mary that Nan had given him for his Confirmation. 'Flick's got one as well.'

'Uh!' Donna let out in disgust. 'I think it's ugly.'

'Bet it ain't even real,' Martin joined in.

Stan glared back at his cousins and reached across and pushed Martin in the chest.

Flick grabbed his brother's arm and swung him around. 'I've already told you to lay off hitting them—'

'I'm gonna do him I am,' Stan replied imitating their old man.

'Look what my dad bought me,' Martin said. As the others gathered around he pulled out a penknife from his pocket. Flicked the blade.

'Wow,' Stan said, his eyes mesmerised by the sharp knife.

'Put it away,' Flick said quickly. 'Before Nan sees it. You know she don't like no funny business in her house.'

But Martin ignored him. Flick stood up and moved towards the door. 'Right, I'm getting myself a drink from the kitchen, so who else fancies one?' But the others were too caught up in Martin showing off his knife. Flick wandered into the kitchen and mixed himself an orange squash. On his way back to the bedroom he noticed Nan slumped in her favourite chair, fast asleep. He smiled. He loved his nan. He loved spending nights over at hers, listening to her talking about the good ol' days; watching her put her make-up on and do her hair.

He snapped out of his happy thoughts when he heard the noise coming from the bedroom, shouts and something falling over. He'd bloody well told them to keep the noise down and behave. When he got back to the room Martin and Stan were going at each other on the bed fighting like a couple of five-year-olds.

'Stop it!' he yelled as he slammed his drink on the bedside table.

But the boys wouldn't listen. He tried to pull them apart. Tried to . . . Picked up the . . .

Sweating heavily, Flick shot out of his nightmare. But one image wouldn't leave him. The one of Nan standing in the doorway, staring at his cousins lying on the floor; at the knife in his hand; at the blood all over his Confirmation suit.

After Nanny Nikki left him, Darius slipped out of bed, got on his knees and started to pray. Telling God that he was going to keep his promise and take back his and Molly's secret tomorrow because God had let his brother live.

fifty

The next morning Anna was up early, which wasn't her usual style. She loved cuddling up to Bell under the duvet, and then when her girlfriend was gone she loved nothing better than to roll around in bed for an hour or two just soaking up the warmth. A girl who partied as hard as she did needed to get her beauty sleep. But not this morning, she'd hit the street looking for the brothel. Number 50 Claremont Road. And as soon as she stepped onto Claremont Road she knew why it was familiar. It was the same street where the Lewis girls had been killed. Fancy the brothel being on the same street, Anna thought. She wore large, Jackie-O style shades and a Baker Boy cap to keep as much of her face hidden as possible. Her amber gaze scanned the street – a sweetshop on the corner, the school where Jackie's kids went and large Victorian houses. Houses with huge, jutting bay windows, decorative plaster work, attic rooms tucked up at the top and memories of what this capital city was like a hundred years ago. Most people would kill to get a house like that, but not her. She was a modern girl and needed a modern flat, so the warehouse conversion she shared with Bell overlooking the Regent's Canal in King's Cross was right up her street. She did a full sweep of the houses, wondering which one was the brothel Daisy was after.

She checked out the number of the first house. Number 1. Odd numbers. The brothel must be on the same side of the street as the school. She crossed over and started walking and checking door numbers as she went. Number 2. 4. 6. 8. 10. She kept going until the houses became the school. The happy yells and shouts of kids fooling around in the playground sounded in the background as she peered at the number above the closed, iron entrance gate of the school. Number 48. So she was near. It must be one of the next two houses coming up.

She left the school and carried on walking. Hit the next house. Number 52. She froze. Can't be. Where the heck was number 50? Maybe it was on the other side of the road. No, those were all odd numbers. She stared at the houses opposite. But just in case she'd got it wrong she moved to cross the road. She stepped into the road as a car came tearing down the street. She jackknifed back as the car beeped its horn furiously at her, just missing her.

'Oi,' she yelled out. 'There's a bloody school here.' But the car kept on going. She flipped her finger at the back of the car. Then she could've kicked herself. She was not meant to be attracting any attention to herself. She scurried across the remainder of the road. Checked the first house she came to. Number 53. Moved back to the next house. Number 51. What the hell was going on? Where was number 50? Baffled, she rubbed her hand over her chin, wondering what she should do next. She might blow her cover but she was going to need to ask someone. She walked towards the green gloss door of number 51 and knocked. Immediately the rough bark of a dog sounded. She stepped back. A dog might be a man's best friend, but they weren't no friend of hers. She hadn't like the mutts since that incident at Schiphol Airport in Holland years ago. As she debated whether to leg-it the door opened. A woman, maybe in her thirties, face red and cross, aggressively asked, 'What do you want? If you're a reporter you can piss off. The school's had enough to deal with without you bastards sniffing around.'

Anna realised that the woman was referring to the Lewis girls' death. They must've had Grub Street parked up here at one stage. She moved closer and settled a tiny smile on her face. 'I ain't no journalist—'

'Journalist?' The woman's mouth curled as if she'd just cursed. 'Bunch of word rats, that's what they are, the lot of 'em. Sticking their hooters where no one wants them to. I'll stick my Harvey onto the next one that comes knocking.'

Anna swallowed hard, knowing that Harvey was the name of the dog inside and she didn't need to see him to know that he'd be some motherfucker with huge canines. 'Like I said, I ain't a reporter. Just wanted to know if you knew where number 50 is.'

The woman poked her head further out of the doorway. 'Number 50 what?'

'The houses on the street. I can't find number 50.'

The woman let out a long sigh. 'All I know is this is number 51. Number 50 I don't know about. I don't stick my nose into anyone else's business.' And with that she slammed the door making Harvey bark his head off again.

Anna moved back into the street. She was going to find the brothel if it killed her. She pushed her Jackie-O's further up her nose and with determined strides, went up the street. Down the street. Up again. Down again. No number 50. As the voices of the kids in the school died away, as they left the playground to go back to their lessons to learn, Anna pulled off her cap in frustration, wondering if Kimmie had got the wrong address.

Bliss was suited and booted as he waited nervously for his brief, Daisy Sullivan, to arrive. He sat sandwiched between two screws in a back room of the court building. Both of them had been part of the crew that had done him over yesterday. He didn't know what he was going to do, but he couldn't go back to Oldgate. He knew he wasn't ever going to see the sun rise again if he did.

Suddenly one of the screws shoved his face into Bliss's. 'When we get back I'm going to finish you off.'

Bliss tensed as he felt warm, heavy breath on the other side of his face. He didn't need to look around to know that it was bastard screw number two. 'Nah, I say leave him in the gym for the others to get him.'

'Or what about in the shower?' the other taunted.

They went on and on, playing where best to kill someone ping-pong. Their faces getting closer. Their breaths getting hotter. He could feel his heartbeat jacking so hard he thought it was going to pop straight out of his chest. He clenched his handcuffed fists. He was going to explode if they didn't stop. If they didn't . . .

'Excuse me gentlemen.' All three men looked up at the figure in the doorway. Daisy Sullivan. She looked relaxed and cool in a just below the knee navy blue suit, polished black heels and her gleaming hair tied back into a knot. 'I hope that you've been looking after my client,' she carried on softly as she stepped into the room.

The prison officers moved out of Bliss's space, one of them rubbing his teeth together like he was getting ready to spit.

'I'd like a word with my client.' She took in the other two men's faces, her expression clearly saying she wasn't about to take any shit. 'In private.'

The POs got up. 'You've got five minutes.'

Once they were gone, Daisy eased herself into a seat next to Bliss and placed her leather briefcase on the floor. She scanned his face. 'You aren't looking too good. Has something happened?'

'Something happened?' He stared back at her as if she'd just arrived from Mars. 'I'm doing time for a crime I didn't commit.'

'You've not been convicted of anything yet—'

'Well the judge is going to send me back and I can't go back.'

Daisy checked him out more closely, the worry showing on her face. 'What's happened?'

He almost told her about being roughed up, but he didn't. He'd never been a grass and he wasn't about to start now. No, if he went back he'd have to find a way to handle things. 'All you need to know is I can't go back.'

Daisy said nothing as she just kept watching him. Then she leaned towards him. 'I might be able to help you. You might not like it though.'

'Just tell me,' he growled.

'OK. This is what we're going to have to do . . .'

They should've been celebrating Preston's recovery, but the women weren't. All they could think about was what had happened last night. They sat at the bar in the Shim-Sham-Shimmy, Misty at her usual spot behind the bar, facing the TV screen on the wall opposite and the others sitting on stools with drinks on their Doris Day and Rock Hudson 'Pillow Talk' place mats.

It was Anna who finally broke their gloomy silence. 'Well, at least Roxy ain't a goner.'

That should've cheered them up but it didn't because they all thought about who was dead. Poor Kimmie.

Misty looked sadly into the clear depths of her G&T. 'Know what Mickey said to me when I told him about his sister?' No one answered. 'She was a goner years ago he says, but he was cut up about it alright.' Suddenly she flicked her intense, grey eyes up at the others. 'We've got two choices ladies, we can either find out who was behind last night's mad movie or we can take this back to Kenny and wash our hands of it.'

Silence settled into the room as each woman sank into her own thoughts. It was Ollie who broke it. 'This needs to be Jackie's decision. It was her son who was hurt. She was the one who wanted justice.' What she didn't say to the others was that she just couldn't get out of her head what the dead woman Doris Hunter had meant when she'd told Jackie she'd seen all those men. What men?

The others all turned their gazes onto Jackie. She looked back at each of them in turn. Last night had been a hell of a night. Preston was alright now and maybe that should be enough for her. And how would she feel if she continued and her mates got hurt this time around? What if it *had* been Roxy who had been on *Miss Josephine*? How would she feel if she had to stand by a grave and watch Roxy being lowered into it? She shivered and answered, 'I say we turn our backs on this and leave it alone.'

No one made a sound but the air of relief blew into the room. Misty straightened. 'Right.' She pushed an easy smile onto her lips. 'I think we should plan a bash, like we were going to, to celebrate Preston and Darius's Confirmation. What do you say?'

Anna piped up, 'That's what we were going to do before and that's what we should do now. It's time to celebrate the living.'

Jackie knew they were all waiting for her response. She didn't feel much like partying. Just wanted to get her boys home and lock the doors and keep them safe. But hey, why not? Her boys deserved it. A full-grown grin spread across her face. 'Yeah. That's what we're gonna do, say cheers to life. Say . . .' She stopped when she saw the look on Misty's face. Misty looked pale, her eyes glued to the plasma TV screen. Jackie twisted around the same time as her friends. They all gasped when they read the breaking news headline running across the bottom of the screen:

Paul Bliss pleads guilty to dangerous driving. Bail granted.

fifty-one

Kenny heard the news the same time he got his first letter in his new prison cell. The inmate who delivered the letter was young and doing the last stretch of a sentence for ABH. Big-headed sort, Kenny had decided, who he didn't like much, but the lad was obviously out to impress Kenny because of his reputation. As he passed the letter over he said, 'Heard something you want to know.'

'Oh yeah?' Kenny kept his reply casual. He hadn't come in here to make any new mates.

'Bliss is on the streets again.'

'You what?' Kenny grabbed him by the throat and dragged him forward.

The other man choked as Kenny pressed down against his windpipe. 'You better not be shitting me about lad.'

The youth spluttered, 'Honest, I ain't.'

Kenny relaxed his hold and waited. 'Heard the screws chatting this morning when I got the post. Said he's pleaded guilty. Something about dangerous driving. They let him out on bail.'

Kenny shoved the boy away with anger as he yelled, 'Bastard.' Bliss had sworn to him that he'd never done it. Never touched a hair on the head of his own nieces. What the fuck was going on? And when Stan found out . . . Kenny knew he had to get out of here.

The other prisoner staggered to the door just as a screw came in. His eyes took in the situation. 'Everything OK in here?'

Kenny's eyes turned to the younger prisoner and dared him to open his mouth. The boy knew better and kept it well shut. So

Kenny answered, nice and easy. 'Yes, boss. Just passing the time of day.'

The screw nodded. 'Just reminding you that we have got a guest speaker in tonight. Hope you're going to sign up for it.'

As part of its programme to get residents ready to re-join the outside world, the open prison ran a programme of events that included guest speakers. Kenny didn't have a clue what he was going on about. He didn't have time to think about bloody guest speakers. If he didn't get out of here there was going to be major league trouble on the streets. His sons were going to be out to kill each other.

The screw was still talking, the other prisoner long gone. 'The Number One likes everyone to show their face at these things. Even lets one of the prisoners drive the guest to the station after. Of course, that ain't going to be you because you haven't been here long enough, but impress the Number One and you could make it onto the special privileges list.'

Fuck the Number One, Kenny wanted to growl but he didn't, he kept it nice and cool. It wouldn't do for this screw to know he'd heard the news about Bliss. ''Course I'll be there, sir.'

And with that the screw left him alone. He pulled his pillow up and took out his mobile. Called Bliss. Voicemail. Shit. Called Stan. No fucking response. He whispered down the phone, 'Don't do nuthin' stupid.' Then he cut the call.

He sank onto his narrow bed next to the letter. He should get up and do his Tai Chi, get back into feeling calm all over again. But his mind just kept turning and turning and turning. Absently his hand reached for the letter. Ripped it open. But instead of a letter out popped a photo. Old. Showed him with his arms around his mum in his club in Hoxton years back. But what caught his eye was someone had drawn a pink circle around his head. There was a line running from the circle to another circle around someone's head in the background. Mo, Bliss's mum. The air caught in his throat as he saw the pink love heart someone had drawn above the line linking him and Mo. Fucking hell. Someone knew about him and her. Did they know that he was Bliss's dad?

*

Stan got the news the same time that his new child came, bawling its head off, into the world. All the other new dads were in the delivery rooms with their partners, probably with tears in their eyes as they witnessed birth first hand. Not Stan. He was waiting in the corridor. He'd been there at the birth of the twins and it had all been a bit messy for him; all that screaming, for crying out loud. No, he didn't need any of that this time round.

He'd been waiting a good few hours already when a pretty nurse, all rosy cheeks and smiles, brought the baby out to him. As soon as she reached him he pushed away the clothing wrapped around the kid. Looked down. Grinned like the mad hatter. 'A boy.' He laughed out loud. A son.

'Your partner has been calling for you,' the nurse said, gently securing the sheet around the baby again.

'Yeah sure,' he replied. 'Just got to make a call.'

She smiled assuming she knew that he was getting on the blower to his family. But he wasn't. He pulled out his mobile. As soon as the line connected he hissed, 'I've got a son you bitch. You hear that. A son. Something you were never able to give me—'

'Oh yeah,' his ex-wife screamed back. 'You sure he's yours? The way I hear, that tart Tiffany was spreading it for anyone who would pay her cab fare home at night.'

His hand tightened on the phone. 'He's mine alright. Looks just like me.' He cut the call. She might be biting back but he could hear the tears in her voice.

Just as he turned towards the delivery room he saw Flick walking down the corridor towards him.

'I've got a boy,' he said proudly.

But Flick wasn't smiling. 'You need to stay calm.'

All the joy left Stan. 'What's up?'

'Bliss is out. Says he did it.'

'That fucker.' Stan bolted forward, but Flick caught his arm and held on tight. 'If you do something stupid now, you're going to mess up all our plans.' Stan looked at him, rage clouding his face. But he didn't move. 'Just think about it. He needed to get out because he's got something coming through—'

'He's got a shipment coming through tonight,' Stan cut in harshly. 'How do you know?'

Stan sniggered. 'Let's just say I know a man who knows.'

'Where?'

Stan shook his head. 'That, you don't need to know . . .'

'You're going to need someone there beside you.'

Stan just laughed. 'Don't worry, I will. Last breath Bliss takes will be tonight.'

'Sir, I just heard,' Detective Sonny Begum said quietly as she popped her head around Ricky's office door.

She could tell from the hard set of her boss's features that he was as mad as hell. She moved inside and closed the door behind her. Approached his desk. 'What are we going to do about it?'

Ricky gazed down at Bliss's open file on his desk. Shit. He'd never thought this would happen in a million years. Mind you, why was he surprised, Daisy was a top of the range lawyer.

He pulled his eyes away from the file and leaned back in his seat. 'There isn't much we can do. All we should do is wait for the trial. My big problem at the moment is Stanley Lewis's reaction when he—' The sound of Sonny's mobile going stopped his words.

With a look of irritation she pulled out her mobile. Turned her back on him and whispered into the phone. He leaned forward trying to pick up her words, but he couldn't. She was quick and as soon as she finished she swung around to him. He didn't like the pale look on her face. What was going on with her?

He shoved himself up. 'There isn't going to be any blood spilled on my patch. We need to find Bliss before Stan Lewis does.'

Sonny coughed, an uncomfortable expression covering her face. 'I'm really sorry, sir, but I need to get away for a few hours.'

Ricky moved around the desk never taking his dark gaze off her. 'What's going on Sonny?'

She avoided his eyes. 'Nothing, sir. Just something personal I've got to sort out.'

'We don't do personal, not on the job. People like *us* need to give it more than one hundred per cent if we want to get to the top.'

She knew what he meant by us. Black people. High flying jobs in the Met didn't come to them easy. If they wanted the top brass to take notice of them they had to work twice as hard as their white colleagues. That's just how it was.

'I'm sorry, sir. I need to do this.' And without waiting for his consent she left the office.

Ricky gave it a few minutes then headed for the door. He rushed down the corridor. Headed for his car as soon as he got outside. He should've started hunting for Bliss but he didn't. Instead he began to tail Detective Sonny Begum in her car.

Paul Bliss knew he had to stay low until tonight. So he'd been holed-up in the back seat of his car in a motorway service station off the M25 since he'd got bail. Not even Sean knew where he was. He still couldn't believe it but his bird brief had got him out. If his hands hadn't been cuffed when she suggested the only way out was to plead guilty he would've backhanded her one. Guilty? No way. But she'd calmed him down and told him that the judge he was up before was an advocate of rehabilitation, so if he pleaded guilty to dangerous driving and showed a wagonload of remorse the judge might buy it. If he didn't cop to doing it, the judge was likely to be unsympathetic and sling him back in a place where he knew he'd be a goner by the end of the day. So he'd done the whole 'I didn't mean to do it, sir' routine, swearing blind that he was sorry from the bottom of his heart. And that old codger of a judge had swallowed the lot.

Now he was back out he could take care of business. All he had to do in the meantime was stay out of his brother's way. Once the deal was over, Stan could come looking for him alright, and when he did . . .

His mobile went off again. Been buzzing so much he'd been tempted to turn it off. He looked down at the call display. His dad. Again. He should answer it, but he didn't. Instead he waited for the ringing to stop, then picked up the phone.

'Where the fuck are you?'

'I'm coming. It wasn't easy for me to leave—'

'Look doll, you get your arse here. You've got thirty minutes left.'

Ricky sat two cars behind Sonny. He'd been following her for the last twenty-five minutes. He didn't know where she was going except her car was heading out of town. He didn't want to believe what his instincts were telling him, that his right-hand woman was hiding something from him. Shit, what was he going to do if it was true? What if she was mixed up in all of this?

His mobile pinged. One hand still on the wheel he pulled it out. Text. From Daisy.

Don't 4rget dinner 2nite.

He smiled. It was their anniversary. Two years together. Two years of pure bliss. Bliss. Shit, he thought about the aggro she'd unleashed by getting Bliss out. The lights ahead turned red. The car ahead of him stopped. He watched as Sonny's car motored ahead. Bollocks. He slammed his fist on his horn, but the car in front wasn't moving. He watched as she disappeared in the distance knowing there was no way he was going to be able to follow her now.

A weary Daisy threw the shopping bags on the kitchen table. She braced her hands on the table and took a deep breath. What a day. She knew that Jackie was going to be upset with her, but she'd only been doing her job. If she'd left Bliss inside he wouldn't be coming out alive. He hadn't said a word, but she suspected that someone had beaten the shit out of him. So she'd got him out and she didn't question herself about whether it was right or wrong. She closed her eyes as a wave of dizziness hit her and smiled. Her hand touched her tummy. She still couldn't believe that she was going to be a mum. Thoughts of her own mum came to her and she pinched her lip with her teeth. It always hurt when she thought about the woman who'd given birth to her. Who'd abandoned her. She'd never leave her own child, never.

She jumped when she heard the ping of the intercom. Couldn't be Ricky, it was way too early. Better not be him because she hadn't got their anniversary dinner ready yet.

She smiled when she saw who was on the video screen. She pressed for them to come on up.

She opened the door to a flustered looking Auntie Anna. 'Jackie is one unhappy lady,' Anna said as soon as she came in.

'You know I can't discuss my clients.'

Anna just made a scoffing sound as she tilted her hip and popped a fist onto it. 'I found it.'

'The brothel?'

Anna nodded. 'Well sort of. A working girl I know. She texted me but also went to see me at the boat—'

'Oh no.' Daisy covered her lips in dismay. 'She wasn't the one who died?'

'Yeah. I feel well shit about it. If it weren't for me she wouldn't have been there. But like I said she sent me a text with the knocking shop's address. 50 Claremont Road. I went looking for it, but couldn't find it anywhere.'

Daisy frowned. 'Isn't that the same street the school's on?'

'Yep. The numbers of the houses went from 2 to 48 then jumped to 52. Couldn't find it anywhere.'

Daisy thought for a minute. 'But where could it be?'

Anna shrugged. 'Maybe Kimmie got the wrong road or something. I can ask around some more for you if you want.'

Daisy shook her head making her black hair move like a shimmering curtain. 'No. Don't worry.'

'Told lover boy about the baby yet?'

Daisy smiled. 'I'm going to do it tonight. We're having an anniversary dinner.'

'Well you make sure he pops the question or he's gonna have to answer to me.' Anna headed for the door, but stopped when she heard Daisy's words.

'Tell Jackie I'm sorry about Bliss.'

Anna arched her perfectly shaped eyebrow. 'You need to be doing that yourself.'

*

Schoolboy stared at the gun as he stood in the study at home. Even in his days on the street he'd stayed away from shooters. Getting tooled up was a mug's game. But what father wouldn't do what he was doing now? Some scumbag admits to running your kid over and now he's running around town as free as a bird? Now that just wasn't right, was it? How could the justice system have let him back on the street? Justice? Schoolboy felt like taking the gun and going to find the judge first and then Bliss. And he was going to do it. If the law wasn't going to sort this out, he was.

He picked the gun up . . .

'You can't do it.'

He spun around to find Jackie standing in the doorway. The light from the passage formed behind her and for the first time in ages he saw how small she was. Barely a couple of inches above five foot. And he saw the toll the last few weeks had taken on her. Her freckles stood out on her pale skin, her green eyes had lost their shine and the hair above the front of her forehead, which she loved to punch up, lay flat and lifeless.

He knew what she was asking him to do, but he didn't put the gun down.

'What are you going to do if the kids lose their dad?' She stepped inside, remained at the door. 'What am I going to tell the boys?'

'That their dad did the only thing any man would do for his sons. I know Preston's alright now, but it ain't right that Bliss should be walking around town. No fucking way.'

'No.' She moved closer to him. Kept her eyes steady on his tense face. 'You're not doing this. I won't—'

'You need to get out of my way, Jackie.' His tone was rock hard like steel.

Her hands formed into fists by her side. 'Do you remember what that life was like?' He knew what life she was referring to. Hadn't been much of a life. 'Shit, that's what. Selling gear on some street corner, knowing that if you trod on the wrong toes you'd be yesterday's news. And don't give me no BS coz that's what nearly happened.' She took the last step into his space. 'I knew you when you were nearly a dead bloke. I don't want you to ever go back to being that.'

Suddenly he squeezed his eyes tight. He knew she was right. His days lived in the cracks and grime of London city were ones he'd tried to put behind him; never thought about any more. And now here he was, full circle, with a shooter in his hand.

'Please.'

He pushed his eyes back open. She held her hand out to him. Leaned forward. Took the gun from his hand. Let it drop on the floor. Then he started shaking. Really shaking, like every bone in his body was coming apart.

'Baby,' Jackie whispered seeing his distress. She wrapped her arms around him. His arms came around her and they clung to each other in a way they hadn't done for a long time. Then the phone in the study rang.

'Leave it,' she said.

So they did. Just let it ring, saying nothing, but finding each other all over again.

Then the ringing stopped. The answerphone clicked on:

'This is a message for Ms Jackie Jarvis. This is Mandy from the clinic, your results will be back by the end of this week . . .'

Schoolboy jerked back and held Jackie's arms. The space was back between them again. 'Results?' He checked her over with disbelieving eyes. 'What's going on?'

fifty-two

'This is the last time.'

Bliss stared at the woman as she threw her defiant words at him. He half smiled. Who the fuck did she think she was chatting to? Some little boy who was in danger of getting his arse spanked? His smile became full grown as he remembered how she'd loved him spanking her behind when they had it off. Repressed bitch. Until he came along she didn't even know what it meant to come for Christ's sake. He heard her little whimpers and pleading words in his mind . . .

Fuck me Paul. That's it. Harder. Deeper. Make me come . . .

She weren't begging him now as she sat beside him in his car. But she would be soon. All he had to do was dangle his cock in front of her and she'd do anything he'd want. So he ran his thumb over the smooth skin of her flushed cheek. 'Now don't be like that, babe.'

She shook him off before he could finish. 'I mean it. I don't want to be involved in this any more.'

Now she was making him mad. He screwed his mouth up. 'I don't want to be involved in this any more,' he mimicked the sound of her voice. Who did the cunt think she was? 'Listen up.' His voice was deadly. 'I say when this ends. Not an over-the-hill tart like you.'

He heard her wince. He knew she hated swearing. So he said the C word three times on the trot just so he could see her squirm. Shocked she tried to reach for the door but he grabbed her arm and swung her around. Yanked her into his body. That old-style perfume she wore swam all over his face. 'The shipment that's coming through tonight is important, got it?' He shook her, snapping her head back. She nodded. 'So I don't need to hear your bellyaching right now. Stay in the background and shut the fuck up.' He pinched his fingers around her jaw squeezing her flesh. 'If this goes Pete Tong coz of you I'm gonna dice you up into bite-sized pieces.'

As soon as she was back in her car she dialled 999. She should've done this ages ago. What had she been thinking to become involved with a psycho like Paul Bliss? Sex that's what, her inner voice answered back. Even when she'd found out he liked men as well she still wanted him warming her bed. Bed? That almost made her laugh. They hadn't done it in a bed once. It was always somewhere sleazy, like that time in the garage at the petrol station; or him screwing her doggy style on the bonnet of her car in an open country lane. Just the way she liked it, the thrill of only being able to have an orgasm if she knew she might be caught. Dirty, nasty, panty-wetting heaven.

'Emergency,' a female voice said on the other end of the line.

And how would she feel if Bliss told everyone about her sexual fantasies? Told everyone about all the other things she'd let him do? Told everyone that the death of the Lewis girls might be her fault?

She cut the call. The line went dead.

'I might have cancer.'

Jackie knew the words were stark and cold but Schoolboy had to hear it the way it was. But when she saw him rock back on his heels she wished she'd been more gentle. He slumped onto the sofa. She pushed herself down beside him but didn't touch him. He gazed at her bleakly. 'Where?'

She swallowed. This was the bit she was dreading. Talking about her thrupenny bits. What if he got all disgusted thinking she might have it cut off. She couldn't say it, so she touched her right boob.

'Breast cancer?' His mouth just kept working but no more words came out.

'I found a lump a couple of months back. Went to see the quack and she got me an appointment up at the ozzie. I was meant to go the same day that Preston got run down, but I didn't—'

'Why the hell didn't you tell me?' He yelled.

'Coz you had enough on your plate already. Coz I was scared!' she screamed back. Her voice caught. 'And I'm still scared.'

He grabbed her by the arm. 'You listen to me and listen good. You get up that clinic . . .'

'I've done it. The test results will be back by the end of this week. They think it might be a cyst but they ain't sure.'

'Jackie.' Then she was in his arms. And before she knew it he was kissing her, really kissing her. Then their hands were all over each other. They hit the bare floorboards half naked. His hand lifted her top. She froze. Stopped him. Tried to get out of his arms. But he held her tight.

'Is that why you ain't been coming to bed with me? Coz you didn't want me to see it?'

The tears pricked her eyes. 'I thought you might not fancy me any more.'

'You could have an arm missing, a leg, and I'd still want to knock you off. There ain't no one like you, girl.'

Gently his hand raised her top. Pulled her bra out of the way. Then he lowered his head and kissed her right breast.

Ollie knew they had decided not do anything else but she just couldn't leave this alone. Finding out who had killed those two girls was her way of trying to atone for all the bad things she'd done as a child soldier. This was one loose end that had kept on bugging her over and over again. Doris Hunter. She ran her fingers through her mini afro as she stared up at the tower block that Doris had lived in, brought her kids up in and been murdered in.

I saw lots of men. That's what Jackie had said Doris Hunter had told her. What men? Ollie knew they were missing something and only Doris Hunter knew what it was. She pulled out her mobile and called Jackie.

After a small bit of chit-chat she got down to what she was after. 'Jackie, I know you want us to leave this alone, but there's one thing that keeps bothering me.'

'Ollie,' Jackie groaned. She felt as snug as a bug in bed next to a snoozing Schoolboy. 'I'm not sure we should. Plus, I just want to stay at home with my family.'

'Look,' Ollie persisted. 'How about this? If we find anything we give the information to Ricky.'

Jackie groaned. 'What information?'

Ollie's glasses slid slightly down her nose. 'I don't know yet. I'm standing outside Doris Hunter's building.'

'Why?'

'She said she saw something on the street. Men. It doesn't make any sense.'

'The woman was a bit cuckoo.'

Ollie's response was hard. 'Someone killed her because she knew something. What if she left some clue to what she meant in her flat?'

Candlelight flickered in the middle of the table. Daisy grinned with delight at the dining table on the balcony of her duplex. The balcony had an eye-popping view of the Thames as it moved gently in the summer evening light. Daisy grinned as she thought of Ricky's surprise when he came through the door and saw the cosy dinner for two she'd lovingly prepared to celebrate their second anniversary of being together. Her grin disappeared as her teeth tucked at her bottom lip thinking of the other surprise she had for him tonight. Her palm rested gently against her tummy. She hoped he was as pleased as her about becoming a dad. They hadn't really discussed the whole becoming a parent thing, but she was over the moon about it. Having her own family was one of the most important things to Daisy. That's why she'd worked so hard at her career to make sure that when babies came along she had enough to make them feel safe and secure. A thrill ran through her as the evening air kicked up around her.

She gave the dining table one last look and then walked back inside. She put on a Dido track and checked her watch. She still had enough time to check over those papers from Bliss before Ricky came through the door. She headed for her study, a neat, square room upstairs on the mezz floor. The papers were waiting for her in front of the computer on the dark wooden desk next to a half drunk glass of white wine. She eased herself down, flicked on the table lamp and reached for the wine. As she sipped she opened the folder. She scanned the first sheet – Bliss's property holdings. She turned to the next sheet. Mostly clubs, bars and a couple of houses. Nothing unusual there. She drained the glass as she got to the final page, her mind only half on it as she thought of the evening and the no doubt naughty night ahead. She couldn't wait to see Ricky. Couldn't wait to get him starkers in bed. She began to flick the folder shut when something caught her eye on the page. She jerked forward as she read the details of another of Bliss's properties.

Number 50 Claremont Road.

Wasn't that the address Anna had told her that the brothel was located at? The one that Anna couldn't find? Her gaze skidded down to the rest of the writing. Her mouth fell open. It couldn't be. No way in hell could she be reading the right thing. 50 Claremont Road couldn't be . . . ?

The front door buzzed, almost making her jump. Still reeling from what she'd read she headed for the front door. Pressed the intercom link to see who was downstairs. She was shocked to see the person on the other side of the door. What was she doing here? Daisy opened the door to face Kate, the former forced-sex worker she was representing. She looked shattered, dark circles under her eyes as if she hadn't slept in a week.

'I'm sorry, Miss Sullivan, I needed to see you.' Her voice was clipped and tight.

'No worries. Come on up.' It was only then that Daisy wondered how the other woman had found out where she lived. She never gave out her private details to her clients.

Just over a minute later Daisy let the younger woman into her home. Daisy led her into the main room, where the evening breeze fluttered through the open French doors to the balcony. As soon as they got inside, the words gushed from Kate's mouth. 'I couldn't sleep. I have nightmares. I'm frightened that he will find me.'

Daisy rushed over to her and drew the other woman into a deep embrace. 'Hey, hey. Don't worry. I think I might've found it?' Daisy eased Kate away from her slowly so she could see her face.

'The place?' Daisy knew that Kate found it hard to call it anything else. It was as if saying the word brothel took her back to the horrors she'd been through.

Daisy gave a tiny, triumphant smile. 'Yes.' The smile fell from her face. 'I think the man who may have kept you was called Paul Bliss.' Kate sucked in a sharp breath. 'But we will need to verify where the br . . . the place is because I think there must be a mistake.' Daisy shook her head. 'It just can't be where I think it is.'

'What you mean?' Kate stepped closer.

'Look I'll go and get the papers upstairs so that you can see.' Daisy quickly turned and headed back up the stairs to her office. She picked the paper up and stared at the information with disbelief again. This just couldn't be true. As she moved to the door clutching the paper in her hand she realised that something was on the back of the sheet. She turned it over never missing a step. She froze at what she saw. A picture of a house. A house she had seen herself before. Oh my God, it was true. What was she going to do with this explosive piece of information? Maybe she shouldn't show it to Kate. What if she did and she dropped the word to other people? There was no way that Daisy could let this get out, not yet anyway. Right, what she was going to do was go downstairs and give Kate some wrong information. She rushed back inside and placed the sheet of paper on the desk. Left the room. Reached the top of the stairs and peered down. She couldn't see Kate anywhere. She leaned over and peered over the side and called the other woman's name. No response. She twisted around and almost jumped out of her skin when she found Kate standing behind her.

Daisy's hand fluttered to her chest. 'You gave me a shock,' she uttered breathlessly.

Kate's gaze drifted down to Daisy's hand, which was empty. 'You say you bring paper.'

Daisy swallowed. 'Look I think I've got it wrong. Let's just—' But she never finished because Kate's hands came up and pushed her hard in the chest. Daisy wobbled and rocked at the top of the stairs. Her arms shot out as if to find something to hang onto. But it was too late. She was already falling.

fifty-three

Pinkie Lewis made the sign of the cross as she stared at the cross-shaped palm on the bedroom door, then she knocked. Without waiting for an answer she opened the door. Flick was lying on the bed.

'There's a young lady to see you.'

His heart lurched when he thought it might be Jackie. He moved past Pinkie into the passage. But it wasn't Jackie that waited for him. He started to speak but could feel his nan's eyes on them. He turned his eyes to Pinkie. 'Thanks, Nan. Why don't you go back and watch your show on the box.' She stared back at him and as always, since he'd been back, he could see the sadness in her eyes. He hated to see that. He didn't want her pity or no one else's. Pity wasn't why he'd come back. Finally his nan's pink slippers slapped against the carpet as she went back into the sitting room.

Flick turned to the woman who clutched her bag nervously. 'What are you doing here? You were meant to give me a bell on the blower.'

'I found it,' was all she said. Her hand dived into her bag and pulled something out. She handed it to him. He read. His head slammed back up. 'Fucking hell,' he said with disbelief. He looked at the woman. 'You done good, girl.'

'Kate' smiled back at him.

As soon as Flick had found out that Bliss was operating a brothel in his stash house to entertain his new business associates, he'd got his old mate, Cecilia, to go to Bliss's brief with the sob story of being a Tom on the run. Got her to pretend to be one of the women in the refuge that Daisy Sullivan occasionally gave free advice to. All Cecilia had to do was find out from Daisy where this brothel was. And bingo, she had. He and Cecilia went back years, to their days dealing blackjack in the casinos in Ibiza. Cecilia had been up for it, for the right price of course.

Flick grinned. Now he knew exactly where Bliss's stash house was; where the deal was going down in a few hours' time.

Ricky leaned against the back of the lift feeling bone weary. He usually never took work home with him but the murder of the Lewis kids just wouldn't leave him alone. Now Bliss was claiming he was guilty, now why would he do that? After sticking to his 'I never done it' story why would he confess? Mind you he was only holding his hands up to dangerous driving and because of that Daisy had managed to get him off. He should've known she'd have something up her sleeve. She was smart and that was one of the reasons he was totally potty about her. And Sonny hadn't come back to the station. Called in sick someone said. Shit, what was going on?

As the lift opened he dumped thoughts of the case from his mind as he thought about what Daisy had up her sleeve for their anniversary tonight. He knew she was planning something and couldn't wait to find out what it was. Mind you he was a bit worried about her lately because she hadn't been herself. Looked a little too pale for his liking. He reached the door of their home and pushed his key into the door. As soon as he got inside the smell of the cooking in the air made him smile. He knew what she was going to try and seduce him with tonight – bangers and mash, their favourite dish. He pulled his jacket off and slung it on the floor. Just the thought of the woman waiting for him made him feel as horny as hell. Maybe he should get naked in the hallway and surprise her with his own banger? He laughed at that. No, plenty of time later for him to peel his clothes off one at a time in front of her as she lay looking and licking her lips at him from the bed.

'Daisy baby,' he called in his roughest, ghetto-boy voice. She liked that voice, it really turned her on. No response. She must be on the balcony.

Whistling he swaggered into the lounge and stopped dead. Daisy was lying at an awkward angle on the floor at the bottom of the stairs. With shock he called out her name as he ran over to her. Dropped desperately to his knees. He knew he shouldn't move her, but for fuck's sake this was the woman he loved, his one and only, so gently he placed his palm against her shoulders.

'Daisy.' He shook her slightly. No response. He did it again. No response. Just as he got ready to flip his mobile out to dial 999 her beautiful blue eyes opened, filled with pain.

'Don't move, babe,' he let out breathlessly as he caressed her pale cheek.

With pleading eyes she groaned, 'Pushed me.'

'What?' His hand stopped moving. 'Someone pushed you down the stairs?' Christ what was going on here? If some shithead had put their hands on her he was going to . . .

Breath hitching high and loud in her throat she nodded. He dropped his lips close to her face. 'Who?'

But instead of answering her hands gripped the front of her tummy as she let out a sharp groan of pain. She caught his gaze as the tears filled her eyes. 'Ricky . . . Oh my God . . . the baby.'

The baby? What baby? She couldn't mean . . . ? But he never finished the thought as Daisy let out a shocking scream, then went limp. That's when Ricky noticed the blood spreading between her legs.

Ollie was waiting outside the block of flats where Doris Hunter had once lived when Jackie got there.

'I've checked the place over. No cops,' Ollie said.

Without speaking they made their way to the lift. Rode up in silence. Soon they were outside Doris Hunter's door. The police tape had been removed and there was an eerie quiet. They knocked. Waited. No response. Ollie assessed the lock on the front door. Pulled out a credit card from her purse and slipped it between the flimsy lock. The lock gave away easily.

'And where did you learn to do that?' Jackie whispered as they entered.

'You don't want to know . . .'

The flat was bathed in darkness except for a shaft of light coming in from the window in the sitting room. Jackie said, 'And what are we looking for exactly?'

Ollie's gaze darted around. 'Anything that might tell us what Doris knew. Maybe she wrote it on a notebook, a piece of paper.'

Jackie's gaze shifted to the closed bedroom door where she'd discovered Doris's body. She shivered as she remembered the blood and the smell. And the tongue. Ollie must've realised what she was thinking because she said, 'I'll do that room, why don't you look in the sitting room.'

They spent the next thirty minutes going over the place, looking in drawers, cupboards, behind furniture. Nothing. Finally they both slumped on the lumpy settee in the main room.

'Bloody fool's errand,' Jackie grumbled as she pulled out a fag.

Jackie puffed quickly on her ciggie as Ollie asked, 'Have you told Schoolboy yet about your lump?'

Jackie winced at hearing the word lump. Other people would have skirted around it, but not Ollie. She was direct as she'd always been. 'Yeah.'

'He loves you.'

'Yeah I know. He wants to come with me when I go to get the results.' She stopped. Took a deep breath. 'I'm still shit scared.'

Ollie reached for her hand and squeezed it. 'If it's the wrong news you're going to be alright. And you know why? Because you're a fighter.'

Jackie couldn't tell Ollie how grateful she was for the faith she had in her. Ollie was right she was a fighter. But if it was the big C would she win?

Suddenly she wanted to get out of the flat and the smell of death. She heaved herself to her feet. 'Let's get out of here.'

But instead of moving towards the door Ollie walked towards the window where the curtain was drawn back. She peered down at the street. 'What do you think she saw outside?'

Jackie walked over to join her at the window and looked down as well. 'She said she saw men. The woman was off her rocker.'

But Ollie didn't reply. Her body stiffened as she leaned forward. Jackie looked at her. 'What is it?'

Without turning around, Ollie quickly answered, 'Look at the street and tell me what you see.'

Puzzled, Jackie did as asked. Cars going along the road. What the heck was Ollie going on about? She shifted her head back at Ollie. She didn't get it. Ollie swung her head to gaze at Jackie, her face set in shock. Jackie's heart galloped. 'What is it?'

Ollie pointed. 'What's going on over there?' Jackie followed her finger. And stopped. The school. A group of men were getting out of a large van outside it.

'That's just the school. It's just the workmen carrying out some work for Mrs Moran. At night must be the best time for them to work. You know, when the kids ain't there.'

Ollie looked at her. 'Didn't Doris Hunter tell you that she saw men?'

'Yeah. But . . .' Jackie's words fell away as she continued to watch the men and the van. She peered closer. The men were unloading something. Two of them carried something large into the playground. But they didn't head for the scaffolding area of the playground but to a building in the playground.

'What building is that?'

'That's the old school keeper's house. The school sold it a year ago to make some money so Mrs Moran wouldn't have to let some staff go. Why would they be going in there?'

Ollie gripped Jackie's arms and turned her to face her. 'What if this has all been about something happening in the school?'

Jackie shook her head. 'No way. Mrs Moran is on the level.' She swallowed. 'I can't—'

'But what if the head teacher doesn't know about it? She isn't here at night. Plus the school keeper's house no longer belongs to the school.' Jackie continued to shake her head in disbelief. 'Look,' Ollie continued. 'This is the chair.' She pointed at the high-back chair on the side of the window. 'Where Doris Hunter most probably sat, staring at the street every day. And every night. She tells you she's been seeing men and now she's dead.'

Jackie's gaze fell back outside the window. She didn't want to believe what Ollie was saying. But Ollie was right, Doris had talked about men. Even Ricky had said when he'd spoken to her that's all she'd talked about. And they had all told her to piss off. But what did this have to do with the Lewis girls' murder? Then Jackie's heart almost stopped when she saw another figure walking across the playground towards the school keeper's house. 'No fucking way.'

'What is it?'

Jackie swung her head to face Ollie. 'I think that's the Chair of Governors, Scott Miller.'

'The man we followed the other day who met the Polish teaching assistant?'

Dazed, Jackie nodded and said, 'We need to get inside the school.'

'How?'

Jackie thought for a minute. Then looked back at Ollie. 'I know someone who was once one of the best burglars around.'

fifty-four

'I grew up on a council estate. Same as many of you I guess. And back in the day I thought I was some kinda bad boy ...' Self-proclaimed role model to the working-class man, Matthew Heller, started his talk at Bronswick Centre Open Prison. Tonight he was playing to a packed house of the prisons' residents in a white-painted room that also doubled up as the prison's chapel. He stood before them telling his story. A tale of a young man who had spent some of his youth behind bars and was, some said, on his way to becoming a best-selling author of action books about East London's gangland. His story never failed to grip and tonight was no different. He had them all on the edge of their seat, especially a muscular looking older man sporting a short, no nonsense haircut.

Ten minutes later he finished his talk with the same rousing words he ended on every time:

'If I can do it so can you!' And with that the room erupted into resounding applause. He smiled. Yeah, he could feel proud of himself tonight.

The man who had invited him stood up and moved away from the two prison officers at the back and made his way to the front. Cedric Fletcher ran the prison's education programme and addressed the gathered group, rubbing his hands together. 'I'm sure that some of you will have some questions you would like to ask Matthew.'

Immediately, the muscular man Matthew had noticed stuck his hand into the air. 'Your words have really touched me tonight.'

Matthew liked the sincerity he heard in his voice. 'Made me think about my future. Some people in my family died recently and it's got me thinking about my life. About the bad things I've done. How I've been a bad example to my sons. I ain't getting any younger and I want to spend the rest of my life being someone my family can look up to. How am I going to do it?'

Matthew launched into the usual advice he gave about turning your life around. Then the man asked another question and another. Matthew was impressed, this man really wanted to change. Finally Cedric Fletcher brought the talk to an end asking the men to once again show their appreciation. As the prison officers told the men to assemble in a line the man who had asked the questions came towards Matthew. He wasn't tall but there was something about him that screamed criminal. But Matthew didn't flinch, he held his ground.

'Thanks,' was all he said as he held out his hand. Matthew took it and was surprised at the power he felt in the grip.

'OK, Lewis,' Cedric Fletcher said. 'You can join the others.'

As he turned to follow the instruction, Cedric Fletcher grinned at Matthew. 'You should feel proud of yourself. That is one of our newer residents. A very hardened criminal indeed. Thank you so much for coming. Now let's see if we can get your driver to take you back to the station.' Fletcher scanned the room and frowned. 'Where's Johnson?' He caught the eye of one of the prison officers who nodded and then spoke into his radio. As he did this, Kenny Lewis joined the end of the line. The prison officer on the radio stopped speaking and made his way to Fletcher. And whispered in his ear.

'Problem?' Matthew asked.

'Sounds like Johnson is ill. I'll have to take you myself.'

'Is Johnson one of the residents?'

'Yes. The prison has a policy of letting the men do activities that slowly re-introduce them back into everyday life. But no need to worry because I'll—'

'I'll take him.'

Surprised they both looked over to the line of men. Matthew saw that it was the big prisoner he had spoken to. Cedric Fletcher spoke. 'Thank you Lewis, but I'll take him.'

'No trouble at all, sir. In fact it would be an honour.' Kenny Lewis looked at the visitor. 'I can't tell you how grateful I am that you came today. You've changed my life.'

Fletcher didn't answer as his mind ticked away. He knew who Kenneth Lewis was and the idea that some programme he had initiated in a prison might change one of London's most feared hard men would look fantastic on his CV. He might even get a top job with the government's prison reform programme.

'I'll need to check it out with the Governor first.'

One of the POs moved Kenny out of the line as Fletcher walked their visitor out of the room and back into the reception area. 'Let me just make a call.' A few minutes later he was back and spoke to the nearest PO. 'Get Kenneth Lewis.'

A sombre-faced Kenny was escorted into the room a few minutes later. Fletcher passed him the key. 'Make sure Matthew is in the back for insurance reasons.'

Kenny grinned. 'Thank you, sir. You won't regret this.'

Matthew Heller smiled as they made their way in the darkness outside towards a black car. Kenny opened the back door and Matthew got in. Quietly he closed the door and headed for the driver's side. A few seconds later they were heading into the night. For the first few minutes Matthew said nothing then he thought about asking the question he knew he shouldn't. But he'd been curious about the prisoner – resident he corrected himself – since he'd asked all those questions during his talk. So he asked.

'Why are you inside?'

'Little bit of this, a little bit of that.'

Matthew understood his reluctance to speak about his life, most probably so ashamed of what he had become. But he wanted this man to know that he could turn his life around so he started doing a mini version of the talk he'd just given. 'Growing up in a poor area is no disgrace. You don't have to continue being a criminal. You can always go back to college. You might become a role model yourself one day—'

'Bollocks to that mate.'

'I beg your pardon?'

'Role model my big, fat arse.'

Suddenly Matthew didn't feel comfortable with this man any more. He noticed the darkness of the night outside. The bleak-looking wooded area they were passing through. His heart started to gallop. Something told him to keep his mouth shut as the station came into view. All he wanted to do now was get out of the car as quickly as possible. And when he got out he was going to phone . . . He bolted upright in his seat as the car shot past the station.

'What the hell are you doing?' he shouted as he leaned forward. The central locking clicked into place. Desperately he tried the handle. The door wouldn't budge. Oh Jesus.

'Ease back and enjoy the ride,' the prisoner growled. 'Let me tell you about my role model. It's a semi-automatic and it's in my pocket. And unless you want to meet it you'll shut your face and do as you're told.' Kenny swung the car into a swift right. 'Chuck your mobile phone to me.'

Matthew's heart lost its rhythm he was that scared. He didn't hesitate to follow Kenny's instruction. The mobile landed on the front passenger seat. Kenny swiped it up. Steered with one hand as he punched in the number. Spoke:

'It's me . . . Look I ain't got no time for chit-chat. This is where I want you to meet me . . .'

Ricky paced like a caged animal outside the emergency room in the hospital. The room where Daisy was losing their baby. The baby he'd not known anything about. He felt like screaming; crying; shooting his mouth off to the world. How could this have happened to them? Daisy had wanted a family so badly and he knew why. To make up for the years that she'd been without a mum and dad. He wanted to barge into the room and hold her close, but the nurse had said it was better this way, for him to wait outside until it was over. Until the baby that Daisy had wanted so much had finally slipped away. What a way to find out you might have been a father.

Ricky jumped out of his thoughts as the doctor came towards him. The doctor wore a grim expression. 'I'm sorry there was nothing that we could do.' Ricky felt like ramming his fist into the wall.

The doctor's expression grew grimmer. 'This was a very bad miscarriage and there are some complications—'

'What complications?' Ricky's furious words pushed him closer to the doctor.

'Miss Sullivan is still bleeding internally and I'm afraid that the only way to stop it is either to remove one of her ovaries or a full hysterectomy. We just don't know yet until we—'

Now Ricky did slam his fist into the wall. 'No, no, no.' He leaned his forehead against the cold wall.

'Miss Sullivan is still heavily sedated,' the doctor ploughed on. 'We need the consent of her next of kin to operate.'

Ricky swung around, shaking his head. 'I won't let you do it. I won't let you take away her chance of having a family.' Tears filled his eyes. 'It's not fair.'

'I know,' the doctor soothed. 'But she could die if she doesn't have this procedure.'

'You want me to do what?' Schoolboy asked as he stared at his wife and Ollie as if they'd lost their marbles. Neither of the women were sitting down.

They were in the main room of his and Jackie's house. Darius was as snug as a bug sleeping upstairs.

Jackie quickly filled her husband in on what they had found out. 'You used to be one of the best burglars around, both commercial and residential.' Schoolboy winced at the reminder of his days breaking into both businesses and homes. Yeah he'd been good, the right size to slip easily through a broken window and quick enough fingers to swipe what he needed in a flash.

He thought for a minute. No, he didn't like this, not one bit. 'We should take this to Ricky—'

'No.' It was Ollie this time. 'We don't really have any evidence for him to work on, all we've seen are men at the school with Scott Miller.'

He interrupted her. 'So maybe nothing's going on—'

'That's what we have to find out,' Jackie cut in. 'Say there is something?'

Schoolboy leaned forward as his mind went like the clappers. What if Jackie was right and he sat on his arse and did nothing about it? 'Alright.' Both women let out a collective sigh of relief. 'But I'm going on my own.'

Jackie stepped towards him. 'If we're doing this, we're in it together.'

Schoolboy didn't like it but he knew from the stubborn tilt of her chin there was no point getting into a row about it; when Jackie made up her mind it was like trying to move a mountain. He stood up and moved out of the room into the study at the end of the hallway. Jackie and Ollie watched from the doorway as he opened a drawer.

'I hope we don't, but we might need this.' The air pumping out of Jackie's body caught in her throat when she saw what he held – the shooter that Window had given to him.

Without waiting for a response Schoolboy looked up towards the ceiling. 'What about Darius?'

Jackie jumped up. 'I'll see if Mum can stay with him.'

Twenty minutes later Nikki arrived. She and Jackie went upstairs to check on Darius. They saw the outline of his shape in the bed.

'Sh,' Nikki uttered softly as she closed the door. 'I'll stay downstairs until you get back. Where are you off to?'

Jackie dipped her head down, so her mum couldn't see her expression. If Nikki knew what they were going to do she'd hit the roof.

Darius listened at his bedroom door. Mum and dad were still chatting with Auntie Ollie and Granny Nikki. Good. That meant he could do it now. He threw the duvet back. He was all dressed ready to go. He placed Preston's guitar under the duvet, then stepped back to make sure it looked like the outline of him sleeping in the bed. He tiptoed towards his Confirmation suit. Pulled out his and Molly's secret from the pocket. Picked up his Arsenal rucksack and popped the secret inside. Then he moved towards the window.

Opened it and shinned down the pipe that led to the ground outside. Easy, he and Preston had done this before.

He hit the ground. Pulled the rucksack off his back. Unzipped it. Looked at the secret he and Molly had found inside the house in the playground. He'd promised God he would put it back if Preston woke up. Now he was going to do it.

'You can see her now.'

Ricky looked up at the doctor who now stood beside him in the corridor. Ricky pulled himself wearily out of the chair. His legs felt stiff after sitting there like a zombie for over an hour. 'Did you have to . . . ?'

The doctor shook his head. 'We managed to save her womb, but we had to take an ovary.'

Ricky didn't know what that meant. Seeing the troubled expression on his face the doctor explained, 'Her chances of having a child are much slimmer, but she may still be able to conceive.' Ricky nodded gratefully. 'She's very weak so please don't keep her talking for long.'

Shattered, Ricky entered Daisy's room. Her blue eyes were large against the paleness of her face.

'Oh Ricky,' she sobbed. She was soon in his arms.

'I'm so sorry,' he whispered over and over again. And he was. If only he'd got home half an hour earlier; fifteen minutes. They cried together for a while.

Suddenly Daisy pushed him back. 'I need to tell you something,' she said.

'It can wait—'

She clung to his hand. 'No. Listen.' She swallowed. 'I've been helping this young woman who was forced into the sex trade to stay in this country. Remember?' He let her talk although he was puzzled. 'I'd been looking for the brothel she was kept in. I found it and told her I knew where it was. But because I wouldn't tell.' Her breath hitched in her throat. 'She pushed me down the stairs.'

What? Ricky shoved to his feet, but Daisy wouldn't let his hand go. 'You don't understand. I found out that the brothel belongs to Paul Bliss. And where it is.'

Bliss bloody Bliss. He should've known that Daisy being anywhere near that scumbag was going to be bad news.

Ricky sat back down beside her. 'Where?'

'It's in the school.'

Now he was baffled. 'What school?'

'The one where the Lewis girls were killed and Preston hurt.' Ricky sucked in his breath in total shock. 'It's in the former school keeper's house. 50 Claremont Road.'

fifty-five

The window. That was another of his and Molly's secrets. And that's how he got into the school tonight, through the window that was in the old block that had years ago housed the school's now disused swimming pool. He and Molly had discovered that the window was never locked when they had sneaked into the disused building one lunchtime. He crept along the dusty floor. The place was full of bits of old, broken school furniture. He coughed as the dust settled in the back of his throat and quickly put his hand over his mouth just in case someone was nearby and heard him.

He reached the door and opened it. Crept outside into the night. Opened the black door that led into the playground. Popped his head around the corner. Grinned. No one in sight. He ran across the playground. Towards the former school keeper's house. He was surprised that the door was already open. He tiptoed inside.

Darius's heart beat like mad when he heard the voices and laughter coming from upstairs. He told himself he wasn't scared but he was really. He just needed to put it back and get out of here. Mrs Moran had told everyone at assembly never, ever to go inside the house. Never, ever was like a dare to him and Molly and all they'd talked about was getting inside the house, just once. So they'd done it during one lunchtime when Mrs Ahmed and Mrs Leech were chatting away on the bench. They'd crept up the stairs at the back. If his mum and dad ever found out ... He moved quietly inside the dark main room and headed for the kitchen. He didn't turn the light on, just went straight to the cupboard under the

sink, where they'd found it. He got on his knees. Unzipped his bag.
Pulled out the secret. He opened the cupboard the same time the
door opened in the main room. He dived for cover in a corner as
he heard voices. He trembled as he drew his knees up and huddled
in the dark. He clutched his and Molly's secret tight in his hand.

A gun.

Schoolboy, Jackie and Ollie were all decked out in black to blend in
with the darkness of the night. They stopped outside the tall, solid
iron gate next to the broken streetlight. Schoolboy stepped back as
he checked over the security at the school – razor-sharp barbed wire
ran across the top of the brick wall that circled the building. He kept
looking because his days as a low-level burglar had taught him that
there was always a way in. He fixed on a long black pipe that ran
up the wall. He moved back until he was in the road to get the best
view of where the pipe ended up. His gaze became grim when he
saw where it stopped, at a large skylight in the school's roof.

He moved back to the women. 'Wait here for me.'

'What are you going to do?' Jackie lightly touched his arm.

'Just do what I say.' Before she could say anything more he
headed towards the black pipe. He lunged up and caught the
second bracket that secured the pipe against the wall. He heard a
gasp behind him, Jackie or Ollie he wasn't sure, but he didn't have
the time to look back. He dug his trainers into the wall and began
to climb like a monkey going up a tree. He winced as the skin
on the inside of one of his hands scraped against an unexpected
rough part of the pipe. He stopped. Took a breath. Started again.
The sweat started to pour down his face as he pulled his weight
higher. And higher. His right foot skidded off the wall shifting his
weight to the side. The movement made his other foot slip. His
hands gripped the pipe as he dangled in the air, his legs swinging
beneath him. Shit. The sweat dropped into one of his eyes making
it sting. He rapidly blinked. His vision blurred for a few seconds,
then everything came back into focus again. He settled his body,
trying to get his weight balanced evenly again. He eased the swing
of his legs. Hung there still.

With a huge breath he yanked his feet back against the wall. Tested their grip. Heaved his body upwards. Tested the grip of his feet again. Heaved himself up. Sure of his footing he climbed more quickly getting into a rhythm. Finally he reached the top, but remained still, trying to regularise his breathing. He looked up at the rectangular tiled roof. Luckily the skylight was positioned not far from the roof's edge. He stretched up and caught the edge of the window. Pulled himself forward and used his elbow to shatter the window. He waited expecting an alarm to go off, but none did. He smiled at that. He pulled himself further up, knowing he would need to be really careful because all it took was one slip . . .

He pushed his arm slowly through the broken section of the window feeling around for the catch to open it. As his arm moved, the window slightly lifted and he realised that the window hadn't been locked. Stupid, he cursed himself, the first rule of breaking and entering was to see if a window, a door was open. He lifted the skylight. Pulled himself until he was peering down into the school. Smiled again when he noticed the ladder underneath the window. He drew himself further forward, keeping his grip tight on the window's edge. He tucked his legs under his body. Counted in his head.

One.

Two.

Three.

Swung himself down until he dangled inside. Waited until the rocking of his body grew still. Inched his body towards the ladder. His feet touched a rung. He kept them there while he moved one arm inside and caught the top of the ladder and did the same to the other arm. Holding the ladder tight he climbed down. Reached the ground. Looked around. The space was small, but he saw the top of a staircase to the side. Headed to it and carefully made his way down. At the bottom was a door. This time he remembered the first rule of burglary – tried the handle. Turned. The door opened. He found himself in the corridor that he knew led to the top hall where he'd been before to see the kids get their end of year presentations. He moved to the swing doors and rushed downstairs. Ended up at one of the doors that led to the playground. He peeped out of the door's glass panel into the playground. No one outside. He pushed the door and ran quickly towards the back gate. Unbolted the lock at the bottom and the top. Eased the gate back. Grinned when he saw Jackie and Ollie.

'We're in.'

Without another word they ran across the playground towards the former school keeper's house. Slammed their bodies against the wall, near the old iron staircase that led to the upper floors of the house. Schoolboy moved towards the staircase, but Jackie grabbed his arm. Startled, he looked at her.

'I'll do this,' she insisted and before he could argue she moved. He caught the back of the top of her tracksuit but she shook him off. Reached the start of the stairs. Took the steps slowly moving on her tiptoes. Finally she reached the top where there was a door. The night air circled her as she moved towards it. Slowly she turned the round, metal knob. It opened. She heard laughter as soon as she got inside the narrow hallway. Sounded like a man and a woman. She quickly scanned the hallway. Two doors and two windows. She headed for the first window, on the front of her toes again. She flattened her body on the wall near the window. Steadied her breathing. Pushed her head so she could look inside.

What she saw nearly made her gasp out loud. She clamped her hand over her mouth to hold the shock back. Her boys' Polish teaching assistant, Ms Karska, was decked out in black stockings, frothy pink suspenders and blood-red spiked heels and fuck all else in front of a man stood in his birthday suit. The guy was hairy, a right gut bucket, and as for his dick . . . The room was pretty bare except for a good-sized bed and table. On the table were two glasses filled with what Jackie suspected must be hard liquor. Suddenly Ms Karska dropped to her knees, her mouth headed for the man's . . .

Jackie whipped her head away from the window. She heard groaning and moaning coming from the other room at the end of the hallway. For a few seconds she remained paralysed on the wall. Bloody hell if she didn't know better she'd think she was in a knocking shop. She shot off the wall and eased back downstairs. Reached Schoolboy and Ollie.

'Did you see anything?' Ollie asked.

Jackie nodded, getting her breath back. 'One of the teaching assistants was in there showing some bloke a good time.'

'Didn't Anna say that she couldn't find the brothel Daisy was after on this street?' Ollie said. 'What if this is 50 Claremont Road? And this is the brothel?'

'No way,' Jackie answered. 'Mrs Moran—'

'What if she doesn't know anything about this?' Schoolboy spoke this time. 'She just sold the place to make money for the school, what goes on inside doesn't have anything to do with her any more.'

'Bloody hell.' Jackie shook her head in disbelief. 'Let's get out of here . . .'

But her words froze in her throat when she heard voices downstairs. They slammed themselves back against the wall. Listened. Male voices. This time it was Schoolboy who inched towards the nearest window. Shifted his head to the side and looked in.

His head reared back from the window. 'Fuck.' He shook his head as if he couldn't believe who he'd seen.

'What is it?' He heard Jackie's insistent whisper on the wind.

He turned to her. Mouthed, 'Bliss.'

Without waiting to see her reaction he twisted back to the window. Bliss was talking to another man as they studied something. The men moved to another part of the room. Schoolboy inched his head closer trying to see what they had been looking at. A box. Now Schoolboy had a clear view of what the box contained – guns. He shuffled away from the window and back to Jackie and Ollie.

He drew them around the side of the building. 'We need to get out of here now and turn this one over to the cops.'

'What did you see?' Jackie's question was frantic.

But before he could answer a voice behind them coldly said, 'Don't matter what he saw because you're all gonna be dead.'

They turned to find Stanley Lewis pointing an Uzi at them.

fifty-six

Stan marched them towards the front door of the house.

'You,' he said to Schoolboy. 'Kick it in.'

For a second Schoolboy hesitated. Stan shifted the gun onto Jackie. Schoolboy did what he was told and rammed his foot into the door. The door burst open.

'What the . . . ?' someone shouted inside.

Stanley hustled the women and Schoolboy forward into the house as he rushed inside behind them. Bliss was reaching for one of the guns inside the box, but Stan's voice stopped him.

Stan pointed the Uzi at him. 'Well, well, well, if it ain't the scumbag who murdered my kids.'

Jackie, Schoolboy and Ollie were huddled together in a corner. With them were a terrified Ms Karska and, to Jackie's shock, Mrs Moran's Polish admin manager and the two men they'd been entertaining upstairs, one of which was Scott Miller, the Chair of Governors. Stan had soon got it out of the man who Jackie had seen with Ms Karska upstairs that he was Bliss's contact for the guns. Bliss and his right-hand man Sean McCarthy were in the middle of the room. Stan stood in front of the door so that he had a good view of everyone.

Without warning Ms Karska started crying and babbling. 'Please let me go. I helped you. It was me who saw her.' She pointed at Jackie. 'With that Doris woman so I told—'

Suddenly the pieces about Doris Hunter's murder began to shift into place inside Jackie's mind. Of course, the teaching assistant had spoken to her on the street just before Doris Hunter had arrived. She must've seen them and told . . .

Stan turned the Uzi onto the teaching assistant and the room tore up as he sprayed her with a round of bullets. The other Polish woman screamed and everyone else hit the ground as her bloody, bullet-ridden body crashed to the floor. Jackie turned away from the awful sight.

'The next person to open their gob gets some of the same.' His voice was hard. 'Now get back on your feet.'

They all scrambled up, Schoolboy pulling Jackie close to his side.

Stan eyeballed Bliss and sneered, 'Nice little set-up you've got here. Keeping your importers sweet with a little bit of pussy upstairs and hiding your stash downstairs.' He let out a cruel laugh. 'I should've thought of it myself shouldn't I?' His laughter stopped. 'Was it worth killing my kids for?'

'I never done your kids,' Bliss slammed out.

Stan tightened his finger against the trigger, his face turning red with rage. 'I should—'

But he never finished because the front door burst open. That's when everything happened at once. Schoolboy moved the same time that Sean did. Schoolboy lunged for Stan as Sean dived towards the box with the guns. Everyone else hit the deck as Mrs Moran walked into the chaos. She screamed, frozen in the doorway as Stan managed to step back and kick Schoolboy in the face. As Sean grabbed a gun Jackie jumped to her feet and ran towards her groaning husband.

Stan and Sean pointed their guns at each other.

Silence. The others watched the two men. Watched the guns. Who was going to . . . ?

'Shoot him!' Bliss ordered Sean.

Sean kept his gun raised, his chest heaving. Stan didn't move an inch. Suddenly Stan laughed as he lowered his gun.

'Do it,' Bliss yelled.

But instead Sean twisted to the side and pointed the gun at his boss. The air tightened in Jackie's chest in shock.

'What you doing?' shouted Bliss, clearly dazed.

Now Stan pointed his gun again at Bliss. 'How do you think I knew where your stash house was?'

'Sorry, boss,' Sean said as he moved to stand with Stan.

'You cunt,' Bliss growled back. 'I'm gonna—'

'Kill him?' Stan jumped in. 'I think you're forgetting who's holding the shooter.'

'In here,' Sean ordered Mrs Moran, who stared with shock at the body of her teaching assistant.

'Leave her alone.' Jackie spoke for the first time. If there was one thing she was going to do it was protect this woman. 'She ain't got nothin' to do with this.'

Stan started chuckling. Suddenly he stopped as he grabbed the head teacher by the arm and yanked her inside. 'You gonna tell her or should I?'

What did he mean? Jackie gazed with confusion at one of the women she respected most in the world.

'I'm sorry.' Mrs Moran's voice was tiny.

'Shut up,' Bliss belted at her.

'Head teacher,' Stan scoffed. 'More like head gun runner.' With horror, Jackie realised what was being said. Mrs Moran was part of this. She caught the other woman's eyes and saw the truth in them. Jackie looked away in disgust, tightening her arms around Schoolboy.

'What we gonna do?' Sean asked Stan nervously.

'Only thing we can do.' Stan stepped nearer Bliss. Aimed the Uzi at him.

'Put that fucking gun away you prat.'

They all looked up at the voice coming from the stairs. Kenny Lewis. And behind him stood his son, Flick.

fifty-seven

'D . . . a . . . d?' Stan stammered, stunned.

Kenny just shook his head as he took the last step entering the room. The gun wavered in Stan's hand as his dad took centre stage in the room. He turned his gaze to Stan. Then Bliss. Finally Flick. Shook his head again.

'What a right fucking family I've got here.' He rubbed his lips together like he was going to spit.

'He ain't family.' Stan waved his gun at Bliss.

With a resigned sigh Kenny said, 'You had to find out sometime. Bliss is your brother.' Shocked gasps filled the room. 'Half-brother. Had a bit of slap and tickle with his mum years back.'

Bliss confidently stepped forward. 'And dad has been in this with me from the beginning.'

Stan shook his head as if trying to clear it. 'I don't believe you.'

'Shut. Up.' Jackie swung her gaze between Kenny and his three sons. And that's when she realised why Kenny wasn't frightened that he wasn't tooled up – he didn't need to be, because he was the all-powerful father telling off his three sons like they were naughty school kids.

'A right mess you lot have made of the business,' Kenny said. He turned to Flick. 'And you can stop looking all innocent like, coz I know exactly what you've been up to. Double-crossing everyone behind their back. Meeting Stan, meeting Bliss.' Flick just coolly lifted his eyebrows. 'Just coz I was banged up don't mean I don't know what's happening.' He switched his gaze once again on all his sons in turn. 'You're a disgrace to the Lewis name the lot of you and as far as I'm concerned you can all blow each other to bits for all I care.' His tone became deadly. 'But there's something we've all got to sort out first – who killed my kids?'

Bliss was the first to jump in. 'I've already told you, Dad, it weren't me. On my life, I would never have touched a hair on those girls' heads.'

'And you know how much I loved my nieces,' Flick added.

'Hold up a minute.' Stan looked his dad straight in the eye. 'What do you mean *your kids*?'

Kenny looked unsettled for the first time. 'You knew Marina was a whore when you tied the knot with her, you didn't want to listen to me. The truth is, son, she'd been banging me for a while before she turned her baby blues onto you. She only married you coz she was carrying my kids.'

A strange look spread across Stan's face as he continued to watch his father. Suddenly he raised the gun up and pointed it at him. 'What you going to do?' Kenny said softly. 'Take me out over some tart? You're my boy and she's nothin' to me.' Slowly Kenny walked over to Stan. Stan didn't lower the gun. Kenny reached him. Pulled the gun easily from his grasp. 'Good boy,' Kenny whispered.

'So that's why you wanted us to find out who killed the girls,' Jackie said. 'Because they were yours all the time.'

Kenny ignored her and stepped back so he had a view of all his sons. He flicked his gaze to Bliss. 'You said you killed them.'

Bliss rapidly shook his head. 'I only said that to get out of the poke. My lawyer said putting my hands up to dangerous driving was my only chance of getting out.' He turned to Flick. 'It must've been you because you were trying to set me up.'

'Got the wrong guy *brother*,' Flick responded contemptuously. 'The only thing I did was to get my mate Cecilia to play cards with you to take your car.' He nodded at Stan. 'He asked me to get your car so I organised it. I didn't do nothin' else, didn't have a clue why he'd want it. It was *you* wasn't it, Stan? We're a sick family but there's only one of us sick enough to kill a couple of children, and let's face it Stan you've done it before.'

'What do you mean he's done it before?' Kenny stormed, his hand tightening on the gun at his side.

'I never killed Donna and Martin.' There was real sorrow in Flick's voice. 'It was Stan. He got mad coz they were having a go at him so he took Martin's penknife and stabbed them. You always told me I had to look after Stan so I took the blame for him.'

Kenny's lips quivered. All these years he'd cut his eldest out of his life like a cancer and he hadn't even done it.

'You ask Nan,' Flick flung at him. 'She knew, but I told her not to say anything. He killed those girls, Dad, believe me—'

'No way.' Stan stepped back. 'I wouldn't have done that. You said yourself that Flick has been double-crossing everyone. Maybe he was working with Sean—'

'You what?' Sean let out.

But Stan carried on. 'Flick must've given the car to him to kill my . . . your girls—'

'Nah!' Sean yelled. 'That ain't how it happened. It was Stan that made me do it. Said that his wife was threatening to take his kids away from him, plus he knew that Bliss's stash house was at the school. He said that he could sort out his missus and get Bliss to take the blame for his kids' death and get him out of the way and take over his business. See, Bliss weren't meant to be here tonight. It was just going to be me and Stan would just waltz in and taken over.'

'I never—' Stan started.

'Shut up!' Kenny ordered. He turned to Sean. 'Go on.'

Sean swallowed. 'He said it didn't matter if the girls died coz he already had another bird knocked up and so had another family already on the way.'

Instead of looking at Stan, Kenny sauntered over to Sean, the gun banging at his side. When he reached him he smiled. 'I like a man who tells me the truth.' He patted the younger man on the cheek as if he'd been his mate for years. 'I know it was Stan's doing. Relax.' He moved away, turned his back. Took two steps then swivelled around and let off a round of bullets in Sean's chest. The impact of the bullets made Sean's body move as if he was doing some funky new dance. Then he slumped to the floor, the blood pooling around him. Kenny picked up Sean's handgun.

Stan rushed for the door, but Kenny fired a round by his feet stopping him. 'Come here,' Kenny said. Stan shook as he walked over to him. 'On your knees.'

'Dad, please.'

'You heard me.'

Stan dropped to his knees in front of his dad. He started sobbing as he looked up, his eyes pleading with his father. 'Please.'

Kenny thrust the dead man's gun at him. 'Take it. You're a tough guy killing kids for a living. Now do the right thing.'

Stan took the gun knowing exactly what his dad was telling him to do. He started really blubbing. No one in the room felt an ounce of pity for him. Especially Jackie. Stan had murdered those girls as if he'd been driving the car himself. Almost killed her little boy. Just as well it turned out his blood hadn't run in those girls' veins. If she had that shooter . . .

Stan leapt to his feet surprising everyone. No one had time to react before he pumped his newly found brother full of lead. Bliss hit the floor and Jackie didn't need to see him to know he was dead. Everyone dived for cover, but Flick wasn't fast enough. That's when Jackie knew what Stan was trying to do – get rid of his brothers first and foremost. Flick dived the same time a bullet ripped through his arm.

A scream sounded somewhere in the room next door. What the . . . ? Jackie's heart stopped when she saw Darius running into the room. Without thinking of her own protection she jumped up, along with Schoolboy.

'Mum! Mum!' he screamed.

Stan sprayed a volley at her making her duck for cover. She had to get her boy. She had to get her boy.

The next time she reared her head her heart surely did stop. She was thrust back to her wedding day eleven years ago, to another scene, her oldest boy Ryan, someone with a gun against his head. Stan had hold of her boy with the handgun in his back.

'Let him go, son.' Kenny straightened up.

Sirens sounded somewhere in the distance.

Stan just held tight to Jackie's son. 'Weren't you the one that said I was good at killing kids? Anyone follow me and you'll soon find out how good I am.' The terrified look in Darius's face held everyone back as Stan dragged him towards the door. Silent pleading entered his dark eyes as he shot past his parents. 'I love you,' Jackie whispered to his back. The wind kicked inside as Stan smashed the door back. The sirens grew closer. Stan flew out across the playground, shoved Darius away and ran.

Jackie and Schoolboy bolted outside to their son as Scott Miller, the gun importer and the Polish office manager-cum-call girl took off. Only Kenny, Flick and Mrs Moran remained.

Flick picked himself up, one hand covering the bleeding hole in his arm.

'We should get out of here,' Kenny said.

Flick calmly walked over to him. 'Nah we don't. The Bill ain't got nothing on us—'

'But I killed Sean—'

'Who says you did? She,' he nodded at the shattered head teacher still crouching on the floor. 'Ain't gonna say nothin'. Ain't that right, bitch?'

Dazed she just nodded as if she wasn't really there.

Jackie hugged Darius tight. 'What were you doing here?'

Hiccupping cries tore between his words. 'I took it back, Mum. Me and Molly's secret. A gun we found in that house. I promised God I would take it back.'

Jackie swung to the side when Schoolboy leapt to his feet. 'Leave it alone.' She didn't need to ask him what he was planning to do – go after Stan. 'We've got both our boys back now. Please.'

As he fought with his decision the cops swam into the playground. They saw Ricky first who started running towards them. 'What happened?' he asked, his eyes growing wide when he saw Darius.

Jackie answered him in a rush. 'Haven't got time to tell you. Kenny and Flick Lewis are inside, but you need to get Stanley. He organised the killing of the girls.'

Stan ran down the back streets of Mile End. Where he was heading he wasn't sure. But he had to get out of here, now. He ran around Tredegar Square. Past its upstanding Georgian houses, towards the Mile End Road. His breathing accelerated like crazy as the bright lights and sounds of the main road grew louder. As he neared the end a cop car appeared out of nowhere. He whirled and tore off the other way, but the car just revved its engine behind him. The first corner he came to, he twisted into it. Heard the car skid to a halt. Heard a voice say, 'Go the other way.'

He knew that voice – Detective Inspector Ricardo Smart was on his tail. He heard pounding feet behind him. He could do this – he just had to get to the Tube station. He ducked and dived around every corner he came to. Waved the gun like a lunatic at anyone that had the nerve to get in his way. He could feel the cop getting closer. He was so intent on Ricky behind him that he never heard the sound of the vehicle roaring down the street. He skidded around a corner. Rushed into the road.

Bang. The vehicle, a 4x4, smashed into him, sending his body like an acrobat out of control into the air. He landed head first in the road, his head crashing against the ground.

fifty-eight

'Can we go now?' Schoolboy asked Ricky. He was bone tired and it showed in his voice. He sat with Jackie and Darius in Ricky's office in Unity Road nick. Darius was still trembling.

'Are you sure that it was Stanley Lewis who killed Sean McCarthy?' Ricky looked at them deeply.

Jackie and Schoolboy had agreed their lie in the police car – Kenny had the right to do what he did because Sean had killed his kids. 'Yes,' Jackie finally answered. 'What's going to happen to Flick and Kenny?'

'From what you and Mrs Moran have said they arrived to stop Bliss and Stanley. The only thing we can pin on Kenny is absconding from prison. The others won't get far.'

'How's Daisy?' Jackie winced as she saw the pain cloud Ricky's face.

'She'll be alright. She's a fighter.' He stood up and wandered to his desk. Pulled out the top drawer. 'This is for you.' He held an envelope in his hand and gave it to Jackie. Puzzled she stared back at him. 'Just something I've been meaning to give you for a while. Nothing important.' Ricky made his voice sound light. 'When you've got some time *on your own* open it.'

She heard the way he said on your own and wondered what he was going on about. But the envelope would have to wait, there was one more thing she had to do before she left.

'Can I see Mrs Moran?'

Both Schoolboy and Ricky looked at her startled. 'I can't do that,' Ricky finally said.

'I won't interfere with your investigation.'

Ricky thought for a minute. 'You've got five minutes.'

Jackie entered interview room number two still clutching the envelope. A uniformed policewoman stood in a corner, but Jackie had eyes only for the woman at the table – Mrs Moran, the person she had trusted to look after her boys. The other woman raised her head. She had lost her cool, teacher knows best look, her eyes were bloodshot, her hair clinging to her face, and her glasses were slightly at an angle.

Jackie approached the table but didn't sit down. 'Why?'

Mrs Moran kept her gaze level with Jackie. She inhaled deeply. 'When the recession hit, the local authority said that all the schools had to make drastic cuts. Parkhurst was no different. I was in the position where I was going to have to lay off at least two teachers and most probably all the teaching assistants. That would have really damaged the work we'd done to change the school.' Her eyes pleaded with Jackie. 'People now wanted to send their children to the school.' Jackie didn't interrupt her. 'So I decided to sell the school keeper's house. You know what houses are worth in that part of Mile End. The word got out and a local businessman, Paul Bliss–' Jackie scoffed at that. 'I didn't know who he was, I swear. He offered to buy it well above the asking price. I took it to the governing body and they agreed.' She shook her head. 'What a fool I was. He started coming around and before I knew it, asking me out. I couldn't believe that such a young man was interested in me. But I thought why not, my husband had been dead for five years and I was lonely. He treated me so well.' She linked her fingers and twisted them. 'Then one night I came back to the school to finish some paperwork and saw him and a few other men at the house. So I went over . . . they were using the place to store drugs. I told him he couldn't do it, but he said he'd let me have a cut of the profits. And all I could think about was what that extra money would mean for the school – another teacher, more books for the library, more outings for the children, not just in the summer. I talked to Scott Miller, the Chair of Governors, about it and he agreed we should do it.'

'How could you even think of doing that?' Jackie cut in horrified.

Mrs Moran slipped into her head teacher's voice. 'Because my school, your children's school, deserved the money to keep it going. As far as I was concerned the children and the school community deserved the best.' The sternness left her as quickly as it had come. 'But I didn't understand Bliss as well as I thought I did. Before I knew it he was demanding that the upper floor of the house be used to . . .' She coughed. 'To entertain men. He'd heard about the need for the school to have some Polish members of staff to meet the needs of the growing Polish community. I wouldn't allow it at first but he threatened me and I was frightened of him.' Funny, Jackie thought, the one woman every parent in that school was terrified of was herself living under a rule of terror. 'So we had one Polish teaching assistant and my office manager who doubled up as prostitutes at night. That's what eventually sucked Scott Miller in, the free sex.' Mrs Moran's face crumbled. 'I don't care what happens to me, but what's going to happen to the school now?'

Jackie could understand the temptation this woman had faced and all she'd wanted to do was help the children in her school.

'Were you involved in Doris Hunter's murder as well?' Jackie suddenly asked.

Mrs Moran's face became paler. 'I had to tell him what Ms Karska told me. That she'd seen the two of you talking together.'

Jackie shook her head. She spoke quietly. 'You might've thought you were helping your kids but in the end it led to two of them dying. A mother losing her children.'

And with that Jackie turned and left. Only when she collapsed against the wall outside did she realise that her fingers were white as they gripped the envelope that Ricky had given her. Who would've thought it, the one place children should've been safe was the most dangerous place of all. She absently opened the envelope while she tried to get her mind to ease down. She didn't look down as she shoved her fingers inside. Pulled out what felt like a couple of sheets of paper. Finally she looked down. And nearly slid down the wall.

Three snaps of her and Flick deepthroating each other on *Miss Josephine*'s roof. So Ricky had known about this all the time. She didn't even think, just tore up the pictures into small pieces.

'You OK, babe?' Her head shot up to find Schoolboy looking at her with Darius by his side.

'Yeah.' She shoved the torn-up pieces into the envelope. Moved towards him. 'Let's go home.' He smiled at her. They linked arms and started walking down the corridor. On the way out she threw the envelope into the first bin she passed.

fifty-nine

'Happy Confirmation to you.
Happy Confirmation to you.
Happy Confirmation Darius and Preston.
Happy Confirmation to you.'

The crowd gathered around Preston's hospital bed sent out three riotous cheers after their rendition to the tune of 'Happy Birthday'. Jackie knew there might be some rule in the Catholic Church that said they couldn't sing the song, but she was doing this her way. She grinned at Father Tom, who winked back, then turned her smile on all the others in the room. Schoolboy, Darius, Daisy, Ricky, Jackie and her trusted mates, Ollie, Misty, Anna and Roxy. Ryan and Foxy. And her mum Nikki. Jackie's chest moved with pride as she watched her boys, in their suits. The hospital had advised them to keep Preston in for a while longer, just to be on the safe side, so Jackie had asked Father Tom if he'd do the service in the hospital.

Jackie watched as the others surged forward to congratulate the boys. She scanned every face. This was her family and they were all finally safe. She still shuddered when she thought of what might've been. She felt Schoolboy's arm go around her. She looked up at him and knew that she was the luckiest girl alive to have a man like him by her side.

He drew her away and whispered, 'Ready?'

The smile dropped from her face as nerves cramped her tummy. The pressure of his arm increased. 'It's going to be alright, babe.'

She took a deep breath. Steadied her nerves. 'Let's go.'

They tried to leave the room without anyone noticing but Misty saw them and shouted, 'Where you two lovebirds off to?'

Schoolboy's arm tightened around Jackie as she lied, 'Just off for some fresh air.'

'Well don't be too long, we've got a party to plan.'

Jackie forced a smile onto her face, she didn't want the others to know where they were off to.

Silently they held hands as they left the joy of the room behind. Made their way to the lift. It opened and out walked Marina Lewis.

'Marina.' Jackie smiled and hugged the other woman. Considering she'd finally found out who'd killed her daughters, her own ex-husband, Marina was looking good. No make-up, no false eyelashes, no frills, just a woman who seemed to be saying she was happy not to stand out of the crowd. But from the slightly glazed look in her blue eyes Jackie could tell she was still on some heavy-duty medication.

'I'm really pleased you could come,' Jackie continued. She'd invited Marina to join them to celebrate the boys' Confirmation. Jackie hadn't thought she would come because she knew it must be really hard for the other woman to see Jackie's sons when her own daughters were dead. But Jackie had given her the invitation just so she knew that she wasn't alone, that Jackie was there for her anytime she wanted a chat.

'I'm sorry I'm late—'

Jackie gently cut in, 'That don't matter, you're here now.'

Suddenly Marina's hand dropped into her open shoulder bag. She shoved a white envelope into Jackie's hand. 'Open this later. Just my way of saying cheers for all your help.'

Jackie nodded. 'We're just off for a bit.' She grasped Marina's hand and gently squeezed. 'But we'll be back soon, so wait around for us.'

As the other woman walked away from them they pressed the lift again. Got in. Less than a minute later Schoolboy and Jackie walked into the breast clinic. Jackie was finally going to get her results. She was sure the lump in her boob lurched. She cast her gaze around and was surprised to see Ricky's detective, Sonny Begum, sitting there. Sonny got up and approached them. Jackie knew you didn't ask questions so she just smiled.

'This is a bit embarrassing,' Sonny started. 'But I haven't told the Guv'nor about this. I sorta don't want him to know, if you get me?'

'Sure,' Jackie responded.

The other woman smiled gratefully and walked back to her seat.

'OK?' Schoolboy asked.

Jackie drew her gaze back to him, but instead of answering she moved confidently towards the desk, her hand still in his. 'Jackie Jarvis,' she told the receptionist. As she waited for the receptionist to find her appointment on the computer, she noticed another patient's form lying carelessly on the desk.

Name: Sunita Begum

Procedure: Breast reduction.

Jackie was glad that the younger woman wasn't there for anything more drastic. Now knowing the other woman's health problem, Jackie felt guilty about what she'd implied about her to Ricky.

A couple of minutes later Jackie's name was called. Schoolboy and Jackie got up and walked, hand-in-hand, towards the room that might change their lives forever.

The laughing, chatting crowd in the hospital room never noticed when Marina slipped out of the room.

An ecstatic Schoolboy twisted Jackie around in the air as they stood in the corridor outside the clinic.

'Put me down, you idiot,' she said, but her voice brimmed with joy. But he just covered her face with kisses. It had been a bloody cyst all along. A strange cyst but nothing to worry about, the doctor had said. They wanted her to come back for a simple op to remove it.

Schoolboy finally eased Jackie back to her feet. Suddenly his face became very serious. 'The next time you've got a problem you share it with me. We're a family. We've been a partnership since you told me to stop bleeding all over your Bermuda Beech floor.'

She nodded. He was right. They were a family, who might have their ups and downs, but what mattered was sticking together through the good and bad times.

She grabbed his hand, pulled him towards the lift like a young girl in love for the first time, and said, 'Let's go and join the rest of our family then.'

As they waited for the lift a group of nurses ran past them. Sonny Begum rushed from inside the breast clinic into the corridor and from the look on her face something was seriously wrong. Jackie caught her arm. 'What's going on?'

'Someone has just taken one of the babies from the maternity ward.'

Jackie gasped. 'Who?'

'A woman. She's on the roof.'

A funny feeling ran through Jackie. 'What does she look like?'

Sonny just shook her head and pulled away from Jackie and rushed off.

Schoolboy pulled Jackie to face him. 'Didn't you say that Stanley Lewis's new baby boy was born here recently?'

'Ohmygod. Marina!'

Jackie and Schoolboy hurtled up the stairs to the roof, puffing and panting when they got there. In the entrance stood Sonny.

Sonny stepped in front of Jackie and held up her hands. 'You can't go any further.'

'It's Marina isn't it?' Sonny just tightened her lips. 'She's got Stan's baby out there. I'm the only one who might be able to help you with this. She trusts me.'

'Let her through,' Ricky called from the roof behind Sonny.

Sonny got out of the way and Jackie rushed outside. Froze at what she saw. Marina held a baby snugly to her chest, her feet tottering on the edge of the ledge. Ricky stood a good few metres back. He nodded at Jackie.

She stepped forward. And stopped. 'Marina?'

The other woman looked up. Sent Jackie a sad smile. 'The baby's sleeping.' She lightly caressed the baby's forehead.

Jackie took another tentative step closer. 'The baby's going to be cold up here, why don't you bring him inside.'

The smile dropped from Marina's face. 'He said I never gave him a boy, that's what he always wanted, someone to carry on his name.'

'Marina—'

'He knew I couldn't have any more kids. He killed mine you know.' She looked directly at Jackie. 'I should take this baby as revenge—'

'No.' Jackie stepped closer. 'It ain't this little one's fault who his dad was. He's innocent, you can't blame him for what Stan did.'

Suddenly the baby woke up and started screaming. Marina hugged him tighter as she looked down at the crowd below. Then she rocked the baby and started cooing to him. Soothing him. But the baby's bawling got louder.

'He needs his mum.' Jackie took another step. And another. Then held her arms out.

'I hate Stan for what he did.'

'I know.' Jackie kept her arms in the air.

Marina rubbed her chin across the baby's head. Inhaled his pure smell. Then she held the baby out to Jackie. Tenderly Jackie took Stan Lewis's son into her arms.

'You tell that tart Tiffany to bring him up right,' Marina said.

Ricky jumped forward yelling out, 'No!'

Only then did Jackie realise what was happening. But it was too late. Marina leapt to her death from the rooftop of the hospital.

Jackie snuggled against Schoolboy as they lay on the bed. She desperately needed his warmth after the harrowing events of the day. Poor Marina. If she'd realised that things had been that bad with her she would've done something about it.

As if reading her thoughts Schoolboy said, 'It weren't your fault.'

'I know. But—'

'You couldn't have done anything for her.' She knew he was right, but that didn't make her feel any better. 'Didn't she give you something. In an envelope.'

'Yeah. She said it was a thank you for all my help.'

Jackie pushed out of his arms and padded towards her bag on the white, cane chair by the fitted wardrobe. She picked it up and plonked herself on the side of the bed. Schoolboy sat up as she pulled out the envelope. Opened it. A single piece of folded paper. She unfolded it. Read:

Put the prettiest flowers that you can find on my girls' grave when it's their birthday.

Across the country Flick Lewis entered the prison visiting room. No one had shopped his dad for Sean McCarthy's murder and the only thing they could do to Flick was to warn him to keep his fingernails clean.

He saw his dad straight away. Took a seat opposite him.

For a few seconds there was silence as they both looked at each other. Finally Kenny spoke. 'I was wrong, son—'

'I did what I had to do to protect Stan. You told me to look out for him and that's what I did.'

'Not many men would've done what you did.'

'But not many men are the mighty Kenny Lewis's son.'

Kenny puffed out his chest. 'I want you to look after the business for me . . .'

Flick smiled.

sixty

A week later Jackie and Schoolboy were smiling, their oldest son, Ryan, was trying to look bored in a cool way while the two youngest boys both looked uncomfortable in their Confirmation suits. They were standing in front of a sky blue backdrop while a photographer fiddled with his lenses and adjusted his tripod. The cheerful, good-looking young man with the camera was dressed in a smart suit and an open-necked shirt and had his hair slicked back. He looked down his viewfinder and then at the group he was trying to picture and pleaded with a smile.

'Oh, come on folks, try a bit harder, I've seen guys looking happier posing for mug shots down the nick . . .'

Schoolboy playfully cuffed Ryan and told him to smile while Jackie told the two boys that their Happy Meal afterwards depended on them looking happy in this family photo. The photographer looked down his lens and again and said, 'That's better! Now can we all move a little bit closer together . . . that's it . . . and smile . . . West Ham 6 Millwall 0? If that doesn't make you smile, nothing will . . . Perfect!'

The camera turned a few times, some recomposing was done and some more photos.

Suddenly Schoolboy took hold of Jackie's hand. She looked up at him. They both smiled at each other. She squeezed his hand as she whispered, 'We ain't done too bad for ourselves. Two kids from the wrong end of East London.'

Schoolboy squeezed her hand back. 'No, we ain't done bad at all.'